PRAISE
The Schopenl

"Yalom's melding of philosophy, pedantry, psychiatry, and literature results in an engaging novel of ideas."

—*San Francisco Chronicle*

"Yalom has fashioned a slick braid: strands of Schopenhauer's troubled biography, a twirl of philosophical apologia from Epictetus to Nietzsche, and real-time psychotherapy sessions."

—*Seattle Times*

"A beautifully wrought tale of a therapy group's final year and a moving debate about the end of life." —*Kirkus Reviews*

"[*The Schopenhauer Cure*] considers the value and limits of therapy and those points at which philosophy and psychology converge."

—*Washington Post*

"Yalom's enthusiasm is contagious, and his knack for presenting complex ideas and theories in clear, engaging prose makes him a popularizer in the finest sense. And he certainly knows how to tell a page-turning story." —*Los Angeles Times*

"Meticulous. Yalom often refers to his books as 'teaching novels,' and his re-creation of a working therapy group is utterly convincing."

—*Publishers Weekly*

"As a novel of ideas, this book effectively explores loss, sexual desire, and the search for meaning." —*Library Journal*

"The world's first accurate group-therapy novel, a mesmerizing story of two men's search for meaning."

—*Greensboro News & Record*

ALSO BY IRVIN D. YALOM

Lying on the Couch

When Nietzsche Wept

The Gift of Therapy

Momma and the Meaning of Life

Love's Executioner

Every Day Gets a Little Closer

The Theory and Practice of Group Psychotherapy

Existential Psychotherapy

Inpatient Group Psychotherapy

The Yalom Reader

Encounter Groups: First Facts
(with Morton Lieberman and Matt Miles)

The Schopenhauer Cure

A Novel

Irvin D. Yalom

NEW YORK • LONDON • TORONTO • SYDNEY

HARPER PERENNIAL

A hardcover edition of this book was published in 2005 by HarperCollins Publishers.

P.S.™ is a trademark of HarperCollins Publishers.

FIRST HARPER PERENNIAL EDITION PUBLISHED 2006.

Designed by Nancy Singer Olaguera

The Library of Congress has catalogued the hardcover edition as follows:
Yalom, Irvin.
The Schopenhauer cure: a novel / Irvin D. Yalom.—1st ed.
p. cm.
ISBN 978-0-06-621441-2
1. Schopenhauer, Arthur, 1788–1860—Influence—Fiction.
2. Group psychotherapy—Fiction. I. Title.
PS3575.A39S36 2005
813'.54—dc22 2004047580

ISBN 978-0-06-093810-9 (pbk.)

24 25 26 27 28 LBC 40 39 38 37 36

To my community of older buddies who grace me with their friendship, share life's inexorable diminishments and losses, and continue to sustain me with their wisdom and dedication to the life of the mind: Robert Berger, Murray Bilmes, Martel Bryant, Dagfinn Føllesdahl, Joseph Frank, Van Harvey, Julius Kaplan, Herbert Kotz, Morton Lieberman, Walter Sokel, Saul Spiro, and Larry Zaroff.

Acknowledgments

This book has had a long gestation and I am indebted to many who helped along the way. To editors who assisted me in this odd amalgam of fiction, psychobiography and psychotherapy pedagogy: Marjorie Braman (a tower of support and guidance at HarperCollins), Kent Carroll, and my extraordinary in-house editors—my son, Ben, and my wife, Marilyn. To many friends and colleagues who read parts or all of the manuscript and offered suggestions: Van and Margaret Harvey, Walter Sokel, Ruthellen Josselson, Carolyn Zaroff, Murray Bilmes, Julius Kaplan, Scott Wood, Herb Kotz, Roger Walsh, Saul Spiro, Jean Rose, Helen Blau, David Spiegel. To my support group of fellow therapists who, throughout this project, offered unwavering friendship and sustenance. To my amazing and multitalented agent, Sandy Dijkstra, who among other contributions suggested the title (as she did for my preceding book, *The Gift of Therapy*). To my research assistant, Geri Doran.

Much of the Schopenhauer correspondence that exists either remains untranslated or has been clumsily rendered into English. I am indebted to my German research assistants, Markus Buergin and Felix Reuter, for their translation services and their prodigious library research. Walter Sokel offered exceptional intellectual guidance and helped translate many of the Schopenhauer epigrams preceding each chapter into English that more reflects Schopenhauer's powerful and lucid prose.

In this work, as in all others, my wife, Marilyn, served as a pillar of support and love.

Many fine books guided me in my writing. By far, I am most heavily indebted to Rudiger Safranski's magnificent biography, *Schopenhauer and the Wild Years of Philosophy* (Harvard University Press, 1989) and grateful to him for his generous consultation in our long conversation in a Berlin café. The idea of bibliotherapy—curing oneself through reading the entire corpus of philosophy—comes from Bryan Magee's excellent book, *Confessions of a Philosopher* (New York: Modern Library, 1999). Other works that informed me were Bryan Magee's *The Philosophy of Schopenhauer* (Oxford: Clarendon Press, 1983; revised 1997; John E. Atwell's *Schopenhauer: The Human Character* (Philadelphia: Temple University Press, 1990); Christopher Janeway's *Schopenhauer* (Oxford, U.K.: Oxford Univ. Press, 1994); Ben-Ami Scharfstein's *The Philosophers: Their Lives and the Nature of their Thought* (New York: Oxford University Press, 1989); Patrick Gardiner's *Schopenhauer* (Saint Augustine's Press, 1997); Edgar Saltus's *The Philosophy of Disenchantment* (New York: Peter Eckler Publishing Co., 1885); Christopher Janeway's *The Cambridge Companion to Schopenhauer* (Cambridge, UK: Cambridge University Press, 1999); Michael Tanner's *Schopenhauer* (New York: Routledge, 1999); Frederick Copleston's *Arthur Schopenhauer: Philosopher of Pessimism* (Andover, UK: Chapel River Press, 1946); Alain de Botton's *The Consolations of Philosophy* (New York: Vintage, 2001); Peter Raabe's *Philosophical Counseling* (Westport, Conn.: Praeger); Shlomit C. Schuster's *Philosophy Practice: An Alternative to Counseling and Psychotherapy* (Westport, Conn.: Praeger, 1999); Lou Marinoff's *Plato Not Prozac* (New York: HarperCollins, 1999); Pierre Hadot and Arnold I. Davidson, eds., *Philosophy as a Way of Life: Spiritual Exercises from Socrates to Foucault* (Michael Chase, trans., New Haven: Blackwell, 1995); Martha Nussbaum's *The Therapy of Desire* (Princeton, N.J.: Princeton Univ. Press, 1994); Alex Howard's *Philosophy for Counseling and Psychotherapy: Pythagoras to Postmodernism* (London: Macmillan, 2000).

The Schopenhauer Cure

Every breath we draw wards off the death that constantly impinges on us. . . . Ultimately death must triumph, for by birth it has already become our lot and it plays with its prey only for a short while before swallowing it up. However, we continue our life with great interest and much solicitude as long as possible, just as we blow out a soap-bubble as long and as large as possible, although with the perfect certainty that it will burst.

1

Julius knew the life-and-death homilies as well as anyone. He agreed with the Stoics, who said, "As soon as we are born we begin to die," and with Epicurus, who reasoned, "Where I am, death is not and where death is, I am not. Hence why fear death?" As a physician and a psychiatrist, he had murmured these very consolations into the ears of the dying.

Though he believed these somber reflections to be useful to his patients, he never considered that they might have anything to do with him. That is, until a terrible moment four weeks earlier which forever changed his life.

The moment occurred during his annual routine physical examination. His internist, Herb Katz—an old friend and medical school classmate—had just completed his examination and, as always, told Julius to dress and come to his office for a debriefing.

Herb sat at his desk, rifling through Julius's chart. "On the whole, you look pretty good for an ugly sixty-five-year-old man. Prostate is getting a little swollen, but so is mine. Blood chemistries, cholesterol, and lipid levels are well-behaved—the meds and your diet are doing their job. Here's the prescription for your Lipitor, which, along with your jogging, has lowered your cholesterol enough. So you can give yourself a break: eat an egg once in a while. I eat two for breakfast every Sunday. And here's the prescription for your synthyroid. I'm raising the dose a bit. Your thyroid gland is slowly closing down—the good thyroid cells are dying and being replaced by fibrotic material. Perfectly benign condition, as you know. Happens to us all; I'm on thyroid meds myself.

"Yes, Julius, no part of us escapes the destiny of aging. Along with your thyroid, your knee cartilage is wearing out, your hair follicles are dying, and your upper lumbar disks are not what they used to be. What's more, your skin integrity is obviously deteriorating: your epithelial cells are just plain wearing out—look at all those senile keratoses on your cheeks, those brown flat lesions." He held up a small mirror for Julius to inspect himself. "Must be a dozen more on you since I last saw you. How much time you spending in the sun? Are you wearing a broad-brimmed hat like I suggested? I want you to see a dermatologist about them. Bob King's good. He's just in the next building. Here's his number. Know him?"

Julius nodded.

"He can burn off the unseemly ones with a drop of liquid nitrogen. I had him remove several of mine last month. No big deal—takes five, ten, minutes. A lot of internists are doing it themselves now. Also there's one I want him to look at on your back: you can't see it; it's just under the lateral part of your right scapula. It looks different from the others—pigmented unevenly and the borders aren't sharp. Probably nothing, but let's have him check it. Okay, buddy?"

"Probably nothing, but let's have him check it." Julius heard the strain and forced casualness in Herb's voice. But, let there be no mistake, the phrase "pigmented differently and borders aren't sharp," spoken by one doc to another, was a cause for alarm. It was code for potential melanoma, and now, in retrospect, Julius identified that phrase, that singular moment, as the point when carefree life ended and death, his heretofore invisible enemy, materialized in all its awful reality. Death had come to stay, it never again left his side, and all the horrors that followed were predictable postscripts.

Bob King had been a patient of Julius's years ago, as had a significant number of San Francisco physicians. Julius had reigned over the psychiatric community for thirty years. In his position as professor of psychiatry at the University of California he had trained scores of students and, five years before, had been president of the American Psychiatric Association.

His reputation? The no-bullshit doctor's doctor. A therapist of last resort, a canny wizard willing to do anything he had to do to help his patient. And that was the reason why, ten years earlier, Bob King had consulted Julius for treatment of his long-standing addiction to Vicodin (the physician-addict's drug of choice because it is so easily accessible). At that time King was in serious trouble. His Vicodin needs had dramatically increased: his marriage was in jeopardy, his practice was suffering, and he had to drug himself to sleep every night.

Bob tried to enter therapy, but all doors were closed for him. Every therapist he consulted insisted that he enter an impaired physician recovery program, a plan which Bob resisted because he was loath to compromise his privacy by attending therapy groups with other physician-addicts. The therapists wouldn't budge. If they treated a practicing addicted physician without using the official recovery program, they would place themselves at risk of punitive action by the medical board or of personal litigation (if, for example, the patient made an error of judgment in clinical work).

As a last resort before quitting his practice and taking a leave of absence to be treated anonymously in another city, he appealed to Julius, who accepted the risk and trusted Bob King to withdraw on his own from Vicodan. And, though therapy was difficult, as it always is with addicts, Julius treated Bob for the next three years without the help of a recovery program. And it was one of those secrets that every psychiatrist had—a therapeutic success that could in no way be discussed or published.

Julius sat in his car after leaving his internist's office. His heart pounded so hard the car seemed to shake. Taking a deep breath to quell his mounting terror, then another and another, he opened his cell phone and, with trembling hands, called Bob King for an urgent appointment.

"I don't like it," said Bob the next morning, as he studied Julius's back with a large round magnifying glass. "Here, I want you to look at it; we can do it with two mirrors."

Bob stationed him by the wall mirror and held a large hand mirror next to the mole. Julius glanced at the dermatologist through the mirror: blond, ruddy faced, thick spectacles resting on his long imposing nose—he remembered Bob telling him how the other kids taunted him with cries of "cucumber nose." He hadn't changed much in ten years. He looked harried, much as when he had been Julius's patient, huffing and puffing, arriving always a few minutes late. The White Rabbit's refrain, "I'm late, I'm late for a very important date," often had come to mind when Bob rushed into his office. He had gained weight but was as short as ever. He looked like a dermatologist. Whoever saw a tall dermatologist? Then Julius glanced at his eyes—oh oh, they seemed apprehensive—the pupils were large.

"Here's the critter." Julius looked through the mirror as Bob pointed with an eraser-tipped stylus. "This flat nevus below your right shoulder under your scapula. See it?"

Julius nodded.

Holding a small ruler to it, he continued, "It's a shade less than one centimeter. I'm sure you remember the ABCD rule of thumb from your med school dermatology—"

Julius interrupted, "I don't remember squat from medical school dermatology. Treat me like a dummy."

"Okay. ABCD. *A* for asymmetry—look here." He moved the stylus to parts of the lesion. "It's not perfectly round like all these others on your back—see this one and this one." He pointed to two nearby small moles.

Julius tried to break his tension by taking a deep breath.

"*B* for borders—now, look here, I know it's hard to see." Bob pointed again to the subscapular lesion. "See in this upper area how sharp the border is, but all around here on the medial side it's indistinct, just fades into the surrounding skin. *C* for coloration. Here, on this side, see how it's light brown. If I magnify it, I see a tad of red, some black, maybe even some gray. *D* for diameter; as I say, perhaps seven-eighths of a centimeter. That's good-sized, but we can't be sure how old it is, I mean how fast it's growing. Herb Katz says it wasn't there at last year's physical. Lastly, under magnification, there is no doubt that the center is ulcerated."

Putting down the mirror, he said, "Put your shirt back on, Julius." After his patient finished buttoning up, King sat down on the small stool in the examining room and began, "Now, Julius, you know the literature on this. The concerns are obvious."

"Look, Bob," replied Julius, "I know our previous relationship makes this hard for you, but please don't ask me to do your work. Don't assume I know anything about this. Keep in mind that right now my state of mind is terror veering toward panic. I want you to take charge, to be entirely honest with me, and take care of me. Just as I did for you. And, Bob, look at me! When you avoid my gaze like that, it scares the shit out of me."

"Right. Sorry." He looked him straight in the eyes. "You took damn good care of me. I'll do the same for you." He cleared his throat, "Okay, my strong clinical impression is that it's a melanoma."

Noting Julius's wince, he added, "Even so, the diagnosis itself tells you little. Most—remember that—*most* melanomas are easily treated, though some are bitches. We need to know some things from the pathologist: Is it melanoma for certain? If so, how deep is it? Has it spread? So, first step is biopsy and getting a specimen to the pathologist.

"Soon as we finish I'll call a general surgeon to excise the lesion. I'll be by his side throughout. Next, an examination of a frozen section by the pathologist, and if it's negative, then great: we're finished. If it's positive, if it is a melanoma, we'll remove the most suspicious node or, if necessary, do a multiple node resection. No hospitalization required—the whole procedure will be done in the surgery center. I'm pretty sure no skin graft will be needed, and, at most, you miss only a day of work. But you'll feel some discomfort at the surgical site for a few days. Nothing else to say now until we learn more from the biopsy. As you asked, I'll take care of you. Trust my judgment on this; I've been involved with hundreds of these cases. Okay? My nurse will call you later today with all the details about time and place and prep instruction. Okay?"

Julius nodded. They both rose.

"I'm sorry," Bob said, "I wish I could spare you all this but I can't." He held out a folder of reading material. "I know you may not want this stuff, but I always distribute it to patients in your situation. Depends on the person: some are comforted by information, others would rather not know and just toss it on the way out of the office. Hope after the surgery to tell you something brighter."

But there was never to be anything brighter—the later news was darker yet. Three days after the biopsy procedure, they met again. "Do you want to read this? said Bob, holding out the final pathologist's report. Seeing Julius shake his head, Bob scanned the report again and began: "Okay let's go over it. I gotta tell you: it's not good. Bottom line is that it *is* a melanoma and it has several . . . uh . . . notable characteristics: it's deep, over four millimeters, ulcerated, and there are five positive nodes."

"Meaning? Come on, Bob, don't talk around this. 'Notable,' four millimeters, ulcerated, five nodes? Be straight. Talk to me as if I were a layman."

"Meaning bad news. It's a sizable melanoma, and it has spread to the nodes. The real danger here is more distant spread, but we won't know that till the CT scan which I've arranged for tomorrow at eight."

Two days later they continued their discussion. Bob reported that the CT scan was negative—no evidence of spread elsewhere in the body. That was the first good news. "But even so, Julius, this adds up to a dangerous melanoma."

"How dangerous?" Julius's voice cracked. "What are we talking about? What kind of survival rate?"

"You know we can only address that question in terms of statistics. Everyone is different. But for an ulcerated melanoma, four millimeters deep, with five nodes, the statistical charts show a five-year survival of less than twenty-five percent."

Julius sat for several moments with head bowed, heart pounding, tears in his eyes, before asking, "Keep going. You're being straight. I need to know what to tell my patients. What will my course be like? What's going to happen? "

"It's impossible to be precise because nothing more will happen to you until the melanoma recurs somewhere in the body. When it does, especially if it metastasizes, then the course might be quick, perhaps weeks or months. As for your patients, hard to say, but it would not be unreasonable to hope for at least a year of good health ahead of you."

Julius nodded slowly, head down.

"Where's your family, Julius? Shouldn't you have brought someone in with you?"

"I think you know about my wife's death ten years ago. My son is on the East Coast and my daughter in Santa Barbara. I've said nothing to them yet; I didn't see any sense in disrupting their lives unnecessarily. I generally do better licking my wounds in private anyway, but I'm pretty sure that my daughter will come up immediately."

"Julius, I'm so sorry to have to tell you all this. Let me end with a little good news. There's a lot of energetic research going on now—perhaps a dozen very active labs in this country and abroad. For unknown reasons the incidence of melanoma has risen, almost doubled in the last ten years, and it's a hot research area. It's possible that breakthroughs are close at hand."

For the next week Julius lived in a daze. Evelyn, his daughter, a classics professor, canceled her classes and drove up immediately to spend several days with him. He spoke at length to her, his son, his sister and brother, and to intimate friends. He often woke in terror at 3 A.M., crying out, and gasping for air. He canceled his hours with his individual patients and with his therapy group for two weeks and spent hours pondering what and how to tell them.

The mirror told him he didn't look like a man who had reached the end of his life. His three-mile daily jog had kept his body young and wiry, without an ounce of fat. Around his eyes and mouth, a few wrinkles. Not many—his father had died with none at all. He had green eyes; Julius had always been proud of that. Strong and sincere eyes. Eyes that could be trusted, eyes that could hold anyone's gaze. Young eyes, the eyes of the sixteen-year-old Julius. The dying man and the sixteen-year-old gazed at each other across the decades.

He looked at his lips. Full, friendly lips. Lips that, even now in his time of despair, were on the edge of a warm grin. He had a full head of unruly black curly hair, graying only in his sideburns. When he was a teenager in the Bronx, the old white-haired, red-faced, anti-Semitic barber, whose tiny shop was down his street between Meyer's candy store and Morris's butcher shop, cursed his tough hair as he tugged at it with a steel comb and cut it with thinning shears. And now Meyer, Morris, and the barber were all dead, and little sixteen-year-old Julius was on death's call sheet.

One afternoon he tried to attain some sense of mastery by reading the melanoma literature in the medical school library, but that proved futile. Worse than futile—it made things more horrendous. As Julius apprehended the truly ghastly nature of his disease, he began to think of melanoma as a voracious creature sinking ebony tendrils deep into his flesh. How startling it was to realize that suddenly he was no longer the supreme life form. Instead he was a host; he was nourishment, food for a fitter organism whose gobbling cells divided at a dizzying pace, an organism that blitzkrieged and annexed adjacent protoplasm and was now undoubtedly outfitting clusters of cells for cruises into the bloodstream and colonization of distant organs, perhaps the sweet friable feeding grounds of his liver or the spongy grassy meadows of his lungs.

Julius put aside the reading. Over a week had gone by, and it was time to move past distraction. The hour had come to face what was really happening. Sit down, Julius, he told himself. Sit down and meditate upon dying. He closed his eyes.

So death, he thought, has finally made its appearance on stage. But what a banal entrance—the curtains jerked open by a roly-poly dermatologist with a cucumber nose, magnifying glass in hand, and costumed in white hospital coat with his name stitched in dark blue letters upon his upper breast pocket.

And the closing scene? Destined, most likely, to be equally banal. His costume would be his wrinkled pinstriped New York Yankees nightshirt with DiMaggio's number 5 on the back. The stage set? The same queen-sized bed in which he had slept for thirty years, crumpled clothes on the chair beside the bed and, upon his bedside table, a stack of unread novels unaware that their time would now never come. A whimpering, disappointing finale. Surely, Julius thought, the glorious adventure of his life deserved something more . . . more . . . more what?

A scene he had witnessed a few months ago on a Hawaiian vacation came to mind. While hiking he had quite by chance come upon a large Buddhist retreat center and saw a young woman walking though a circular labyrinth, constructed of small lava stones. Reaching the center of the labyrinth she stopped and remained motionless in a lengthy standing meditation. Julius's knee-jerk reaction to such religious ritual was not charitable, generally falling somewhere in the territory between ridicule and revulsion.

But, now, as he thought about that meditating young woman, he experienced softer feelings—a flood of compassion for her and for all his fellow humans who are victims of that freakish twist of evolution that grants self-awareness but not the requisite psychological equipment to deal with the pain of transient existence. And so throughout the years, the centuries, the millennia, we have relentlessly constructed makeshift denials of finiteness. Would we, would any of us, ever be done with our search for a higher power with whom we can merge and exist forever, for God given instruction manuals, for some sign of a larger established design, for ritual and ceremony?

And yet, considering his name on death's roster, Julius wondered whether a little ceremony might not be such a bad thing. He jerked away from his own thought as if scorched—so thoroughly dissonant was it with his lifelong antagonism to ritual. He had always despised the tools by which religions strip their followers of reason and freedom: the ceremonial robes, incense, holy books, mesmerizing Gregorian chants, prayer wheels, prayer rugs, shawls and skullcaps, bishop's miters and crosiers, holy wafers and wines, last rites, heads bobbing and bodies swaying to ancient chants—all of which he considered the paraphernalia of the most powerful and longest-running con game in history, a game which empowered the leaders and satisfied the congregation's lust for submission.

But now, with death standing next to him, Julius noted that his vehemence had lost its bite. Maybe it was simply *imposed* ritual he disliked. Perhaps a good word could be found for a little personal creative ceremony. He was touched by the newspaper descriptions of the firemen at ground zero in New York, stopping, standing, and removing hats to honor the dead as each pallet of newly discovered remains was brought to the surface. Nothing wrong with honoring the dead . . . no, not the dead, but honoring the life of the one who died. Or was it something more than honoring, more than sanctifying? Wasn't the gesture, the ritual of the firemen, also signifying connectivity? The recognition of their relationship, their unity with each victim?

Julius had a personal taste of connectivity a few days after his fateful meeting with his dermatologist when he attended his support group of fellow psychotherapists. His fellow doctors were stunned when Julius revealed the news of his melanoma. After encouraging him to talk himself out, each group member expressed his shock and sorrow. Julius couldn't find any more words, nor could anyone else. A couple of times someone started to talk but did not, and then it was as if the group agreed nonverbally that words were not necessary. For the final twenty minutes all sat in silence. Such prolonged silences in groups are almost invariably awkward, but this one felt different, almost comforting. Julius was embarrassed to admit, even to himself, that the silence felt "sacred." Later it occurred to him that the members not only were expressing grief but were also removing their hats, standing at attention, joining and honoring his life.

And perhaps this was a way of honoring their own lives, Julius thought. What else do we have? What else other than this miraculous blessed interval of being and self-awareness? If anything is to be honored and blessed, it should simply be this—the priceless gift of sheer existence. To live in despair because life is finite or because life has no higher purpose or embedded design is crass ingratitude. To dream up an omniscient creator and devote our life to endless genuflection seems pointless. And wasteful, too: why squander all that love on a phantasm when there seems too little love to go around on Earth as it is? Better to embrace Spinoza's and Einstein's solution: simply bow one's head, tip one's hat to the elegant laws and mystery of nature, and go about the business of living.

These were not new thoughts for Julius—he had always known of finiteness and the evanescence of consciousness. But there is knowing and *knowing*. And death's presence on the stage brought him closer to really knowing. It was not that he had grown wiser: it was only that the removal of distractions—ambition, sexual passion, money, prestige, applause, popularity—offered a purer vision. Wasn't such detachment the Buddha's truth? Perhaps so, but he preferred the path of the Greeks: everything in moderation. Too much of life's show is missed if we never take off our coats and join in the fun. Why rush to the exit door before closing time?

• • •

After a few days, when Julius felt calmer with fewer sweeps of panic, his thoughts turned to the future. "One good year" Bob King had said, "no guarantees, but it would not be unreasonable to hope for at least a year of good health." But how to spend that year? One thing he resolved was not to make that one good year a bad year by grieving that it was not more than a year.

One night, unable to sleep and craving some comfort, he restlessly browsed in his library. He could find nothing written in his own field that seemed even remotely relevant to his life situation, nothing pertaining to how should one live, or find meaning in one's remaining days. But then his eye fell upon a dog-eared copy of Nietzsche's *Thus Spake Zarathustra.* Julius knew this book well: decades ago he had thoroughly studied it while writing an article on the significant but unacknowledged influence of Nietzsche on Freud. *Zarathustra* was a brave book which more than any other, Julius thought, teaches how to revere and celebrate life. Yes, this might be the ticket. Too anxious to read systematically, he flipped the pages randomly and sampled some of the lines he had highlighted.

"To change 'it was' into 'thus I willed it'—that alone shall I call redemption."

Julius understood Nietzsche's words to mean that he had to choose his life—he had to live it rather than be lived by it. In other words he should love his destiny. And above all there was Zarathustra's oft-repeated question whether we would be willing to repeat the precise life we have lived again and again throughout eternity. A curious thought experiment—yet, the more he thought about it, the more guidance it provided: Nietzsche's message to us was to live life in such a way that we would be willing to repeat the same life eternally.

He continued flipping the pages and stopped at two passages highlighted heavily in neon pink: "Consummate your life." "Die at the right time."

These hit home. Live your life to the fullest; and then, and only then, die. Don't leave any unlived life behind. Julius often likened Nietzsche's words to a Rorschach exam; they offered so many opposing viewpoints that the readers' state of mind determined what they took from them. Now he read with a vastly different state of mind. The presence of death prompted a different and more enlightened reading: in page after page, he saw evidence of a pantheistic connectedness not previously appreciated. However much Zarathustra extolled, even glorified solitude, however much he required isolation in order to give birth to great thoughts, he was nonetheless committed to loving and lifting others, to helping others perfect and transcend themselves, to sharing his ripeness. *Sharing his ripeness*—that hit home.

Returning *Zarathustra* to its resting place, Julius sat in the dark staring at the lights of cars crossing the Golden Gate Bridge and thinking about Nietzsche's words. After a few minutes Julius "came to": he knew exactly what to do and how to spend his final year. *He would live just the way he had lived the previous year—and the year before that and before that.* He loved being a therapist; he loved connecting to others and helping to bring something to life in them. Maybe his work was sublimation for his lost connection to his wife; maybe he needed the applause, the affirmation and gratitude of those he helped. Even so, even if dark motives played their role, he was grateful for his work. God bless it!

Strolling over to his wall of file cabinets, Julius opened a drawer filled with charts and audiotaped sessions of patients seen long ago. He stared at the names—each chart a monument to a poignant human drama that had once played itself out in this very room. As he surfed through the charts, most of the faces immediately sprang to mind. Others had faded, but a few paragraphs of notes evoked their faces, too. A few were the truly forgotten, their faces and stories lost forever.

Like most therapists, Julius found it difficult to seal himself off from the unremitting attacks on the field of therapy. Assault came from many directions: from pharmaceutical companies and managed care, which sponsored superficial research orchestrated to validate the effectiveness of drugs and briefer therapies; from the media, which never tired of ridiculing therapists; from behaviorists; from motivational speakers; from the hordes of new age healers and cults all competing for the hearts and minds of the troubled. And, of course, there were doubts from within: the extraordinary molecular neurobiological discoveries reported with ever-increasing frequency caused even the most experienced therapists to wonder about the relevance of their work.

Julius was not immune to these attacks and often entertained doubts about the effectiveness of his therapy and just as often soothed and reassured himself. *Of course* he was an effective healer. *Of course* he offered something valuable to most, perhaps even all, of his patients.

Yet the imp of doubt continued to make its presence known: *Were you really, truly, helpful to your patients? Maybe you've just learned to pick patients who were going to improve on their own anyway.*

No. Wrong! Wasn't I the one who always took on great challenges?

Huh, you've got your limits! When was the last time you really stretched yourself—took a flagrant borderline into therapy? Or a seriously impaired schizophrenic or a bipolar patient?

Continuing to thumb through old charts, Julius was surprised to see how much post-therapy information he had—from occasional follow-up or "tune-up" visits, from chance encounters with the patient, or from messages delivered by new patients they had referred to him. But, still, had he made an enduring difference to them? Maybe his results were evanescent. Maybe many of his successful patients had relapsed and shielded that information from him out of sheer charity.

He noted his failures, too—folks, he had always told himself, who were not ready for his advanced brand of deliverance. Wait, he told himself, give yourself a break, Julius. How do you know they were *really* failures? *permanent* failures? You never saw them again. We all know there are plenty of late bloomers out there.

His eye fell upon Philip Slate's thick chart. You want failure? he said to himself. *There* was failure. Old-time major-league failure. Philip Slate. More than twenty years had passed, but his image of Philip Slate was crisp. His light brown hair combed straight back, his thin graceful nose, those high cheekbones that suggested nobility, and those crisp green eyes that reminded him of Caribbean waters. He remembered how much he disliked everything about his sessions with Philip. Except for one thing: the pleasure of looking at that face.

Philip Slate was so alienated from himself that he never thought to look within, preferring to skate on the surface of life and devote all his vital energy to fornication. Thanks to his pretty face, he had no end of volunteers. Julius shook his head as he rifled through Philip's chart—three years of sessions, all that relating and support and caring, all those interpretations without a whisper of progress. Amazing! Perhaps he wasn't the therapist he thought he was.

Whoa, don't jump to conclusions, he told himself. Why would Philip continue for three years if he had gotten nothing? Why would he continue to spend all that money for nothing? And God knows Philip hated to spend money. Maybe those sessions had changed Philip. Maybe he *was* a late bloomer—one of those patients who needed time to digest the nourishment given by the therapist, one of those who stored up some of the therapist's good stuff, took it home, like a bone, to gnaw on later, in private. Julius had known patients so competitive that they hid their improvement just because they didn't want to give the therapist the satisfaction (and the power) of having helped them.

Now that Philip Slate entered his mind, Julius could not get him out. He had burrowed in and taken root. Just like the melanoma. His failure with Philip became a symbol embodying *all* his failures in therapy. There was something peculiar about the case of Philip Slate. From where had it drawn all that power? Julius opened his chart and read his first note written twenty-five years before.

PHILIP SLATE—Dec. 11, 1980

26 yr old single white male chemist working for DuPont—develops new pesticides—strikingly handsome, carelessly dressed but has a regal air, formal, sits stiffly with little movement, no expression of feelings, serious, absence of any humor, not a smile or grin, strictly business, no social skills whatsoever. Referred by his internist, Dr. Wood.

CHIEF COMPLAINT: "I am driven against my will by sexual impulses."

> *Why now? "Last straw" episode a week ago which he described as though by rote.*
>
> *I arrived by plane in Chicago for a professional meeting, got off the plane, and charged to the nearest phone and went down my list of women in Chicago looking for a sexual liaison that evening. No luck!*

> *They were all busy. Of course they were busy: it was a Friday evening. I knew I was coming to Chicago; I could have phoned them days, even weeks earlier. Then, after calling the last number in my book, I hung up the phone and said to myself, "Thank God, now I can read and get a good night's sleep, which is what I really wanted to do all along."*
>
> *Patient says that phrase, that paradox—"which is what I really wanted to do all along"—haunted him all week and is the specific impetus for seeking therapy. "That's what I want to focus on in therapy," he says. "If* that *is what I want—to read and to get a good night's sleep—Dr. Hertzfeld, tell me—why can't I, why don't I, do it?"*

Slowly more details of his work with Philip Slate coasted into mind. Philip had intellectually intrigued him. At the time of their first meeting he had been working on a paper on psychotherapy and the will, and Philip's question—*why can't I do what I truly want to do?*—was a fascinating beginning for the article. And, most of all, he recalled Philip's extraordinary immutability: after three years he seemed entirely untouched and unchanged—and as sexually driven as ever.

Whatever became of Philip Slate? Not one word from him since he abruptly bailed out of therapy twenty-two years ago. Again Julius wondered whether, without knowing it, he had been helpful to Philip. Suddenly, he had to know; it seemed a matter of life and death. He reached for the phone and dialed 411.

Ecstasy in the act of copulation. That is it! That is the true essence and core of all things, the goal and purpose of all existence.

2

"Hello, is this Philip Slate?"

"Yes, Philip Slate, here."

"Dr. Hertzfeld here. Julius Hertzfeld."

"Julius Hertzfeld?"

"A voice from your past."

"The deep past. The Pleistocene past. Julius Hertzfeld. I can't believe it—it must be what? . . . at least twenty years. And why this call?"

"Well, Philip, I'm calling about your bill. I don't believe you paid in full for our last session."

"What? The last session? But I'm sure . . ."

"Just kidding, Philip. Sorry, some things never change—the old man is still jaunty and irrepressible. I'll be serious. Here, in a nutshell, is why I'm calling. I'm having some health problems, and I'm contemplating retirement. In the course of making this decision I've developed an irresistible urge to meet with some of my ex-patients—just to do some follow-ups, to satisfy my own curiosity. I'll explain more later if you wish. Soooo—here's my question to you: would you be willing to meet with me? Have a talk for an hour? Review our therapy together and fill me in on what's happened to you? It'll be interesting and enlightening for me. Who knows?—maybe for you as well."

"Um . . . an hour. Sure. Why not? I assume there's no fee?"

"Not unless you want to charge me, Philip—I'm asking for your time. How about later this week? Say, Friday afternoon?"

"Friday? Fine. That's satisfactory. I'll give you an hour at one o'clock. I shan't request payment for my services, but this time let's meet in my office—I'm on Union Street—four-thirty-one Union. Near Franklin. Look for my office number on the building directory—I'll be listed as Dr. Slate. I am now also a therapist."

Julius shivered as he hung up the phone. He swiveled his chair around and craned his neck to catch a glimpse of the Golden Gate Bridge. After that call he needed to see something beautiful. And feel something warm in his hands. He filled up his meerschaum pipe with Balkan Sobranie, lit the match, and sucked.

Oh baby, Julius thought, that warm earthy taste of latakia, that honeyed, pungent fragrance—like nothing else in the world. Hard to believe that he'd been away from it for so many years. He sank into a reverie and mused about the day he stopped smoking. Had to be right after that visit to his dentist, his next-door neighbor, old Dr. Denboer who had died twenty years ago. Twenty years—how could it be? Julius could still see his long Dutch face and gold-rimmed spectacles so clearly. Old Dr. Denboer beneath the soil now for twenty years. And he, Julius, still above ground. For now.

"That blister on your palate," Dr. Denboer shook his head slightly, "looks worrisome. "We'll need a biopsy." And though that biopsy had been negative, it caught Julius's attention because that very week he had gone to Al's funeral, his old cigarette-smoking tennis buddy, who died of lung cancer. And it didn't help then that he was in the midst of reading *Freud, Living and Dying,* by Max Schur, Freud's doctor—a graphic account of how Freud's cigar-spawned cancer gradually devoured his palate, his jaw, and, finally, his life. Schur promised Freud to help him die when the time came, and when Freud finally told him that the pain was so great that it no longer made sense to continue, Schur proved a man of his word and injected a fatal dose of morphine. Now *that* was a doctor. Where do you find a Dr. Schur nowadays?

Over twenty years of no tobacco, and also no eggs or cheese or animal fats. Healthy and happily abstinent. Until that God-dammed physical exam. Now everything was permitted: smoking, ice cream, spare ribs, eggs, cheese . . . everything. What difference did any of that matter any longer? What difference did anything make?—in another year Julius Hertzfeld would be leached into the soil, his molecules scattered, awaiting their next assignment. And sooner or later, in another few million years, the whole solar system would lie in ruins.

Feeling the curtain of despair descending, Julius quickly distracted himself by turning his attention back to his phone call with Philip Slate. Philip a therapist? How was that possible? He remembered Philip as cold, uncaring, oblivious of others, and, judging from that phone call, he was still much the same. Julius drew on his pipe and shook his head in silent wonder as he opened Philip's chart and continued reading his dictated note of their first session.

PRESENT ILLNESS—Sexually driven since thirteen—compulsive masturbation throughout adolescence continuing till present day—sometimes four, five times daily—obsessed with sex continually, masturbates to give himself peace. Huge hunk of life spent on obsessing about sex—he says "the time I've wasted chasing women—I could have gotten Ph.D.s in philosophy, Mandarin Chinese, and astrophysics."

RELATIONSHIPS: A loner. Lives with his dog in a small flat. No male friends. Zero. Nor any contacts with acquaintances from past—from high school, college, grad school . Extraordinarily isolated. Never had a long-term relationship with a woman—consciously avoids ongoing relationships—prefers one-night stands—occasionally sees a woman as long as a month—usually woman breaks it off—either she wants more from him, or she gets angry at being used or gets upset about his seeing other women. Desires novelty—wants the sexual chase—but never satiated—sometimes when he travels he picks up a woman, has sex, gets rid of her, and an hour later leaves his hotel room on the prowl again. Keeps a record of partners, a score sheet, and in past twelve months has had sex with ninety different women. Tells all this with flat affect—no shame, no boasting. Feels anxious if he is alone for an evening. Usually sex acts like Valium. Once he has sex, he feels peaceful for the rest of the evening and can read comfortably. No homosexual activities or fantasies.

HIS PERFECT EVENING? Out early, picks up woman in bar, gets laid (preferably before dinner), dumps woman as quickly as possible, preferably without having to buy her dinner but usually ends up having to feed her. Important to have as much evening time as possible for reading before going to bed. No TV, no movies, no social life, no sports. Only recreation is reading and classical music. Voracious reader of classics, history, and philosophy—no fiction, nothing current. Wanted to talk about Zeno and Aristarchus, his current interests.

PAST HISTORY: Grew up in Connecticut, only child, upper middle class. Father investment banker who committed suicide when Philip was thirteen. He knows nothing about circumstances or reasons behind father's suicide, some vague ideas that it was aggravated by mother's continual criticism. Blanket childhood amnesia—remembers little of his first several years and nothing about his father's funeral. Mother remarried when he was 24. A loner in school, fanatically immersed in studies, never had close friends, and since starting Yale at 17, has cut himself off from family. Phone contact with mother once or twice a year. Has never met stepfather.

WORK: Successful chemist—develops new hormonal-based pesticides for DuPont. Strictly an eight-to-five job, no passion about field, recently growing bored with his work. Keeps current with the research in field but never during his off hours. High income plus valuable stock options. A hoarder: enjoys tabulating his assets and managing his investments and spends every lunch hour alone, studying stock market research.

IMPRESSION: Schizoid, sexually compulsive—very distant—refused to look at me—not once did he meet my gaze—no sense of anything personal between us—clueless about interpersonal relations, responded to my here-and-now question about his first impressions of me with a look of bewilderment—as though I were speaking Catalan or Swahili. He seemed edgy, and I felt uncomfortable with him. Absolutely no humor. Zero. Highly intelligent, articulate but stingy with words—makes me work hard. Tenaciously concerned about therapy cost (though he can easily afford it). Requested fee reduction, which I refused. Seemed unhappy about my starting a couple minutes late and did not hesitate to inquire whether we'd make up this time at end of session to get full value. Questioned me twice about precisely how much advance notice he needed to give to cancel a session and avoid being charged.

Closing the chart, Julius thought: *Now, twenty-five years later, Philip is a therapist. Could there be a more unsuitable person in the world for that job? He seems very much the same: still no sense of humor, still hung up about money (maybe I shouldn't have made that crack about his bill). A therapist without a sense of humor? And so cold. And that edgy request to meet at* his *office.* Julius shivered again.

Life is a miserable thing. I have decided to spend my life thinking about it.

3

Union Street was sunny and festive. The clatter of silverware and the buzz of animated luncheon conversation streamed from the packed sidewalk tables at Prego, Betelnut, Exotic Pizza, and Perry's. Aquamarine and magenta balloons tethered to parking meters advertised a weekend sidewalk sale. But as Julius strolled toward Philip's office he barely glanced at the diners or the outdoor stalls heaped with the leftover designer clothes from the summer season. Nor did he linger at any of his favorite shop windows, not at Morita's antique Japanese furniture shop, the Tibetan shop, or even Asian Treasures with the gaily colored eighteenth-century roof tile of a fantastical woman warrior that he rarely passed without admiring.

Nor was dying in his mind. The riddles connected with Philip Slate offered diversion from those disquieting thoughts. First there was the riddle of memory and why he could so easily conjure up Philip's image with such eerie clarity. Where had Philip's face, name, story been lurking all these years? Hard to get his mind around the fact that the memory of his whole experience with Philip was contained neurochemically somewhere in the cortex of his brain. Most likely Philip dwelled in an intricate "Philip" network of connected neurons that, when triggered by the right neurotransmitters, would spring into action and project an image of Philip upon a ghostly screen in his visual cortex. He found it chilling to think of harboring a microscopic robotic projectionist in his brain.

But even more intriguing was the riddle of why he chose to revisit Philip. Of all his old patients, why choose Philip to lift out of deep memory storage? Was it simply because his therapy had been so dismally unsuccessful? Surely there was more to it than that. After all, there were many other patients he had not helped. But most of the faces and names of the failures had vanished without a trace. Maybe it was because most of his failures had dropped out of therapy quickly; Philip was an unusual failure in that he had continued to come. God, how he continued! For three frustrating years he never missed a session. Never late, not one minute—too cheap to waste any paid time. And then one day, without warning, a simple and irrevocable announcement at the end of an hour that this was his last session.

Even when Philip terminated, Julius had still regarded him as treatable; but then, he always erred in the direction of thinking everyone was treatable. Why did he fail? Philip was serious about working on his problems; he was challenging, smart, with intelligence to burn. But thoroughly unlikable. Julius rarely accepted a patient he disliked, but he knew there was nothing personal in his dislike of Philip: *anyone* would dislike him. Consider his lifelong lack of friends.

Though he may have disliked Philip, he *loved* the intellectual riddle Philip presented. His chief complaint ("Why can't I do what I really want to do?") was an enticing example of will-paralysis. Though the therapy may not have been useful for Philip, it was marvelously facilitative for Julius's writing, and many ideas emerging from the sessions found their way into his celebrated article "The Therapist and the Will" and into his book *Wishing, Willing, and Acting*. The thought flashed though his mind that perhaps he had exploited Philip. Perhaps now, with his heightened sense of connectivity, he might redeem himself, might yet accomplish what he had failed to do before.

Four-thirty-one Union was a modest stucco two-story corner building. In the vestibule Julius saw on the directory Philip's name: "Philip Slate Ph.D. Philosophical Counseling." Philosophical counseling? What the hell is that? Next, Julius snorted, it'll be barbers offering tonsorial therapy and greengrocers advertising legume counseling. He ascended the stairs and pressed the bell.

A buzz sounded as the door lock clicked open, and Julius entered a tiny bare-walled waiting room furnished only with an uninviting black vinyl loveseat. A few feet away, in the doorway to his office, Philip stood and, without approaching, beckoned Julius to enter. No handshake was offered.

Julius checked Philip's appearance against his memory. Pretty close match. Not much change in the past twenty-five years except for some soft wrinkles about the eyes and slight flabbiness in the neck. His light brown hair still combed straight back, those green eyes still intense, still averted. Julius recalled how rarely their gaze had met in all their years together. Philip reminded him of one of those supremely self-sufficient kids in class who sat in lectures and never took notes, while he and everyone else hustled to jot down every fact that might make an appearance on an exam.

Entering Philip's office, Julius considered a wisecrack about the Spartan furnishings—a scuffed cluttered desk, two uncomfortable-looking, nonmatching chairs, and a wall adorned only with a diploma. But he thought better of it, sat in the chair Philip indicated, played it straight, and waited for Philip's lead.

"Well, it has been a long time. Really long." Philip spoke in a formal, professional voice and gave no sign of nervousness about taking charge of the interview and thereby switching roles with his old therapist.

"Twenty-two. I just looked over my records."

"And why now, Dr. Hertzfeld?"

"Does this mean we've finished the small talk?" No, no! Julius chided himself. Cut it out! He remembered that Philip had no sense of humor.

Philip seemed unperturbed. "Basic interview technique, Dr. Hertzfeld. You know the routine. Establish the frame. We've already set the place, the time—I offer a sixty-minute session, incidentally, not the fifty-minute psych hour—and the fees, or lack thereof. So, next step is to move to purpose and goals. I'm trying to be at your service, Dr. Hertzfeld, to make this session as efficient as possible for you."

"All right, Philip. I appreciate it. Your 'why now?' is never a bad question—I use it all the time. Focuses the session. Gets us right down to business. As I told you on the phone, some health problems, significant health problems, have resulted in my wanting to look back, appraise things, evaluate my work with patients. Perhaps it's my age—a summing up. I believe when you reach sixty-five you'll understand why."

"I'll have to take your word on that summing-up process. The reason for your wish to see me or any of your clients again is not immediately apparent to me, and I experience no inclinations in that direction. My clients pay me a fee, and, in return, I give them my expert counsel. Our transaction ends. When we part, they feel they got good value, I feel I gave them full measure. I can't possibly imagine wanting to revisit them in the future. But, I am at your service. Where to start?"

Julius characteristically held little back in interviews. That was one of his strengths—people trusted him to be a straight shooter. But today he forced himself to hold back. He was stunned by Philip's brusqueness, but he wasn't there to give Philip advice. What he wanted was Philip's honest version of their work together, and the less Julius said about his state of mind, the better. If Philip knew about his despair, his search for meaning, his longing to have played some enduring instrumental role in Philip's life, he might, out of a sense of charity, give him just the affirmation he wanted. Or, perhaps, because of his contrariness, Philip might do just the opposite.

"Well, let me start by thanking you for humoring me and agreeing to meet. Here's what I want: first, your view of our work together—how it helped and how it didn't—and, second—and this is a tall order—I'd like very much to get a full briefing about your life since we last met. I always like to hear the end of stories."

If surprised by this request, Philip gave no sign but sat silently for a few moments, eyes closed, the fingertips of his two hands touching. In a carefully measured pace, he began. "The story's not at an end yet—in fact my life has had such a remarkable turn in the last few years that I feel it's just now beginning. But I'll maintain a strict chronology and start with my therapy. Overall, I'd have to say that my therapy with you was a complete failure. A time-consuming and expensive failure. I think I did my job as a patient. As far as I can recall, I was fully cooperative, worked hard, came regularly, paid my bills, remembered dreams, followed any leads you offered. Would you agree?"

"Agree that you were a cooperative patient? Absolutely. I'd even say more. I remember you as a dedicated patient."

Looking again at the ceiling, Philip nodded and continued: "As I recall, I saw you for three full years. And much of that time we met twice a week. That's a lot of hours—at least two hundred. About twenty thousand dollars."

Julius almost leaped in. Whenever a patient made a statement like that, his reflex was to reply "a drop in the bucket." And then point out that the issues being worked on in therapy had been problematic for so much of the patient's life that one could hardly expect them to yield quickly. He often added a personal note—that his first course of therapy, an analysis during his training, had been five times a week for three years—a total of over seven hundred hours. But Philip was not his patient now, and he was not there to persuade Philip of anything. He was there to listen. He bit his lips in silence.

Philip continued. "When I started with you I was at the nadir of my existence; 'in the trough' might be more apt. Working as a chemist and developing new ways to kill insects, I was bored with my career, bored with my life, bored with everything except reading philosophy and pondering the great riddles of history. But the reason I came to you was my sexual behavior. You remember that, of course?"

Julius nodded.

"I was out of control. All I wanted was sex. I was obsessed with it. I was insatiable. I shudder to think of the way I was, the life I led. I attempted to seduce as many women as possible. After coitus I had a brief respite from the compulsion, but in a short while my desire took over again."

Julius suppressed a smile at Philip's use of *coitus*—he remembered now the strange paradox of Philip wallowing in carnality but eschewing all four-letter words.

"It was only in that brief period—immediately after coitus," Philip continued, "that I was able to live fully, harmoniously—that was when I could connect with the great minds of the past."

"I remember you and your Aristarchus and Zeno."

"Yes, those and many others since, but the respites, the compulsion-free times, were all too brief. Now I'm liberated. Now I dwell in a higher realm all the time. But let me continue to review my therapy with you. Isn't that your primary request?"

Julius nodded.

"I remember being very attached to our therapy. It became another compulsion, but unfortunately it didn't replace the sexual compulsion but merely coexisted with it. I remember anticipating each hour with eagerness and yet ending with disappointment. It's difficult to remember much of what we did—I think we strove to understand my compulsion from the standpoint of my life history. Figuring it out—we always tried to figure it out. Yet every solution seemed suspect to me. No hypothesis was well-argued or well-grounded, and, worse, not one had the slightest impact on my compulsion.

"And it *was* a compulsion. I knew that. And I knew that I had to stop cold turkey. It took me a long time, but eventually I realized you didn't know how to help me and I lost faith in our work together. I recall that you spent inordinate amounts of time exploring my relationships—with others and especially with you. That never made sense to me. It didn't then. It still doesn't. As time went by, it became painful to meet with you, painful to keep on exploring our relationship as though it were real or enduring or anything other than what it truly was: *a purchase of service."* Philip stopped and looked at Julius with his palms up as though to say, "You wanted it straight—there it is."

Julius was stunned. Someone else's voice answered for him: "That's straight, all right. Thanks, Philip. Now, the rest of your story. What's happened to you since?"

Philip placed his palms together, rested his chin on his fingertips, stared up at the ceiling to collect his thoughts, and continued. "Well, let's see. I'll start with work. My expertise in developing hormonal agents to block insect reproduction had important implications for the company, and my salary escalated. But I grew profoundly bored with chemistry. Then, at age thirty, one of my father's trust funds matured and was turned over to me. It was a gift of freedom. I had enough to live on for several years, and I canceled my subscriptions to the chemistry journals, dropped out of the work force, and turned my attention to what I really wanted in life—the pursuit of wisdom.

"I was still miserable, still anxious, still sexually driven. I tried other therapists, but none helped me any more than you had. One therapist, who had studied with Jung, suggested I needed more than psychological therapy. He said that for an addict like me the best hope for release was a spiritual conversion. His suggestion led me to religious philosophy—especially the ideas and practices of the Far East—they were the only ones that made any sense. All other religious systems failed to explore the fundamental philosophical questions but instead used God as a method of avoiding true philosophical analysis. I even put in a few weeks at meditation retreats. That was not without interest. It didn't halt the obsession, but nonetheless I had a feeling that there was something important there. I just wasn't yet ready for it.

"Meanwhile, except for the interlude of forced chastity in the ashram, and even there I managed to find a few sliding doors, I continued the sexual hunt. As before, I had sex with a lot of women, by the dozens, by the hundreds. Sometimes two a day, anywhere, anytime I could find them—the same as when I was seeing you. Sex once, occasionally twice, with a woman and then moving on. Never exciting after that; you know the old saying: 'You can only have sex for the first time with the same girl once.'" Philip lifted his chin from his fingertips and turned to Julius.

"That last comment was meant to be humor, Dr. Hertzfeld. I remember you once said it was remarkable that, in all our hours together, I never once told you a joke."

Julius, now in no mood for levity, forced his lips into a grin even though he recognized Philip's little bon mot as something he himself had once said to Philip. Julius imagined Philip as a mechanical doll with a large key jutting from the top of his head. Time to wind him up again. "And then what happened?"

Gazing at the ceiling, Philip continued. "Then one day I reached a momentous decision. Since no therapist had helped in any way—and, sorry to say, Dr. Hertzfeld, that included you—"

"I'm beginning to get that particular point," Julius interjected, then quickly added, "No apologies needed. You're simply answering my questions honestly."

"Sorry, didn't mean to dwell on that. To continue, since therapy had not been the answer, I decided to heal myself—a course of bibliotherapy, assimilating the relevant thoughts of the wisest men who ever lived. So I began systematically reading the entire corpus of philosophy starting with the Greek pre-Socratics and working my way up to Popper, Rawls, and Quine. After a year of study my compulsion was no better, but I arrived at some important decisions: namely, that I was on the right track and that philosophy was my home. This was a major step—I remember how much you and I had talked about my never being at home anywhere in the world."

Julius nodded. "Yes, I remember that, too."

"I decided that, as long as I was going to spend years reading philosophy, I might as well make a profession of it. My money wouldn't last forever. So I entered the Ph.D. program in philosophy at Columbia. I did well, wrote a competent dissertation, and five years later had a doctorate in philosophy. I embarked on a teaching career and then, just a couple of years ago, became interested in applied or, as I prefer to think of it, 'clinical philosophy.' And that brings me up to today."

"You haven't finished telling me about being healed."

"Well, at Columbia, midway through my reading, I developed a relationship with a therapist, the perfect therapist, the therapist who offered me what no one else had been able to give."

"In New York, eh? What was his name? At Columbia? What institute did he belong to?"

"His name was Arthur . . ." Philip paused and watched Julius with a trace of a grin on his lips.

"Arthur?"

"Yes, Arthur Schopenhauer, my therapist."

"Schopenhauer? You're putting me on, Philip."

"I've never been more serious."

"I know little about Schopenhauer: just the clichés about his gloomy pessimism. I've never heard his name mentioned in the context of therapy. How was he able to help? What—?"

"I hate to cut you off, Dr. Hertzfeld, but I have a client coming and I still refuse to be late—that hasn't changed. Please give me your card. Some other time I'll tell you more about him. He was the therapist meant for me. I don't exaggerate when I say I owe my life to the genius of Arthur Schopenhauer."

Talent is like a marksman who hits a target which others cannot reach; genius is like a marksman who hits a target which others cannot see.

4

1787—The Genius: Stormy Beginning and False Start

Stormy Beginning—The genius was only four inches long when the storms began. In September of 1787 his enveloping amniotic sea roiled, tossed him to and fro, and threatened his fragile attachment to the uterine shore. The sea waters reeked of anger and fear. The sour chemicals of nostalgia and despair enveloped him. Gone forever were sweet balmy bobbing days. With nowhere to turn and no hope of comfort, his tiny neural synapses flared and fired in all directions.

What is young-learned is best-learned. Arthur Schopenhauer never forgot his early lessons.

False Start (or How Arthur Schopenhauer almost became an Englishman)—Arthurrr. Arthurrr, Arthurrrr. Heinrich Florio Schopenhauer scratched each syllable with his tongue. Arthur—a good name, an excellent name for the future head of the great Schopenhauer mercantile house.

It was 1787, and his young wife, Johanna, was two months pregnant when Heinrich Schopenhauer made a decision: if he had a son, he would name him Arthur. An honorable man, Heinrich allowed nothing to take precedence over duty. Just as his ancestors had passed the stewardship of the great Schopenhauer mercantile house to him, he would pass it to his son. These were perilous times, but Heinrich was confident that his yet unborn son would guide the firm into the nineteenth century. Arthur was the perfect name for the position. It was a name spelled the same in all major European languages, a name which would slip gracefully through all national borders. But, most important of all, it was an English name!

For centuries Heinrich's ancestors had guided the Schopenhauer business with great diligence and success. Heinrich's grandfather once hosted Catherine the Great of Russia and, to ensure her comfort, ordered brandy to be poured over the floors of the guest quarters and then set afire to leave the rooms dry and aromatic. Heinrich's father had been visited by Frederick, the king of Prussia, who spent hours attempting, unsuccessfully, to persuade him to shift the company from Danzig to Prussia. And now the stewardship of the great merchant house had passed to Heinrich, who was convinced that a Schopenhauer bearing the name of Arthur would lead the firm into a brilliant future.

The Schopenhauer mercantile house, dealing in the trade of grains, timber, and coffee, had long been one of the leading firms of Danzig, that venerable Hanseatic city which had long dominated the Baltic trade. But bad times had come for the grand free city. With Prussia menacing in the west and Russia in the east, and with a weakened Poland no longer able to continue guaranteeing Danzig's sovereignty, Heinrich Schopenhauer had no doubt that Danzig's days of freedom and trading stability were coming to an end. All of Europe was awash in political and financial turmoil—save England. England was the rock. England was the future. The Schopenhauer firm and family would find safe haven in England. No, more than safe haven, it would prosper if its future head should be born an Englishman and bear an English name. Herr Arthurrr Schopenhauer, no—Mister

Arthurrr Schopenhauer—an English subject heading the firm: that was the ticket to the future.

So, paying no heed to the protests of his teenaged pregnant wife, who pleaded to be in her mother's calming presence for the birth of her first child, he set off, wife in tow, for the long trip to England. The young Johanna was aghast but had to submit to the unbending will of her husband. Once settled in London, however, Johanna's ebullient spirit returned and her charm soon captivated London society. She wrote in her travel journal that her new English loving friends offered comforting reassurance and that before long she was the center of much attention.

Too much attention and too much love for the dour Heinrich, apparently, whose anxious jealousy shortly escalated into panic. Unable to catch his breath and feeling as though the tension in his chest would split him asunder, he had to do something. And so, reversing his course, he abruptly left London, carting his protesting wife, now almost six months pregnant, back to Danzig during one of the century's most severe winters. Years later Johanna described her feelings at being yanked from London: "No one helped me, I had to overcome my grief alone. The man dragged me, in order to cope with his anxiety, halfway across Europe."

This, then, was the stormy setting of the genius's gestation: a loveless marriage, a frightened, protesting mother, an anxious, jealous father, and two arduous trips across a wintry Europe.

A happy life is impossible; the best that a man can attain is a heroic life.

5

Leaving Philip's office, Julius felt stunned. He gripped the banister and unsteadily descended the stairs and staggered into the sunlight. He stood in front of Philip's building and tried to decide whether to turn left or right. The freedom of an unscheduled afternoon brought confusion rather than joy. Julius had always been focused. When he was not seeing patients, other important projects and activities—writing, teaching, tennis, research—clamored for his attention. But today nothing seemed important. He suspected that nothing had *ever* been important, that his mind had arbitrarily imbued projects with importance and then cunningly covered its traces. Today he saw through the ruse of a lifetime. Today there was nothing important to do, and he ambled aimlessly down Union Street.

Toward the end of the business section just past Fillmore Street, an old woman approached him noisily pushing a walker. *God, what a sight!* Julius thought. He first averted his face, then turned back to take inventory. Her clothes—several layers of sweaters capped by a burly overcoat—were preposterous for the sunny day. Her chipmunk cheeks churned hard, no doubt to keep dentures in place. But worst of all was the huge excrescence of flesh that buttressed one of her nostrils—a translucent pink wart the size of a grape, out of which sprouted several long bristles.

Stupid old lady was Julius's next thought, which he immediately amended: "She's probably no older than me. In fact, she's my future—the wart, the walker, the wheelchair. As she came closer, he heard her mumbling: "Now, let's see what's in these shops ahead. What will it be? What will I find?"

"Lady, I have no idea, I'm just walking here," Julius called out to her.

"I weren't talking to you."

"I don't see anyone else here."

"That still don't mean I'm talking to you."

"If not me, who?" Julius put his hands above his eyes and pantomimed looking up and down the empty street.

"What's it your business? Goddamn street freaks," she muttered as she clanked her walker past him.

Julius froze for a moment. He looked about him to make certain that no one had witnessed that interaction. My God, he thought, I'm losing it—what the fuck am I doing? Good thing I have no patients this afternoon. No doubt about it: spending time with Philip Slate is not good for my disposition.

Turning toward the intoxicating aroma emanating from Starbucks, Julius decided that an hour with Philip called for indulgence with a double espresso. He settled into a window seat and watched the passing show. No gray heads to be seen, inside or outside. At sixty-five he was the oldest person around, the oldest of the old, and rapidly growing older inside as his melanoma continued its silent invasion.

Two pert counter clerks flirted with some of the male customers. These were the girls that had never looked his way, never flirted with him when he was young nor caught his gaze as he aged. Time to realize that his time would never come, that those nubile, breasty girls with the Snow White faces would never turn his way with a coy smile and say, "Hey, haven't seen you here for a while. How's it going?" It was not going to happen. Life was seriously linear and not reversible.

Enough. Enough self-pity. He knew what to say to whiners: find a way to turn your gaze outward, stretch beyond yourself. Yes, that was the way—find the route to turn this shit into gold. Why not write about it? Perhaps as a personal journal. Then something more visible—who knows what?—maybe an article for the *Journal of the American Psychiatric Association* on "The Psychiatrist Confronting

Mortality." Or maybe something commercial for the *Sunday Times Magazine.* He could do it. Or why not a book? Something like *Autobiography of a Demise.* Not bad! Sometimes when you find a dynamite title, the piece just writes itself. Julius ordered an espresso, took out his pen and unfolded a paper bag he found on the floor. As he began to scribble, his lips curled into a slight smile at the humble origins of his powerful book.

Friday November 2, 1990. DDD (death-discovery day) + 16

No doubt about it: searching out Philip Slate was a bad idea. A bad idea to think I could get something from him. A bad idea to meet with him. Never again. Philip a therapist? Unbelievable—a therapist sans empathy, sensitivity, caring. He heard me say on the phone that I had health problems and that these problems were part of the reason I wanted to meet with him. Yet not one personal question about how I was doing. Not even a handshake. Frigid. Inhuman. Kept ten feet away from me. I worked like hell for that guy for three years. Gave him everything. Gave him my best stuff. Ungrateful bastard.

Oh yes, I know what he would say. I can hear that disembodied precise voice of his: "You and I had a commercial transaction: I gave you money and you provided your expert services. I paid promptly for every hour of your consultation. Transaction over. We're even; I owe you nothing."

Then he'd add, "Less than nothing, Dr. Hertzfeld, you had the best of our bargain. You received your full fee, whereas I received nothing of value in return."

The worst thing is, he's right. He owes me nothing. I crow about psychotherapy being a life of service. Service lovingly given. I have no lien on him. Why expect something from him? And, anyway, whatever it is I crave, he does not have it to give.

"He does not have it to give"—how many times have I said that to how many patients—about husbands or wives or fathers. Yet I can't let Philip go, this unrelenting, callous, ungiving man. Shall I write an ode about the obligation patients owe in later years to their therapists?

And why does it matter so much? And why, of all my patients, choose to contact him? I still don't know. I found a clue in my case notes—the feeling that I was talking to a young phantasm of myself. Perhaps there's more than a trace of Philip in me, in the me who in my teens and twenties and thirties was whipped around by hormones. I thought I knew what he was going through, I thought that I had an inside track to healing him. Is that why I tried so hard? Why he got more attention and energy from me than most of my other patients combined? In every therapist's practice, there is always some patient who consumes a disproportionate amount of the therapist's energy and attention—Philip was that person for me for three years.

Julius returned home that evening to a cold dark house. His son, Larry, had spent the last three days with him but that morning had returned to Baltimore, where he did neurobiological research at Johns Hopkins. Julius was almost relieved that Larry had left—the anguished look on his face and his loving but clumsy efforts to comfort his father had brought more sorrow than serenity. He started to phone Marty, one of his colleagues in his support group, but felt too despondent, hung up the phone, and instead turned on his computer to enter the notes scribbled on the crumpled Starbucks paper bag. "You have e-mail," greeted him, and, to his surprise, there was a message from Philip. He read it eagerly:

> At the end of our discussion today you asked about Schopenhauer and how I was helped by his philosophy. You also indicated that you might want to learn more about him. It occurs to me that you might be interested in my lecture at Coastal College next Monday evening at 7 P.M. (Toyon Hall, 340 Fulton St.). I am teaching a survey course on European philosophy, and on Monday I will give a brief overview of Schopenhauer (I must cover two thousand years in twelve weeks). Perhaps we can chat a bit after the lecture. Philip Slate

Without hesitation Julius e-mailed Philip: *Thanks. I'll be there.* He opened his appointment book to the following Monday and penciled in "Toyon Hall, 340 Fulton 7 P.M."

• • •

On Mondays Julius led a therapy group from four-thirty till six. Earlier in the day he had pondered whether to tell the group about his diagnosis. Though he had decided to postpone telling his individual patients until he regained his equilibrium, the group posed a different problem: group members often focused upon him, and the chances of someone spotting some change in his mood and commenting upon it were much greater.

But his concerns were unfounded. The members had readily accepted his excuse of the flu for having canceled the two previous meetings and then moved on to catch up on the last two weeks of each other's lives. Stuart, a short, pudgy pediatrician who perpetually seemed distracted, as though he were in a rush to get to his next patient, seemed pressured and asked for time from the group. This was a most unusual occurrence; in Stuart's year in the group he had rarely asked for help. He had originally entered the group under duress: his wife informed him by e-mail that unless he entered therapy and made some significant changes she was going to leave him. She added that she had conveyed this via e-mail because he paid more attention to electronic communication than anything said to him directly. During the past week his wife had upped the ante by moving out of their bedroom, and much of the meeting was spent on helping Stuart explore his feelings about her withdrawal.

Julius loved this group. Often the courage of the members took his breath away as they regularly broke new ground and took great risks. Today's meeting was no exception. Everyone supported Stuart for his willingness to show his vulnerability, and the time whizzed by. By the end of the meeting Julius felt much better. So caught up was he by the drama of the meeting that for an hour and a half he forgot his own despair. That was not unusual. All group therapists know about the wonderfully healing qualities inherent in the atmosphere of the working group. Time and again Julius had entered a meeting disquieted and left considerably better even though he had not, of course, explicitly addressed any of his personal issues.

He had barely time for a quick dinner at We Be Sushi a short distance from his office. He was a regular there and was greeted loudly by Mark, the sushi chef, as he took his seat. When alone, he always preferred sitting at the counter—like all of his patients, he was uncomfortable eating by himself at a restaurant table.

Julius ordered his usual: California rolls, broiled eel, and a variety of vegetarian maki. He loved sushi but carefully avoided raw fish because of his fear of parasites. That whole battle against outside marauders—now, what a joke it seemed! How ironic that, in the end, it would be an inside job. To hell with it; Julius threw caution to the wind and ordered some ahi sushi from the astonished chef. He ate with great relish before rushing out to Toyon Hall and to his first meeting with Arthur Schopenhauer.

The solid foundations of our view of the world and thus its depth or shallowness are formed in the years of childhood. Such a view is subsequently elaborated and perfected, yet essentially it is not altered.

6

Mom and Pop Schopenhauer—Zu Hause

What kind of a man was Heinrich Schopenhauer? Tough, dour, repressed, unyielding, proud. The story is told that in 1783, five years before Arthur's birth, Danzig was blockaded by the Prussians and food and fodder were scarce. The Schopenhauer family was forced to accept the billeting of an enemy general at their country estate. As a reward, the Prussian officer offered to grant Heinrich the privilege of forage for his horses. Heinrich's reply? "My stable is well stocked, sir, and when the food supply runs out I will have my horses put down."

And Arthur's mother, Johanna? Romantic, lovely, imaginative, vivacious, flirtatious. Though all of Danzig in 1787 considered the union of Heinrich and Johanna a brilliant event, it proved to be a tragic mismatch. The Troiseners, Johanna's family, came from a modest background and had long regarded the lofty Schopenhauers with awe. Hence, when Heinrich, at the age of thirty-eight, came to court the seventeen-year-old Johanna, the Troiseners were jubilant and Johanna acquiesced to her parents' choice.

Did Johanna regard her marriage as a mistake? Read her words written years later as she warned other young women facing a matrimonial decision: "Splendor, rank, and title exercise an all too seductive power over a young girl's heart luring women into tying a marriage knot . . . a false step for which they must suffer the hardest punishment the rest of their lives."

"Suffer the hardest punishment the rest of their lives"—strong words from Arthur's mother. In her journals she confided that before Heinrich courted her she had had a young love, which fate took from her, and it was in a state of resignation that she had accepted Heinrich Schopenhauer's marriage proposal. Did she have a choice? Most likely not. This typical eighteenth-century marriage of convenience was arranged by her family for reasons of property and status. Was there love? There was no question of love between Heinrich and Johanna Schopenhauer. Never. Later, in her memoirs, she wrote, "I no more pretended ardent love than he demanded it." Nor was there abundant love for others in their household—not for the young Arthur Schopenhauer, nor for his younger sister, Adele, born nine years later.

Love between parents begets love for the children. Occasionally, one hears tales of parents whose great love for each other consumes all the love available in the household, leaving only love-cinders for the children. But this zero-sum economic model of love makes little sense. The opposite seems true: the more one loves, the more one responds to children, to everyone, in a loving manner.

Arthur's love-bereft childhood had serious implications for his future. Children deprived of a maternal love bond fail to develop the basic trust necessary to love themselves, to believe that others will love them, or to love being alive. In adulthood they become estranged, withdraw into themselves, and often live in an adversarial relationship with others. Such was the psychological landscape that would ultimately inform Arthur's worldview.

If we look at life in its small details, how ridiculous it all seems. It is like a drop of water seen through a microscope, a single drop teeming with protozoa. How we laugh as they bustle about so eagerly and struggle with one another. Whether here, or in the little span of human life, this terrible activity produces a comic effect.

7

At five minutes to seven Julius knocked out the ashes from his meerschaum pipe and entered the auditorium in Toyon Hall. He took a seat in the fourth row on the side aisle and looked about the amphitheater: Twenty rows rose sharply from the entry level where the lecture podium stood. Most of the two hundred seats were vacant; roughly thirty were broken and wrapped with yellow plastic ribbon. Two homeless men and their collections of newspapers sprawled across seats in the last row. Approximately thirty seats were occupied by unkempt students randomly sprinkled throughout the auditorium with the exception of the first three rows which remained vacant.

Just like a therapy group, Julius thought, no one wants to sit near to the leader. Even in his group meeting earlier that day the seats on either side of him had been left vacant for the late members, and he had joked that a seat next to him seemed to be the penalty for tardiness. Julius thought of the group therapy folklore about seating; that the most dependent person sits to the leader's right, whereas the most paranoid members sit directly opposite; but, in his experience, the reluctance to sit next to the leader was the only rule that could be counted on with regularity.

The shabbiness and dilapidation of Toyon Hall was typical of the entire campus of California Coastal College, which had begun life as an evening business school, then expanded and flowered briefly as an undergraduate college, and was now obviously in a phase of entropy. On his walk to the lecture through the unsavory Tenderloin, Julius had found it difficult to distinguish unkempt students from homeless denizens of the neighborhood. What teacher could avoid demoralization in this setting? Julius began to understand why Philip wanted to switch careers by moving into clinical work.

He checked his watch. Seven o'clock exactly and right on cue Philip entered the auditorium, dressed in the professorial uniform of khaki pants, checkered shirt, and a tan corduroy jacket with sewed-on elbow patches. Extracting his lecture notes from a properly scuffed briefcase and, without so much as a glance at his audience, he began:

> This is the survey of Western philosophy—lecture eighteen—Arthur Schopenhauer. Tonight I shall proceed differently and stalk my prey more indirectly. If I appear desultory, I ask your forbearance—I promise I shall soon enough return to the matter at hand. Let us begin by turning our attention to the great debuts in history.

Philip scanned his audience for some nod of comprehension and, failing to find it, crooked his forefinger at one of the students sitting nearest him and pointed to the blackboard. He then spelled out and defined three words, *d-e-s-u-l-t-o-r-y, f-o-r-e-b-e-a-r-a-n-c-e,* and *d-e-b-u-t,* which the student dutifully copied onto the blackboard. The student started to return to his seat, but Philip pointed to a first-row seat, instructing him to remain there.

> Now for great debuts; trust me—my purpose for beginning in such a fashion will, in time, become apparent. Imagine Mozart stunning the Viennese royal court as he performed flawlessly on the harpsichord at the age of nine. Or, if Mozart does not strike a familiar chord *(here the faintest trace of a smile),* imagine something more familiar to you, the Beatles at nineteen playing their own compositions to Liverpool audiences.
>
> Other amazing debuts include the extraordinary debut of Johann Fichte. *(Here a signal to the student to write* F-i-c-h-t-e *on*

the board.) Does any one of you remember his name from my last lecture in which I discussed the great German idealist philosophers who followed Kant in the late eighteenth and early nineteenth centuries: Hegel, Schelling, and Fichte? Of these, Fichte's life and his debut was the most remarkable for he began life as a poor uneducated goose shepherd in Rammenau, a small German village whose only claim to fame was its clergyman's inspired sermons every Sunday.

Well, one Sunday a wealthy aristocrat arrived at the village too late to hear the sermon. As he stood, obviously disappointed, outside the church, an elderly villager approached him and told him not to despair because the gooseherd, young Johann, could repreach the sermon to him. The villager fetched Johann, who, indeed, repeated the entire lecture verbatim. So impressed was the baron by the gooseherd's astoundingly retentive mind that he financed Johann's education and arranged for him to attend Pforta, a renowned boarding school later attended by many eminent German thinkers, including the subject of our next lecture, Friedrich Nietzsche.

Johann excelled in school and later at the university, but when his patron died, Johann had no means of support and took a tutoring job in a private home in Germany where he was hired to teach a young man the philosophy of Kant, whom he had not yet read himself. Soon he was entranced by the work of the divine Kant . . .

Philip suddenly looked up from his notes to survey his audience. Seeing no glint of recognition in any eyes, he hissed at his audience as he motioned to the blackboard scribe to write *K-a-n-t:*

Hello, anybody home? Kant, Immanuel Kant, Kant, Kant, remember? We spent two hours on him last week? Kant, the greatest, along with Plato, of all the world's philosophers. I give you my word: Kant will be on the final. Ah ha, there's the ticket . . . I see stirrings of life, movement, one or two eyes opening. A pen making contact with paper.

So where was I? Ah, yes. The gooseherd. Fichte was next

tendered a position as a private tutor in Warsaw and, penniless, walked all the way only to have the job denied him when he arrived. Since he was only a few hundred miles from Königsberg, the home of Kant, he decided to walk there to meet the master in person. After two months he arrived at Königsberg and, audaciously, knocked on Kant's door but was not granted an audience. Kant was a creature of habit and not inclined to receive unknown visitors. Last week I described to you the regularity of his schedule—so exact that the townspeople could set their watches by seeing him on his daily walk.

Fichte assumed he was refused entry because he had no letters of recommendation and decided to write his own in order to gain an audience with Kant. In an extraordinary burst of creative energy he wrote his first manuscript, the renowned *Critique of All Revelation,* which applied Kant's views on ethics and duty to the interpretation of religion. Kant was so impressed with the work that he not only agreed to meet with Fichte but encouraged its publication.

Because of some curious mishap, probably a marketing ploy of the publisher, the *Critique* appeared anonymously. The work was so brilliant that critics and the reading public mistook it for a new work by Kant himself. Ultimately, Kant was forced to make a public statement that it was not he who was the author of this excellent manuscript but a very talented young man named Fichte. Kant's praise ensured Fichte's future in philosophy, and a year and a half thereafter he was offered a professorship at the University of Jena.

"That," Philip looked up from his notes with an ecstatic look on his face and then jabbed the air with an awkward show of enthusiasm, "that is what I call a debut!" No students looked up or gave a sign of registering Philip's brief awkward display of enthusiasm. If he felt discouraged by his audience's unresponsiveness, Philip did not show it and, unperturbed, continued:

And now consider something closer to your hearts—athletic debuts. Who can forget the debut of Chris Evert, Tracy Austin,

> or Michael Chang, who won grand-slam professional tennis tournaments at fifteen or sixteen? Or the teenaged chess prodigies Bobby Fischer or Paul Morphy? Or think of José Raoul Capablanca, who won the chess championship of Cuba at the age of eleven.
>
> Finally, I want to turn to a literary debut—the most brilliant literary debut of all time, a man in his midtwenties who blazed onto the literary landscape with a magnificent novel . . .

Here, Philip stopped in order to build the suspense and looked up, his countenance shining with confidence. He felt assured of what he was doing—that was apparent. Julius watched in disbelief. What was Philip expecting to find? The students on the edge of their seats, trembling with curiosity, each murmuring, "Who was this literary prodigy?"

Julius, in his fifth-row seat, swiveled his head to survey the auditorium: glazed eyes everywhere, students slumped in chairs, doodling, poring over newspapers, crossword puzzles. To the left, a student stretched out asleep over two chairs. To the right, two students at the end of his row embraced in a long kiss. In the row directly in front of him, two boys elbowed each other as they leered upward, toward the back of the room. Despite his curiosity, Julius did not turn to follow their gaze—probably they were staring up some woman's skirt—and turned his attention back to Philip, who droned on:

> And who was the prodigy? His name was Thomas Mann. When he was your age, yes, your age, he began writing a masterpiece, a glorious novel called *Buddenbrooks* published when he was only twenty-six years old. Thomas Mann, as I hope and pray you know, went on to become a towering figure in the twentieth-century world of letters and was awarded the Nobel Prize for Literature. *(Here Philip spelled* M-a-n-n *and* B-u-d-d-e-n-b-r-o-o-k-s *to his blackboard scribe.) Buddenbrooks,* published in 1901, traced the life of one family, a German burgher family, through four generations and all the associated vicissitudes of the life cycle.
>
> Now what does this have to do with philosophy and with the real subject of today's lecture? As I promised, I have

strayed a bit but only in the service of returning to the core with greater vigor.

Julius heard rustling in the auditorium and the sound of footsteps. The two elbowing voyeurs directly in front of Julius noisily collected their belongings and left the hall. The embracing students at the end of the row had departed, and even the student assigned to the blackboard had vanished.

Philip continued:

To me, the most remarkable passages in *Buddenbrooks* come late in the novel as the protagonist, the paterfamilias, old Thomas Buddenbrook, approaches death. One is astounded by a writer in his early twenties having such insight and such sensibility to issues concerned with the end of life. *(A faint smile played on his lips as Philip held up the dog-eared book.)* I recommend these pages to anyone intending to die.

Julius heard the strike of matches as two students lit cigarettes while exiting the auditorium.

When death came to claim him, Thomas Buddenbrook was bewildered and overcome by despair. None of his belief systems offered him comfort—neither his religious views which had long before failed to satisfy his metaphysical needs, nor his worldly skepticism and materialistic Darwinian leaning. Nothing, in Mann's words, was able to offer the dying man "in the near and penetrating eye of death a single hour of calm."

Here, Philip looked up. "What happened next is of great importance and it is here that I begin to close in on the designated subject of our lecture tonight."

In the midst of his desperation Thomas Buddenbrooks chanced to draw from his bookcase an inexpensive, poorly sewn volume of philosophy bought at a used book stand years before. He began to read and was immediately soothed.

He marveled by how, as Mann put it, "a master-mind could lay hold of this cruel mocking thing called life."

The extraordinary clarity of vision in the volume of philosophy enthralled the dying man, and hours passed without his looking up from his reading. Then he came upon a chapter titled "On Death, and Its Relation to Our Personal Immortality" and, intoxicated by the words, read on as though he were reading for his very life. When he finished, Thomas Buddenbrooks was a man transformed, a man who had found the comfort and peace that had eluded him.

What was it that the dying man discovered? *(At this point Philip suddenly adopted an oracular voice.)* Now listen well, Julius Hertzfeld, because this may be useful for life's final examination. . . .

Shocked at being directly addressed in a public lecture, Julius bolted upright in his seat. He glanced nervously about him and saw, to his astonishment, that the auditorium was empty: everyone, even the two homeless men, had left.

But Philip, unperturbed by his vanished audience, calmly continued:

I'll read a passage from *Buddenbrooks. (He opened a tattered paperback copy of the book.)* "Your assignment is to read the novel, especially part nine, with great care. It will prove invaluable to you—far more valuable than attempting to extract meaning from patients' reminiscences of long ago.

> Have I hoped to live on in my son? In a personality yet more feeble, flickering, and timorous than my own? Blind, childish folly! What can my son do for me? Where shall I be when I am dead? Ah, it is so brilliantly clear. I shall be in all those who have ever, do ever, or ever shall say "I"—especially, however, in all those who say it most fully, potently, and gladly! . . . Have I ever hated life—pure, strong, relentless life? Folly and misconception! I have but hated myself because I could not bear it. I love you all, you blessed, and soon, soon, I shall cease to be cut off from you by all the narrow bonds of myself; soon that

> in me which loves you will be free and be in and with you—in and with you all.

Philip closed the novel and returned to his notes.

Now who was the author of the volume which so transformed Thomas Buddenbrooks? Mann does not reveal his name in the novel, but forty years later he wrote a magnificent essay which stated that Arthur Schopenhauer was the author of the volume. Mann then proceeds to describe how, at the age of twenty-three, he first experienced the great joy of reading Schopenhauer. He was not only entranced by the ring of Schopenhauer's words, which he describes as "so perfectly consistently clear, so rounded, its presentation and language so powerful, so elegant, so unerringly apposite, so passionately brilliant, so magnificently and blithely severe—like never any other in the history of German philosophy," but by the essence of Schopenhauerian thought, which he describes as "emotional, breathtaking, playing between violent contrasts, between instinct and mind, passion and redemption." Then and there Mann resolved that discovering Schopenhauer was too precious an experience to keep to himself and straightaway used it creatively by offering the philosopher to his suffering hero.

And not only Thomas Mann but many other great minds acknowledged their debt to Arthur Schopenhauer. Tolstoy called Schopenhauer the "genius par excellence among men." To Richard Wagner he was a "gift from Heaven." Nietzsche said his life was never the same after purchasing a tattered volume of Schopenhauer in a used-book store in Leipzig and, as he put it, "letting that dynamic, dismal genius work on my mind." Schopenhauer forever changed the intellectual map of the Western world, and without him we would have had a very different and weaker Freud, Nietzsche, Hardy, Wittgenstein, Beckett, Ibsen, Conrad.

Philip pulled out a pocketwatch, studied it for a moment, and then, with great solemnity:

> Here concludes my introduction to Schopenhauer. His philosophy has such breadth and depth it defies a short summary. Hence I have chosen to pique your curiosity in the hope that you will read the sixty-page chapter in your text carefully. I prefer to devote the last twenty minutes of this lecture to audience questions and discussion. Are there questions from the audience, Dr. Hertzfeld?

Unnerved by Philip's tone, Julius once again scanned the empty auditorium and then softly said, "Philip, I wonder if you're aware that your audience has departed?"

"What audience? Them? Those so-called students?" Philip flicked his wrist in a disparaging manner to convey that they were beneath his notice, that neither their arrival nor their departure made the slightest difference to him. "You, Dr. Hertzfeld, are my audience today. I intended my lecture for you alone," said Philip, who in no way seemed discomfited by holding a conversation with someone thirty feet away in a cavernous deserted auditorium.

"All right, I'll bite. Why am I your audience today?"

"Think about it, Dr. Hertzfeld . . ."

"I'd prefer you'd call me Julius. If I refer to you as Philip, and I'm assuming that's okay with you, then it's only right that you call me Julius. Ah, déjà vu all over again—how clearly I recall saying so very very long ago, 'Call me Julius, please—we're not strangers.'"

"I am not on a first-name basis with my clients because I am their professional consultant, not their friend. But, as you wish, Julius it is. I'll start again. You inquire why you alone are my intended audience. My answer is that I am merely responding to your request for help. Think about it, Julius, you came to see me with a request for an interview and embedded in that request were other requests."

"Oh?"

"Yes. Let me expand upon this matter. First, there was a tone of urgency in your voice. It was particularly important to you that I meet with you. Obviously, your request did not arise from simple curiosity about how I was doing. No, you wanted something else. You mentioned that your health was imperiled, and, in a sixty-five-year-old man, that means you must be confronting your death. Hence, I could only assume that you were frightened and searching for some kind of consolation. My lecture today is my response to your request."

"An oblique response, Philip."

"No more oblique than your request, Julius."

"Touché! But, as I recall, you've never minded obliquity."

"And I'm comfortable with it now. You made a request for help, and I responded by introducing you to the man who, of all men, can be most helpful to you."

"And so your intent was to offer me solace by describing how Mann's dying Buddenbrooks received comfort from Schopenhauer?"

"Precisely. And I offered that to you only as an appetizer, a sampler of what is to come. There is a great deal that I, as your guide to Schopenhauer, can offer you, and I would like to make a proposal."

"A proposal? Philip, you continue to surprise. My curiosity is piqued."

"I've completed my course work in a counseling program and all other requirements to obtain a state counseling license, except that I need two hundred more hours of professional supervision. I can continue practicing as a clinical philosopher—that field is not regulated by the state—but a counselor's license would offer me a number of advantages, including the ability to buy malpractice insurance and to market myself more effectively. Unlike Schopenhauer, I have neither an independent source of financial support nor any secure academic support—you've seen with your own eyes the disinterest in philosophy displayed by the clods who attend this pigsty of a university."

"Philip, why must we shout to one another? The lecture is over. Would you mind taking a seat and continuing this discussion more informally."

"Of course." Philip collected his lecture notes, stuffed them into his briefcase, and eased into a seat in the front row. Though they were closer, four rows of seats still separated them, and Philip was forced to swivel his neck awkwardly to see Julius.

"So, am I correct in assuming that you propose a swap—I supervise you and you teach me about Schopenhauer?" Julius now asked in a low voice.

"Right!" Philip turned his head but not enough to make eye contact.

"And you've given thought to the precise mechanics of our arrangement?"

"I've given much thought to it. In fact, Dr. Hertzfeld . . ."

"Julius."

"Yes, yes—Julius. What I was going to say is that I'd been considering the idea of calling you for several weeks to try to arrange supervision but kept putting it off, primarily for financial reasons. So I was startled by the remarkable coincidence of your call. As for mechanics, I suggest meeting weekly and splitting our hour: half the time you provide expert advice about my patients, and half the time I am your guide to Schopenhauer."

Julius closed his eyes and lapsed into thought.

Philip waited two or three minutes and then: "What say you to my offer? Even though I'm certain no students will appear, I'm scheduled for office hours after my lecture and so must head back to the administration building."

"Well Philip, it's not your everyday offer. I need more time to think it through. Let's meet later this week. I take off Wednesday afternoons. Can you do four o'clock?"

Philip nodded. "I finish at three on Wednesday. Shall we meet in my office?"

"No, Philip. My office. It's in my home at two-forty-nine Pacific Avenue, not too far from my old office. Here, take my card."

Excerpts from Julius's Journal

After his lecture Philip's proposal for a supervision-tutoring swap stunned me. How quickly one moves back into the familiar force field of another person! So much like the state-dependent memories in dreams in which the landscape's eerie familiarity reminds you that you've visited the identical locale before in other dreams. Same with marijuana—a couple of hits and suddenly you're in a familiar place thinking familiar thoughts that exist only in the marijuana state.

And it's the same with Philip. Only a little time in his presence and—presto—my deep memories of him plus a peculiar Philip-induced state of mind reappear in a flash. How arrogant, how disdainful he is. How uncaring about others. And yet there is something, something strong—I wonder what?—that draws me to him. His intelligence? His loftiness and otherworldliness coupled to such extraordinary naïveté? And how unchanged he is after twenty-two years. No, that's not true! He's liberated from the sexual compulsion, no longer doomed to walk nose-to-ground forever sniffing for pussy. He lives much more in the higher places he's always longed for. But his manipulativeness—that's still there, and so patent, and he's so clueless about its visibility, about how I should leap at his offer, how I should give him two hundred hours of my time in return for his teaching me Schopenhauer, and brazenly presenting it as though it was I who suggested it, who want and need it. Can't deny that I have some slight interest in Schopenhauer, but spending a couple hundred hours with Philip to learn about Schopenhauer right now is low on my wish list. And if that excerpt he read about the dying Buddenbrooks is a prime example of what Schopenhauer has to offer me, then it leaves me cold. The idea of rejoining the universal oneness without any persistence of me and my memories and unique consciousness is the coldest of comfort. No, it's no comfort at all.

And what draws Philip to me? That's another question. That crack the other day about the twenty thousand dollars he wasted on his therapy with me—maybe he is still looking for some return on his investment.

Supervise Philip? Make him a legitimate, kosher therapist? There's a dilemma. Do I want to sponsor him? Do I want to give him my blessing when I don't believe that a hater (and he is a hater) can help anyone grow?

Religion has everything on its side: revelation, prophecies, government protection, the highest dignity and eminence . . . and more than this, the invaluable prerogative of being allowed to imprint its doctrines on the mind at a tender age of childhood, whereby they become almost innate ideas.

8

Halcyon Days of Early Childhood

Johanna wrote in her diary that after Arthur's birth in February 1788 she, like all young mothers, enjoyed playing with her "new doll." But new dolls soon become old dolls, and within months Joanna wearied of her toy and languished in boredom and isolation in Danzig. Something new was emerging in Johanna—some vague sense that motherhood was not her true destiny, that some other future awaited her. Her summers at the Schopenhauer country estate were particularly difficult. Though Heinrich, accompanied by a clergyman, joined her for weekends, Johanna spent the rest of her time alone with Arthur and her servants. Because of his fierce jealousy, Heinrich forbade his wife to entertain neighbors or to venture from home for any reason.

When Arthur was five, the family encountered great stress. Prussia annexed Danzig, and, shortly before the advancing Prussian troops arrived under the command of the very general Heinrich had insulted years before, the entire Schopenhauer family fled to Hamburg. There, in 1797, in a strange city, Johanna gave birth to her second child, Adele, and felt ever more trapped and despairing.

Heinrich, Johanna, Arthur, Adele—Father, mother, son, daughter—the four bound together yet unconnected.

To Heinrich, Arthur was a chrysalis destined to emerge as the future head of the Schopenhauer mercantile house. Heinrich was the traditional Schopenhauer father; he attended to business and put his son out of mind, intending to spring into action and assume fatherly duties when Arthur had finished his childhood.

And the wife, what was Heinrich's plan for her? She was the Schopenhauer family seedpod and cradle. Dangerously vital, she had to be contained, protected, and restrained.

And Johanna? What did she feel? Trapped! Her husband and provider, Heinrich, was her lethal mistake, her joyless jailer, the grim evacuator of her vitality. And her son, Arthur? Was he not part of the trap, the seal to her coffin? A talented woman, Johanna had a desire for expression and self-realization that was growing at a ferocious pace, and Arthur would prove a woefully inadequate recompense for self-renunciation.

And her young daughter? Little noticed by Heinrich, Adele was assigned a minor role in the family drama and was destined to spend her entire life as Johanna Schopenhauer's amanuensis.

And so the Schopenhauers each went their separate ways.

Father Schopenhauer, heavy with anxiety and despair, lumbered to his death, sixteen years after Arthur's birth, by climbing to the upper freight window of the Schopenhauer warehouse and leaping into the frigid waters of the Hamburg canal.

Mother Schopenhauer, sprung from her matrimonial trap by Heinrich's leap, kicked the grime of Hamburg from her shoes and flew like the wind to Weimar, where she quickly created one of Germany's liveliest literary salons. There she became the dear friend of Goethe and other outstanding men of letters, and authored a dozen best-selling romantic novels, many about women who were forced into unwanted marriages but refused to bear children and continued to long for love.

And young Arthur? Arthur Schopenhauer was to grow up into one of the wisest men who ever lived. And one of the most despairing and life-hating of men, a man who at the age of fifty-five would write:

Could we foresee it, there are times when children might seem like innocent prisoners condemned not to death but to life and as yet all too unconscious of what their sentence means. Nevertheless every man desires to reach old age . . . a state of life of which it may be said "it is bad today, and every day it will get worse, until the worst of all happens."

In endless space countless luminous spheres, round each of which some dozen smaller illuminated ones revolve, hot at the core and covered with a cold hard crust on which a mouldy film has produced living and knowing beings—this is . . . the real, the world.

9

Julius's spacious Pacific Heights home was far grander than any he could now possibly afford to buy: he was one of the lucky millionaires in San Francisco who had the good fortune to buy a house, any house, thirty years earlier. It was his wife, Miriam's, thirty-thousand-dollar-inheritance money that had made the purchase possible, and, unlike any other investment Julius and Miriam had ever made, the house's value had rocketed upward. After Miriam's death, Julius considered selling the house—it was far too large for one person—but instead he moved his office into the first floor of the house.

Four steps led from the street to a landing with a blue-tiled fountain. On the left, a few stairs led to Julius's office, on the right was a longer stairway to his home. Philip arrived precisely on time. Julius greeted him at the door, escorted him into the office, and gestured toward an auburn leather chair.

"Some coffee or tea?"

But Philip did not look around as he took his seat and, ignoring Julius's offer, said, "I await your decision about supervision."

"Ah, once again, straight to the business at hand. I'm having a difficult time with that decision. Lots of questions. There's something about your request—a deep contradiction—that puzzles the hell out of me."

"Undoubtedly, you want to know why I'm asking you for supervision after being so dissatisfied with you as a therapist?"

"Precisely. In exceedingly clear language you claimed that our therapy was a colossal failure, a waste of three years and a great deal of your money."

"There's no true contradiction," Philip replied instantaneously. "One can be a competent therapist and supervisor even though one fails with a particular patient. Research shows that therapy, in any hands, is unsuccessful for about a third of patients. Besides, there's no doubt I played a significant role in the failure—my stubbornness, my rigidity. Your only error was to choose the wrong type of therapy for me and then persist in it far too long. However, I'm not incognizant of your effort, even your interest, in helping me."

"Sounds good, Philip. Sounds logical. But still, to ask for supervision from a therapist who gave you nothing in therapy. Damned if I'd do it—I'd find someone else. I have a feeling that there's something more, something you're not saying."

"Perhaps a modest retraction is in order. It is not entirely accurate to say I got nothing from you. You did make two statements that stuck with me and may have played some instrumental role in my recovery."

For a moment Julius fumed about having to ask for details. Did Philip think he wouldn't be interested? Could he be that much of a space cadet? Finally, he gave in and said, "And which two statements?"

"Well, the first statement doesn't sound like much, but it had some power. I had been telling you about one of my typical evenings—you know, picking up a woman somewhere, taking her to dinner, the seduction scene in my bedroom with the same routine and the same mood music. I remember asking your opinion of my evening and whether you found it distasteful or immoral."

"I don't remember my answer."

"You said you found it neither distasteful nor immoral, only boring. It jolted me to think that I was living a boring, repetitious life."

"Ah, interesting. So that was one statement. The other?"

"We were discussing tombstone epitaphs. I don't remember why, but I believe you had raised the question of what epitaph I might select for myself . . ."

"Very possible. I've used that question when I feel at an impasse and need some shocking intervention. And . . . ?"

"Well, you suggested that I might have my tombstone engraved with the phrase "He liked to fuck." And then you added that the phrase could be a good epitaph for my dog too—that I could use the same stone for both me and the dog."

"Pretty strong stuff. Was I really that harsh?"

"Whether it is harsh or not is irrelevant. What's important is its effectiveness and persistence. Much later, maybe ten years later, I made use of it."

"Time-delayed interventions! I've always had a hunch they're more important than usually thought. Always meant to do a study of that. But for our purposes today tell me, why were you reluctant at our last meeting to mention these, to acknowledge that I had in some way, even some small way, been useful to you?"

"Julius, I'm not sure I see the relevance of this to the issue at hand—that is, whether you are or are not willing to be my psychotherapy supervisor? And to permit me in return to be your Schopenhauerian adviser?"

"The fact that you don't see the relevance makes it all the more relevant. Philip, I'm not going to attempt to be diplomatic. Here it is straight: I'm not certain you're basically equipped to be a therapist, and hence I have some doubts that supervision makes sense."

"You say, not 'equipped'? Clarify please," said Philip with no trace of discomfort.

"Well, let me put it this way. I've always regarded therapy more as a calling than a profession, a way of life for people who care about others. I don't see sufficient caring in you. The good therapist wants to alleviate suffering, wants to help people grow. But I see in you only disdain for others—look at the way you dismissed and insulted your students. Therapists need to relate to their patients, whereas you care little about how others feel. Take the two of us. You tell me that, on the basis of my phone call to you, you made the assumption that I had a fatal illness. Yet never did you utter a word of consolation or sympathy."

"Would that have helped—mumbling some vacuous words of sympathy? I gave you more, much more. I constructed and delivered an entire lecture for you."

"I understand that now. But it was all so oblique, Philip. It made me feel like I was being managed, not cared about. Better for me, much better, if you had been direct, if you had sent some message from your heart to mine. Nothing monumental, maybe just some simple inquiry into my situation or state of mind, or, Christ, you might have simply said, 'I'm sorry to hear you're dying.' How hard would that have been?"

"If I were sick, that's not what I'd want. I would have wanted the tools, the ideas, the vision that Schopenhauer offered in the face of death—and that's what I delivered to you."

"Even now, Philip, you still don't bother to check your assumption that I have a fatal illness."

"Am I mistaken?"

"Come again, Philip. Say the words—it won't hurt."

"You said you had significant health problems. Can you tell me more?"

"Good start, Philip. An open-ended comment is by far the best choice." Julius paused to collect his thoughts and to consider how much to reveal to Philip. "Well, I've very recently learned that I have a form of skin cancer called malignant melanoma which poses a serious threat to my life, though my doctors assure me that for the next year I should remain in good health."

"I feel even more strongly," Philip responded, "that the Schopenhaurian vision I offered in my lecture would be of value to you. In our therapy I remember you once said that life was a 'temporary condition with a permanent solution'—that is pure Schopenhauer."

"Philip, that perspective was meant in jest."

"Well we know, don't we, what your own guru, Sigmund Freud, had to say about jesting. My point still stands: Schopenhauer's wisdom contains much that will serve you well."

"I'm not your supervisor, Philip, that's still to be determined, but I'll give you psychotherapy lesson number one, gratis. *It's not ideas, nor vision, nor tools that truly matter in therapy.* If you debrief patients at the end of therapy about the process, what do they remember? *Never* the ideas—it's *always* the relationship. They rarely remember an important insight their therapist offered but generally fondly recall their personal relationship with the therapist. And I'm going to venture a guess that this is even true for you. Why did you remember me so well and value what happened between us so much that you now, after all these years, turn to me for supervision? It's not because of those two comments—however provocative they were—no, I believe it was because of some bond you felt with me. I believe you might have some deep affection for me, and because our relationship, however difficult though it might have been, was meaningful, you are now turning to me again in the hope of some form of embrace."

"Wrong on all counts, Dr. Hertzfeld . . ."

"Yeah, yeah, so wrong that the mere mention of an embrace sends you scurrying back to formal titles again."

"Wrong on all counts, Julius. First, I want to caution you against the error of assuming that your view of reality is the real thing—the *res naturalis*—and that your mission is to impose this vision on others. You crave and value relationships, and you make the erroneous assumption that I, indeed everyone, must do the same and that if I claim otherwise, I've repressed my relationship-craving.

"It seems likely," Philip continued, "that a philosophical approach may be far preferable for someone like me. The truth is—you and I are fundamentally different. I have *never* drawn pleasure from the company of others—their drivel, their demands, their ephemeral petty strivings, their pointless lives—are a nuisance and an obstacle to my communion with the handful of great world spirits who have something of significance to say."

"Then why sign on to be a therapist? Why not remain with the great world spirits? Why busy yourself offering help to these pointless lives?"

"If, like Schopenhauer, I had an inheritance to support myself, I assure you I would not be here today. It's entirely a matter of economic need. My educational expenses have depleted my bank account, my teaching pays a pittance, the college is near bankruptcy, and I doubt that I will be rehired. I need to see only a few clients a week to meet my expenses: I live frugally, I wish to acquire nothing except the freedom to pursue what is truly important to me: my reading, thinking, meditation, music, chess, and my walks with Rugby, my dog."

"You have still not answered my question: why come to see me when it is clear I work in quite a different fashion from the way you want to work? And you haven't responded to my conjecture that there's something about our past relationship drawing you to me."

"I didn't respond because it's so far off the mark. But since it seems important to you, I'll continue to ponder your conjecture. Don't conclude that I'm questioning the presence of basic interpersonal needs. Schopenhauer himself said that bipeds—his term—need to huddle together by the fire for warmth. He cautioned, however, about getting singed by too much huddling. He liked porcupines—they huddled for warmth but used their quills to keep their separateness. He treasured his separateness and depended on nothing outside himself for his happiness. And he wasn't alone on this; other great men, Montaigne, for example, shared this way of thinking.

"I also fear bipeds," Philip continued, "and I agree with his observation that a happy man is one who can avoid most of his fellow creatures. And how can you not agree that bipeds create a hell here on Earth? Schopenhauer believed 'Homo homini lupus'—*man is a wolf to man*; I'm certain that he was the inspiration for Sartre's *No Exit.*"

"All well and good, Philip. But you're confirming my very point: that you may not be equipped to work as a therapist. Your point of view leaves no room for friendships."

"Every time I reach out to another, I end up with less of myself. I have not had a friendship in adulthood, nor do I care to form one. You may remember I was a solitary child with a disinterested mother and an unhappy father who eventually took his life. To be frank, I've never met anyone who has anything of interest to offer me. And it's not because I haven't looked. Every time I've tried to befriend someone, I've had the same experience as Schopenhauer, who said he only found miserable wretches, men of limited intelligence, bad heart, and mean disposition. I'm referring to living persons—not to the great thinkers of the past.

"You met me, Philip."

"That was a professional relationship. I refer to social encounters."

"These attitudes are visible in your behavior. With your contempt and lack of social skills spawned by this contempt, how can you possibly interact with others in a therapeutic manner?"

"We're not in disagreement there—I agree I need to work on social skills. A little friendliness and warmth, Schopenhauer said, makes it possible to manipulate people just as we need to warm wax if we wish to work it."

Julius rose, shaking his head. He poured a cup of coffee for himself and paced back and forth. "Working wax is not just a bad metaphor;—it's about the worst goddamn metaphor for therapy I've ever encountered—in fact it *is* the worst. You sure as hell are not pulling your punches. Nor, incidentally, are you making your friend and therapist, Arthur Schopenhauer, endearing to me."

Taking his seat again and sipping his coffee, Julius said, "I'm not repeating my offer of coffee because I'm assuming you want nothing to do with anything except the answer to your singular question about supervision. You seem very strongly focused, Philip, so I will be merciful and cut to the chase. Here's my decision about supervising you . . ."

Philip, who had been averting his gaze throughout this discussion, looked directly at Julius for the first time.

"You've got a fine mind, Philip. You know a great deal. Maybe you'll find a way to harness your knowledge in the service of therapy. Maybe you'll end up making real contributions. I hope so. *But you're not ready to be a therapist.* And you're not ready for supervision. Your interpersonal skills, sensitivity, and awareness need work—a lot of work. But I want to be helpful to you. I failed once, and now I've got a second chance. Can you think of me as your ally, Philip?"

"Let me answer that question after I hear your proposal, which I assume is imminent."

"Jesus! All right, here it is. I, Julius Hertzfeld, agree to be Philip Slate's supervisor if, *and only if,* he first spends six months as a patient in my psychotherapy group."

For once, Philip was startled. He had not anticipated Julius's response. "You're not serious."

"Never been more."

"I tell you that after so many years of sloshing about in the sewers I've finally got my life together. I tell you that I want to earn a living as a therapist and that to do so I need a supervisor—that's the one thing I need. Instead you offer me what I don't want and can't afford."

"I repeat, you're not ready for supervision, not ready to be a therapist, but I think that group therapy can begin to address your deficits. Those are my conditions. First, a course of group therapy and then, and only then, will I supervise you."

"Your group therapy fees?"

"Not high. Seventy dollars for a ninety-minute session. And, incidentally, that's billed even if you miss a meeting."

"How many patients in the group?"

"I try to keep it about seven."

"Seven times seventy dollars—that's four hundred and ninety dollars. For an hour and a half. That's an interesting commercial venture. And what's the point of group therapy—the way you do it?"

"The point? What have we been talking about? Look, Philip, I'll be blunt: how can you be a therapist when you don't know what the fuck is going on between you and other people?"

"No, no. I've gotten *that* point. My question was imprecise. I've had no training in group therapy and am asking for clarification about how it operates. How will it profit me to hear others describe their lives and problems en masse? The very idea of such a chorus of misery appalls me, although, as Schopenhauer points out, there is always pleasure in learning that others suffer more than you."

"Oh, you're asking for an orientation. That's a justified request. I make a point of providing an orientation to group therapy to every patient entering a group. Every therapist should do that. So let me give you my spiel. First, my approach is rigorously interpersonal, and I make the assumption that each member is in the group because of difficulties in establishing sustaining relationships . . ."

"But, that's not true. I neither wish nor need . . ."

"I know, I know. Just humor me on this, Philip. I merely said I make the assumption that these interpersonal difficulties are present—I assume it's the case whether you agree or not. As for my goal in the therapy group, I can be real clear about that: *it is to help each member understand as much as possible about how he or she relates to each person in the group, including the therapist.* I maintain a here-and-now focus—that's an essential concept for you to master as a therapist, Philip. In other words, the group works ahistorically: we focus on the *now*—there's no need to investigate each member's past history in depth—we focus on the current moment in the group; and on the *here*—forget about what members say has gone wrong in other relationships—I make the assumption that group members will manifest the same behavior in the group that has created difficulties for them in their social life. And I further assume that ultimately they will generalize what they learn about their group relationships to their relationships outside. Is that clear? I can give you reading material if you wish."

"It's clear. What ground rules does the group have?"

"First confidentiality—you speak to no one about other members of the group. Second—you strive to reveal yourself and to be honest in expressing your perceptions of other members and your feelings about them. Third—everything must go on inside the group. If there is contact between members outside the group, it must be brought back into the group and discussed."

"And this is the only way you're willing to supervise me?"

"Absolutely. You want me to train you? Well, this is my prerequisite."

Philip sat silently with eyes closed and his forehead resting on his clasped hands. Then he opened his eyes and said, "I'll go along with your suggestion only if you are willing to credit the group therapy sessions as supervisory hours."

"That's a stretch, Philip. Can you imagine the ethical dilemma that creates for me?"

"Can you imagine the dilemma your proposal creates for me? To turn my attention to my relations with others when I never wish for anyone to be anything to me. Besides, did you not imply that improving my social skills will make me more effective as a therapist?"

Julius stood up, took his coffee cup to the sink, shook his head, wondered about what he had gotten himself into, returned to his seat, exhaled slowly, and said, "Fair enough, I'll agree to sign off the group therapy hours as supervision."

"One other thing: we haven't discussed the logistics of the exchange—of my offering you guidance on Schopenhauer."

"Whatever we do on that matter will have to wait, Philip. Another therapy pointer: avoid dual relationships with patients—they will interfere with therapy. I refer to all kinds of ancillary relationships: romantic, business, even teacher and student. So I much prefer, and this is for your sake, to keep our relationship clean and clear. That's why I am suggesting we start with the group and then, in the future, enter into a supervisory relationship, and then, possibly—I make no promises—a philosophy tutorial. Though at the moment I feel no great desire to study Schopenhauer."

"Still, can we establish a fee for my future philosophical consultation with you."

"That's iffy, and a long way off, Philip."

"I'd still like to set the fee."

"You continue to amaze me, Philip. The goddamnedest things you worry about! And the things you don't!"

"Just the same, what's a fair fee?"

"My policy is to charge the supervisee the same fee I charge for individual therapy—with some reduction for beginning students."

"Done," said Philip, nodding.

"Hold on, Philip, I want to be certain you've heard me say that the idea of a Schopenhauer tutorial arrangement is not of great import to me. When the topic first arose between us, all I did was to voice some slight interest in how Schopenhauer had provided so much help to you, and you ran with the ball and assumed we had made a contractual arrangement."

"I hope to increase your interest in his work. He had much to say of great value to our field. In so many ways he anticipated Freud, who borrowed his work wholesale, without acknowledgement."

"I'll keep an open mind, but, I repeat, many of the things you've said about Schopenhauer do not pique my desire to know more about his work."

"Including what I said in my lecture about his views on death?"

"Especially that. The idea that one's essential being will ultimately be reunited with some vague, ethereal universal life force offers me zero comfort. If there is no persistence of consciousness, what possible solace could I draw from that? By the same token, I get little comfort from knowing that my bodily molecules will be dispersed into space and that ultimately my DNA will end up being a part of some other life-form."

"I'd like us to read together his essays on death and on the indestructibility of being. If we did, I'm certain—"

"Not now, Philip. At the moment I'm not as much interested in death as I am in living the rest of my life as fully as possible—that's where I am."

"Death is always there, the horizon of all these concerns. Socrates said it most clearly, 'to learn to live well, one must first learn to die well.' Or Seneca, 'No man enjoys the true taste of life but he who is willing and ready to quit it.'"

"Yes, yes, I know these homilies, and maybe in the abstract they are true. And I have no quarrel with incorporating the wisdom of philosophy into psychotherapy. I'm all for it. And I also know that Schopenhauer has served you well in many ways. But not in all ways: there's a possibility that you may need some remedial work. And that's where the group comes in. I look forward to seeing you here for your first meeting next Monday at four-thirty."

Just because the terrible activity of the genital system still slumbers, while that of the brain already has its full briskness, childhood is the time of innocence and happiness, the paradise of life, the lost Eden, on which we look back longingly through the whole remaining course of our life.

10

The Happiest Years of Arthur's life

When Arthur turned nine, his father decided the time had come to take over the direction of his son's education. His first step was to deposit him for two years in Le Havre at the home of a business partner, Gregories de Blesimaire. There, Arthur was to learn French, social graces, and, as Heinrich put it, "become read in the books of the world."

Expelled from home, separated from his parents at the age of nine? How many children have regarded such exile as a catastrophic life event? Yet, later in life, Arthur described these two years as "by far the happiest part of his childhood."

Something important happened in Le Havre: perhaps for the only time in his life Arthur felt nurtured and enjoyed life. For many years afterward he cherished the memory of the convivial Blesimaires, with whom he found something resembling parental love. His letters to his parents were so full of praise for them that his mother felt compelled to remind him of his father's virtues and largesse. "Remember how your father permits you to buy that ivory flute for one louis-d'or."

Another important event took place during his sojourn in Le

Havre. Arthur found a friend—one of the very few of his entire life. Anthime, the Blesimaire son, was the same age as Arthur. The two boys became close in Le Havre and exchanged a few letters after Arthur returned to Hamburg.

Years later as young men of twenty they met once again and on a few occasions went out together searching for amorous adventures. Then their paths and their interests diverged. Anthime became a businessman and disappeared from Arthur's life until thirty years later when they had a brief correspondence in which Arthur sought some financial advice. When Anthime responded with an offer to manage his portfolio for a fee, Arthur abruptly ended the correspondence. By that time he suspected everyone and trusted no one. He put Anthime's letter aside after jotting on the back of the envelope a cynical aphorism from Gracian (a Spanish philosopher much admired by his father): "Make one's entry into another's affair in order to leave with one's own."

Arthur and Anthime had one final meeting ten years later—an awkward encounter during which they found little to say to one another. Arthur described his old friend as "an unbearable old man" and wrote in his journal that the "feeling of two friends meeting after a generation of absence will be one of great disappointment with the whole of life."

Another incident marked Arthur's stay in Le Havre: he was introduced to death. A childhood playmate in Hamburg, Gottfried Janish, died while Arthur was living in Le Havre. Though Arthur seemed undemonstrative and said that he never again thought of Gottfried, it is apparent that he never truly forgot his dead playmate, nor the shock of his first acquaintance with mortality, because thirty years later he described a dream in his journal: "I found myself in a country unknown to me, a group of men stood on a field, and among them a slim, tall, adult man who, I do not know how, had been made known to me as Gottfried Janish, and he welcomed me."

Arthur had little difficulty interpreting the dream. At that time he was living in Berlin in the midst of a cholera epidemic. The dream image of a reunion with Gottfried could only mean one thing: a warning of approaching death. Consequently, Arthur decided to escape death by immediately leaving Berlin. He chose to move to Frankfurt, where he was to live the last thirty years of his life, largely because he thought it to be cholera-proof.

The greatest wisdom is to make the enjoyment of the present the supreme object of life because that is the only reality, all else being the play of thought. But we could just as well call it our greatest folly because that which exists only a moment and vanishes as a dream can never be worth a serious effort.

11

Philip's First Meeting

Philip arrived fifteen minutes early for his first group therapy meeting wearing the same clothes as in his two previous encounters with Julius: the wrinkled, faded checkered shirt, khaki pants, and corduroy jacket. Marveling at Philip's consistent indifference to clothes, office furnishings, his student audience, or, seemingly, anyone with whom he interacted, Julius once again began to question his decision to invite Philip into the group. Was it sound professional judgment, or was his chutzpah raising its ugly head again?

Chutzpah: raw nervy brashness. *Chutzpah:* best defined by the renowned story of the boy who murdered his parents and then pleaded for mercy from the court on the grounds that he was an orphan. *Chutzpah* often entered Julius's mind when he reflected upon his approach to life. Perhaps he had been imbued with chutzpah from the start, but he first consciously embraced it in the autumn of his fifteenth year when his family relocated from the Bronx to Washington, D.C. His father, who had had a financial setback, moved the family into a small row house on Farragut Street in northwest Washington. The nature of his father's financial difficulties was off limits to any inquiry, but Julius was convinced that it had something to do with Aqueduct racetrack and She's All That, a horse he owned with Vic Vicello, one of his poker cronies. Vic was an elusive figure who wore a pink handkerchief in his yellow sports jacket and took care never to enter their home if his mother was present.

His father's new job was managing a liquor store owned by a cousin felled at forty-five by a coronary, that dark enemy which had either maimed or killed a whole generation of fifty-year-old male Ashkenazi Jews raised on sour cream and fat-flaked brisket. His dad hated his new job, but it kept the family solvent; not only did it pay well, but its long hours kept Dad away from Laurel and Pimlico, the local racetracks.

On Julius's first day of school at Roosevelt High in September 1955, he made a momentous decision: he would redo himself. He was unknown in Washington, a free soul unencumbered by the past. His past three years at P.S. 1126, his Bronx junior high school, were nothing to be proud of. Gambling had been so much more interesting than other school activities that he spent every afternoon at the bowling alley lining up challenge games betting on himself or on his partner, Marty Geller—he of the great left-handed hook. He also ran a small bookie operation, where he offered ten-to-one odds to anyone picking any three baseball players to get six hits among them on any given day. No matter who the pigeons picked—Mantle, Kaline, Aaron, Vernon, or Stan (the Man) Musial—they rarely won, at best once in twenty to thirty bets. Julius ran with like-minded punks, developed the aura of a tough street fighter in order to intimidate would-be welchers, dumbed himself down in class to remain cool, and cut many a school afternoon to watch Mantle patrol the Yankee Stadium center field.

Everything changed the day he and his parents were called into the principal's office and confronted with his bookie ledger-book, for which he had been frantically searching the previous couple of days. Though punishment was meted out—no evenings out for the remaining two months of the school year, no bowling alley, no trips to Yankee Stadium, no after-school sports, no allowance—Julius could see his father's heart wasn't in it: he was entirely intrigued by the details of Julius's three-player, six-hit caper. Still, Julius had admired the principal, and falling from his grace was such a wake-up call that he attempted to reclaim himself. But it was too little, too late; the best he could do was to move his grades up to low Bs. It wasn't possible to form new friendships—he was role-locked, and no one could relate to the new boy Julius had decided to become.

As a consequence of this episode, the latter-day Julius had an exquisite sensitivity to the phenomenon of "role-lock": how often had he seen group therapy patients change dramatically but continue to be perceived as the same person by the other group members. Happens also in families. Many of his improved patients had a hell of a time when visiting their parents: they had to guard against being sucked back into their old family role and had to expend considerable energy persuading parents and siblings that they were indeed changed.

Julius's great experiment with reinvention commenced with his family's move. On that first day of school in Washington, D.C., a balmy Indian summer September day, Julius crunched through the fallen sycamore leaves and strode into the front door of Roosevelt High, searching for a master strategy to make himself over. Noticing the broadsides posted outside the auditorium advertising the candidates for class president, Julius had an inspired thought, and even before he learned the location of the boys' room he had posted his name for the election.

The election bid was a long shot, beyond long shot—longer odds than betting on the tightfisted Clark Griffith's inept Washington Senators to climb out of last place. He knew nothing about Roosevelt High and had yet to meet a single classmate. Would the old Julius from the Bronx have run for office? Not in a thousand years. But that was the point; precisely for this reason, the new Julius took the plunge. What was the worst that could happen? His name would be out there, and all would recognize Julius Hertzfeld as a force, a potential leader, a boy to be reckoned with. What's more, he loved the action.

Of course, his opponents would dismiss him as a bad joke, a gnat, an unknown know-nothing. Expecting such criticism, Julius readied himself and prepared a riff about the ability of a newcomer to see fault lines invisible to those living too close to the corruption. He had the gift of gab, honed by long hours in the bowling alley of wheedling and cajoling suckers into match games. The new Julius had nothing to lose and fearlessly strolled up to clusters of students to announce, "Hi, I'm Julius, the new kid on the block, and I hope you'll support me in election for class president. I don't know crap about school politics, but, you know, sometimes a fresh look is the best look. Besides, I'm absolutely independent—don't belong to any cliques because I don't know anybody."

As things turned out, not only did Julius recreate himself, but he damn near won the election. With a football team that had lost eighteen straight games and a basketball team almost as hapless, Roosevelt High was demoralized. The two other candidates were vulnerable: Catherine Shumann, the brainy daughter of the diminutive long-faced minister who led the prayer before each school assembly, was prissy and unpopular, and Richard Heishman, the handsome, red-haired, rednecked football halfback, had a great many enemies. Julius rode the crest of a robust protest vote. In addition, to his great surprise, he immediately was embraced vigorously by virtually all the Jewish students, about 30 percent of the student body, who had heretofore kept a low, apolitical profile. They loved him, the love of the timid, hesitant, make-no-waves Mason-Dixon Yid for the gutsy, brash New York Jew.

That election was the turning point of Julius's life. So much reinforcement did he receive for his brazenness that he rebuilt his whole identity on the foundation of raw chutzpah. The three Jewish high school fraternities vied for him; he was perceived as having both guts and that ever so elusive holy grail of adolescence, "personality." Soon he was surrounded by kids at lunch in the cafeteria and was often spotted walking hand in hand after school with the lovely Miriam Kaye, the editor of the school newspaper and the one student smart enough to challenge Catherine Schumann for valedictorian. He and Miriam were soon inseparable. She introduced him to art and aesthetic sensibility; he was never to make her appreciate the high drama of bowling or baseball.

Yes, chutzpah had taken him a long way. He cultivated it, took great pride in it, and, in later life, beamed when he heard himself referred to as an original, a maverick, the therapist who had the guts to take on the cases that had defeated others. But chutzpah had its dark side—grandiosity. More than once Julius had erred by attempting to do more than could be done, by asking patients to make more change than was constitutionally possible for them, by putting patients through a long and, ultimately, unrewarding course of therapy.

So was it compassion or sheer clinical tenacity that led Julius to think he could yet reclaim Philip? Or was it grandiose chutzpah? He truly did not know. As he led Philip to the group therapy room, Julius took a long look at his reluctant patient. With his straight light brown hair combed straight back without a part, his skin stretched tight across his high cheekbones, his eyes wary, his step heavy, Philip looked as though he were being led to his execution.

Julius felt a wave of compassion and, in his softest, most comforting voice, offered solace. "You know, Philip, therapy groups are infinitely complex, but they possess one absolutely predictable feature."

If Julius expected the natural curious inquiry about the "one absolutely predictable feature," he gave no sign of disappointment at Philip's silence. Instead he merely continued speaking as though Philip had expressed appropriate curiosity. "And that feature is that the first meeting of a therapy group is invariably less uncomfortable and more engaging than the new member expects."

"I have no discomfort, Julius."

"Well then, simply file what I said. Just in case you run across some."

Philip stopped in the hallway at the door to the office in which they had met a few days before, but Julius touched his elbow and guided him down the hall to the next door, which opened into a room lined on three sides with ceiling-to-floor bookshelves. Three windows of wood-lined panes on the fourth wall looked out into a Japanese garden graced by several dwarf five-needle pines, two clusters of tiny boulders, and a narrow eight-foot-long pond in which golden carp glided. The furniture in the room was simple and functional, consisting only of a small table next to the door, seven comfortable Rattan chairs arranged in a circle, and two others stored in corners.

"Here we are. This is my library and group room. While we're waiting for the other members, let me give you the nuts-and-bolts housekeeping drill. On Mondays, I unlock the front door about ten minutes before the time of the group, and the members just enter on their own into this room. When I come in at four-thirty, we start pretty promptly, and we end at six. To ease my billing and bookkeeping task, everyone pays at the end of each session—just leave a check on the table by the door. Questions?"

Philip shook his head no and looked around the room, inhaling deeply. He walked directly to the shelves, put his nose closely to the rows of leather-bound volumes, and inhaled again, evincing great pleasure. He remained standing and industriously began perusing book titles.

In the next few minutes five group members filed in, each glancing at Philip's back, before taking seats. Despite the bustle of their entrance, Philip did not turn his head or in any way interrupt his task of examining Julius's library.

Over his thirty-five years of leading groups, Julius had seen a lot of folks enter therapy groups. The pattern was predictable: the new member enters heavy with apprehension, behaving in a deferential manner to the other members, who welcome the neophyte and introduce themselves. Occasionally, a newly formed group, which mistakenly believes that benefits are directly proportional to the amount of attention each receives from the therapist, may resent newcomers, but established groups welcome them: they appreciate that a full roster adds to, rather than detracts from, the effectiveness of the therapy.

Once in a while newcomers jump right into the discussion, but generally they are silent for much of the first meeting as they try to figure out the rules and wait until someone invites them to participate. But a new member so indifferent that he turns his back and ignores the others in the group? Never before had Julius seen *that.* Not even in groups of psychotic patients on the psychiatric ward.

Surely, Julius thought, he had made a blunder by inviting Philip into the group. Having to tell the group about his cancer was more than enough on his plate for the day. And he felt burdened by having to worry about Philip.

What was going on with Philip? Was it possible that he was simply overcome by apprehension or shyness? Unlikely. No, he's probably pissed at my insisting on his entering a group, and, in his passive-aggressive way, he's giving me and the group the finger. God, Julius thought, I'd just like to hang him out to dry. Just do nothing. Let him sink or swim. It would be a pleasure to sit back and enjoy the blistering group attack that will surely come.

Julius did not often remember joke punch lines, but one that he had heard years ago returned to him now. One morning a son said to his mother, "I don't want to go to school today."

"Why not?" asked his mother.

"Two reasons: I hate the students, and they hate me."

Mother responds, "There are two reasons you have to go to school: first, you're forty-five years old and, second, you're the principal."

Yes, he was all grown up. And he was the therapist of the group. And it was his job to integrate new members, to protect them from others and from themselves. Though he almost never started a meeting himself, preferring to encourage the members to take charge of running the group, today he had no choice.

"Four-thirty. Time to get started. Philip, why don't you grab a seat." Philip turned to face him but made no movement toward a chair. Is he deaf? Julius thought. A social imbecile? Only after Julius vigorously gestured with his eyeballs to one of the empty chairs did Philip seat himself.

To Philip he said, "Here's our group. There's one member who won't be here tonight, Pam, who's on a two-month trip." Then, turning to the group, "I mentioned a few meetings ago that I might be introducing a new member. I met with Philip last week, and he's beginning today." Of course he's beginning today, Julius thought. Stupid, shithead comment. That's it. No more handholding. Sink or swim.

Just at that moment Stuart, rushing in from the pediatric clinic at the hospital and still wearing a white clinical coat, charged into the room and plunked himself down, muttering an apology for being late. All members then turned to Philip, and four of them introduced themselves and welcomed him: "I'm Rebecca, Tony, Bonnie, Stuart. Hello. Great to see you. Welcome. Glad to have you. We need some new blood—I mean new input."

The remaining member, an attractive man with a prematurely bald pate flanked by a rim of light brown hair and the hefty body of a football linesman somewhat gone to seed, said, in a surprisingly soft voice, "Hi, I'm Gill. And, Philip, I hope you won't feel I'm ignoring you, but I absolutely, urgently need some time in the group today. I've never needed the group as much as today."

No response from Philip.

"Okay, Philip?" Gill repeated.

Startled, Philip opened his eyes widely and nodded.

Gill turned toward the familiar faces in the group and began. "A lot has happened, and it all came to a head this morning following a session with my wife's shrink. I've been telling you guys over the past few weeks about how the therapist gave Rose a book about child abuse that convinces her that she was abused as a child. It's like a fixed idea—what do you call it . . . an idea feexed?" Gill turned to Julius.

"An idée fixe," Philip instantaneously interjected with perfect accent.

"Right. Thanks," said Gill, who shot a quick look at Philip and added, sotto voce, "Whoa, that was fast," and then returned to his narrative. "Well, Rose has an idée fixe that her father sexually molested her when she was young. She can't let it go. Does she remember any sexual event happening? No. Witnesses? No. But her therapist believes that if she's depressed, fearful about sex, has stuff like lapses in attention and uncontrollable emotions, especially rage at men, then she *must* have been molested. That's the message of that goddamned book. And her therapist swears by it. So, for months, as I've told you ad nauseam, we've been talking about little else. My wife's therapy is our life. No time for anything else. No other topic of conversation. Our sex life is defunct. Nothing. Forget it. A couple of weeks ago she asked me to phone her father—she won't talk to him herself—and invite him to come to her therapy session. She wanted me to attend, too—for 'protection,' she said.

"So I phoned him. He agreed immediately. Yesterday he took a bus down from Portland and appeared at the therapy session this morning carrying his beat-up suitcase because he was going to head right back to the bus station after we met. The session was a disaster. Absolute mayhem. Rose just unloaded on him and kept on unloading. Without limits, without letup, without a word of acknowledgment that her old man had come several hundred miles for her—for her ninety-minute therapy session. Accusing him of everything, even of inviting his neighbors, his poker chums, his coworkers at the fire department—he was a fireman back then—to have sex with her when she was a child."

"What did the father do?" asked Rebecca, a tall, slender, forty-year-old woman of exceptional beauty who had been leaning forward, listening intently to Gill.

"He behaved like a mensch. He's a nice old man, about seventy years old, kindly, sweet. This is the first time I met him. He was amazing—God, I wish I had a father like that. Just sat there and took it and told Rose that, if she had all that anger, it was probably best to let it out. He just kept gently denying all her crazy charges and took a guess—a good one, I think—that what she is really angry about is his walking out on the family when she was twelve. He said her anger was fertilized—his word, he's a farmer—by her mother, who had been poisoning her mind against him since she was a child. He told her he had had to leave, that he had been depressed out of his gourd living with her mother and would be dead now if he had stayed. And let me tell you, I know Rose's mother, and he's got a point. A good one.

"So, at the end of the session he asked for a ride to the bus terminal, and before I could answer, Rose said she wouldn't feel safe in the same car with him. 'Got it,' he said, and walked away, lugging his suitcase.

"Well, ten minutes later Rose and I were driving down Market Street, and I see him—a white-haired, stooped old man pulling his suitcase. It was starting to rain, and I say to myself, 'This is the shits.' I lost it and told Rose, 'He comes here for you—for your therapy session—he comes all the way from Portland, it's raining, and goddamnit I'm taking him to the bus station.' I pulled over to the curb and offered him a lift. Rose stares daggers at me. 'If he gets in, I get out,' she says. I say, 'Be my guest.' I point to Starbucks on the street and tell her to wait there and I'll come back in a few minutes. She gets out and stalks off. That was about five hours ago. She never did show up at Starbucks. I drove over to Golden Gate Park and been walking around since. I'm thinking of never going home."

With that, Gill flopped back in his chair, exhausted.

The members—Tony, Rebecca, Bonnie, and Stuart—broke out into a chorus of approval: "Great, Gill." "About time, Gill." "Wow, you really did it." "Whoa, good move." Tony said, "I can't tell you how glad I am that you tore yourself loose from that bitch." "If you need a bed," said Bonnie, nervously running her hands through her frizzy brown hair and adjusting her goggle-shaped, yellow-tinted spectacles, "I've got a spare room. Don't worry, you're safe," she added with a giggle, "I'm too old for you and my daughter's home."

Julius, not happy with the pressure the group was applying (he had seen too many members drop out of too many therapy groups because they were ashamed of disappointing the group), made his first intervention, "Strong feedback you're getting, Gill. How do you feel about it?"

"Great. It feels great. Only I . . . I don't want to disappoint everybody. This is happening so fast—this all just happened this morning . . . I'm shaky and I'm fluid . . . don't know what I'm going to do."

"You mean," said Julius, "you don't want to substitute your wife's imperatives with the group's imperatives."

"Yeah. I guess. Yeah, I see what you mean. Right. But it's a mixed bag. I really want, really really need this encouragement . . . grateful for it . . . I need guidance—this may be a turning point in my life. Heard from everyone but you, Julius. And of course from our new member. Philip, is it?"

Philip nodded.

"Philip, I know you don't know about my situation, but *you* do." Gill turned to face Julius. "What about it? What do *you* think I should do?"

Julius involuntarily flinched and hoped it had not been visible. Like most therapists, he hated that question—the "damned if you do, damned if you don't" question. He had seen it coming.

"Gill, you're not going to like my answer. But here it is. I can't tell you what to do: that's your job, your decision, not mine. One reason you're here in this group is to learn to trust your own judgment. Another reason is that everything I know about Rose and your marriage has come to me through you. And you can't avoid giving me biased information. What I can do is help you focus on how you contribute to your life predicament. We can't understand or change Rose; it's *you*—your feelings, your behavior—that's what counts here because *that's* what you can change."

The group fell silent. Julius was right; Gill did not like that answer. Neither did the other members.

Rebecca, who had taken out two barrettes and was flouncing her long black hair before replacing them, broke the silence by turning to Philip. "You're new here and don't know the backstory that the rest of us know. But sometimes from the mouth of newborn babes. . . ."

Philip sat silent. It was unclear whether he had even heard Rebecca.

"Yeah, you have a take on this, Philip?" said Tony, in what was, for him, an unusually gentle tone. Tony was a swarthy man with deep acne scars on his cheeks and a lean, graceful athletic body exhibited to good advantage in his black San Francisco Giants T-shirt and tight jeans.

"I have an observation and a piece of advice," said Philip, hands folded, head tilted back, and eyes fixed on the ceiling. "Nietzsche once wrote that a major difference between man and the cow was that the cow knew how to exist, how to live without angst—that is, *fear*—in the blessed now, unburdened by the past and unaware of the terrors of the future. But we unfortunate humans are so haunted by the past and future that we can only saunter briefly in the now. Do you know why we so yearn for the golden days of childhood? Nietzsche tells us it's because those childhood days were the carefree days, days *free of care*, days before we were weighted down by leaden, painful memories, by the debris of the past. Allow me to make one marginal note: I refer to a Nietzsche essay, but this thought was not original—in this, as in so much else, he looted the works of Schopenhauer."

He paused. A loud silence rang out in the group. Julius squirmed in his chair, thinking, Oh shit, I must have been out of my fucking mind to bring this guy here. This is the goddamnedest, most bizarre way I've ever seen a patient come into a group.

Bonnie broke the silence. Turning her gaze squarely upon him, she said, "That's fascinating, Philip. I know I keep yearning for my childhood, but I never understood it that way, that childhood feels free and golden because there's no past to weigh you down. Thanks, I'm going to remember that."

"Me too. Interesting stuff," said Gill. "But you said you had advice for me?"

"Yes, here's my advice." Philip spoke evenly, softly, still making no eye contact. "Your wife is one of those people who is particularly unable to live in the present because she is so heavily laden with the freight of the past. She is a sinking ship. She's going down. My advice to you is to jump overboard and start swimming. She'll produce a powerful wake when she goes under, so I urge you to swim away as fast and as hard as you can."

Silence. The group seemed stunned.

"Hey, no one is going to accuse you," said Gill, "of pulling your punches. I asked a question. You gave an answer. I appreciate that. A lot. Welcome to the group. Any other comments you got—I want to hear them."

"Well," said Philip, still looking upward, "in that case let me add one additional thought. Kierkegaard described some individuals as being in 'double despair,' that is, they are in despair but too self-deceived to know even that they are in despair. I think you may be in double despair. Here's what I mean: most of my own suffering is a result of my being driven by desires, and then, once I satisfy a desire, I enjoy a moment of satiation, which soon is transformed into boredom, which is then interrupted by another desire springing up. Schopenhauer felt this was the universal human condition—wanting, momentary satiation, boredom, further wanting.

"Back to you—I question whether you've yet explored this cycle of endless desires within yourself. Perhaps you've been so preoccupied with your wife's wishes it's kept you from becoming acquainted with your own desires? Isn't that why others here were applauding you today? Wasn't it because you were finally refusing to be defined by her wishes? In other words, I'm asking whether your work on yourself has been delayed or derailed by your preoccupation with your wife's wishes."

Gill listened, mouth gaping, gaze fixed on Philip. "That's deep. I know there's something deep and important in what you're saying—in this double despair idea—but I'm not getting it all."

All eyes were now on Philip, who continued to have eyes only for the ceiling. "Philip," said Rebecca, now finished with replacing her barrettes, "weren't you saying that Gill's personal work won't really begin until he liberates himself from his wife?"

"Or," Tony said, "that his involvement with her prevents him from knowing how fucked-up he really is? Hell, I know this is true for me and the way I relate to my work—I been thinking this past week that I'm so busy being ashamed of being a carpenter—being blue-collar, being low-income, being looked down on—that I never get around to thinking about the real shit I should be dealing with."

Julius watched in amazement as others, thirsty for Philip's every word, chimed in. He felt competitive urges rising but quelled them by reminding himself that the group's purposes were being served. *Cool it, Julius,* he said to himself, *the group needs you; they're not going to desert you for Philip. What's going on here is great; they are assimilating the new member, and they are also each laying out agendas for future work.*

He had planned to talk about his diagnosis in the group today. In a sense his hand was now forced because he had already told Philip he had a melanoma and, to avoid the impression of a special relationship with him, had to share it with the whole group. But he had been preempted. First there was Gill's emergency, and then there was the group's total fascination with Philip. He checked the clock. Ten minutes left. Not enough time to lay this on them. Julius resolved that he would absolutely begin the next meeting with the bad news. He remained silent and let the clock run out.

The kings left their crowns and scepters behind here, and the heroes their weapons. Yet the great spirits among them all, whose splendor flowed out of themselves, who did not receive it from outward things, they take their greatness across with them.

—*Arthur Schopenhauer, age sixteen at Westminster Abbey*

12

1799—Arthur Learns about Choice and Other Worldly Horrors

When the nine-year-old Arthur returned from Le Havre, his father placed him in a private school whose specific mandate was to educate future merchants. There he learned what good merchants of the time had to know: to calculate in different currencies, to write business letters in all the major European languages, to study transport routes, trade centers, yields of the soil, and other such fascinating topics. But Arthur was not fascinated; he had no interest in such knowledge, formed no close friendships at school, and dreaded more each day his father's plan for his future—a seven-year apprenticeship with a local business magnate.

What did Arthur want? Not the life of a merchant—he loathed the very idea. He craved the life of a scholar. Though many of his classmates also disliked the thought of a long apprenticeship, Arthur's protests ran far deeper. Despite his parents' strong admonitions—a letter from his mother instructed him to "put aside all these authors for a while . . . you are now fifteen and have already read and studied the best German, French and, in part, also English authors"—he spent all his available free time studying literature and philosophy.

Arthur's father, Heinrich, was tormented by his son's interests. The headmaster of Arthur's school had informed him that his son had a passion for philosophy, was exceptionally suited for the life of a scholar, and would do well to transfer to a gymnasium which would prepare him for the university. In his heart, Heinrich may have sensed the correctness of the schoolmaster's advice; his son's voracious consumption and comprehension of all works of philosophy, history, and literature in the extensive Schopenhauer library was readily apparent.

What was Heinrich to do? At stake was his successor, as well as the future of the entire firm and his filial obligation to all his ancestors to maintain the Schopenhauer lineage. Moreover, he shuddered at the prospect of a male Schopenhauer subsisting on the limited income of a scholar.

First, Heinrich considered setting up a lifelong annuity through his church for his son, but the cost was prohibitive; business was bad, and Heinrich also had obligations to guarantee the financial future of a wife and daughter.

Then gradually a solution, a somewhat diabolical solution, began to form in his mind. For some time he had resisted Johanna's pleas for a lengthy tour of Europe. These were difficult times; the international political climate was so unstable that the safety of the Hanseatic cities was threatened and his constant attention to business was required. Yet because of weariness and his yearning to shed the weight of business responsibilities, his resistance to Johanna's request was wavering. Slowly there swiveled into mind an inspired plan that would serve two purposes; his wife would be pleased, and the dilemma of Arthur's future would be resolved.

His decision was to offer his fifteen-year-old son a choice. "You must choose," he told him. "Either accompany your parents on a year's grand tour of all of Europe or pursue a career as a scholar. Either you give me a pledge that on the day you return from the journey you will begin your business apprenticeship *or* forego this journey, remain in

Hamburg, and immediately transfer to a classical educational curriculum which will prepare you for the academic life."

Imagine a fifteen-year-old facing such a life-altering decision. Perhaps the ever-pedantic Heinrich was offering existential instruction. Perhaps he was teaching his son that alternatives exclude, that for every yes there must be a no. (Indeed, years later Arthur was to write, "He who would be everything cannot be anything.")

Or was Heinrich exposing his son to a foretaste of renunciation, that is, if Arthur could not renounce the pleasure of the journey, how could he expect himself to renounce worldly pleasures and live the impecunious life of a scholar?

Perhaps we are being too charitable to Heinrich. Most likely his offer was disingenuous because he knew that Arthur would not, could not, refuse the trip. No fifteen-year-old could do that in 1803. At that time such a journey was a priceless once-in-a-lifetime event granted only to a privileged few. Before the days of photography, foreign places were known only through sketches, paintings, and published travel journals (a genre, incidentally, that Johanna Schopenhauer was later to exploit brilliantly).

Did Arthur feel he was selling his soul? Was he tormented by his decision? Of these matters history is silent. We know only that in 1803, at the age of fifteen, he set off with his father, mother, and a servant on a journey of fifteen months throughout all of western Europe and Great Britain. Adele, his six-year-old sister, was deposited with a relative in Hamburg.

Arthur recorded many impressions in his travel journals written, as his parents required, in the language of the country visited. His linguistic aptitude was prodigious; the fifteen-year-old Arthur was fluent in German, French, and English and had working knowledge of Italian and Spanish. Ultimately, he was to master a dozen modern and ancient languages, and it was his habit, as visitors to his memorial library have noted, to write his marginal notes in the language of each text.

Arthur's travel journals offer a subtle prefiguring of interests and traits which were aggregating into a persistent character structure. A powerful subtext in the journals is his fascination with the horrors of humanity. In exquisite detail Arthur describes such arresting sights as starving beggars in Westphalia, the masses running in panic from the impending war (the Napoleonic campaigns were incubating), thieves, pickpockets, and drunken crowds in London, marauding gangs in Poitiers, the public guillotine on display in Paris, the six thousand galley slaves, on view as in a zoo, in Toulon doomed to be chained together for life in landlocked naval hulks too decrepit to put out to sea ever again. And he described the fortress in Marseilles, which once housed the Man in the Iron Mask, and the Black Death museum, where letters from quarantined sections of the city were once required to be dipped into vats of hot vinegar before being passed on. And, in Lyon, he remarked on the sight of people walking indifferently over the very spot where their fathers and brothers were killed during the French Revolution.

At a boarding school in Wimbledon where Lord Nelson had once been a student in England, Arthur perfected his English and attended public executions and naval floggings, visited hospitals and asylums, and walked by himself through the massive teeming slums of London.

The Buddha as a young man lived in his father's palace, where the common lot of mankind had been veiled from him. It was only when he first journeyed outside of his father's palace that he saw the three primal horrors of life: a diseased person, a decrepit old man, and a corpse. His discovery of the tragic and terrible nature of existence led the Buddha to his renunciation of the world and the search for a relief from universal suffering.

For Arthur Schopenhauer, too, early views of suffering profoundly influenced his life and work. The similarity of his experience to that of the Buddha was not lost on him, and years later, when writing about his journey, he said, "In my seventeenth year, without any learned school education, I was gripped by the misery of life, just like Buddha in his youth, when he saw sickness, pain, aging, and death."

Arthur never had a religious phase; he had no faith but, when young, had a will to faith, a wish to escape the terror of a totally unobserved existence. Had he a belief in the existence of God, though, it would have been sorely tested by his teenaged tour of the horrors of European civilization. At the age of eighteen he wrote, "This world is supposed to have been made by a God? No, much better by a devil!"

When, at the end of their lives, most men look back they will find that they have lived throughout ad interim. They will be surprised to see that the very thing they allowed to slip by unappreciated and unenjoyed was just their life. And so a man, having been duped by hope, dances into the arms of death.

13

The trouble with a kitten is that
Eventually it becomes a cat.
The trouble with a kitten is that
Eventually it becomes a cat.

Jerking his head to dislodge the annoying couplet from his mind, Julius sat up in bed and opened his eyes. It was 6 A.M., a week later, the day of the next group meeting, and those odd Ogden Nash lines looping around in his mind had been the background music for yet another night of unsatisfying sleep.

Though everyone agrees that life is one goddamned loss after another, few know that one of the most aggravating losses awaiting us in later decades is that of a good night's sleep. Julius knew that lesson all too well. His typical night consisted of tissue-thin dozing which almost never entered the realm of deep, blessed delta-wave slumber, a sleep that was interrupted by so many awakenings that he often dreaded going to bed. Like most insomniacs, he awoke in the morning believing either that he had slept far fewer hours than he actually had or that he had been awake all night long. Often he could assure himself that he had slept only by carefully reviewing his nocturnal thoughts and realizing that he would never, in a waking state, have ruminated at such length about such bizarre, irrational things.

But this particular morning he was entirely confused about how much he had slept. The kitten-cat couplet must have emerged from the dream realm, but his other nocturnal thoughts fell into a no-man's-land, with neither the clarity and purposefulness of full-fledged consciousness nor the quirky caprice of dream thoughts.

Julius sat in bed, reviewing the couplet with his eyes closed, following the instructions he offered patients to facilitate the recall of nighttime fantasies, hypnagogic images, and dreams. The poem was pointed at those who loved kittens but not their coming to age as cats. But what did that have to do with him? He loved kittens and cats alike, had loved the two adult cats in his father's store, loved their kittens and their kittens' kittens, and couldn't understand why the couplet lodged in his mind in such tiresome fashion.

On second thought, perhaps the verse was a grim reminder of how, all his life, he had embraced the wrong myth: namely, that everything about Julius Hertzfeld—his fortune, stature, glory—was spiraling upward, and that life would always get better and better. Of course, now he realized that the reverse was true—that the couplet had it right—that the golden age came first, that his innocent, kittenly beginnings, the playfulness, the hide-and-seek, the capture-the-flag games, and the building of forts out of the empty liquor boxes in his father's store, while unburdened by guilt, guile, knowledge, or duty, was the very best time of life and that as the days and years passed, the intensity of his flame dimmed, and existence grew inexorably more grim. The very worst was saved for last. He recalled Philip's words about childhood in the last meeting. No doubt about it: Nietzsche and Schopenhauer had that part right.

Julius nodded his head sadly. It was true he had never truly savored the moment, never grasped the present, never said to himself, "This is it, this time, this day—this is what I want! These are the good old days, right now. Let me remain in this moment, let me take root in this place for all time." No, he had always believed that the juiciest meat of life was yet to be found and had always coveted the future—the time of being older, smarter, bigger, richer. And then came the upheaval, the time of the great reversal, the sudden and cataclysmic deidealization of the future, and the beginning of the aching yearning for what used to be.

When was that reversal? When did nostalgia replace the golden promise of tomorrow? Not in college, where Julius considered everything as prelude (and obstacle) to that grand prize: admission to medical school. Not in medical school, where, in his first years, he yearned to be out of the classrooms and onto the wards as a clinical clerk, with white jacket and stethoscope hanging out of pocket or slung casually about his neck like a steel-and-rubber shawl. Not in the clerkships of his third and fourth medical school years, when he finally took his place on the wards. There he yearned for more authority—to be important, to make vital clinical decisions, to save lives, to dress in blue scrubs and careen a patient on a gurney down the corridor to the OR to perform emergency trauma surgery. Not even when he became chief resident in psychiatry, peeked behind the curtain of shamanism, and was stunned at the limits and uncertainty of his chosen profession.

Without doubt Julius's chronic and persistent unwillingness to grasp the present had played havoc with his marriage. Though he had loved Miriam from the moment he laid eyes on her in the tenth grade, he simultaneously resented her as an obstacle blocking him from the multitude of women he felt entitled to enjoy. He had never completely acknowledged that his mate-search was over or that his freedom to follow his lust was in the slightest way curtailed. When his internship began he found that the house staff sleeping quarters were immediately adjacent to the nursing school dorm brimming with nubile young nurses who adored doctors. It was a veritable candy store, and he stuffed himself with a rainbow of flavors.

It was only after Miriam's death that the reversal must have occurred. In the ten years since the car crash took her from him, he had cherished her more than while she was alive. Julius sometimes heaved with despair when he thought of how his lush contentment with Miriam, the true idyllic soaring moments of life, had come and gone without his fully grasping them. Even now, after a decade, he could not speak her name quickly but had to pause after each syllable. He knew also that no other woman would ever really matter to him. Several women temporarily dispelled his loneliness, but it didn't take long for him, and for them, to realize they would never replace Miriam. More recently, his loneliness was attenuated by a large circle of male friends, several of whom belonged to his psychiatric support group, and by his two children. For the past few years he had taken all his vacations *en famille* with his two children and five grandchildren.

But all these thoughts and reminiscences had been only nocturnal trailers and short subjects—the main feature of the night's mentation had been a rehearsal of the speech he would deliver to the therapy group later that afternoon.

He had already gone public about his cancer to many of his friends and his individual therapy patients, yet, curiously, he was painfully preoccupied with his "coming out" in the group. Julius thought it had something to do with his being in love with his therapy group. For twenty-five years he had looked forward eagerly to every meeting. The group was more than a clump of people; it had a life of its own, an enduring personality. Though none of the original members (except, of course, he himself) was still in the group, it had a stable persisting self, a core culture (in the jargon, a unique set of "norms"—unwritten rules) that seemed immortal. No one member could recite the group norms, but everyone could agree whether a certain piece of behavior was appropriate or inappropriate.

The group demanded more energy than any other event of his week, and Julius had labored mightily to keep it afloat. A venerable mercy ship, it had transported a horde of tormented people into safer, happier harbors. How many? Well, since the average stay was between two and three years, Julius figured at least a hundred passengers. From time to time, memories of departed members wafted through his mind, snippets of an interchange, a fleeting visual image of a face or incident. Sad to think that these wisps of memory were all that remained of rich vibrant times, of events bursting with so much life, meaning, and poignancy.

Many years ago Julius had experimented with videotaping the group and playing back some particularly problematic interchanges at the next meeting. These old tapes were in an archaic format no longer compatible with contemporary video playback equipment. Sometimes he fancied retrieving them from his basement storage room, having them converted, and bringing departed patients back to life again. But he never did; he couldn't bear exposing himself to proof of the illusory nature of life, how it was warehoused on shiny tape and how quickly the present moment and every moment to come will fade into the nothingness of electromagnetic wavelets.

Groups require time to develop stability and trust. Often a new group will spin off members who are unable, for reasons of either motivation or ability, to engage in the group task (that is, interacting with other members and analyzing that interaction). Then it may go through weeks of uneasy conflict as members jockey for position of power, centrality, and influence, but eventually, as trust develops, the healing atmosphere grows in strength. His colleague, Scott, had once likened a therapy group to a bridge built in battle. Many casualties (that is, dropouts) had to be taken during the early formative stage, but once the bridge was built it conveyed many people—the remaining original members and all those who subsequently joined the group—to a better place.

Julius had written professional articles about the various ways that therapy groups helped patients, but he always had difficulty in finding the language to describe the truly crucial ingredient: the group's healing ambience. In one article he likened it to dermatological treatments of severe skin lesions in which the patient was immersed into soothing oatmeal baths.

One of the major side benefits of leading a group—a fact never stated in the professional literature—is that a potent therapy group often heals the therapist as well as the patients. Though Julius had often experienced personal relief after a meeting, he never was certain of the precise mechanism. Was it simply a result of forgetting himself for ninety minutes, or of the altruistic act of therapy, or of enjoying his own expertise, feeling proud of his abilities, and enjoying the high regard of others? All of the above? Julius gave up trying to be precise and for the past few years accepted the folksy explanation of simply dipping into the healing waters of the group.

Going public with his melanoma to his therapy group seemed a momentous act. It was one thing, he thought, to be open with family, friends, and all the other folks residing backstage, but quite another to unmask himself to his primary audience, to that select group for whom he had been healer, doctor, priest, and shaman. It was an irreversible step, an admission that he was superannuated, a public confession that his life no longer spiraled upward toward a bigger, brighter future.

Julius had been thinking a good bit of the missing member, Pam, now traveling and not due to return for a month. He regretted she would not be there today for his disclosure. For him, she was the key member of the group, always a comforting, healing presence for others—and for him as well. And he felt chagrined by the fact that the group had not been able to help with her extreme rage and obsessional thinking about her husband and an ex-lover and that Pam, in desperation, had sought help at a Buddhist meditation retreat in India.

And so, heaving and churning with all these feelings, Julius entered the group room at four-thirty that afternoon. The members were already seated and poring over sheets of paper which were whisked out of sight when Julius entered.

Odd, he thought. Was he late? He took a quick look at his watch. Nope, four-thirty on the dot. He put it out of mind and began the recitation of his prepared statement.

"Well, let's get started. As you know, I never make a practice of starting the meeting, but today's an exception because there's something I need to get off my chest, something that's hard for me to say. So here goes.

"About a month ago I learned that I have a serious, I'll be frank, more than serious—a life-threatening form of skin cancer, malignant melanoma. I thought I was in good health; this turned up at a recent routine physical exam. . . ."

Julius stopped. Something was off kilter: The members' facial expression and nonverbal language weren't right. Their posture was wrong. They should have been turned toward him; focusing on him; instead no one fully faced him, no one met his gaze, all eyes were averted, unfocused, except for Rebecca, who covertly studied the sheet of paper in her lap.

"What's happening?" asked Julius. "I feel like I'm not making contact. You all seem preoccupied with something else today. And, Rebecca, what is it that you're reading?"

Rebecca immediately folded the paper, buried it in her purse, and avoided Julius's gaze. Everyone sat quietly until Tony broke the silence.

"Well, I gotta talk. I can't talk for Rebecca but I'll talk for myself. My problem when you were speaking was that I already know what you're going to tell us about your . . . health. So it was hard to look at you and pretend I was hearing something new. And yet I just couldn't interrupt you to tell you that I knew it already."

"How? What do you mean you knew what I was going to say? What in hell is going on today?"

"Julius, I'm sorry, let me explain," said Gill. "I mean, in a way I'm to blame. After the last meeting I was still frazzled and not clear about when or whether to go home or where to sleep that night. I really put pressure on everyone to come to the coffee shop, where we continued the meeting."

"Yeah? And?" Julius coaxed, moving his hand in a small circle as though conducting an orchestra.

"Well, Philip told us what the score was. You know—about your health and about the malignant myeloma—"

"Melanoma," Philip softly interjected.

Gill glanced at the paper in his hand. "Right, melanoma. Thanks, Philip. Keep doing that. I get mixed up."

"Multiple myeloma is a cancer of the bone," said Philip. "Melanoma is a cancer of the skin, think of melanin, pigment, skin coloring—"

"So those sheets are . . . ," interrupted Julius, gesturing with his hands to invite Gill or Philip to explain.

"Philip downloaded information about your medical condition and prepared a summary, which he handed out just as we entered the room a few minutes ago." Gill extended his copy toward Julius, who saw the heading: Malignant Melanoma.

Staggered, Julius sat back in his chair. "I . . . uh . . . don't know how to put it . . . I feel preempted, I feel like I had a big news story to tell you and I've been scooped, scooped on my own life story—or death story." Turning and speaking directly to Philip, Julius said, "Had you any guesses about how I'd feel about that?"

Philip remained impassive, neither replying nor looking at Julius.

"That's not entirely fair, Julius," said Rebecca, who removed her barrette, loosened her long black hair, and twisted it into a coil on the top of her head. "He's not at fault here. First of all, Philip did not, in the worst way, want to go to the coffee shop after the meeting. Said he didn't socialize, said he had a class to prepare. We had to practically drag him there."

"Right." Gill took over. "We talked mostly about me and my wife and where I should sleep that night. Then, of course, we all asked Philip about why he was in therapy, which is only natural—every new member gets asked that—and he told us about your phone call to him which was prompted by your illness. That news jolted us, and we couldn't let it pass without pressing him to tell us what he knew. Looking back, I don't see how he could have withheld that from us."

"Philip even asked," Rebecca added, "whether it was kosher for the group to meet without you."

"Kosher? Philip said *that*?" asked Julius.

"Well, no," said Rebecca, "come to think of it, *kosher* was my term, not his. But that was his meaning, and I told him that we often had a postgroup session at the coffee shop and that you've never raised objections about it except to insist that we debrief everyone who wasn't there in the next meeting so that there be no secrets."

It was good that Rebecca and Gill gave Julius time to calm himself. His mind churned with negativity: *That ungrateful prick, that undercutting bastard. I try to do something for him, and this is what I get for it—no good deed goes unpunished. And I can just imagine how little he told the group about himself and why he had been in therapy with me in the first place. . . . I'd lay big money that he conveniently forgot to tell the group that he had screwed about a thousand women without an ounce of care or compassion for a single one of them.*

But he kept all these thoughts to himself and gradually cleansed his mind of rancor by considering the events following the last meeting. He realized that *of course* the group would have pressured Philip to attend a postgroup coffee and that Philip would have been swayed by the group pressure to attend—indeed he himself was at fault for not having informed Philip about these periodic postgroup get-togethers. And, *of course,* the group would have questioned Philip about why he was in therapy—Gill was right—the group never failed to pose this question to a new member, and *of course* Philip would have to reveal the story of their unusual history and subsequent contract for therapy—what choice did he have? As for his distributing medical information on malignant melanoma—that was Philip's own idea, no doubt his way of ingratiating himself with the group.

Julius felt wobbly, couldn't pull off a smile, but braced himself and continued. "Well, I'll do my best to talk about this. Rebecca, let me take a good look at that sheet." Julius quickly scanned it. "These medical facts seem accurate so I won't repeat them, but I'll just fill you in on my experience. It started with my doctor spotting an unusual mole on my back, which a biopsy confirmed was a malignant melanoma. Of course that's why I canceled the group—had a rough couple of weeks, really rough, letting it sink in." Julius's voice quavered. "As you see, it's still rough." He paused, took a deep breath, and continued. "My doctors can't predict my future, but what is important here is they feel strongly that I have at least a year of good health ahead. So this group will be open for business as usual for the twelve months. No, wait, let me put it this way: health permitting, I commit myself to meet with you for one more year, at which time the group will terminate. Sorry to be clumsy about it, but I've had no practice at this."

"Julius, is this seriously life threatening?" asked Bonnie. "Philip's Internet information . . . all these statistics based on stages of the melanoma."

"Straight question and the straight answer is 'yes'—definitely life threatening. The chances are good that this thing will get me in the future. I know that wasn't an easy question to ask, but I appreciate your straightforwardness, Bonnie, because I'm like most people with major illness—I hate everyone to be pussyfooting around. That would just isolate and frighten me. I've got to get used to my new reality. I don't like it, but life as a healthy carefree person—well, *that* life is definitely coming to an end."

"I'm thinking of what Philip said to Gill last week. I wonder—is there something of value in there for you, Julius? asked Rebecca. "I'm not sure if it was in the coffee shop or here in the group—but it had to do with defining yourself or your life by your attachments. Do I have it right, Philip?"

"When I spoke to Gill last week," said Philip, speaking in a measured tone and avoiding eye contact, "I pointed out that the more attachments one has, the more burdensome life becomes and the more suffering one experiences when one is separated from these attachments. Schopenhauer and Buddhism both hold that one must release oneself from attachments and—"

"I don't think that is helpful to me," interrupted Julius, "and I'm also not sure if this is where this meeting should be going." He noted a quick pregnant glance passing between Rebecca and Gill but continued, "I come in on that in the opposite way: attachments, and plenty of them, are the indispensable ingredients of a full life, and to avoid attachments because of anticipated suffering is a sure recipe for being only partially alive. I don't mean to cut you off, Rebecca, but I think it more to the point to go back to your reactions, everyone's reactions, to the announcement I've made. Obviously, learning of my cancer has got to stir up strong feelings. I've known many of you for a long time." Julius stopped talking and looked around at his patients.

Tony, who had been slumped in his chair, stirred himself. "Well, I had a jolt when you said earlier that what should be important to us was how long you could continue to lead this group—that comment got under my skin, thick-skinned as I've been accused of being. Now, I don't deny that crossed my mind, but, Julius, I'm mostly upset at what this means for *you*. . . . I mean, let's face it, you've been pretty, I mean . . . *really*, important to me, helped me get over some really bad stuff. . . . I mean, is there something I, we, can do for you? This has gotta be terrible for you."

"Ditto for me," said Gill, and all the others (save Philip) joined in assent.

"I'm going to respond, Tony, but first say how touched I am and how impossible it would have been for you, a couple of years ago, to be so direct and to reach out so generously. But to answer your question, it's been terrible. My feelings come in waves. I hit bottom the first couple of weeks when I canceled the group. Did a lot of nonstop talking to my friends, my whole support network. Right now, at this moment, I'm doing better. You get used to everything, even mortal illness. Last night the refrain 'Life is just one goddamned loss after another' kept passing through my mind."

Julius stopped. No one spoke. Everyone stared at the floor. Julius added, "I want to deal with it openly . . . willing to discuss everything . . . I won't shy away from anything . . . but unless you ask something specific, I'm talked out now plus I don't feel I need the whole meeting to be given to me today. I want to say I have energy to work with you here in my usual way. In fact it's important to me that we go on as we always have."

After a short silence Bonnie said, "I'll be honest, Julius, there's something I could work on, but I don't know . . . my problems seem insignificant compared to what you're going through."

Gill looked up and added, "Me, too. My stuff—whether or not I learn to talk to my wife, stay with her, or leave the sinking ship—all that seems trivial in comparison."

Philip took that as his cue. "Spinoza was fond of using a Latin phrase, *sub specie aeternitatis,* meaning 'from the aspect of eternity.' He suggested that disturbing quotidian events become less unsettling if they are viewed from the aspect of eternity. I believe that concept may be an underappreciated tool in psychotherapy. Perhaps," and here Philip turned and addressed Julius directly, "it may offer a form of solace to even the kind of serious assault you're facing."

"I can see you're trying to offer me something, Philip, and I appreciate that. But right now the idea of taking a cosmic-eye view of life is the wrong flavor of medicine. Let me tell you why. Last night I didn't sleep well and got to feeling sad for not having appreciated what I had at the very moment it was happening. When I was young, I always regarded the present as a prelude to something better that was going to occur. And then, the years passed, I suddenly found myself doing the opposite—I was bathing myself in nostalgia. What I've not done enough of is to treasure each moment, and that's the problem with your solution of detachment. I think it faces life through the wrong end of the telescope."

"I gotta come in here, Julius," said Gill, "with an observation: I don't think there's much chance you're going to accept anything that Philip says."

"An observation I'll always pay attention to, Gill. But that's an opinion. Where's the observation?"

"Well, the observation is that you're just not respecting anything he offers."

"I know what Julius would say about that, Gill," said Rebecca. "It's still not an observation; it's a guess about his feelings. What I observe"—she turned to Julius—"is that this is the first time you and Philip have addressed one another even halfway directly and that you have interrupted Philip a few times today, something I never see you do with anyone else."

"Touché, Rebecca," answered Julius. "Right on—a direct and accurate observation."

"Julius," said Tony, "I'm not getting the picture at all. You and Philip—what's going on?—I don't get it. Is he right when he says you phoned him out of the blue?"

Julius sat with his head bowed for a few minutes and then said, "Yes, I can see how confusing this must be for all of you. Okay, here it is straight. Or as straight as my memory permits. After my diagnosis, I fell into real despair. I felt I had gotten a death sentence, and I was staggered by it. Among other dark thoughts I began to question whether anything I had done in my life had any enduring meaning whatsoever. I slogged around in that question for a day or two, and, since my life is so intertwined with my work, I began thinking of patients I'd seen in the past. Had I really, permanently, affected anyone's life? I felt I had no time to waste, and so, on the spot, I decided to contact some of my old patients. Philip was the first person, and so far the only one, I reached."

"And why select Philip?" asked Tony.

"That's the sixty-four-thousand-dollar question—or maybe that's dated—is it the sixty-four-million-dollar question these days? Short answer: I'm not sure. I've wondered about it a lot. It wasn't smart of me because if I wanted reassurance of my worth, there are a lot of better candidates. Try as hard as I did for a full three years, I didn't help Philip. Maybe I was hoping that he would report some delayed effect of therapy—some patients report such a thing. But it didn't turn out that way for him. Maybe I was being masochistic—wanted to rub my nose in it. Maybe I chose my biggest failure in order to give myself a second chance. I admit it—I frankly don't know my motives. And then during the course of our discussion Philip told me of his career change and asked if I would be willing to be his supervisor. Philip," Julius turned to face Philip, "I assume you filled the group in on this?"

"I provided the necessary details."

"Can you be a little more cryptic?"

Philip looked away, the rest of the group looked uncomfortable, and after a long silence Julius said, "I apologize for the sarcasm, Philip, but can you see where your answer left me?"

"As I said, I provided the necessary details to the others," Philip said.

Bonnie turned to face Julius: "I'll be upfront. This feels unpleasant, and I'm rescuing you. I don't think you need to be hassled today—I think you need to be taken care of. Please, what can we do for you, today?"

"Thanks, Bonnie, you're right, I am shaky today—your question's a lovely one, but I'm not sure I can answer it. I'll tell you all a big secret: there have been times I've entered this room feeling bad because of some personal issues and left feeling better just as a result of being a part of this terrific group. So maybe that's the answer to your question. The best thing for me is simply for all of you to use the group and not let my situation bring us to a total stop."

After a short silence Tony said, "Tough assignment with what's gone down today."

"Right," said Gill. "It'll feel awkward to talk about anything else."

"These are the times I miss Pam," said Bonnie. "She was the one who always knew what to do—no matter how awkward the situation."

"Funny, I was thinking about her earlier too," said Julius.

"It must be telepathy," said Rebecca. "Just a minute ago Pam went through my mind also. It was when Julius talked about successes and failures." She turned to Julius: "I know she was your favorite child in our family here—and that's not a question—it's so obvious. What I'm wondering is whether you feel like you failed with her—you know, her taking a couple of months off to seek another kind of therapy because we couldn't help her. That can't be great for your self-esteem."

Julius gestured toward Philip. "Maybe you should fill him in."

"Pam's a real force here," Rebecca said to Philip, who did not meet her eyes. "Both her marriage and a relationship with a lover fell apart. She decided to leave her marriage but then the lover opted not to leave his wife. She got upset with both men and obsessed about them day and night. Try as we could, we never found a way to help her. In desperation she took off for India to seek help from a famous guru at a Buddhist meditation retreat."

Philip made no response.

Rebecca turned back to face Julius. "So how did you feel about her taking off?"

"You know, up to about fifteen years ago I would have been very uptight—more than that, I might even have taken a strong stand against it and insisted that her search for another form of enlightenment was just resistance to change. I've changed. Now I feel I need all the help I can get. And I've found that participation in some other mode of growth, even flaky stuff, can often open up new areas for our therapeutic work. And I sure hope that will be true for Pam."

"It may have been not a flaky but an excellent choice for her," said Philip. "Schopenhauer felt positive about Eastern meditative practice and its emphasis on mind clearing, on seeing through illusion, and its approach to relieving suffering by teaching the art of letting go of attachments. In fact, he was the first to introduce Eastern thought into Western philosophy."

Philip's comment was made to no one in particular, and no one responded. Julius felt irritated about hearing Schopenhauer's name so often but kept it to himself as he noted several members nodding in appreciation of Philip's remarks.

After a brief silence Stuart commented, "Shouldn't we go back to where we were a few minutes ago when Julius said that what would be best for him would be for us to get to work in the group?"

"I agree," said Bonnie, "but where to start? How about a follow-up on you and your wife, Stuart? Last we heard she e-mailed you that she was thinking of leaving the marriage."

"It's settled down and we're back to status quo. She's keeping her distance, but at least things are no worse. Let's see what else is pending in the group." Stuart looked around the room. "I can think of two items. Gill, how about you and Rose—what's been happening there? And, Bonnie, you said earlier today you had something to work on, but it felt too trivial."

"I want to pass today," said Gill, looking downward. "I took too much time last week. But the bottom line is defeat and capitulation. I'm ashamed to be back home in the same situation. All that good advice from Philip, from all of you, was wasted on me. How about you, Bonnie?"

"My stuff feels like small potatoes today."

"Remember my version of Boyle's law," said Julius. "A small amount of anxiety will expand to fill our whole anxiety cavity. Your anxiety feels just as awful as anxiety in others that comes from more obviously calamitous sources." He looked at his watch. "We're just about out of time, but do you want to open it up? Get it on the agenda?"

"To stop me from chickening out next week, you mean?" asked Bonnie. "Well, that's not a bad idea. What I was going to bring up has to do with my being homely and fat and clumsy and Rebecca—and also Pam—being beautiful and . . . and stylish. But, Rebecca, you, especially, open up a lot of painful old feelings for me—feelings I've always had about being klutzy, homely, unchosen." Bonnie stopped and looked at Julius. "There, it's out."

"And on the agenda for next week," said Julius, rising to signal the end of the meeting.

A person of high, rare mental gifts who is forced into a job which is merely useful is like a valuable vase decorated with the most beautiful painting and then used as a kitchen pot.

14

1807—How Arthur Schopenhauer Almost Became a Merchant

The Schopenhauer family's grand tour ended in 1804, and the sixteen-year-old Arthur, with a heavy heart, honored his pledge to his father by commencing his seven-year apprenticeship with Senator Jenisch, an eminent Hamburg merchant. Slipping into a double life, Arthur fulfilled all the quotidian tasks of his apprenticeship but surreptitiously spent every spare moment studying the great ideas of intellectual history. He had so internalized his father, however, that these stolen moments filled him with remorse.

Then, nine months later came the staggering event that marked Arthur's life forever. Though Heinrich Schopenhauer was only sixty-five, his health had rapidly deteriorated: he appeared jaundiced, fatigued, depressed, and confused, often not recognizing old acquaintances. On the twentieth of April, 1805, he managed, despite his infirmity, to travel to his Hamburg warehouse, slowly climb to the upper loft of the granary, and hurl himself out of the window into the

Hamburg Canal. A few hours later his body was found floating in the icy water.

Every suicide leaves a wake of shock, guilt, and anger in the survivors, and Arthur experienced all these sentiments. Imagine the complexity of feelings Arthur must have experienced. His love for his father resulted in intense grief and loss. His resentment of his father—later he often spoke of his suffering from his father's excessive hardness—evoked remorse. And the wonderful possibility of liberation must have evoked much guilt: Arthur realized that his father would have forever blocked the path to his becoming a philosopher. In this regard one thinks of two other great free-thinking moral philosophers, Nietzsche and Sartre, who lost their fathers early in life. Could Nietzsche have become the Antichrist if his father, a Lutheran minister, had not died when Nietzsche was a child? And in his autobiography Sartre expresses his relief that he was not burdened with the search for his father's approbation. Others, Kierkegaard and Kafka, for example, were not so fortunate: all their lives they were oppressed by the weight of their fathers' judgment.

Though Arthur Schopenhauer's work contains an enormous range of ideas, topics, historical and scientific curiosities, notions, and sentiments, there are to be found only a couple of personal tender passages, and each pertains to Heinrich Schopenhauer. In one passage Arthur expresses pride in his father's honest admission that he was in business to make money and compares his father's forthrightness to the duplicity of many of his fellow philosophers (particularly Hegel and Fichte), who grasp for wealth, power, and fame all the while pretending they are working for humanity.

At the age of sixty he planned to dedicate his complete works to the memory of his father. He worked and reworked the wording of his dedication, which ultimately was never published. One version began: "Noble, excellent spirit to whom I owe everything that I am and that I achieve . . . any one finding in my work any kind of joy, consolation, instruction, let him hear your name and know that, if Heinrich Schopenhauer had not been the man he was, Arthur Schopenhauer would have perished a hundred times."

The strength of Arthur's filial devotion remains puzzling, given Heinrich's lack of any overt affection toward his son. His letters to

Arthur are laced with criticism. For example: "Dancing and riding do not make for a livelihood for a merchant whose letters have to be read and must therefore be well written. Now and then I find that the capital letters in your hand are still veritable monstrosities." Or: "Do not acquire a round back, which looks ghastly. . . . if in the dining room one catches sight of someone stooping, one takes him for a disguised tailor or cobbler." In his very last letter Heinrich instructed his son: "With reference to walking and sitting upright, I advise you request everyone you are with to give you a blow whenever you are caught oblivious of this great matter. This is what children of Princes have done, not minding the pain for a short time, rather than appear as oafs all their lives."

Arthur was his father's son, resembling him not only physically but temperamentally. When he was seventeen, his mother wrote him: "I know too well how little you had of a happy sense of youth, how large the disposition for melancholic brooding you received as a sad share of your inheritance from your father."

Arthur also inherited his father's deep sense of integrity, which played a decisive role in the dilemma that confronted him following his father's death: should he stay in the apprenticeship even though he hated the world of commerce? Eventually, he decided to do what his father would have done: honor his pledge.

He wrote of his decision, "I continued to hold my position with my merchant patron, partly because my excessive grief had broken the energy of my spirit, partly because I would have had a guilty conscience were I to rescind my father's decision so soon after his death."

If Arthur felt immobilized and duty-bound after his father's suicide, his mother had no such inclinations. With the speed of a whirlwind she changed her entire life. In a letter to the seventeen-year-old Arthur she wrote: "Your character is so completely different from mine: you are by nature undecided, I myself am too fast, too resolute." After a few months of widowhood she sold the Schopenhauer mansion, liquidated the venerable family business, and moved away from Hamburg. She boasted to Arthur, "I will always choose the most exciting option. Consider my choice of residence: instead of moving to my hometown, back to my friends and relatives, like every other woman would have done in my stead, I chose Weimar, which was almost unknown to me."

Why Weimar? Johanna was ambitious and yearned to be close to the epicenter of German culture. Supremely confident of her social abilities, she knew she could make good things happen, and, indeed, within months she had created an extraordinary new life for herself: she established the liveliest salon of Weimar and developed a close friendship with Goethe and many other leading writers and artists. Soon she began a career, first as a successful writer of travel journals chronicling the Schopenhauer family's tour and a trip to southern France; then, with Goethe's urging, she turned to fiction and wrote a series of romantic novels. She was one of the first truly liberated women and was Germany's first woman to earn her living as a writer. For the next decade Johanna Schopenhauer became a renowned novelist, the Danielle Steel of nineteenth-century Germany, and for decades Arthur Schopenhauer was known only as "Johanna Schopenhauer's son." In the late 1820s Johanna's complete works were published in a twenty-volume edition.

Though history (based greatly on Arthur's scathing criticism of his mother) has generally presented Johanna as narcissistic and uncaring, there is no doubt that she, and only she, liberated Arthur from his servitude and started him on his way to philosophy. The instrument of delivery was a fateful letter she wrote to Arthur in April 1807, two years after his father's suicide.

> Dear Arthur,
>
> The serious and calm tone of your March 28th letter, flowing from your mind into my mind, woke me up and revealed that you might be on your way to totally missing your vocation! That is why I have to do each and every thing to save you, however possible; I know what it means to live a life repugnant to one's soul; and if it is possible, I will spare you, my dear son, this misery. Oh, dear dear Arthur, why was it that my voice counted so little; what you want now, was in fact then my warmest wish; how hard I strove to make it happen, despite everything one said against me. . . . if you do not wish to be taken into the honourable Philistine order, I, my dear Arthur, truly don't want to put any obstacle into your way; it is just you who have to seek your own way and choose it. Then I will advise and help, where and how I can. First try to come to peace with yourself . . .

remember you must choose studies that promise you a good salary, not only because it is the only way you can live, for you will never be rich enough to live from your inheritance alone. If you have made your choice, tell me so, but you have to take this decision on your own. . . . If you feel the strength and heart to do this, I will willingly give you my hand. But just don't imagine life as a complete learned man to be too delightful. I now see it around me, dear Arthur. It is a tiring, troublesome life full of work; only the delight in doing it gives it its charm. One doesn't get rich with it; as a writer, one acquires with difficulty what one needs for survival. . . . To make your life as a writer you have to be able to produce something excellent. . . . now, more than ever, there is a need of brilliant heads. Arthur, think about it carefully, and choose, but then stay firm; let your perseverance never fail, and you will safely achieve your goal. Choose what you want . . . but with tears in my eyes I implore you: do not cheat on yourself. Treat yourself seriously and honestly. The welfare of your life is at stake, as well as the happiness of my old days; because only you and Adele can hopefully replace my lost youth. I couldn't bear it to know that you are unhappy, especially if I had to blame myself for having let this great misfortune happen to you out of my too large pliability. You see, dear Arthur, that I dearly love you, and that I want to help you in everything. Reward me by your confidence and by, having once made up your mind, following my advice in fulfilling your choice. And don't hurt me by rebelliousness. You know that I am not stubborn. I know how to give way by arguments, and I will never demand anything from you I won't be able to support by arguments. . . .

Adieu, dear Arthur, the post is urgent and my fingers hurt. Bear in mind all I send and write to you, and answer soon.

Your mother
J. Schopenhauer

In his old age Arthur wrote, "When I finished reading this letter I shed a flood of tears." By return mail he opted for liberation from his apprenticeship, and Johanna responded, "That you have so quickly come to a decision, against your wont, would disquiet me in anyone else. I should fear rashness; with you it reassures me, I regard it as the power of your innermost desires that drives you.'

Johanna wasted no time; she notified Arthur's merchant patron and his landlord that Arthur was leaving Hamburg, she organized his move and arranged for him to attend a gymnasium in Gotha, fifty kilometers from his mother's home in Weimar.

Arthur's chains were broken.

It is noteworthy and remarkable to see how man, besides his life in the concrete, always lives a second life in the abstract . . . (where) in the sphere of calm deliberation, what previously possessed him completely and moved him intensely appears to him cold, colorless, and distant: he is a mere spectator and observer.

15

Pam in India

As the Bombay-Igatpuri train slowed for a stop at a small village, Pam heard the clangs of ceremonial cymbals and peered through the grimy train window. A dark-eyed boy of about ten or eleven, pointing to her window, ran alongside holding aloft a raised rag and yellow plastic water pail. Since she had arrived in India two weeks ago, Pam had been shaking her head no. No to sightseeing guides, shoe shines, freshly squeezed tangerine juice, sari cloth, Nike tennis shoes, money exchange. No to beggars and no to numerous sexual invitations, sometimes offered frankly, sometimes discreetly by winking, raising eyebrows, licking lips, and flicking tongues. And, finally, she thought, someone has actually offered me something I need. She vigorously nodded yes, yes to the young window washer, who responded with a huge toothy grin. Delighted with Pam's patronage and audience, he washed the pane with long theatrical flourishes.

Paying him generously and shooing him away as he lingered to stare at her, Pam settled back and watched a procession of villagers snake their way down a dusty street following a priest clad in billowing scarlet trousers and yellow shawl. Their destination was the center of the town square and a large papier-mâché statue of Lord Ganesha, a short plump Buddha-like body bearing an elephant's head. Everyone—the priest, the men dressed in gleaming white, and the women robed in saffron and magenta—carried small Ganesha statues. Young girls scattered handfuls of flowers, and pairs of adolescent boys carried poles holding metal burners emitting clouds of incense. Amid the clash of cymbals and the roll of drums, everyone chanted, "Ganapathi bappa Moraya, Purchya varshi laukariya."

"Pardon me, can you tell me what they're chanting?" Pam turned to the copper-skinned man sitting opposite her sipping tea, the only other passenger sharing the compartment. He was a delicate winsome man dressed in a loose white cotton shirt and trousers. At the sound of Pam's voice he swallowed the wrong way and coughed furiously. Her question delighted him since he had been attempting, in vain, since the train commenced in Bombay to strike up a conversation with the handsome woman sitting across from him. After a vigorous cough he replied, with a squeak, "My apologies, madam. Physiology is not always at one's command. What the people here, and throughout all of India today, are saying is 'Beloved Ganapati, lord of Moraya, come again early next year.' "

"Ganapati?"

"Yes, very confusing, I know. Perhaps you know him by his more common name, Ganesha. He has many other names, as well, for example, Vighnesvara, Vinayaka, Gajanana."

"And this parade?"

"The beginning of the ten-day festival of Ganesha. Perhaps you may be fortunate enough to be in Bombay next week at the end of the festival and witness the entire population of the city walk into the ocean and immerse their Ganesha statues in incoming waves."

"Oh, and that? A moon? Or sun?" Pam pointed to four children carrying a large yellow papier-mâché globe.

Vijay purred to himself. He welcomed the questions and hoped the train stop would be long and that this conversation would go on and on. Such voluptuous women were common in American movies, but never before had he had the good fortune to speak to one. This woman's grace and pale beauty stirred his imagination. She seemed to have stepped out of the ancient erotic carvings of the Kama Sutra. And where might this encounter lead? he wondered. Could this be the life-changing event for which he had long sought? He was free, his garment factory had, by Indian standards, made him wealthy. His teenaged fiancée died of tuberculosis two years ago, and, until his parents selected a new bride, he was unencumbered.

"Ah, it is a moon the children hold. They carry it to honor an old legend. First, you must know that Lord Ganesha was renowned for his appetite. Note his ample belly. He was once invited for a feast and stuffed himself with dessert pastries called laddoos. Have you eaten laddoos?"

Pam shook her head, fearing that he might produce one from his valise. A close friend had contracted hepatitis from a tea shop in India, and thus far she had heeded her physician's advice to eat nothing but four-star-hotel food. When away from the hotel she had limited herself to food she could peel—mainly tangerines, hard-boiled eggs, and peanuts.

"My mother made wonderful coconut almond laddoos," Vijay continued. "Essentially, they are fried flour balls with a sweet cardamom syrup—that sounds prosaic, but you must believe me when I say they are far more than the sum of their ingredients. But back to Lord Ganesha, who was so stuffed that he could not stand up properly. He lost his balance, fell, his stomach burst, and all the laddoos tumbled out.

"This all took place at night with only one witness, the moon, who found the event hilarious. Enraged, Ganesha cursed the moon and banished him from the universe. However, the whole world lamented the moon's absence, and an assembly of gods asked Lord Shiva, Ganesha's father, to persuade him to relent. The penitent moon also apologized for his misbehavior. Finally, Ganesha modified his curse and announced that the moon need be invisible only one day a month, partially visible the remainder of the month, and for one day only would be permitted to be visible in its full glory."

A brief silence and Vijay added, "And now you know why the moon plays a role in Lord Ganesha festivals."

"Thank you for that explanation."

"My name is Vijay, Vijay Pande."

"And mine is Pam, Pam Swanvil. What a delightful story, and what a fantastical droll god—that elephant head and Buddha body. And yet the villagers seem to take their myths so seriously . . . as though they were really—"

"It's interesting to consider the iconography of Lord Ganesha," Vijay gently interrupted as he pulled from his shirt a large neck pendant on which was carved the image of Ganesha. "Please note that every feature on Ganesha has a serious meaning, a life instruction. Consider the large elephant head: it tells us to think big. And the large ears? To listen more. The small eyes remind us to focus and to concentrate and the small mouth to talk less. And I do not forget Ganesha's instruction—even at this moment as I talk to you I remember his counsel and I warn myself not to talk too much. You must help by telling me when I tell you more than you wish to know."

"No, not at all. I'm most interested in your comments on iconography."

"There are many others; here, look closer—we Indians are very serious people." He reached into the leather bag he wore on his shoulder and held out a small magnifying lens.

Taking the glass, Pam leaned over to peer at Vijay's pendant. She inhaled his aroma of cinnamon and cardamon and freshly ironed cotton cloth. How was it possible for him to smell so sweet and so fresh in the close dusty train compartment? "He has only one tusk," she observed.

"Meaning: retain the good, throw away the bad."

"And what's that he holds? An ax?"

"To cut off all bonds of attachment."

"That sounds like Buddhist doctrine."

"Yes, remember that the Buddha emerged from the mother ocean of Shiva."

"And Ganesha holds something in the other hand. It's hard to see. A thread?"

"A rope to pull one ever closer to your highest goal."

The train suddenly lurched and began to move forward.

"Our vehicle is alive again," said Vijay. "Note Ganesha's vehicle—there under his foot."

Pam moved closer to look through the lens and inhale Vijay's scent discreetly. "Oh, yes, the mouse. I've seen it in every statue and painting of Ganesha. I've never known why a mouse."

"That's the most interesting attribute of all. The mouse is desire. You may ride it but only if you keep it under control. Otherwise it causes havoc."

Pam fell silent. As the train chugged on past scrawny trees, occasional temples, water buffalo in muddy ponds, and farms whose red soil had been exhausted by thousands of years of work, she looked at Vijay and felt a wave of gratitude. How unobtrusively, how gently, he had taken out his pendant and saved her from the embarrassment of speaking irreverently about his religion. When had she ever been so graced by a man? But no, she reminded herself, don't shortchange other dear men. She thought about her group. There was Tony, who would do anything for her. And Stuart, too, could be generous. And Julius, whose love seemed unending. But Vijay's subtlety—that was uncommon, that was exotic.

And Vijay? He too fell into a reverie, reviewing his conversation with Pam. Uncommonly excited, his heart raced, and he sought to calm himself. Opening his leather shoulder pouch, he took out an old wrinkled cigarette package, not to smoke—the package was empty, and besides he had heard of how peculiar Americans were about smoking. He merely wished to study the blue-and-white package, which bore the silhouette of a man wearing a top hat and, in firm black letters, the brand name, The Passing Show.

One of his first religious teachers had called his attention to the Passing Show, a brand of cigarettes his father smoked, and instructed him to begin his meditation by thinking of all of life as a passing show, a river carrying all objects, all experience, all desires, past his unswerving attention. Vijay meditated on the image of a flowing river and listened to his mind's soundless words, *anitya, anitya*—impermanence. Everything is impermanent, he reminded himself; all of life and all experience glide by as surely and irrevocably as the passing landscape seen through the train window. He closed his eyes, breathed deeply, and rested his head upon his seat; his pulse slowed as he entered the welcome harbor of equanimity.

Pam, who had been eyeing Vijay discreetly, picked up the wrapping that had fallen to the floor, read the label, and said, "The Passing Show—that's an unusual name for cigarettes."

Vijay slowly opened his eyes and said, "As I said, we Indians are very serious. Even our cigarette packages have messages for the conduct of life. Life *is* a passing show—I meditate on that whenever I feel inner turbulence."

"Is that what you were just doing a minute ago? I should not have disturbed you."

Vijay smiled and gently shook his head. "My teacher once said that one can not be disturbed by another. It is only oneself who can disturb one's equanimity." Vijay hesitated, realizing even as it happened that he was awash in desire: he so craved the attention of his traveling companion that he had turned his meditation practice into a mere curiosity—all for the sake of a smile from this lovely woman who was simply an apparition, part of the passing show, soon to pass out of his life and to dissolve into the nonbeing of the past. And knowing, too, that his next words would only take him farther from his path, Vijay nonetheless rashly plunged ahead.

"There is something I would like to say: I shall long treasure our meeting and our conversation. Shortly I shall depart from this train to an ashram where I must face silence for the next ten days, and I am immeasurably grateful for the words we have exchanged, the moments we have shared. I am reminded of American prison films where the condemned man is permitted to order anything he wishes for his last meal. May I say that I have had my wishes for a last conversation fully granted."

Pam simply nodded. Rarely at a loss for words, she did not know how to respond directly to Vijay's courtliness. "Ten days at an ashram? Do you mean Igatpuri? I'm on my way there to a retreat."

"Then we have the same destination and the same goal—to be taught Vipassana meditation by the honored guru Goenka. And very soon, too—it is the next stop."

"Did you say 'ten days of silence'?"

"Yes, Goenka always requires noble silence—aside from necessary discussions with the staff, the students are to utter no words. Are you experienced in meditation?"

Pam shook her head no. "I'm a university professor. I teach English literature, and last year one of my students had a healing and transformative experience at Igatpuri. This student has become very active in organizing Vipassana retreats in the United States and she is currently helping to plan an American tour by Goenka."

"Your student hoped to offer her teacher a gift. She wished that you, too, would undergo a transformation?"

"Well, something like that. It wasn't that she felt I needed to change some particular thing about myself; it was more that she had profited so much that she wanted me, and others, to have the same experience."

"Of course. My question was ill put; in no way did I mean to suggest that you need transformation. I was interested in your student's enthusiasm. But did she prepare you for this retreat in any way?"

"She pointedly did not. She herself stumbled upon this retreat quite by accident and said that it would be best if I too entered it with an entirely open mind. You're shaking your head. You disagree."

"Ah, remember that Indians shake their heads from side to side when they agree and up and down when they disagree—the reverse of the American custom."

"Oh my God. I think I've sensed this unconsciously because so much of my interaction with people here has been slightly askew. I must have confused people I spoke with."

"No, no, many Indians who come into contact with Westerners make that adaptation. As for your student's advice to you, I am not certain I agree that you should be entirely unprepared. Let me point out that this is not a beginner's retreat. Noble silence, meditation beginning at four A.M., little sleep, one meal a day. A difficult regimen. You must be strong. Ah, the train slows. We are at Igatpuri."

Vijay stood, collected his belongings, and lifted Pam's valise down from the overhead rack. The train stopped. Vijay prepared to leave and said, "The experience begins."

Vijay's words offered little comfort, and Pam was growing more apprehensive. "Does that mean we will not be able to speak to one another during the retreat?"

"No communication, not written, not sign language."

"E-mail?"

Vijay did not smile. "Noble silence is the correct path to benefit from Vipassana." He seemed different. Pam felt him already drifting away.

"At least," she said, "it will offer me comfort to know you are there. It's less foreboding to imagine being alone together."

"Alone together. A felicitous phrase," Vijay responded without looking at her.

"Perhaps," Pam said, "we may meet again on this train after the retreat."

"Of that we must not think. Goenka will teach us that it is only the present we must inhabit. Yesterday and tomorrow do not exist. Past remembrances, future longings, only produce disquiet. The path to equanimity lies in observing the present and allowing it to float undisturbed down the river of our awareness." Without looking back, Vijay hoisted his bag onto his shoulder, opened the doors of the compartment, and walked away.

Only the male intellect, clouded by the sexual impulse, could call the undersized, narrow-shouldered, broad-hipped, and short-legged sex the fair sex.

—*Arthur Schopenhauer on women*

Your eternal quibbles, your laments over the stupid world and human misery, give me bad nights and unpleasant dreams. . . . I have not had a single unpleasant moment I did not owe to you.

—*A letter to Arthur Schopenhauer from his mother*

16

Schopenhauer's Main Woman

The most important woman, by far, in Arthur's life was his mother, Johanna, with whom he had a tormented and ambivalent relationship which ended in cataclysm. Johanna's letter liberating Arthur from his apprenticeship contained admirable motherly sentiments: her concern, her love, her hopes for him. Yet all these required a proviso: namely, that he remain at a convenient distance from her. Hence her letter of liberation advised him to move from Hamburg to Gotha rather than to her home in Weimar, fifty kilometers away.

The glow of warm feelings between the two following Arthur's emancipation from servitude evaporated quickly because of the brevity of Arthur's stay at the preparatory school in Gotha. After only six months the nineteen-year-old Arthur was expelled for writing a clever but cruelly mocking poem about one of the teachers and beseeched his mother for permission to live with her and continue his studies at Weimar.

Johanna was not amused; in fact the prospect of Arthur living with her sent her into a frenzy. He had visited her briefly a few times during his six-month stay at Gotha, and each visit had been the source of much displeasure for her. Her letters to him following his expulsion are among the most shocking letters ever written by a mother to a son.

> . . . I am acquainted with your disposition . . . you are irritating and unbearable and I consider it most difficult to live with you. All your good qualities are darkened by your super-cleverness and thus rendered useless to the world . . . you find fault everywhere except in yourself . . . thereby you embitter the people around you—no one wishes to be improved or illuminated in such a forcible manner, least of all by such an insignificant individual as you still are. No one can tolerate being criticized by someone who displays so many personal weaknesses, especially your derogatory manner which, in oracular tones, proclaims that this is so and so, without even suspecting the possibility of error.
>
> If you were less like you are, you would only be ridiculous but, being as you are, you become most annoying. . . . You might have, like thousands of other students, lived and studied in Gotha . . . but you did not want this and so you are expelled. . . . such a living literary journal as you would like to be is a boring hateful thing because one cannot skip pages or fling the whole rubbishy thing behind the stove, as one can with the printed one.

In time Johanna resigned herself to the fact that she could not avoid accepting Arthur at Weimar while he prepared for the university, but she wrote again, in case he missed the point, and expressed her concerns in even more graphic terms.

> I think it wisest to tell you straight out what I desire and what I feel about matters so we understand one another from the outset. That I am very fond of you, I'm sure you will not doubt. I have proven it to you and will prove it to you as long as I live. It is necessary for my happiness to know you are happy but not to be a witness to it. I have always told you that you are very difficult to live with. . . . The more I get to know you the more strongly I feel this.
>
> I will not hide this from you: as long as you are what you are, I would rather make any sacrifice than consent to be near you. . . . What repels me does not lie in your heart; it is in your outer, not your inner, being. It is in your ideas, in your judgment, your habits; in a word, there is nothing concerning the outer world in which we agree.
>
> Look, dear Arthur, each time you visited me only for a few days there were violent scenes about nothing and each time I only breathed freely again when you were gone because your presence, your complaints about inevitable things, your scowling face, your ill humor, the bizarre opinions you utter . . . all this depresses and troubles me, without helping you.

Johanna's dynamics seem transparent. By the grace of God she had escaped the marriage that she had feared would imprison her forever. Giddy with freedom, she exalted in the idea of never again being answerable to anyone. She would live her own life, meet whomever she wished, enjoy romantic liaisons (but never marry again), and she would explore her own considerable talents.

The prospect of relinquishing her freedom for Arthur's sake was unbearable. Not only was Arthur a particularly difficult, controlling person in his own right, but he was the son of her former jailer: the living incarnation of too many of Heinrich's unpleasant features.

And there was the issue of money. It first surfaced when Arthur, at nineteen, accused his mother of lavish spending, which imperiled the inheritance he was to receive at the age of twenty-one. Johanna bristled, insisted it was well known that she served only bread-and-butter sandwiches at her salons and then excoriated Arthur for living far beyond his means with expensive dining and horseback-riding lessons. Eventually, such quarrels about money were to escalate to unbearable levels.

Johanna's feelings about Arthur and about motherhood are reflected in her novels: a typical Johanna Schopenhauer heroine tragically loses her true love and then resigns herself to an economically sensible, loveless, and sometimes abusive marriage but, in an act of defiance and self-affirmation, refuses to bear children.

Arthur shared his feelings with no one, and his mother later destroyed all his letters. Still, certain trends seem self-evident. The bond between Arthur and his mother was intense, and the pain of its dissolution haunted Arthur his entire life. Johanna was an unusual mother—vivacious, forthright, beautiful, freethinking, enlightened, well read. Surely, she and Arthur discussed his immersion in modern and ancient literature. Indeed it may be that the fifteen-year-old Arthur made his momentous choice in favor of the grand tour rather than university preparation because of his desire to remain in her presence.

It was only after his father's death that the tone of the mother-son relationship changed. Arthur's hopes of replacing his father in his mother's heart must have been crushed by her hasty decision to leave him in Hamburg and move to Weimar. If his hopes were revived when his mother liberated him from his pledge to his dead father, they were again shattered when she sent him to Gotha, despite the vastly superior educational resources available in Weimar. Perhaps, as his mother suggested, Arthur intentionally arranged to be expelled from Gotha. If his actions were based on his wishes to rejoin his mother, he must have been disheartened by her unwillingness to welcome him in her new home and by the presence of other men in her life.

Arthur's guilt about his father's suicide had its origins both in his joy of liberation and in his fear that he may have hastened his father's death by his disinterest in the world of commerce. It was not long before his guilt transformed into a fierce defense of his father's good name, and to vicious criticism of his mother's behavior toward his father.

Years later he wrote:

> I know women. They regard marriage only as an institution for supply. As my father grew wretchedly sick, he would have been abandoned except for the loving charity of a faithful servant who performed the necessary basic acts of caring. My mother held parties, while he lay down in loneliness; my mother had fun, while he was suffering painfully. That's the love of women!

When Arthur arrived in Weimar to study with a tutor for university entrance, he was not permitted to live with his mother but in separate lodgings she had found for him. Awaiting him there was her letter laying out, with ruthless clarity, the rules and boundaries of their relationship.

> Mark now on what footing I wish to be together with you: you are at home in your lodgings, in mine you are a guest . . . who does not interfere in any domestic arrangements. Every day you will come at one o'clock and stay until three, then I shall not see you again all day long, except on my salon days which you may attend if you wish, also eating at my house those two evenings, provided you will abstain from tiresome arguing, which makes me angry. . . . During the midday hours you can tell me everything I need to know about you, the rest of the time you must look after yourself. I cannot provide your entertainment at the expense of mine. Enough, now you know my wishes and I hope you will not repay me for my motherly care and love by giving me opposition.

Arthur accepted these terms during his two-year stay in Weimar and remained strictly an observer at his mother's social evenings, not once engaging the lofty Goethe in conversation. His mastery of Greek, Latin, the classics, and philosophy progressed at a prodigious rate, and, at the age of twenty-one, he was accepted into the University at Göttingen. At the same time he received his inheritance of twenty thousand Reichstalers, enough to provide a sufficient but modest income for the remainder of his life. As his father had predicted, he would have great need of this inheritance—Arthur was never to earn a pfennig from his vocation as a scholar.

As time passed, Arthur viewed his father as an angel and his mother a devil. He believed that his father's jealousy and suspicions about his mother's fidelity were well founded, and he worried that she would fail to revere his father's memory. In his father's name, he demanded that she live a quiet sequestered life. Arthur vehemently attacked those whom he considered his mother's suitors, judging them lesser, "mass-produced creatures," unworthy of replacing his father.

Arthur studied at the Universities of Göttingen and Berlin and then obtained a doctorate in philosophy from the University of Jena. He lived briefly in Berlin but soon fled because of the impending war against Napoleon and returned to Weimar to live with his mother. Soon, the same domestic battles erupted: not only did he upbraid his mother for misusing the money he had made available for his grandmother's care, but he accused her of an improper liaison with her close friend Müller Gerstenbergk. Arthur became so brutally hostile to Gerstenbergk that Johanna was forced to see her friend only when Arthur was absent from the home.

During this period an often-quoted conversation occurred when he gave his mother a copy of his doctoral dissertation, a brilliant treatise on the principles of causation titled "On the Fourfold Root of the Principle of Sufficient Reason."

Glancing at the title page, Johanna remarked: "Fourfold root? No doubt this is something for the apothecary?"

Arthur: "It will still be read when scarcely a copy of your writings can be found."

Johanna: "Yes, no doubt the entire printing of your writings will still be in the shops."

Arthur was uncompromising on his titles, rejecting any considerations of marketability. *On the Fourfold Root of the Principle of Sufficient Reason* should have been more properly titled *A Theory of Explanation*. Nonetheless, two hundred years later, it is still in print. Not many other dissertations can claim that distinction.

Ferocious arguments continued about money and about Johanna's relationships with men until Johanna's patience was exhausted. She let it be known she would never break off her friendship with Gerstenbergk or anyone else for Arthur's sake. She ordered him to move out, invited Gerstenbergk to move into his vacated rooms, and wrote Arthur this fateful letter.

> The door which you slammed so noisily yesterday after your improper behavior toward your mother is now closed forever between you and me. I am leaving for the country and shall not return until I know you are gone. . . . You do not know what a mother's heart is like—the more tenderly it loves, the more painfully it feels every blow from a once loved hand. . . . You yourself have torn away from me: your mistrust, your criticism of my life, of my choice of friends, your desultory behavior toward me, your contempt for my sex, your unwillingness to contribute to my contentment, your greed—this and a lot more makes you seem vicious to me. . . . If I were dead and you had to deal with your father, would you have dared to schoolmaster him? Or try to control his life, his friendships? Am I less than he? Did he do more for you than I did? Loved you more than I did? . . . My duty toward you is at an end. Go your way, I have nothing more to do with you. . . . Leave your address here, but do not write to me, I shall henceforth neither read nor answer any letter from you. . . . So this is the end. . . . You have hurt me too much. Live and be as happy as you can be.

And the end it was. Johanna lived for another twenty-five years, but mother and son were never again to meet.

In old age, reminiscing about his parents, Schopenhauer wrote:

> Most men allow themselves to be seduced by a beautiful face. . . . nature induces women to display all at once the whole of their brilliance . . . and to make a "sensation" . . . but nature conceals the many evils [women] entail, such as endless expenses, the cares of children, refractoriness, obstinacy, growing old and ugly after a few years, deception, cuckolding, whims, crotchets, attacks of hysteria, hell, and the devil. I therefore call marriage a debt that is contracted in youth and paid in old age. . . .

Great sufferings render lesser ones quite incapable of being felt, and conversely, in the absence of great sufferings even the smallest vexations and annoyances torment us.

17

At the start of the next meeting all eyes were upon Bonnie. She spoke in a soft hesitant voice: "It wasn't such a good idea after all to get myself on the agenda because all week long I've been thinking about what to say, rehearsing my lines over and over, even though I know that a canned presentation is not the way to go here. Julius has been saying all along that the group has to be spontaneous if it's going to work. Right?" Bonnie glanced at Julius.

Julius nodded. "Bonnie, try to dump the canned presentation. Try this: Close your eyes and imagine picking up your prepared script, holding it up in front of you and ripping it in half and then in half again. Now put it in the wastebasket. Okay?"

Bonnie, eyes closed, nodded.

"And now in fresh words tell us about homeliness and beauty. Tell us about you and Rebecca and Pam."

Bonnie, still nodding, opened her eyes slowly and began. "You all remember me, I'm sure. I was the little fat girl in your grade-school classroom. Very chubby, very clumsy, hair too curly. The one who was pathetic in gym, got the fewest valentines, cried a lot, never had best friends, always walked home alone, never had a prom invitation, was so terrified that she never raised her hand in class even though she was smart as hell and knew all the right answers. And, Rebecca here, well she was my isomer—"

"Your what?" asked Tony. He sat slouched out nearly horizontally in his seat.

"*Isomer* means like a mirror image," responded Bonnie.

"*Isomer* refers to two chemical compounds," pronounced Philip, "that have the identical constituents in the same proportions but differ in properties because of the way the atoms are arranged."

"Thanks, Philip," said Bonnie. "Maybe that was a pretentious word to use. But, Tony, I want to say that I admire the way you've stuck to your resolution to signal every time you don't understand something. That meeting a couple of months ago when you opened up about your shame about your education and your blue-collar work has really given me permission to talk about some of my stuff. Okay, now back to my school days. Rebecca was my absolute opposite, in every way—you name it. I would have died to have a Rebecca as a friend—I would killed to have *been* a Rebecca. That's what's going on in me. The last couple of weeks I've been flooded with memories of my nightmare childhood."

"That fat little girl went to school a long time ago," said Julius. "What brings her back now?"

"Well, that's the hard part. I don't want Rebecca to get angry with me . . ."

"Best to speak to her directly, Bonnie," Julius interjected.

"Okay," said Bonnie, and turning to face Rebecca. "I want to say something to you, but I don't want you to be angry with me."

"I'm all ears," said Rebecca, her attention fully fixed on Bonnie.

"When I see you operate with men here in the group—how you interest them, how you entice them—I feel totally helpless. All those old bad feelings creep out: chubby, insignificant, unpopular, outclassed."

"Nietzsche," interjected Philip, "once said something to the effect that when we awake discouraged in the middle of the night, enemies that we had defeated long ago come back to haunt us."

Bonnie broke out into a big smile and turned toward Philip. "That's a gift, Philip, a very sweet gift. I don't know why, but the idea of enemies I had once defeated rising again makes me feel better. Just to have something named makes it more—"

"Wait a minute, Bonnie," interrupted Rebecca, "I want to get back to my enticing men here—explain, please."

Bonnie's pupils widened; she avoided Rebecca's gaze. "It's not about you. There's nothing you do that's off—it's all me, it's my response to perfectly normal female behavior."

"What behavior? What are you talking about?"

Bonnie took a deep breath and said, "Preening. You preen. That's the way it seems to me. I don't know how many times in the last meeting you had your barrettes out, your hair down, flouncing your hair, running your fingers through it, but it was more times than I can ever remember before. It's got to be related to Philip's entrance into the group."

"What are you talking about?" asked Rebecca.

"To quote the old sage, Saint Julius, a question ain't a question if you know the answer," interrupted Tony.

"Why don't you let Bonnie speak for herself, Tony?" said Rebecca, her eyes icy.

Tony was unfazed. "It's obvious. Philip enters the group, and you change—you change into a male . . . ah . . . what's the right word? . . . you're coming on to him. Do I got it right, Bonnie?"

Bonnie nodded.

Rebecca reached in her purse for a tissue and dabbed at her eyes, carefully protecting the mascara. "That's really fucking insulting."

"This is exactly where I don't want it to go," pleaded Bonnie. "This is not about you, Rebecca—I keep saying that. You're not doing anything wrong."

"That doesn't wash with me—making an en passant nasty accusation about my behavior and then saying it's not about me doesn't make it less nasty."

"*En passant*?" asked Tony.

"*En passant* means," interjected Philip, "*in passing*—a common term in chess used when the pawn takes two squares in its opening move and passes an opposing pawn."

"Philip, you're a show-off—you know that?" said Tony.

"You threw out a question. I answered it," said Philip, entirely unaffected by Tony's confrontation. "Unless *your* question ain't a question."

"Ouch, you got me there." Tony scanned the rest of the group and said, "I must be gettin' dumber. I feel more out of it. Am I imagining it, or are there more big words getting thrown out here? Maybe having Philip here is getting to others, too—not just Rebecca."

Julius intervened by using the group therapist's most common and most effective tactic—he switched the focus from content to process, that is, away from the words being spoken to the nature of the relationship of the interacting parties. "Lots going on here today. Maybe we can step back a minute and try to understand what's happening. Let me first put out this question to all of you: what do you see going on in the relationship between Bonnie and Rebecca?"

"It's a tough call," said Stuart, who was always the first to respond to questions thrown out by Julius. Using his professional/medical voice, he said, "I really cannot tell if Bonnie has one agenda or two."

"Meaning?" asked Bonnie.

"Meaning, what's your agenda? Do you wish to talk about issues with men and your competition with women? Or, do you wish to take a swipe at Rebecca?"

"I see it from both points of view," said Gill. "I can see how this dredges up Bonnie's old bad memories. And then I can also see why Rebecca is upset—I mean she may have not known she was fixing her hair—and personally I don't think that's such a big issue."

"You're tactful, Gill, " said Stuart. "As usual you try to placate all parties, especially the ladies. But you know if you get so deep into understanding the female point of view, you're never going to speak out in your own voice. That's what Philip said to you last week."

"I resent these sexist comments, Stuart," said Rebecca. "Frankly, a doctor should know better. This 'female point of view' talk is ridiculous."

Bonnie held up her hands and made a *T.* "I've got to call 'time out'—I just cannot go on. This is important stuff, but it's surreal; I cannot go on with it. How can we go on with business as usual when Julius has just announced last week he is dying? This is my fault: I should never have started this topic today about me and Rebecca—it's too trivial. Everything's trivial in comparison."

Silence. Everyone looked down. Bonnie broke the silence.

"I want to back up. The way I should have started this meeting was to describe a dream, a nightmare, I had after the last group. I think it involves you, Julius."

"Go," urged Julius.

"It was night. I was in a dark train station—"

Julius interrupted, "Try using the present tense, Bonnie."

"I should know that by now. Okay—it's night. I'm in a dark train station. I'm trying to catch a train that's just beginning to move. I walk faster to get on. I see the dining car pass by filled with well-dressed people eating and sipping wine. I'm not sure where to board. Now the train starts to move faster, and the last cars get shabbier and shabbier, with their windows boarded up. The final car, the caboose, is just a skeleton car, all falling apart, and I see it pull away from me and I hear the train whistle so loud it wakes me about four A.M. My heart was pounding, I was soaked with sweat, and I never did get back to sleep last night."

"Do you still see that train?" asked Julius.

"Clear as can be. Moving away down the track. The dream is still scary. Eerie."

"You know what I think?" said Tony. "I think the train's the group and that Julius's illness will make it fall apart."

"Right on," said Stuart, "the train's the group—it takes you somewhere, and it feeds you along the way—you know, the folks in the dining car."

"Yeah, but why couldn't you get on? Did you run?" asked Rebecca.

"I didn't run; it was like I knew I couldn't board."

"Strange. Like you wanted to board, but at the same time you didn't want to," said Rebecca.

"I sure didn't try hard to board."

"Maybe you were too scared to board?" asked Gill.

"Did I tell you all that I was in love?" said Julius.

A hush fell upon the group. Dead silence. Julius looked around, mischievously, at the puzzled and concerned faces.

"Yes, in love with this group, especially when it works like it's working today. Great stuff, the way you're working on that dream. You guys are something. Let me add my guess—I'm wondering, Bonnie, if that train isn't a symbol for me as well. That train reeked of dread and darkness. And, as Stuart said, it offers nourishment. I try to do that. But you're frightened of it—as you must be frightened of me or what's happening to me. And that last car, the skeletonlike caboose: isn't that a symbol, a prevision, of my deterioration?"

Bonnie stammered, got tissues from the box in the middle of the room, and wiped her eyes, "I . . . uh . . . I . . . I don't know how to answer—this whole thing is surreal. . . . Julius, you floor me, you knock me out the way you talk about dying so matter-of-factly."

"We're all dying, Bonnie. I just know my parameters better than the rest of you," said Julius.

"That's what I mean, Julius. I always love your flippancy, but now, in this situation, it kind of avoids things. I remember once—it was during that time that Tony was doing weekend jail time and we weren't talking about it—that you said if something big in the group is being ignored, then nothing else of importance gets talked about either."

"Two things," said Rebecca. "First, Bonnie, we *were* talking about something important just now—several important things—and, second, my God, what do you want Julius to do? He *is* talking about this."

"In fact," said Tony, "he even got pissed that we heard it from Philip rather than from him personally."

"I agree," said Stuart. "So Bonnie, what *do* you want from him? He's handling it. He said he's got his own support network to help him deal with it."

Julius broke it off—it had gone far enough. "You know, I appreciate all this support from you guys, but when it's this strong then I begin to worry. Maybe I'm getting loose, but do you know when Lou Gehrig decided to retire? It happened one game when everyone on the team gushed compliments about how he fielded a routine ground ball. Maybe you're considering me too fragile to speak for myself."

"So, where do we go with this?" said Stuart.

"First, let me say to you, Bonnie, that you're showing a lot of guts by jumping in and naming the thing that's too hot to touch. What's more, you're absolutely right: I have been encouraging some . . . no, *a lot of* denial here.

"I'm going to make a short speech and lay it all out for you. I've had some sleepless nights lately and a lot of time to think about everything, including what to do about my patients and this group. I haven't had any practice at this. No one practices endings. They only happen once. No textbooks are written about this situation—so everything is improvisation.

"I'm faced with deciding about what to do with the time I have left. Look, what are my options? Terminate all my patients and end this group? I'm not ready to do that—I've got at least a year of good health, and my work means too much to me. And I get a lot out of it for myself. Stopping all my work would be to treat myself as a pariah. I've seen too many patients with fatal illness who've told me that the isolation accompanying their illness is the worst part of all.

"And the isolation is a dual isolation: first, the very sick person isolates himself because he doesn't want to drag others down into his despair—and I can tell you for a fact that's one of my concerns here—and, second, others avoid him either because they don't know how to talk to him or because they want nothing to do with death.

"So, withdrawing from you is not a good option for me and, what's more, I don't believe for you either. I've seen a lot of terminally ill people who underwent change, grew wiser, riper, and had a great deal to teach others. I think that's already starting to happen to me, and I'm convinced that I'll have a lot to offer you in the next few months. But if we're to keep working together, you may have to face a lot of anxiety. You'll not only have to face my approaching death, but you may be confronted with your own. End of speech. Maybe you all have to sleep on this and see what you want to do."

"I don't need to sleep on it," said Bonnie. "I love this group and you and everyone in it, and I want to work here as long as possible."

After members echoed Bonnie's affirmation, Julius said, "I appreciate the vote of confidence. But group therapy 101 underscores the daunting power of group pressure. It's hard to buck group consensus in public. It would take superhuman resolve for any of you to say today, 'Sorry, Julius, but this is too much for me, and I'd rather find a healthy therapist, someone hale enough to take care of me.'

"So, no commitments today. Let's just stay open and keep evaluating our own work and see how everyone feels in a few weeks. One big danger which Bonnie expressed today is that your problems start to feel too inconsequential to discuss. So we have to figure out the best way for me to keep you working on your own issues."

"I think you're doing it," said Stuart, "by just keeping us informed."

"Okay. Thanks, that helps. Now let's go back to you guys."

A long silence.

"So, maybe I haven't liberated you. Let me try something. Can you, Stuart, or others, lay out our agenda, what's here on the table—what are the open issues today?"

Stuart was the informal group historian: he was blessed with such a retentive memory that Julius could always call on him for an account of past or present group events. He tried not to overuse Stuart, who was in the group to learn how to engage others, not to be a recorder of events. Wonderful with his child patients, Stuart was socially at a loss whenever he left the perimeter of his pediatrician role. Even in the group he often carried some of the accoutrements of the trade stuffed in his shirt pocket: tongue depressors, penlight, lollipops, medication samples. A stable force in the group for the past year, Stuart had made enormous progress in, as he had put it, "project humanization." Yet interpersonal sensitivity was still so undeveloped that his recounting of group events was entirely without guile.

Leaning back in his chair, he closed his eyes before responding. "Well, let's see—we began with Bonnie and her desire to talk about her childhood." Bonnie had been Stuart's frequent critic, and he glanced at her for approval before continuing.

"No, not quite right, Stuart. Right facts, wrong tone. You're making it sound flippant. Like I just want to tell a story for the fun of it. There are a lot of painful memories from my childhood that are now coming up and haunting me. Get the difference?"

"I'm not sure I do get it. I didn't say you were doing it for the fun of it. That's just the kind of thing my wife complains about. But, to continue: next there was some stuff with Rebecca, who felt insulted and angry with Bonnie for pointing out how she was preening and attempting to impress Philip." Stuart ignored Rebecca's slapping her hand to her forehead and muttering, "Goddamnit," and continued, "Then there was Tony's feeling that we were using a more complex vocabulary in order to impress Philip. And then Tony commented that Philip was a show-off. And Philip's sharp response to Tony. And then there was my comment to Gill that he avoided displeasing women so much that he lost his sense of self.

"Let's see what else . . ." Stuart scanned the room. "Well, there's Philip—not what he said but what he didn't say. We don't talk too much about Philip, as though it's taboo. Come to think about it, we don't even talk about *not* talking about him. And, of course, Julius. But we worked on that. Except that Bonnie was particularly concerned and protective, as she often is about Julius. In fact, the Julius part of the meeting started with Bonnie's dream."

"Impressive, Stuart," said Rebecca. "And pretty complete: you left out only one thing."

"And that is?"

"Yourself. The fact that you were being the group camera again, photographing rather than plunging in."

Often the group had confronted Stuart about his impersonal style of participation. Months ago he described a nightmare in which his daughter had stepped into quicksand and he could not save her because he wasted so much time getting his camera out of his backpack to take a snapshot of the scene. That was when Rebecca labeled him the "group camera."

"Right you are, Rebecca. I'll pack my camera away now and say I agree entirely with Bonnie: you are a good-looking woman. But that's not news to you—you know that. And you know I think so. And, *of course,* you were preening for Philip—doing and undoing and stroking your hair. It was obvious. How did I feel about it? I felt a little jealous. No, a lot jealous—you never preened for me. No one ever preened for me."

"That kind of thing makes me feel like I'm in prison," Rebecca shot back. "I hate it when men try to control me like this, like my every movement is under scrutiny." Rebecca broke off each word, showing an edge and a brittleness that had been under wraps for a long time.

Julius remembered his first impressions of Rebecca. A decade ago, long before she entered the group, he had seen her individually for a year. She was a delicate creature with an Audrey Hepburn graceful, slim body and precious, large-eyed face. And who could forget her opening comment in therapy? "Ever since I turned thirty I've noticed that when I enter restaurants, no one stops eating to look at me. I'm devastated."

Two sources of instruction had guided Julius in his work with her both individually and in the group. First, there had been Freud's urging that the therapist should reach out in a human way to a beautiful woman and not withhold himself or penalize her simply because she was beautiful. The second had been an essay he had read as a student titled, "The Beautiful Empty Woman," which made the point that the truly beautiful woman is so often feted and rewarded solely for her appearance that she neglects developing other parts of herself. Her confidence and feelings of success are only skin-deep, and once her beauty fades she realizes she has little to offer: she has developed neither the art of being an interesting person nor that of taking an interest in others.

"I make observations, and I'm called a camera," said Stuart, "and when I say what I feel I'm labeled a controlling man. Talk about feeling cornered."

"I don't get it, Rebecca," said Tony. "What's the big deal here? Why are you freaking out? Stuart's just saying what you've said yourself. How many times have you said you know how to flirt, that it comes naturally to you? I remember your saying that you had an easy time in college and in your law firm because you manipulate men with your sexuality."

"You make me sound like a whore." Rebecca swiveled suddenly to Philip. "Doesn't that make you think I'm a whore?"

Philip, not distracted from gazing at his favorite spot somewhere on the ceiling, answered quickly, "Schopenhauer said that a highly attractive women, like a highly intelligent man, was absolutely destined to living an isolated life. He pointed out that others are blind with envy and resent the superior person. For that reason, such people never have close friends of their same sex."

"That's not necessarily true," said Bonnie. "I'm thinking of Pam, our missing member, who is beautiful too and yet has a large number of close girlfriends."

"Yeah, Philip," said Tony, "you saying that, to be popular, you have to be dumb or ugly?"

"Precisely," said Philip, "and the wise person will not spend his life or her life pursuing popularity. It is a will-o'-the-wisp. Popularity does not define what is true or what is good; quite the contrary, it's a leveler, a dumbing down. Far better to search within for one's values and goals."

"And how about *your* goals and values?" asked Tony.

If Philip noted the surliness in Tony's question, he gave no evidence of it and replied ingenuously, "Like Schopenhauer, I want to will as little as possible and to know as much as possible."

Tony nodded, obviously baffled about how to respond.

Rebecca broke in: "Philip, what you or Schopenhauer was saying about friends was right on the mark for me—the truth is that I've had few close girlfriends. But what about two people with similar interests and abilities? Don't you think that friendship is possible in that case?"

Before Philip could answer, Julius enjoined, "Our time is growing very short today. I want to check in about how you all are feeling about our last fifteen minutes. How are we doing here?"

"We're not on target. We're missing," said Gill. "Something oblique is going on."

"*I'm* absorbed," said Rebecca.

"Nah, too much in our heads," said Tony.

"I agree," said Stuart.

"Well, I'm not in my head," said Bonnie. "I'm close to bursting, or screaming, or . . ." Bonnie suddenly rose, gathered up her purse and jacket, and charged out of the room. A moment later Gill jumped up and ran out of the room to fetch her back. In awkward silence the group sat listening to the retreating footsteps. Shortly Gill returned, and as he sat he reported, "She's okay, said she's sorry but she just had to get out to decompress. She'll go into it next week."

"What *is* going on?" said Rebecca, snapping open her purse to get sunglasses and car keys. "I *hate* it when she does that. That's really pissy."

"Any hunches about what's going on?" asked Julius.

"PMT, I think," said Rebecca.

Tony spotted Philip scrunching his face signifying confusion and jumped in. "PMS—premenstrual syndrome." When Philip nodded,

Tony clenched his hands and poked both thumbs upward, "Hey, hey, I taught *you* something,"

"We've gotta stop," said Julius, "but I've got a guess about what's going on with Bonnie. Go back to Stuart's summary. Remember how Bonnie started the meeting—talking about the chubby little girl at school and her unpopularity and her inability to compete with other girls, especially attractive ones? Well, I wonder if that wasn't recreated in the group today? She opened the meeting, and pretty quickly the group left her for Rebecca. In other words, the very issue she wanted to talk about may have been portrayed here in living color with all of us playing a part in the pageant."

Nothing can alarm or move him any more. All the thousand threads of willing binding us to the world and dragging us (full of anxiety, craving, anger, and fear) back and forth in constant pain: all these he has cut asunder. He smiles and looks back calmly on the phantasmagoria of this world which now stands before him as indifferently as chess-men at the end of a game.

18

Pam in India (2)

It was a few days later at 3 A.M. Pam lay awake, peering into the darkness. Thanks to the intervention of her graduate student, Marjorie, who had arranged VIP privileges, she had a semiprivate room in a tiny alcove with a private toilet just off the women's common dormitory. However, the alcove provided no sound buffer, and Pam listened to the breathing of 150 other Vipassana students. The whoosh of moving air transported her back to her attic bedroom in her parents' Baltimore home when she lay awake listening to the March wind rattling the window.

Pam could put up with any of the other ashram hardships—the 4 A.M. wakeup time, the frugal vegetarian one-meal-a-day diet, the endless hours of meditation, the silence, the Spartan quarters—but the sleeplessness was wearing her down. The mechanism of falling asleep completely eluded her. How did she used to do it? No, wrong question, she told herself—a question that compounded the problem because falling asleep is one of those things that cannot be willed; it must be done unintentionally. Suddenly, an old memory of Freddie the pig floated into her mind. Freddie, a master detective in a series of children's books she hadn't thought about in twenty-five years, was asked for help by a centipede who could no longer walk because his hundred legs were out of sync. Eventually, Freddie solved the problem by instructing the centipede to walk without looking at his legs—or even thinking about them. The solution lay in turning off awareness and permitting the body's wisdom to take over. It was the same with sleeping.

Pam tried to sleep by applying the techniques she had been taught in the workshop to clear her mind and allow all thoughts to drift away. Goenka, a chubby, bronze-skinned, pedantic, exceedingly serious and exceedingly pompous guru, had begun by saying that he would teach Vipassana but first he had to teach the student how to quiet his mind. (Pam endured the exclusive use of the male pronoun; the waves of feminism had yet not lapped upon the shores of India.)

For the first three days Goenka gave instruction in the *anapana-sati*—mindfulness of breathing. And the days were long. Aside from a daily lecture and a brief question-and-answer period, the only activity from 4 A.M. to 9:30 P.M. was sitting meditation. To achieve full mindfulness of breathing, Goenka exhorted students to study in-breaths and out-breaths.

"Listen. Listen to the sound of your breaths," he said. "Be conscious of their duration and their temperature. Note the difference between the coolness of in-breaths and the warmth of out-breaths. Become like a sentry watching the gate. Fix your attention upon your nostrils, upon the precise anatomical spot where air enters and leaves."

"Soon," Goenka said, "the breath will grow finer and finer until it seems to vanish entirely, but, as you focus ever more deeply, you will be able to discern its subtle and delicate form. If you follow all my instructions faithfully," he said, pointing to the heavens, "if you are a dedicated student, the practice of *anapana-sati* will quiet your mind. You will then be liberated from all the hindrances to mindfulness: restlessness, anger, doubt, sensual desire, and drowsiness. You shall awaken into an alert, tranquil, and joyous state."

Mind-quieting was indeed Pam's grail—the reason for her pilgrimage to Igatpuri. For the past several weeks her mind had been a battlefield from which she fiercely tried to repel noisy, obsessive, intrusive memories and fantasies about her husband, Earl, and her lover, John. Earl had been her gynecologist seven years ago when she had become pregnant and decided upon an abortion, electing not to inform the father, a casual sexual playmate with whom she wished no deeper involvement. Earl was an uncommonly gentle, caring man. He skillfully performed the abortion and then provided unusual postoperative follow-up by phoning her twice at home to inquire about her condition. Surely, she thought, all the accounts of the demise of humane, dedicated medical care were hyperbolic rhetoric. Then, a few days later, came a third call which conveyed an invitation to lunch, during which Earl skillfully negotiated the segue from doctor to suitor. It was during their fourth call that she agreed, not without enthusiasm, to accompany him to a New Orleans medical convention.

Their courtship proceeded with astonishing quickness. No man ever knew her so well, comforted her so much, was so exquisitely familiar with her every nook and cranny, nor afforded her more sexual pleasure. Though he had many wonderful qualities—he was competent, handsome, and carried himself well—she conferred upon him (she now realized) heroic, larger-than-life stature. Dazzled at being the chosen one, at being promoted to the head of the line of women packing his office clamoring for his healing touch, she fell wholly in love and agreed to marriage a few weeks later.

At first married life was idyllic. But midway into the second year, the reality of being married to a man twenty-seven years older set in: he needed more rest; his body showed his sixty-five years; white hair appeared in defiance of Grecian formula hair dye. Earl's rotator cuff injury ended their tennis Sundays together, and when a torn knee cartilage put an end to his skiing, Earl put his Tahoe house on the market without consulting her. Sheila, her close friend and college roommate, who had advised her not to marry an older man, now urged her to maintain her own identity and not be in a rush to grow old. Pam felt fast-forwarded. Earl's aging fed on her youth. Each night he came home with barely enough energy to sip his three martinis and watch TV.

And the worst of it was that he never read. How fluently, how confidently he had once conversed about literature. How much his love of *Middlemarch* and *Daniel Deronda* had endeared him to her. And what a shock to realize only a short time later that she had mistaken form for substance: not only were Earl's literary observations memorized, but his repertory of books was limited and static. That was the toughest hit: how *could* she have ever loved a man who did not read? She, whose dearest and closest friends dwelled in the pages of George Eliot, Woolf, Murdoch, Gaskell, and Byatt?

And that was where John, a red-haired associate professor in her department at Berkeley with an armful of books, a long graceful neck, and a stand-up Adam's apple, came in. Though English professors were expected to be well-read, she had known too many who rarely ventured out of their century of expertise and were complete strangers to new fiction. But John read everything. Three years before she had supported his tenure appointment on the basis of his two dazzling books, *Chess: The Aesthetics of Brutality in Contemporary Fiction* and *No Sir!: The Androgynous Heroine in Late Nineteenth-Century British Literature.*

Their friendship germinated in all the familiar romantic academic haunts: faculty and departmental committee meetings, faculty club luncheons, monthly readings in the Norris Auditorium by the poet or novelist in residence. It took root and blossomed in shared academic adventures, such as team teaching the nineteenth-century greats in the Western civilization curriculum or guest lectures in each other's courses. And then permanent bonding took place in the trench warfare of faculty senate squabbles, space and salary sorties, and brutal promotion committee melees. Before long they so trusted each other's taste that they rarely looked elsewhere for recommendations for novels and poetry, and the e-mail ether between them crackled with meaty philosophical literary passages. Both eschewed quotations that were merely decorative or clumsily clever; they settled for nothing less than the sublime—beauty plus wisdom for the ages. They both loathed Fitzgerald and Hemingway, both loved Dickinson and Emerson. As their shared stack of books grew taller, their relationship evolved into ever greater harmony. They were moved by the same profound thoughts of the same writers. They reached epiphanies together. In short, these two English professors were in love.

"You leave your marriage, and I'll leave mine." Who said it first? Neither could remember, but at some point in their second year of team teaching they arrived at this high-risk amorous commitment. Pam was ready, but John, who had two preteen daughters, naturally required more time. Pam was patient. Her man, John, was, thank God, a good man and required time to wrestle with such moral issues as the meaning of the marriage vow. And he struggled, too, with the problem of guilt at abandoning his children and how one goes about leaving a wife, whose only offense had been dullness, a wife transformed by duty from sparkling lover into drab motherhood. Over and over again John assured Pam that he was en route, in process, that he had successfully identified and reconnoitered the problem, and all he needed now was more time to generate the resolve and select the propitious moment to act.

But the months passed, and the propitious moment never arrived. Pam suspected that John, like so many dissatisfied spouses attempting to avoid the guilt and the burden of irreversible immoral acts, was trying to maneuver his wife into making the decision. He withdrew, lost all sexual interest in his wife, and criticized her silently and, occasionally, aloud. It was the old "I can't leave but I pray that she leaves" maneuver. But it wasn't working—this wife wouldn't bite.

Finally, Pam acted unilaterally. Her course of action was prompted by two phone calls beginning with "Dearie, I think you'd like to know . . ." Two of Earl's patients under the pretense of doing her a favor warned her of his sexually predatory behavior. When a summons arrived with the news that Earl was being sued for unprofessional behavior by yet another patient, Pam thanked her lucky stars she had not had a child, and reached for the phone to contact a divorce lawyer.

Might her act force John into decisive action? Even though she would have left her marriage if there had been no John in her life, Pam, in an astounding feat of denial, persuaded herself that she had left Earl for the sake of her lover and continued to confront John with that version of reality. But John dallied; he was still not ready. Then, one day, he took decisive action. It happened in June on the last day of classes just after an ecstatic love fest in their usual bower, an unrolled blue foam mattress situated partially under the tent of his desk on the hardwood floor of his office. (No sofas were to be found in English professors' offices; the department had been so racked by charges of professors preying on their female students that sofas had been banned.) After zipping up his trousers, John gazed at her mournfully. "Pam, I love you. And because I love you, I've decided to be resolute. This is unfair to you, and I've got to take some of the pressure off—off of you, especially, but off me as well. I've decided to declare a moratorium on our seeing one another."

Pam was stunned. She hardly heard his words. For days afterward his message felt like a bolus in her gut too large to digest, too heavy to regurgitate. Hour upon hour she oscillated between hating him, loving and desiring him, and wishing him dead. Her mind played one scenario after another. John and his family dying in an auto accident. John's wife being killed in an airplane crash and John appearing, sometimes with children, sometimes alone, at her doorstep. Sometimes she would fall into his arms; sometimes they would weep tenderly together; sometimes she would pretend there was a man in her apartment and slam the door in his face.

During the two years she had been in individual and group therapy Pam had profited enormously, but, in this crisis, therapy failed to deliver: it was no match for the monstrous power of her obsessional thinking. Julius tried valiantly. He was indefatigable and pulled endless devices out of his toolkit. First, he asked her to monitor herself and chart the amount of time she spent on the obsession. Two to three hundred minutes a day. Astounding! And it seemed entirely out of her control; the obsession had demonic power. Julius attempted to help her regain control of her mind by urging a systematic incremental decrease of her fantasy time. When that failed, he turned to a paradoxical approach and instructed her to choose an hour each morning which she would entirely devote to running the most popular fantasy reels about John. Though she followed Julius's instructions, the unruly obsession refused containment and spilled over into her thoughts just as much as before. Later he suggested several thought-stopping techniques. For days Pam shouted no at her own mind or snapped rubber bands on her wrist.

Julius also attempted to defuse the obsession by laying bare its underlying meaning. "The obsession is a distraction; it protects you from thinking about something else," he insisted. "What is it concealing?" If there were no obsession, what would you be thinking about? But the obsession would not yield.

The group members pitched in. They shared their own obsessive episodes; they volunteered for phone duty so Pam could call them anytime she felt overcome; they urged her to fill her life, call her friends, arrange a social activity every day, find a man, and, for God's sake, get laid! Tony made her smile by requesting an application for that position. But nothing worked. Against the monstrous power of the obsession, all of these therapy weapons were as effective as a BB gun against a charging rhinoceros.

Then came a chance encounter with Marjorie, the starry-eyed graduate student cum Vipassana acolyte, who consulted her about a change in her dissertation topic. She had lost interest in the influence of Plato's concepts of love in the works of Djuna Barnes. Instead she had developed a crush on Larry, Somerset Maugham's protagonist in *The Razor's Edge,* and now proposed the topic of "Origins of Eastern Religious Thought in Maugham and Hesse." In their conversations Pam was struck by one of Marjorie's (and Maugham's) pet phrases, "the calming of the mind." The phrase seemed so enticing, so seductive. The more she thought about it, the more she realized that *mind-calming* was exactly what she needed. And since neither individual nor group therapy seemed capable of offering it, Pam decided to heed Marjorie's advice. So she booked airline passage to India and to Goenka, the epicenter of mind-calming.

The routine at the ashram had indeed begun to offer some mind-calming. Her mind fixated less on John, but now Pam was beginning to feel that the insomnia was worse than the obsession. She lay awake listening to the sounds of the night: a background beat of rhythmic breathing and the libretto of snores, moans, and snorts. About every fifteen minutes she was jolted by the shrill sound of a police whistle outside her window.

But why could she not sink into sleep? It *had* to be related to the twelve hours of meditation every day. What else could it be? Yet the 150 other students seemed to be resting comfortably in the arms of Morpheus. If only she could ask Vijay these questions. Once while furtively looking about for him in the meditation hall, Manil, the attendant who cruised up and down the aisles, poked her with his bamboo rod and commented, "Look inward. Nowhere else." And when she did spot Vijay in the back of the men's section, he seemed entranced, sitting erect in the lotus position, motionless as a Buddha. He must have noticed her in the meditation hall; of the three hundred, she was the only one sitting Western style in a chair. Though mortified by the chair, she had had such a backache from days of sitting that she had no choice but to request one from Manil, Goenka's assistant.

Manil, a tall and slender Indian, who worked hard at appearing tranquil, was not pleased with her request. Without removing his gaze from the horizon, he responded, "Your back? What did you do in past lives to bring this about?"

What a disappointment! Manil's answer belied Goenka's vehement claims that his method lay outside the province of any specific religious tradition. Gradually, she was coming to appreciate the yawning chasm between the nontheistic stance of rarified Buddhism and the superstitious beliefs of the masses. Even teaching assistants could not overcome their lust for magic, mystery, and authority.

Once she saw Vijay at the 11 A.M. lunch and maneuvered herself into a seat next to him. She heard him take a deep breath, as though inhaling her aroma, but he neither looked at her nor spoke. In fact, no one spoke to anyone; the rule of noble silence reigned supreme.

On the third morning a bizarre episode enlivened the proceedings. During the meditation someone farted loudly and a couple of students giggled. The giggle was contagious, and soon several students were caught up in a giggling jag. Goenka was not amused and immediately, wife in tow, stalked out of the meditation hall. Soon one of the assistants solemnly informed the student body that their teacher had been dishonored and would refuse to continue the course until all offending students left the ashram. A few students picked up and left, but for the next few hours meditation was disturbed by the faces of the exiled appearing at windows and hooting like owls.

No mention was ever made again of the incident, but Pam suspected that there had been a late-night purge since the next morning there were far fewer sitting Buddhas.

Words were permitted only during the noon hour when students with specific questions could address the teacher's assistants. On the fourth day at noon Pam posed her question about insomnia to Manil.

"Not for you to be concerned about," he replied, gazing off into the distance. "The body takes whatever sleep it requires."

"Well then," Pam tried again, "could you tell me why shrill police whistles are being blown outside my window all night long?"

"Forget such questions. Concentrate only upon *anapana-sati*. Just observe your breath. When you have truly applied yourself, such trivial events will no longer be disturbances."

Pam was so bored by the breath meditation that she wondered whether she could possibly last the ten days. Other than the sitting, the only available activity was listening to Goenka's nightly tedious discourses. Goenka, garbed in gleaming white, like all the staff, strove for eloquence but often fell short because an underlying shrill authoritarianism shone through. His lectures consisted of long repetitive tracts extolling the many virtues of Vipassana, which, if practiced correctly, resulted in mental purification, a path to enlightenment, a life of calmness and balance, an eradication of psychosomatic diseases, an elimination of the three causes of all unhappiness: craving, aversion, and ignorance. Regular Vipassana practice was like regular gardening of the mind during which one plucked out impure weeds of thought. Not only that, Goenka pointed out; Vipassana practice was portable, and provided a competitive edge in life: while others whiled away the waiting time at bus stops, the practitioner could industriously yank out a few weeds of cognitive impurity.

The handouts for the Vipassana course were heavy with rules which, on the surface, seemed understandable and reasonable. *But there were so many of them.* No stealing, no killing of any living creature, no lies, no sexual activity, no intoxicants, no sensual entertainment, no writing, note taking, or pens or pencils, or reading, no music or radios, no phones, no luxurious high bedding, no bodily decorations of any sort, no immodest clothing, no eating after midday (except for first-time students who were offered tea and fruit at 5 P.M.). Finally, the students were forbidden to question the teacher's guidance and instructions; they had to agree to observe the discipline and to meditate exactly as told. Only with such an obedient attitude, Goenka said, could students gain enlightenment.

Generally, Pam gave him the benefit of the doubt. He was, after all, a dedicated man who had devoted his life to offering Vipassana instruction. Of course he was culture-bound. Who wasn't? And hadn't India always groaned under the weight of religious ritual and rigid social stratification? Besides, Pam loved Goenka's gorgeous voice. Every night she was entranced by his deep sonorous chanting in ancient Pali of sacred Buddhist tracts. She had been moved in similar fashion by early Christian devotional music, especially Byzantine liturgical chants, by the cantors singing in synagogues, and once, in rural Turkey, was transfixed by the hypnotic melodies of the muezzin calling the populace to prayer five times a day.

Though Pam was a dedicated student, it was difficult for her simply to observe her breathing for fifteen straight minutes without drifting off into one of her reveries about John. But gradually changes occurred. The earlier disparate scenarios had coalesced into a single scene: from some news source—either TV, radio, or newspaper—she learned that John's family had been killed in an airplane crash. Again and again she imagined the scene. She was sick of it. But it kept on playing.

As her boredom and restlessness increased, she developed an intense interest in small household projects. When she first registered at the office (and learned to her surprise that there was no fee for the ten-day retreat), she noted small bags of detergent in the ashram shop. On the third day she purchased a bag and thereafter spent considerable time washing and rewashing her clothes, hanging them on the clothesline behind the dormitory (the first clothesline she had seen since childhood), and, at hourly intervals, checking on the drying process. Which bras and which panties were the best dryers? How many hours of night drying were equal to an hour's day drying. Or shade drying versus sun drying? Or hand-wrung clothes versus nonwrung clothes?

On the fourth day came the great event: Goenka began the teaching of Vipassana. The technique is simple and straightforward. Students are instructed to meditate on their scalp until a sensation occurs—an itch, a tingle, a burning, perhaps the feeling of a tiny breeze upon the skin of the scalp. Once the sensation is identified, the student is simply to observe, nothing more. Focus on the itch.

What is it like? Where does it go? How long does it last? When it disappears (as it always does), the meditator is to move to the next segment of the body, the face, and survey for stimuli like a nostril tickle or an eyelid itch. After these stimuli grow, ebb, and disappear, the student proceeds to the neck, the shoulders, until every part of the body is observed right down to the soles of the feet and then returning back to the scalp and repeating the process again and again.

Goenka's evening discourses provided the rationale for the technique. The key concept is *anitya—impermanence.* If one fully appreciates the impermanence of each physical stimulus, it is but a short step to extrapolate the principle of *anitya* to all of life's events and unpleasantries; everything will pass, and one will experience equanimity if one can maintain the observer's stance and simply watch the passing show.

After a couple of days of Vipassana, Pam found the process less onerous as she gained skill and speed at focusing on her bodily sensations. On the seventh day, to her amazement, the whole process slipped into automatic gear and she began "sweeping," just as Goenka had predicted. It was as if someone poured a jug of honey on her head which slowly and deliciously spread down to the bottom of her feet. She could feel a stirring, almost sexual hum, like the buzz of bumblebees enveloping her, as the honey flowed down. The hours zipped by. Soon she discarded her chair and melded with the three hundred other acolytes sitting in the lotus position at the feet of Goenka.

The next two days of sweeping were the same, and each passed quickly. On the ninth night she lay awake—she slept as badly as before but was less concerned about it now after learning from one of the other assistants (having given up on Manil), a Burmese woman, that insomnia in the Vipassana workshop is extremely common; apparently, the prolonged meditative states make sleep less necessary. The assistant also cleared up the mystery of the police whistles. In southern India, night watchmen routinely blow whistles as they circle the perimeter of the territory they guard. It is a preventative measure warning off thieves in the same way the little red light on auto dashboards warns car thieves of the presence of an activated auto alarm.

Often the presence of repetitive thoughts is most apparent when they vanish, and it was with a start that Pam realized that she had not thought about John for two entire days. John had vanished. The entire endless loop of fantasy had been replaced by the honeyed buzz of sweeping. How odd to realize that she now carried around her own pleasure maker which could be trained to secrete feel-good endorphins. Now she understood why people got hooked, why they would go on a lengthy retreat, sometimes months, sometimes years.

Yet now that she had finally cleansed her mind, why was she not elated? On the contrary, a shadow fell upon her success. Something about her enjoyment of sweeping darkened her thoughts. While pondering that conundrum, she dropped off into a light twilight sleep and was aroused a short time later by a strange dream image: a star with little legs, top hat and cane, tap-dancing across the stage of her mind. A dancing star! She knew exactly what that dream image meant. Of all the literary aphorisms that she and John shared and loved, one of her favorites was Nietzsche's phrase from *Zarathustra*: "One must have chaos in oneself to give birth to a dancing star."

Of course. Now she understood the source of her ambivalence about Vipassana. Goenka was true to his word. He delivered exactly what he had promised: equanimity, tranquility, or, as he often put it, *equipoise.* But at what price? If Shakespeare had taken up Vipassana, would *Lear* or *Hamlet* have been born? Would any of the masterpieces in Western culture have been written? One of Chapman's couplets drifted into mind:

No pen can anything eternal write
that is not steeped in the humour of the night

Steeped in the humour of the night—that was the task of the great writer—to immerse oneself in the humour of the night, to harness the power of darkness for artistic creation. How else could the sublime dark authors—Kafka, Dostoyevsky, Virginia Woolf, Hardy, Camus, Plath, Poe—have illuminated the tragedy lurking in the human condition? Not by removing oneself from life, not by sitting back and observing the passing show.

Even though Goenka proclaimed his teaching was nondenominational, his Buddhism shone through. In his nightly discourse cum sales pitch, Goenka could not restrain himself from stressing that Vipassana was the Buddha's own method of meditation, which he, Goenka, was now reintroducing to the world. She had no objection to that. Though she knew little of Buddhism, she had read an elementary text on the plane to India and had been impressed by the power and truth of the Buddha's four noble truths:

1. Life is suffering.
2. Suffering is caused by attachments (to objects, ideas, individuals, to survival itself).
3. There is an antidote to suffering: the cessation of desire, of attachment, of the self.
4. There is a specific pathway to a suffering-free existence: the eight-step path to enlightenment.

Now, she reconsidered. As she looked about her, at the entranced acolytes, the tranquilized assistants, the ascetics in their hillside caves content with a life dedicated to Vipassana sweeping, she wondered whether the four truths were so true after all. Had the Buddha gotten it right? Was the price of the remedy not worse than the disease? At dawn the following morning she lapsed into even greater doubt as she watched the small party of Jainist women walk to the bathhouse. The Jainists took the decree of no killing to absurd degrees: they hobbled down the path in a painfully slow, crablike fashion because they first had to gently sweep the gravel before them lest they step on an insect—indeed they could hardly breathe because of their gauze masks, which prevented the inhalation of any miniscule animal life.

Everywhere she looked, there was renunciation, sacrifice, limitation, and resignation. Whatever happened to life? To joy, expansion, passion, carpe diem?

Was life so anguished that it should be sacrificed for the sake of equanimity? Perhaps the four noble truths were culture-bound. Perhaps they were truths 2,500 years ago in a land with overwhelming poverty, overcrowding, starvation, disease, class oppression, and lack of any hope for a better future. But were they truths for her now? Didn't Marx have it right? Didn't all religions based on release or a better life hereafter target the poor, the suffering, the enslaved?

But, Pam said to herself (after a few days of noble silence she talked to herself a great deal), wasn't she being an ingrate? Give credit where it was due. Hadn't Vipassana done its job—calmed the mind and quashed her obsessive thoughts? Hadn't it succeeded where her own best efforts, and Julius's, and the group members' efforts had all failed? Well, maybe yes, maybe no. Perhaps it was not a fair comparison. After all, Julius had put in a total of about eight group sessions—twelve hours—while Vipassana demanded hundreds of hours—ten full days plus the time, and effort, to travel halfway around the world. What might have happened if Julius and the group had worked on her that many hours?

Pam's growing cynicism interfered with meditation. The sweeping stopped. Where had it gone—that delicious, mellifluous, buzzing contentment? Each new day her meditative practice regressed. The Vipassana meditation progressed no farther than her scalp. Those tiny itches, previously so fleeting, persisted and grew more robust—itches evolved into pinpricks, then into a sustained burning that could not be meditated away.

Even the early work in *anapana-sati* was undone. The dike of calmness built by breath meditation crumbled, and the surf of unruly thoughts, of her husband, John, or revenge and airplane crashes, came breaking through. Well, let them come. She saw Earl for what he was—an aging child, his large lips pursed and lunging for any nipple within range. And John—poor, effete, pusillanimous John, still unwilling to grasp that there can be no yes without a no. And Vijay, too, who chose to sacrifice life, novelty, adventure, friendship upon the altar of the great God, Equanimity. Use the right word for the whole bunch, Pam thought. *Cowards.* Moral cowards. None of them deserved her. Flush them away. Now *there* was a powerful image: all the men, John, Earl, Vijay, standing in a giant toilet bowl, their hands raised imploringly, their squeals for help barely audible over the roar of the flushing water! *That* was an image worth meditating upon.

The flower replied: You fool! Do you imagine I blossom in order to be seen? I blossom for my own sake because it pleases me, and not for the sake of others. My joy consists in my being and my blossoming.

19

Bonnie opened the next meeting with an apology. "Sorry to one and all about my exit last week. I shouldn't have done that but . . . I don't know . . . it was out of my control."

"The devil made you do it." Tony smirked.

"Funny. Funny, Tony. Okay, I know what you want. *I chose to do it because I was pissed.* That better?"

Tony smiled and gave her the thumbs-up signal.

In the gentle voice he always used when addressing any of the women in the group, Gill said to Bonnie, "Last week after you left, Julius suggested you might have felt pissed at being ignored here—that basically the group replayed your description of what routinely happened to you in your childhood."

"Pretty accurate. Except I wasn't pissed. *Hurt* is a better term."

"I know pissed," said Rebecca, "and you were good 'n' pissed at me."

Bonnie's face clouded over as she turned to Rebecca. "Last week you said that Philip had clarified the reason you don't have girlfriends. But I don't buy that. Envy of your good looks is *not* the reason you don't have girlfriends or at least why you and I haven't become close; the real reason is that you're basically not interested in women—or at least you're not interested in me. Whenever you say something to me in the group, it is always to bring the discussion back to you."

"I give you feedback about the way you handle—or, mostly, *don't* handle—anger, and then I get accused of being self-centered." Rebecca bristled. "Do you or don't you want feedback? Isn't that what this group is about?"

"What I want is for you to give me feedback about *me.* Or about me and someone else. It's always about you, Rebecca—or you and me—and you're so attractive it always swings things back to you and away from me. I can't compete with you. But it's not only your fault; the others play into this, and I need to ask all of you a question."

Bonnie swiveled her head looking briefly at each member in turn as she said, "I never really get your interest—why not?"

The men in the room looked down. Bonnie didn't wait for an answer but continued: "And another thing, Rebecca, what I'm saying to you about girlfriends is not news to you. I can remember clear as a bell you and Pam having an identical go-around about this."

Bonnie turned to Julius. "Speaking of Pam, I've been meaning to ask you, any news of her? When is she coming back? I miss her."

"That was fast!" Julius said, "Bonnie, you are the master of the whirlwind segue! But for the moment I'm going to let you get away with it and answer your question about Pam, mainly because I was going to announce that she e-mailed me from Bombay. She's finished her meditation retreat and will be returning soon to the States. She should be here for the next meeting."

Turning to Philip, Julius said, "You remember I mentioned Pam, our missing member, to you?"

Philip replied with a brief nod.

"And, *you,* Philip, are the master of the fast nod," said Tony. "It's amazing how much you stay in the middle of things without ever looking at anyone and without saying very much. Look at all this stuff going on around you. Bonnie and Rebecca squabbling over you. What are you feeling about all this? What are you feeling about the group?"

When Philip did not immediately reply, Tony appeared uncomfortable. He looked around the group: "Shit, what *is* this? I feel like I'm breaking some kind of rule here, like farting in church. I'm just asking him the same kind of question everyone asks everyone else."

Philip broke the short silence. "Fair enough. I require time to collect my thoughts. Here's what I was thinking. Bonnie and Rebecca have similar afflictions. Bonnie cannot tolerate being unpopular, whereas Rebecca cannot tolerate being *no longer* popular. Both are hostages to the caprice of what others think. In other words, happiness, for both of them, lies in the hands and heads of *others.* And for both the solution is the same: *the more one has in oneself, the less one will want from others.*"

In the silence that followed one could almost hear sounds of cerebral mastication as the group attempted to digest Philip's words.

"It doesn't appear that any of you are about to respond to Philip," said Julius, "so I want to address an error I think I made a couple of minutes ago. Bonnie, I shouldn't have gone along with your segue to Pam. I don't want a repeat of last week when your needs were not dealt with. A few minutes ago you were talking about why the group often overlooked you, and I thought you took a courageous step by asking everyone why you could not get their interest. But look what happened then: in the very next breath you switched to Pam's return to the group, and, presto, in a couple of minutes, your question to us faded into history."

"I noticed that, too," said Stuart. "So, Bonnie, it's like you arrange for us to ignore you."

"That's good feedback." Bonnie nodded her head. "Very good. I probably do that a lot. I'll do some thinking about that."

Julius pressed on, "I appreciate the thanks, Bonnie, but I can't help feeling you're doing the same thing now. Aren't you saying, in effect, 'that's enough focus on me.' I should have a Bonnie bell here and ring it every time you switch away from yourself."

"So what do I do?" Bonnie asked.

"Give us the reason you had no right to request feedback from us," Julius suggested.

"I guess I just don't feel important enough."

"But is it okay for others here to make this kind of request?"

"Oh, yes."

"That means that others here are more important than you?"

Bonnie nodded.

"So, Bonnie, try this," Julius continued, "look around at each of the members here and answer this question: *Who in this group is more important than you? And why?"* Julius could hear himself purring. He was coasting in familiar waters. For the first time in a while, certainly since Philip had entered the group, he knew exactly what he was doing. He had done what the good group therapist should do: he had translated one of his patient's central issues into the here-and-now, where it could be explored firsthand. It was always more productive to focus on the here-and-now than to work on the patient's reconstructions of an event from the past or from current outside life.

Swiveling her head to glance briefly at each person in the group, Bonnie said, "*Everyone* here is more important than I am—a lot more important." Her face was flushed, her breathing rapid. As much as she craved attention from others, it was obvious that she now wanted nothing more than invisibility.

"Be specific, Bonnie," Julius urged. "*Who* is more important. *Why?"*

Bonnie looked around, "Everybody here. You, Julius—look how you've helped everyone. Rebecca is drop-dead gorgeous, a successful lawyer, great kids. Gill is the CFO of a large hospital—as well as being a hunk. Stuart—well, he's a busy doctor, helps children, helps parents; he has success written all over him. Tony . . ." Bonnie paused for a moment.

"Wellllll? This'll be interesting." Tony, dressed as always in blue jeans, a black T-shirt, and sneakers splattered with paint stains, leaned back in his chair.

"First of all, Tony, you're you—no posturing, no games, just pure honesty. And you bad-mouth your profession, but I know you're no ordinary carpenter; you're probably an artist at your work—I see that BMW roadster you scoot around in. And you're a hunk, too, I love you in a tight T-shirt. How's that for risk?" Bonnie looked around the group circle. "And, who else? Philip—you've got intelligence to burn, you know everything—a teacher, you're going to be a therapist, your words fascinate everyone. And Pam? Pam is awesome, a university professor, a free spirit; she compels attention; she's been everywhere, knows everyone, has read everything, stands up to anyone."

"Reactions, anyone, to Bonnie's explanation of why she's less important than each of you?" Julius's eyes circled the group.

"Her answer doesn't make sense to me," said Gill.

"Can you tell her?" said Julius.

"Sorry, what I mean is—and I don't want to offend—but Bonnie, your answer sounds regressive . . ."

"Regressive?" Bonnie screwed her face up in puzzlement.

"Well, what this group is about is that we're all just human beings trying to relate in a human way to one another, and that we check our roles, our degrees, our money, and our BMW roadsters at the door."

"Amen," said Julius.

"Amen," chimed in Tony, who added, "I'm with Gill, and, just for the record, I bought that roadster used and it's put me in hock for the next three years."

"And Bonnie," Gill continued, "in your go-round what you did was focus exactly on those external things—professions, money, successful kids. None of those relate to why you are the least important person in this room. I consider you very important. You're a key member; you're engaged with all of us; you're warm, giving; you even offered me a place to sleep a couple of weeks ago when I didn't want to go home. You keep the group focused; you work hard here."

Bonnie held her ground. "I'm a drag; my whole life has been about shame for my alcoholic parents, always lying about my family. Inviting you home, Gill, was a big event for me—I could never invite kids home, full of fear that my father would show up drunk. What's more, my ex-husband was a drunk, my daughter's a heroin addict . . ."

"You're still evading the point, Bonnie," said Julius. "You talk of your past, your daughter, your ex, your family . . . but *you*, where are *you*?"

"I *am* these things, a composite of all these things; what else can I be? I'm a boring pudgy librarian, what I do is to catalog books . . . I . . . I don't know what you mean. I'm confused, I don't know where or who I am." Bonnie began to cry, pulled out a tissue, blew her nose loudly, closed her eyes, raised both hands and drew circles in the air, and, between the sobs, muttered, "This is enough for me; it's all I can take today."

Julius shifted into another gear and addressed the entire group. "Let's take a look at what's happened the past several minutes. Who's got some feelings or observations?" Having succeeded in moving the group into the here-and-now, he advanced to the next step. In his view the work in therapy consisted of two phases: first interaction, often emotional, and second, understanding that interaction. That's the way therapy should proceed—an alternating sequence of evocation of emotions and then understanding. So he now attempted to switch the group into the second phase by saying, "Let's back up and take a dispassionate look at what's just transpired."

Stuart was about to describe the sequence of events when Rebecca jumped in: "I think the important thing was Bonnie giving her reasons for feeling unimportant and then assuming we would all agree. That's when she became confused and cried and said she had had enough—I've seen her do that before."

Tony said, "Yeah, I agree. Bonnie, you do get emotional when you get a lot of attention. Are you embarrassed by the spotlight?"

Still sobbing, Bonnie said, "I should have been appreciative, but look what a mess I made of it. And look at how much better others would've used this time."

"The other day," Julius said, "I had a conversation with a colleague about one of his patients. He said she had a habit of catching spears thrown at her and then stabbing herself with them. Maybe I'm being a little loose here, Bonnie, but that popped in mind when I saw how you take things and punish yourself with them."

"I know you're all feeling impatient with me. I guess I still don't know how to use the group."

"Well, you know what I'm going to say, Bonnie. Exactly *who* here was impatient? Look around the room." The group could absolutely count on Julius asking this question. He had never been known to let such a statement go by without honing in on it and asking for names.

"Well, I think Rebecca wanted me to stop."

"Whhhattt? Why I . . ."

"Hold up a minute, Rebecca," Julius was being unusually directive today. "Bonnie, what exactly did you see? What cues did you pick up?"

"About Rebecca? Well, she was silent. Didn't speak a word."

"I can't win. I was doing my best to be quiet so you couldn't accuse me of taking attention from you. Can't you recognize a gift?"

Bonnie was about to respond when Julius asked her to continue with her descriptions of who was bored.

"Well, nothing I can spell out concretely. But you can just tell when people are bored. I bore myself. Philip wasn't looking at me, but then he never looks at anyone. I know the group was waiting to hear from Philip. What he said about popularity was far more interesting to the group than my whining."

"Well, I wasn't bored with you," replied Tony, "and I didn't see anyone else bored either. And what Philip had to say was *not* more interesting; he stays so much in his head that I don't get real excited by his comments. I don't even remember them."

"I do," said Stuart. "Tony, after you commented about how he was always in the center of things despite saying so little, he said that Bonnie and Rebecca had a very similar problem. They're overinvested in the opinions of others: Rebecca gets too inflated and Bonnie too deflated—it was something like that."

"You're being a clicker again," said Tony, pantomiming holding a camera and taking pictures.

"Right. Keep me honest. I know, I know—less observations, more feelings. Well, I agree that Philip is somehow central without having to say much. And it does feel like breaking the rules to confront Philip about anything."

"That's an observation and an opinion, Stuart," said Julius. "Can you go to the feelings?"

"Well, I guess I have some envy about Rebecca's interest in Philip. I felt that it was odd no one asked Philip how he felt about that—well, that's not quite a feeling, is it?"

"Closer," said Julius. "First cousin to a feeling. Keep going."

"I feel threatened by Philip. He's too smart. Also I feel ignored by him. And don't like being ignored."

"Bingo, Stuart, now you're honing in," said Julius. "Any questions for Philip?" Julius labored to keep his tone soft and delicate. His job was to help the group include, not to threaten and exclude Philip by insisting he perform in a manner not yet possible. It was for that reason he called upon Stuart rather than the more confrontative Tony.

"Sure, but it's hard to ask Philip questions."

"He's right here, Stuart." Another fundamental Julius rule: never allow members to speak of one another in the third person.

"Well, that's the issue. It's hard to talk to him . . ." Stuart turned to

Philip, "I mean, Philip, it's hard to talk to you because you never look at me. Like right now. Why is that?"

"I prefer to keep my own counsel," said Philip, still gazing toward the ceiling.

Julius was poised to leap into the discussion if needed, but Stuart stayed patient.

"I don't follow."

"If you ask something of me, I want to search within myself, free of any distractions, in order to give you my best possible answer."

"But your not looking at me makes me feel we're not in contact."

"But my words must tell you otherwise."

"How about walking and chewing gum?" interjected Tony.

"Pardon?" Philip, puzzled, turned his head but not his eyes toward Tony.

"Like, how about doing both at the same time—looking at him *and* giving a good answer?"

"I prefer to search my own mind. Meeting the gaze of the other distracts me from searching for the answer the other might wish to hear."

Silence prevailed while Tony and the others mulled Philip's response. Stuart then posed another question: "Well, let me ask you, Philip, all that discussion about Rebecca's preening for you—how did that make you feel?"

"You know," Rebecca's eyes showed fire, "I am *really* beginning to resent this, Stuart . . . it's as though Bonnie's fantasy has now passed into the books as gospel."

Stuart refused to be diverted. "Okay, okay. Delete that question. Philip, I'll ask you this: how did you feel about all the discussion about you the last meeting?"

"The discussion was of great interest, and I am unflaggingly attentive." Philip looked at Stuart and continued, "But I have no emotional responses if that's your inquiry."

"None? That doesn't seem possible," replied Stuart.

"Before beginning the group I read Julius's book on group therapy and was well prepared for the events of these meetings. I expected certain things to happen: that I would be an object of curiosity, that some would welcome me and some not, that the established hierarchy of power would be unsettled by my entrance, that the women might look favorably upon me and the men unfavorably, that the more central members might resent my appearance while the less influential ones might be protective of me. Anticipating these things has resulted in my viewing the events in the group dispassionately."

Stuart, as Tony before him, was stunned by Philip's response and lapsed into silence as he digested Philip's words.

Julius said, "I've a bit of a dilemma . . ." He waited a moment. "On the one hand," he continued, "I feel it's important to follow up this discussion with Philip, but I'm also concerned about Rebecca. Where are you, Rebecca? You look distressed, and I know you've been trying to get in."

"I'm feeling a little bruised today and shut out, ignored. By Bonnie, by Stuart."

"Keep going."

"There's a lot of negative stuff coming my way—about being self-centered, not being interested in woman friends, about posturing for Philip. It stings. And I resent it."

"I know what that's like," said Julius. "I have those same knee-jerk reactions to criticism. But let me tell you what I've learned to do. The real trick is to think of feedback as a gift, but first you must decide whether it's accurate. The way I proceed is to check in with myself and ask whether it clicks with my own experience of myself. Does any part, even a tad of it, even five percent, ring true? I try to recall if people in the past had given me this feedback before. I think about other people with whom I can check it out. I wonder if someone is honing in on one of my blind spots, something they see that I do not. Can you try this?"

"That's not easy, Julius. I feel tight about it." Rebecca clasped her hand to her sternum. "Right here."

"Give that tightness a voice. What's it saying?"

"It's saying, 'How will I look?' It's shame. It's being found out. This business about people noticing my playing with my hair. Makes me cringe, makes me want to say, 'It's none of your fucking business—it's my hair—I'll do what I want with it.'"

In his most teacherly voice Julius responded, "Years ago there was a therapist named Fritz Perls who started a school called gestalt therapy. You don't hear much about him nowadays, but, anyway, he did a lot of focusing on the body—you know, 'Look what your left hand is doing right now,' or 'I see you stroking your beard a lot.' He'd ask patients to exaggerate the movement: 'Keep making a tighter fist with your left hand,' or 'Keep stroking that beard more and more vigorously and stay aware of what gets evoked.'

"I always felt there was a lot to Perls's approach because so much of our unconscious is expressed through body movements that lie out of our own awareness. But I've never made much use of it in therapy. The reason? Exactly because of what's happening now, Rebecca. We often get defensive when others spot us doing things of which we are unaware. So I understand how uncomfortable you feel, but even so, can you stay with it and try to learn if there's something of value in the feedback?"

"In other words, you're saying 'be mature.' I'll try." Rebecca sat up straight, took a breath, and with a determined demeanor began, "First, it *is* true that I like attention and that I first came to therapy upset about my aging and about no longer being stared at by men. So I may have been preening for Philip but not consciously." She turned back to the group. "So, mea culpa. I like to be admired, I like to be loved and adored, I like love."

"Plato," Philip interjected, "observed that love is in the one who loves, not in the one who is loved."

"*Love is in the one who loves not in the one who is loved*—That's a great quote, Philip," Rebecca said, flashing a smile. "You see, that's what I like about you. Comments just like that. They open my eyes. I find you interesting. Attractive too."

Rebecca turned to the group. "Does that mean I want to have an affair with him? Nope! The last affair I had just about did my marriage in, and I'm not shopping for trouble."

"So Philip," said Tony, "you have feelings about what Rebecca just said?"

"I said before that my goal in life is to will as little as possible and to know as much as possible. Love, passion, seduction—these are powerful sentiments, part of our hardwiring to perpetuate our species and, as Rebecca has just made clear, they may operate unconsciously. But, all in all, these activities serve to derail reason and interfere with my scholarly pursuits, and I want nothing to do with them."

"Every time I ask you something, you give me an answer that's hard to argue with. But you never answer my question," said Tony.

"I think he answered it," said Rebecca. "He made it clear that he does not want any emotional involvement, that he wants to stay free and clearheaded. I think Julius has made the same point—that's why there's a taboo against romantic involvement in the group."

"What taboo?" Tony addressed Julius. "I never heard that rule said out loud."

"I've never put it just like that. The only ground rule you heard from me about relationships outside of the meetings is that there be no secrets and that if there are any encounters whatsoever outside the group sessions, the members involved must bring it up in the group. If not, if you keep secrets, it almost always gums up the work of the group and sabotages your own therapy. That's my only rule about outside encounters. But, Rebecca, let's not lose the thread of what's going on between you and Bonnie. Check into your feelings about her."

"She's raised some heavy stuff. Is it true I don't relate to women? I want to say no. There's my sister—I'm close to her, sort of—and a couple of other women attorneys in my office, but, Bonnie, you're probably putting your finger on something—there's definitely more charge, more excitement for me in relating to men."

"I'm flashing on college," said Bonnie, "and how I didn't have many dates and how dismissed I felt when some girlfriend thought nothing of canceling out on me, at the last minute, if she got an invitation from a guy."

"Yeah, I probably would have done that," said Rebecca. "You're right—men and dating, that was what it was all about. It made some sense then; now it doesn't."

Tony had been continuing to study Philip and approached him again. "Philip, you know, you're like Rebecca in some ways. You preen, too, but you do it with snappy, deep-sounding slogans."

"I believe your point, " said Philip with eyes closed in deep concentration, "is that my motivation in voicing observations is not what it seems to be: that it is instead self-serving, a form of preening in which, if I understand you, I attempt to evoke Rebecca's and others' interest and admiration. Is that correct?"

Julius felt on edge. No matter what he did, the focus kept going back to Philip. At least three conflicting desires fought for his attention: first, to protect Philip against too much confrontation, second, to prevent Philip's impersonality from derailing the intimate discourse, and, third, to cheer Tony on in his efforts to knock Philip on his ass. But, all in all, he decided to stay on the sidelines for the time being because the group was handling the situation. In fact, something important had just happened: for the first time Philip was responding directly, even personally, to someone.

Tony nodded. "That's about what I meant, except that it may be more than just interest or admiration. Try seduction."

"Yes, that's a good correction. It's implied in your word *preening* and thus you suggest that my motivation parallels Rebecca's, that is, I wish to seduce her. Well, that's a substantial and reasonable hypothesis. Let's see how to test it."

Silence. No one responded, but Philip did not appear to be waiting for a response. After a moment of reflection with his eyes closed he pronounced, "Perhaps it is best to follow Dr. Hertzfeld's procedure . . ."

"Call me Julius."

"Ah, yes. So, to follow Julius's procedure, I must first check whether Tony's hypothesis is consonant with my inner experience." Philip paused, shook his head. "I find no evidence for this. Many years ago I tore myself free from attachment to public opinion. I firmly believe that the happiest of men are those who seek for nothing so much as solitude. I speak of the divine Schopenhauer, of Nietzsche and Kant. Their point, and my point, is that the man of inner wealth wants nothing from the outside except the negative gift of undisturbed leisure which permits him to enjoy his wealth—that is, his intellectual faculties.

"In short, then, I conclude that my contributions do not stem from an attempt to seduce anyone or elevate myself in your eyes. Perhaps there are tatters of this desire left; I can only say I do not consciously experience it. I do recognize regret that I myself have only mastered the great thoughts, not contributed to them."

In his decades of leading therapy groups Julius had experienced many silences, but the silence that followed Philip's response was unlike any other. It was not the silence accompanying great emotion nor the silence signifying dependency, embarrassment, or bafflement. No, this silence was different, as though the group had stumbled upon a new species, a new life-form, perhaps a six-eyed salamander with feathered wings, and, with utmost caution and deliberateness, slowly circled it.

Rebecca was the first to respond, "To be so content, to need so little from others, never to crave the company of others—sounds pretty lonely, Philip."

"On the contrary," said Philip, "in the past, when I craved the company of others, asked for something which they would not, indeed could not, give—*that* was when I knew loneliness. I knew it very well. To need no person is never to be lonely. Blessed isolation is what I seek."

"Yet you're here," said Stuart, "and take it from me—this group is the archenemy of isolation. Why expose yourself to this?"

"Every thinker must support his habit. Either they were fortunate enough to have had a university stipend like Kant or Hegel or independent means like Schopenhauer or a day job like Spinoza, who ground lenses for spectacles to support himself. I have chosen philosophical counseling as my day job, and this group experience is part of my certification experience."

"That means, then," said Stuart, "that you are engaging with us in this group, but your ultimate goal is to help others never to need such engagement."

Philip paused and then nodded.

"Let me be sure I got you right," said Tony. "If Rebecca digs you, comes on to you, turns on her charm, gives you her amazing killer smile, you're saying it has no effect on you? Zero?"

"No, I didn't say 'no effect.' I agree with Schopenhauer when he wrote that beauty is an open letter of recommendation predisposing the heart to favor the person who presents it. I find that an individual of great beauty is wondrous to behold. But I'm also saying that someone else's opinion of me does not, must not, alter my opinion of myself."

"Sounds mechanical. Not quite human," replied Tony.

"What truly felt inhuman was the time when I allowed my estimation of my value to bob up and down like a cork according to the regard flowing from inconsequential others."

Julius stared at Philip's lips. What a marvel they were. How exactly they mirrored Philip's calm composure, how steadfast, how unquavering, as they shaped each passing word into the same perfect roundness of pitch and tone. And it was easy to empathize with Tony's escalating desire to ruffle Philip. But knowing Tony's impulsivity might quickly escalate, Julius decided it was time to steer the discussion into a more benign direction. It was not time to confront Philip; this was only his fourth meeting.

"Philip, earlier in your comments to Bonnie you said that your aim was to be helpful to her. And you've also given counsel to others here—Gill, Rebecca. Can you say more about why you do that? It seems to me there is something in your desire to counsel that goes beyond a day job. After all, there's no financial incentive in offering your help to others here."

"I try always to keep in mind that we are all sentenced to an existence filled with inescapable misery—an existence which none of us would choose if we knew the facts ahead of time. In that sense we are all, as Schopenhauer put it, *fellow sufferers,* and we stand in need of tolerance and love from our neighbors in life."

"Schopenhauer again! Philip, I hear too damn much about Schopenhauer—whoever he is—and too damn little about you." Tony spoke calmly, as though imitating Philip's measured tone, yet his breathing was shallow and rapid. Generally, confrontation came easily to Tony; at the time he began therapy scarcely a week passed without a physical contretemps in a bar, in traffic, at work, or on the basketball court. Though not a large man, he was fearless in confrontation; except for one situation—a clash of ideas with an educated articulate bully, someone exactly like Philip.

Philip gave no sign he intended to respond to Tony. Julius broke the silence. "Tony, you seem deep in thought. What's running through your mind?

"I was thinking about what Bonnie said earlier in the meeting about missing Pam. Me, too. I been missing her today."

Julius was not surprised. Tony had become accustomed to Pam's tutelage and protection. The two of them had struck up an odd-couple relationship—the English professor and the tattooed primitive. Using an oblique approach, Julius said, "Tony, I imagine it's not easy for you to say, '*Schopenhauer, whoever that is.*' "

"Well, we're here to tell the truth," Tony responded.

"Right on, Tony," said Gill, "and, I'll fess up too: I don't know who Schopenhauer is."

"All I know," noted Stuart, "is that he's a famous philosopher. German, pessimistic. Was he nineteenth century?"

"Yes, he died in 1860, in Frankfurt," said Philip, "and, as for pessimism, I prefer to think of it as *realism.* And, Tony, it may be true I speak of Schopenhauer overly often, but I have good reason to do so." Tony seemed shocked that Philip had addressed him personally. Even so, Philip still made no eye contact. No longer staring at the ceiling, he looked out the window, as if intrigued by something in the garden.

Philip continued: "First, to know Schopenhauer is to know me. We are inseparable, twin-brained. Secondly, he has been my therapist and has offered me invaluable help. I have internalized him—of course I mean his ideas—as many of you have done with Dr. Hertzfeld. Wait—I mean Julius." Philip smiled faintly as he glanced at Julius—his first moment of levity in the group. "Last, I harbor a hope that some of Schopenhauer's sentiments will be of benefit to you as they have been to me."

Julius, glancing at his watch, broke the silence that had followed Philip's remark. "It's been a rich meeting, the kind of meeting I hate to bring to an end, but time's up today."

"Rich? What am I missing?" muttered Tony, as he stood and started toward the door.

The cheerfulness and buoyancy of our youth are due partly to the fact that we are climbing the hill of life and do not see death that lies at the foot of the other side.

20

Foreshadowings of Pessimism

Early in their training therapists are taught to focus upon patients' responsibility for their life dilemmas. Mature therapists never accept at face value their patients' accounts of mistreatment by others. Instead, therapists understand that to some extent individuals are cocreators of their social environment and that relationships are always reciprocal. But what about the relationship between young Arthur Schopenhauer and his parents? Surely its nature was primarily determined by Johanna and Heinrich, Arthur's creators and shapers; they were, after all, the adults.

And yet Arthur's contribution cannot be overlooked: there was something primal, inbuilt, tenacious in Arthur's temperament which, even as a child, elicited certain responses from Johanna and from others. Arthur habitually failed to inspire loving, generous, and joyful responses; instead almost everyone responded to him critically and defensively.

Perhaps the template was set during Johanna's tempestuous pregnancy. Or perhaps genetic endowment played the major role in

Arthur's development. The Schopenhauer lineage teemed with evidence of psychological disturbance. For many years before he committed suicide, Arthur's father was chronically depressed, anxious, stubborn, distant, and unable to enjoy life. His father's mother was violent, unstable, and eventually required institutionalization. Of his father's three brothers, one was born severely retarded, and another, according to a biographer, died at age thirty-four "half mad through excesses, in a corner with wicked people."

Arthur's personality, set at an early age, endured with remarkable consistency his entire life. The letters from his parents to the adolescent Arthur contain many passages that indicate their growing concern about his disinterest in social amenities: For example, his mother wrote, ". . . little though I care for stiff etiquette, I like even less a rough, self-pleasing, nature and action. . . . You have more than a slight inclination that way." His father wrote, "I only wish you had learned to make yourself agreeable to people."

Young Arthur's travel diary reveals the man he would become. There, the teenaged Arthur demonstrates a precocious ability to distance himself and view things from a cosmic perspective. In describing a portrait of a Dutch admiral he says, "Next to the picture were the symbols of his life's story: his sword, the beaker, the chain of honor which he wore, and finally the bullet which made all these useless to him."

As a mature philosopher Schopenhauer took pride in his ability to assume an objective perspective, or, as he put it, "viewing the world through the wrong end of the telescope." The appeal of viewing the world from above is already found in his early comments about mountain climbing. At sixteen he wrote, "I find that a panorama from a high mountain enormously contributes to the broadening of concepts. . . . all small objects disappear and only what is big retains its shape."

There is a powerful foreshadowing here of the adult Schopenhauer. He would continue to develop the cosmic perspective that allowed him as a mature philosopher to experience the world as if from a great distance—not only physically and conceptually but temporally. At an early age he intuitively apprehended the perspective of Spinoza's "sub species aeteritatis," to see the world and its events from the perspective of eternity. The human condition, Arthur concluded, could be best understood not from being *a part of* but *apart from* it. As an adolescent he wrote presciently of his future lofty isolation.

> Philosophy is a high mountain road . . . an isolated road and becomes even more desolate the higher we ascend. Whoever pursues this path should show no fear but must leave everything behind and confidently make his own way in the wintry snow. . . . He soon sees the world beneath him; its sandy beaches and morasses vanish from his view, its uneven spots are leveled out, its jarring sounds no longer reach his ear. And its roundness is revealed to him. He himself is always in the pure cool mountain air and beholds the sun when all below is still engulfed in dead of night.

But there is more than a pull toward the heights motivating Schopenhauer; there are pushes from below. Two other traits are also evident in the young Arthur: a deep misanthropy coupled with a relentless pessimism. If there was something about heights, distant vistas, and the cosmic perspective that lured Arthur, then, too, there was much evidence that he was repelled by closeness to others. One day after descending from the crystal-clear sunrise on a mountaintop and reentering the human world in a chalet at the mountain base he reported: "We entered a room of carousing servants. . . . It was unbearable: their animalistic warmth gave off a glowing heat."

Contemptuous, mocking observations of others fill his travel diaries. Of a Protestant service he wrote: "The strident singing of the multitude made my ears ache, and an individual with bleating mouth wide open repeatedly made me laugh." Of a Jewish service: "Two little boys standing next to me made me lose my countenance because at the wide-mouthed roulade with their heads flung back, they always seemed to be yelling at me." A group of English aristocrats "looked like peasant wenches in disguise." The king of England "is a handsome old man but the queen is ugly without any bearing." The emperor and empress of Austria "both wore exceedingly modest clothes. He is a gaunt man whose markedly stupidly face would lead one to guess a tailor rather than an emperor." A school chum aware of Arthur's misanthropic trend wrote Arthur in England: "I am sorry that your stay in England has induced you to hate the entire *nation.*"

This mocking, irreverent young lad would develop into the bitter, angry man who habitually referred to all humans as "bipeds," and would agree with Thomas à Kempis, "Every time I went out among men I came back less human."

Did these traits impede Arthur's goal to be the "clear eye of the world?" The young Arthur foresaw the problem and wrote a memo to his older self: "Be sure your objective judgments are not for the most part concealed subjective ones." Yet, as we shall see, despite his resolve, despite his self-discipline, Arthur was often unable to heed his own youthful, excellent advice.

He is a happy man who can once and for all avoid having to do with a great many of his fellow creatures.

21

At the onset of the following meeting, just as Bonnie was asking Julius whether Pam was back from her trip, Pam opened the door, spread her arms, and loudly called out, "Da Dumm!" Everyone, save Philip, stood and greeted her. In her unique loving fashion she went around the circle, looked into each person's eyes, hugged them, kissed Rebecca and Bonnie, tousled Tony's hair, and, when she got to Julius, held him for a long while and whispered, "Thank you for being so honest on the phone. I'm devastated, so so sorry, so worried about you." Julius looked at Pam. Her familiar, smiling face conveyed courage and radiant energy. "Welcome back, Pam," he said. "God, it's good to see you here. We missed you. I missed you."

Then, when Pam's glance fell on Philip, darkness descended. Her smile and the cheery crinkles around her eyes vanished. Thinking she was jarred by the presence of a stranger in the group, Julius quickly offered an introduction, "Pam, this is our new member, Philip Slate."

"Oh, it's Slate?" said Pam, pointedly not looking at Philip. "Not Philip Sleaze? Or Slimeball? She glanced at the door. "Julius, I don't know if I can stay in the room with this asshole!"

The stunned group members looked back and forth from the agitated Pam to the entirely silent Philip. Julius stepped in. "Fill us in, Pam. Please sit."

As Tony pulled another chair into the group, Pam said, "Not next to him." (The empty seat was next to Philip.) Rebecca immediately stood and guided Pam to her seat.

After a brief silence, Tony said, "What's going on, Pam?"

"God, I can't believe this—is this some monstrous joke? This is the last thing in the world I wanted. Never wanted to see this rodent again."

"What *is* going on?" asked Stuart. "What about *you*, Philip? Say something. What's going on?"

Philip remained silent and shook his head slightly. But his face, now flushed, said volumes. Julius noted to himself that Philip had a functioning autonomic nervous system after all.

"Try to talk, Pam," urged Tony. "You're among friends."

"Of all the men I've ever known, this creature has treated me the worst. And to come home to my therapy group and find him sitting here—it's beyond belief. I feel like bawling or screaming, but I won't—not with him here." Lapsing into silence, Pam looked down, slowly shaking her head.

"Julius," said Rebecca, "I'm getting tense. This is not good for me. Come on, what's going on?"

"Obviously, there's been a former life between Pam and Philip, and, I assure you, that comes as a total surprise to me."

After a short silence, Pam looked at Julius and said, "I've been thinking so much about this group. I've been so eager to come back here, been rehearsing what I would tell you about my trip. But, Julius, I'm sorry, I don't think I can do this. I don't want to stay."

She stood and turned toward the door. Tony jumped up and took her hand.

"Pam, please. You can't just leave. You've done so much for me. Here, I'll sit next to you. You want me to take him out?" Pam smiled faintly and let Tony lead her back to her seat. Gill changed chairs to open the adjoining seat for Tony.

"I'm with Tony. I want to help," said Julius. "We all do. But you've got to let us help you, Pam. Obviously, there's been history, bad history, between you and Philip. Tell us, talk about it—otherwise our hands are tied."

Pam nodded slowly, closed her eyes and opened her mouth, but no words came. Then she stood and walked to the window, rested her forehead against the pane, and waved off Tony, who had started toward her. She turned, took a couple of deep breaths, and began speaking in a disembodied voice: "Over twenty years ago, my girlfriend Molly and I wanted to have a New York experience. Molly had lived next door to me since childhood and was my best friend. We had just finished our freshman year at Amherst and enrolled together for summer classes at Columbia. One of our two courses was on the pre-Socratic philosophers, and guess who was the TA?"

"TA?" asked Tony.

"Teaching assistant," interjected Philip softly but instantaneously, speaking for the first time in the session. "The TA is a graduate student who assists the professor by leading small discussion groups, reading papers, grading exams."

Pam seemed staggered by Philip's unexpected comment.

Tony answered her unspoken question: "Philip's the official answer man here. Put out a question and he answers it. Sorry, once you got started, I should have kept my mouth shut. Go on. Can you join us here in the circle?"

Pam nodded, went back to her seat, closed her eyes again, and continued: "So, there I was at Columbia summer school with Molly, and this man, this creature, sitting here was our TA. My friend Molly was in a bad place: she had just broken up with her long- term boyfriend. And no sooner did the course begin than this . . . this excuse for a man"—she nodded toward Philip—"starts hitting on her. Remember that we were only eighteen, and he was the teacher—oh, a real professor showed up for two formal lectures a week, but the TA was really in charge of the course, including our grades. He was slick. And Molly was vulnerable. She fell for him and for about a week was in a state of bliss. Then one Saturday afternoon, he phones me and asks me to meet with him about an exam essay I had written. He was smooth and ruthless. And I was just stupid enough to be manipulated, and next thing I knew I was naked on the sofa in his office. I was an eighteen-year old virgin. And he was into rough sex. And he did it again to me a couple of days later, and then the pig dropped me, wouldn't even look at me, didn't seem to recognize me, and, worst of all, offered no explanation for dropping me. And I was too scared to ask—he had the power—he did the grading. That was my introduction to the bright wonderful world of sex. I was devastated, so enraged, so ashamed . . . and . . . worst of all, so guilty about betraying Molly. And my view of myself as an attractive woman took a nosedive."

"Oh, Pam," said Bonnie shaking her head slowly. "No wonder you're in shock now."

"Wait, wait. You haven't heard the worst about this monster." Pam was revved up. Julius glanced around the room. Everyone was leaning forward, fixated on Pam, except of course Philip, whose eyes were closed and who looked as though he were in a trance.

"He and Molly were a couple for another two weeks and then he dropped her, just told her he was no longer having fun with her and was going to move on. That was it. Inhuman. Can you believe a teacher saying that to a young student? He refused to say any more or even help her move the things she had left at his flat. His parting gesture was to give her a list of the thirteen women he had screwed that month, many of them in the class. My name was at the top of the list."

"He didn't give her that list," Philip said, eyes still closed. "She found it when burglarizing his living space."

"What sort of depraved creature would even write such a list?" Pam shot back.

Again in a disembodied voice, Philip responded, "The male hardwiring directs men to spread their seed. He was neither the first nor the last to take an inventory of the fields he had plowed and planted."

Pam turned her palms up to the group, shook her head, and muttered, "You see," as if to indicate the bizarreness of this particular life-form. Ignoring Philip, she continued: "There was pain and destruction. Molly suffered tremendously, and it was a long long time before she trusted another man. And she *never* trusted me again. That was the end of our friendship. She *never* forgave my betrayal. It was a terrible loss for me and, I think, for her as well. We've tried to pick it up—even now we e-mail occasionally, keeping each other informed of major life events—but she's never, ever, been willing to discuss that summer with me."

After a long silence, perhaps the longest the group ever sat through, Julius spoke: "Pam, how awful to have been broken like that at eighteen. The fact that you never spoke of this to me or the group confirms the severity of the trauma. And to have lost a lifelong friend in that way! That's truly awful. But let me say something else. It's *good* you stayed today. It's good you talked about it. I know you're going to hate my saying this, but perhaps it's not a bad thing for you that Philip is here. Maybe there is some work, some healing that can be done. For both of you."

"You're right, Julius—I *do* hate your saying that, and, even more, I hate having to look at this insect again. And here he is in my own cozy group. I feel defiled."

Julius's head spun. Too many thoughts clamored for his attention. How much could Philip bear? Even *he* had to have a breaking point. How much longer before he would walk out of the room, never to return? And, as he imagined Philip's departure, he contemplated its consequences—on Philip but primarily on Pam: she mattered far more to him. Pam was a great-souled lady, and he was committed to helping her find a better future. Would she be well served by Philip's departure? Perhaps she'd have some measure of revenge—but what a pyrrhic victory! If I could find a way, Julius thought, to help Pam reach forgiveness for Philip, it would heal her—and perhaps Philip as well.

Julius almost flinched when the buzzword *forgiveness* passed through his mind. Of all the various recent movements swirling through the field of therapy, the hullabaloo around "forgiveness" annoyed him the most. He, like every experienced therapist, had *always* worked with patients who could not let things go, who nurtured grudges, who could find no peace—and he had *always* used a wide variety of methods to help his patients "forgive"—that is, detach from their anger and resentment. In fact, every experienced therapist had an arsenal of "letting-go" techniques they often used in therapy. But the simplistic and canny "forgiveness" industry had magnified, elevated, and marketed this one single aspect of therapy into the whole shebang and presented it as though it were something entirely novel. And the ploy had garnered respectability by implicitly melding with the current social and political forgiveness climate addressing a range of such offenses as genocide, slavery, and colonial exploitation. Even the Pope had recently begged forgiveness for the Crusaders' thirteenth-century sacking of Constantinople.

And if Philip bolted, how would *he,* as the group therapist, feel? Julius was resolved not to abandon Philip, yet it was difficult to locate any compassion toward him. Forty years before, as a young student, he had heard a lecture by Erich Fromm citing Terence's epigram written over two thousand years ago: "I am human, and nothing human is alien to me." Fromm had stressed that the good therapist had to be willing to enter into his own darkness and identify with all of the patient's fantasies and impulses. Julius tried that on. So, Philip had made a list of women he had laid? Hadn't he done that himself when he was younger? Sure he had. And so had many men with whom he'd discussed this matter.

And he reminded himself that he had a responsibility to Philip—and to Philip's future clients. He had invited Philip to become a patient and a student. Like it or not, Philip was going to be seeing many clients in the future, and to forsake him now was bad therapy, bad teaching, bad modeling—and immoral to boot.

With these considerations in mind, Julius pondered what to say. He began to formulate a statement beginning with his familiar, *I have a real dilemma: on the one hand . . . and on the other . . .* But this moment was too loaded for any stock tactics. Finally, he said, "Philip, in your responses to Pam today you referred to yourself in the third person: you didn't say 'I,' you said, 'he.' You said, '*He* didn't give her that list.' I wonder, could you have been implying that you're a different person now from the man you were then?"

Philip opened his eyes and faced Julius. A rare locking of gazes. Was there gratitude in that gaze?

"It's been known for a long time," Philip said, "that the cells of the body age, die, and are replaced at regular intervals. Until a few years ago it was thought that it was only the brain cells that persisted all of one's life—and, of course, in women, the ova. But research has now demonstrated that neural cells, too, die, and new neurons are continuously being generated, including the cells forming the architecture of my cerebral cortex, my mind. I think it can fairly be said that not one cell in me now existed in the man bearing my name fifteen years ago."

"So, Judge, it wasn't me," Tony snarled. "Honest. Ah ain't guilty; somebody else, some other brain cells, did the job before ah even got there."

"Hey, that's not fair, Tony," said Rebecca. "All of us want to support Pam, but there's got to be a better way than 'let's get Philip.' What do you want him to do?"

"Shit, for starters how about a simple 'I'm sorry.' " Tony turned to Philip. "How hard would that be? Would it break your cheeks to say that?"

"I got something to say to both of you," said Stuart. "You first, Philip. I keep current on the latest in brain research, and I want to say your facts about cell regeneration are off. There is some recent research showing that bone marrow stem cells transplanted in another individual can end up as neurons in some select areas of the brain, for example, the hippocampus and the Purkinje cells of the cerebellum, but there is *no* evidence of new neurons forming in the cerebral cortex."

"I stand corrected," said Philip. "I'd appreciate some literature references, please. Could you e-mail them?" Philip drew a card out of his wallet and handed it to Stuart, who pocketed the card without examining it.

"And, Tony," Stuart continued, "you know I'm not against you. I enjoy your no-bullshit directness and irreverence, but I agree with Rebecca: I think you're being too rough—and a little unreal. When I first joined the group you were doing weekend jail equivalent time on the highway cleanup patrols for a sexual assault charge."

"No, it was battery. The sexual assault charge was bullshit, and Lizzy dropped it. And the battery charge was phony, too. But your point?"

"My point was that I never heard *you* talk about being sorry, and no one here got on your case. In fact I saw the opposite—I saw lots of support. Hell, more than support; all the women, even you," Stuart turned to Pam, "got turned on by your . . . your what? Your lawlessness! I remember Pam and Bonnie dropping off sandwiches for you once when you were doing trash pickup duty on Highway 101. I remember Gill and me talking about not being able to compete with your . . . your . . . what was it?"

"Jungle nature," said Gill.

"Yeah." Tony smirked. "Jungle creature. Primitive man. That was pretty cool."

"So, how about giving Philip a break. Jungle man is okay for you but not for him. Let's hear his side of it. I feel awful about what Pam went through, but let's slow down, not rush to lynch. Fifteen years ago—that's a long time."

"Well," said Tony, "I'm not into fifteen years ago; I'm into now." Tony turned to Philip. "Like last week when you . . . Philip—damn, it's hard to talk when you won't make eye contact. Drives me fucking crazy! You claimed that it made no difference to you that Rebecca was interested in you—that she was uh . . . flirting . . . I can't remember that goddamned word."

"Preening!" said Bonnie.

Rebecca clutched her head in both hands. "I can't believe this; I cannot believe we're *still* talking about this. Isn't there a statute of limitations to the ghastly grisly crime of taking my hair down? How long is this going to go on?"

"As long as it takes," responded Tony, who turned back to Philip. "But what about my question, Philip? You put yourself forward as a monk, as someone beyond all this, too pure to be interested in women, even very attractive women . . ."

"Do you see now," Philip addressed Julius, not Tony, "why I was reluctant to enter the group?"

"You anticipated this?"

"It is a true and tested equation," replied Philip, "that the less I have to do with people, the happier I am. When I tried living *in* life, I was drawn into agitation. To stay out of life, to want nothing and to expect nothing, to keep myself engaged in elevated contemplative pursuits—that is the path, my only path, to peace."

"Well and good, Philip," responded Julius, "*but,* if you're going to be in a group or lead groups or try to help clients work on their relationships with others, you absolutely cannot avoid entering into relationships with them."

Julius noted Pam slowly shaking her head in bewilderment. "What's happening here? This is crazy-making. Philip here? Rebecca flirting with him? Philip leading groups, seeing clients? What's going on?"

"Fair enough; let's fill Pam in," said Julius.

"Stuart, that's your cue," said Bonnie.

"I'll give it a crack," said Stuart. "Well, in the two months you were away, Pam—"

Julius interrupted. "This time, why don't you just get us started, Stuart. It's unfair for us to ask you to do all the work."

"Right. But, you know, it's not work—I like to give overviews." Seeing Julius about to interrupt, he quickly said, "Okay, I'll just say one thing and stop. When you left, Pam, it was a downer to me. I felt we had failed you, that we were not good enough or resourceful enough to help you with your crisis. I didn't like that you had to turn elsewhere—to India—for help. Next."

Bonnie quickly said, "The giant issue here was Julius's announcement about his illness. You know all about this, Pam?"

"Yeah." Pam nodded gravely. "Julius told me when I phoned last weekend to tell him I was back."

"Actually," Gill said, "I want to amend that—no offense, Bonnie—but Julius didn't tell us. What happened was that we went out for coffee after Philip's first meeting, and *he* told us since Julius had told him in an individual meeting. Julius was pretty pissed at Philip's preempting him. Next."

"Philip's been here about five sessions. He's in training to be a therapist," said Rebecca, "and, as I understand it, Julius was his therapist many years ago."

Tony said, "We've been talking about Julius's . . . uh . . . condition and uh . . ."

"You mean *cancer*. That's a shocking word, I know," said Julius, "but it's best to look it in the face and say it."

"About Julius's *cancer*. You're one tough old bird, Julius—I gotta hand it to you." Tony went on, "So we talked about Julius's cancer and how hard it was to talk about other things that were small in comparison."

Everyone had spoken but Philip, who now said, "Julius, it would be okay if you were to tell the group about why I first came to see you."

"I'll help, Philip, but it would be better, when you're ready, to describe that yourself."

Philip nodded.

When it became clear that Philip was not going to continue, Stuart said, "Okay, back to me—a second round?"

Looking around at nodding heads, Stuart continued, "In one meeting Bonnie had some reactions to Rebecca's coming on to

Philip." Stuart stopped, looked at Rebecca, and inserted, "Rebecca's *allegedly* coming on to him. Bonnie did some work on her feelings about her self-image, her sense of being unattractive."

"And clumsiness and inability to compete with women like you, Pam, and Rebecca," said Bonnie.

Rebecca said, "While you were away Philip made a lot of constructive comments."

"But revealed nothing about himself," said Tony.

"One last thing: Gill had a serious confrontation with his wife—even considered walking out," said Stuart.

"Don't give me too much credit—I waffled. That resolve lasted about four hours," said Gill.

"A good review," said Julius, looking at his watch. "Before we quit, let me ask you, Pam, how are you handling this—you feel more on board?"

"Still unreal. I'm trying to hang in, but I'm glad to stop. This is all I can deal with today," said Pam, gathering up her things.

"I've got to say something," said Bonnie. "I'm frightened. You all know I love this group, and I feel it's ready to detonate and blow apart. Will we all be back? You, Pam? You, Philip? You guys coming back?"

"A straight question," Philip quickly responded. "I'll respond in kind. Julius invited me come to the group for six months, and I agreed. I also have his commitment for supervisory credit. I plan to pay my bill and honor my contract. I'm not leaving."

"And you, Pam?" said Bonnie.

Pam stood. "This is all I can deal with today."

As the members left, Julius heard some comments about going out for coffee. How would that work? he wondered. Would Philip be invited? He had often told the members that extragroup meetings could be divisive unless everyone was included. Then he noticed that Philip and Pam were heading toward the door on a collision trajectory. This should be interesting, he thought. Philip suddenly took note of it and, realizing that the doorway was too small for two, stopped and softly muttered "please" and stepped back to allow Pam to go through first. She strode out as if he were invisible.

Sex does not hesitate to intrude with its trash, and to interfere with the negotiations of statesmen and the investigations of the learned. Every day it destroys the most valuable relationships. Indeed it robs of all conscience those who were previously honorable and upright.

22

Women, Passion, Sex

After his mother, the next most pervasive female presence in Arthur's life was a querulous seamstress named Caroline Marquet. Few biographical accounts of Schopenhauer fail to spotlight their 1823 midday encounter, which took place on a dimly lit Berlin stairway outside Arthur's flat when he was thirty-five and Caroline forty-five.

On that day Caroline Marquet, living in the adjoining flat, entertained three friends. Irritated by the noisy chattering, Arthur flung open his door, accused the four women of violating his privacy since the anteroom where they stood talking was technically a part of his flat, and sternly ordered them to leave. When Caroline refused, Arthur physically forced her, kicking and screaming, from the anteroom and down the stairs. When she impertinently climbed back up the stairs in defiance, he again removed her, this time more forcefully.

Caroline sued him, claiming that she was pushed down the stairs and suffered grievous injury resulting in trembling and partial paralysis. Arthur was highly threatened by the lawsuit: he knew that he was unlikely ever to earn money from his scholarly pursuits and had always fiercely guarded the capital inherited from his father. When his money was imperiled he became, in the words of his publisher, "a chained dog."

Certain that Caroline Marquet was an opportunistic malingerer, he fought her lawsuit with all his might, employing every possible legal appeal. The bitter court proceedings continued for the next six years before the court ruled against him and ordered him to pay Caroline Marquet sixty talers a year for as long as her injury persisted. (In that era a house servant or cook would have been paid twenty talers annually plus food and board.) Arthur's prediction that she was shrewd enough to tremble as long as the money rolled in proved accurate; he continued to pay for her support until she died twenty-six years later. When he was sent a copy of her death certificate he scrawled across it: *"Obit anus, abit onus"* (the old woman dies, the burden is lifted).

And other women in Arthur's life? Arthur never married but was far from chaste: for the first half of his life he was highly sexually active, perhaps even sexually driven. When Anthime, his childhood friend from Le Havre, visited Hamburg during Arthur's apprenticeship, the two young men spent their evenings searching for amorous adventures, always with women from lower social strata—maids, actresses, chorus girls. If they were unsuccessful in their search, they ended their evening by consoling themselves in the arms of an "industrious whore."

Arthur, lacking in tact, charm, and joie de vivre, was an inept seducer and needed much advice from Anthime. His many rejections ultimately caused him to link sexual desire with humiliation. He hated being dominated by the sexual drive and in subsequent years had much to say about the degradation of sinking to animalistic life. It was not that Arthur didn't want women; he was clear about that: "I was very fond of them—if only they would have had me."

The saddest of love stories in the Schopenhauer chronicles took place when he was forty-three and attempted to court Flora Weiss, a beautiful seventeen-year-old girl. One evening at a boating party he approached Flora with a bunch of grapes and informed her of his attraction to her and his intention of speaking to her parents about marriage. Later, Flora's father was taken aback by Schopenhauer's proposal and responded, "But she is a mere child." Ultimately, he agreed to leave the decision to Flora. The business came to an end when Flora made it clear to all concerned that she vehemently disliked Schopenhauer.

Decades later, Flora Weiss's niece questioned her aunt about that encounter with the famous philosopher and, in her diary, quoted her aunt as saying, "Oh, leave me in peace about this old Schopenhauer." When pressed for more information, Flora Weiss described Arthur's gift of the grapes and said, "But I didn't want them, you see. I felt revolted because old Schopenhauer had touched them. And so I let them slide, quite gently, into the water behind me."

There is no evidence that Arthur ever had a love affair with a woman whom he respected. His sister, Adele, after receiving a letter in which Arthur reported "two love affairs without love," responded, in one of their few interchanges about his personal life, "May you not totally lose the ability to esteem a woman while dealing with the common and base ones of our sex and may Heaven one day lead you to a woman about whom you can feel something deeper than these infatuations."

At thirty-three Arthur entered into an intermittent ten-year liaison with a young Berlin chorus girl named Caroline Richter-Medon, who often carried on affairs with several men simultaneously. Arthur had no objections to that arrangement and said, "For a woman, limitation to one man during the short time of her flowering is an unnatural state. She is expected to save for one what he cannot use and what many others desire from her." He was opposed to monogamy for men as well: "Man at one time has too much and in the long run too little. . . . half their lives men are whoremongers, half cuckolds."

When Arthur moved from Berlin to Frankfurt, he offered to take Caroline with him but not her illegitimate son, whom he insisted was not his. Caroline refused to abandon her child, and after a short correspondence their relationship ended for good. Even so, Arthur, almost thirty years later, at the age of seventy-one, added a codicil to his will leaving Caroline Richter-Medon five thousand talers.

Though he often scorned women and the entire institution of matrimony, Arthur vacillated about marriage. He cautioned himself by reflecting, "All great poets were unhappily married and all great philosophers stayed unmarried: Democritus, Descartes, Plato, Spinoza, Leibniz, and Kant. The only exception was Socrates—and he had to pay for it, for his wife was the shrewish Xanthippe. . . . most men are tempted by the outward appearance of women, that hides their vices. They marry young and pay a high price when they get older for their wives become hysterical and stubborn."

As he aged he gradually relinquished the hope of marriage and gave up the idea completely in his mid-forties. To marry at a late age, he said, was comparable to a man traveling three-fourths of the journey by foot and then deciding to buy the costly ticket for the whole journey.

All of life's most fundamental issues come under Schopenhauer's bold philosophical scrutiny, and sexual passion, a topic avoided by his philosophic predecessors, was no exception.

He launched this discussion with an extraordinary statement about the power and omnipresence of the sexual drive.

> Next to the love of life it [sex] shows itself here as the strongest and most active of all motives, and incessantly lays claim to half the powers and thoughts of the younger portion of mankind. It is the ultimate goal of almost all human effort. It has an unfavorable influence on the most important affairs, interrupts every hour the most serious occupations, and sometimes perplexes for a while the greatest human minds. . . . Sex is really the invisible point of all action and conduct, and peeps up everywhere in spite of all the veils thrown over it. It is the cause of war and the aim and object of peace, . . . the inexhaustible source of wit, the key to all allusions, and the meaning of all mysterious hints, of all unspoken offers and all stolen glances; it is the meditation of the young and often the old as well, the hourly thought of the unchaste and, even against their will, the constantly recurring imagination of the chaste.

The ultimate goal of almost all human effort? The invisible point of all action and conduct? The cause of war and the aim and object of peace? Why so overstated? How much does he draw from his own personal sexual preoccupation? Or is his hyperbole simply a device to rivet the reader's attention on what is to follow?

> If we consider all this, we are induced to exclaim: why all the noise and fuss? Why all the urgency, uproar, anguish and exertion? It is merely a question of every Jack finding his Jill. Why should such a trifle play such an important role, and constantly introduce disturbance and confusion in the life of man?

Arthur's answer to his question anticipates by 150 years much of what is to follow in the fields of evolutionary psychology and psychoanalysis. He states that what is really guiding us is not *our* need but *the need of our species.* "The true end of the whole love story, though the parties concerned are unaware of it, is that a particular child may be begotten," he continues. "Therefore what here guides man is really an instinct directed to what is best in the species, whereas man himself imagines he is seeking merely a heightening of his own pleasure."

He discusses in great detail the principles governing the choice of sexual partner ("everyone loves what they lack") but repeatedly emphasizes that the choice is actually being made by the genius of the species. "The man is taken possession of by the spirit of the species, is now ruled by it, and no longer belongs to himself . . . for ultimately he seeks not his interests but that of a third person who has yet to come into existence."

Repeatedly, he emphasizes that the force of sex is irresistible. "For he is under the influence of an impulse akin to the instinct of insects, which compels him to pursue his purposes unconditionally, in spite of all the arguments of his faculty of reason. . . . He cannot give it up." And reason has little to do with it. Often the individual desires someone whom reason tells him to avoid, but the voice of reason is impotent against the force of sexual passion. He cites the Latin dramatist Terence: "What is not endowed with reason cannot possibly be ruled with reason."

It has often been noted that three major revolutions in thought have threatened the idea of human centrality. First, Copernicus demonstrated that Earth was not the center about which all celestial bodies revolved. Next, Darwin showed us that we were not central in the chain of life but, like all other creatures, had evolved from other life-forms. Third, Freud demonstrated that we are not masters in our own house—that much of our behavior is governed by forces outside of our consciousness. There is no doubt that Freud's unacknowledged co-revolutionary was Arthur Schopenhauer, who, long before Freud's birth, had posited that we are governed by deep biological forces and then delude ourselves into thinking that we consciously choose our activities.

If I maintain silence about my secret it is my prisoner; if I let it slip from my tongue, I am its prisoner. On the tree of silence hang the fruits of peace.

23

Bonnie's concern about the group proved unfounded: at the next meeting everyone was not only present but early—except for Philip, who strode in briskly and took his seat at exactly four-thirty.

A short silence at the beginning of a group therapy session is not unusual. Members learn quickly not to open the meeting capriciously because the first speaker is generally fated to receive much time and attention. But Philip, graceless as ever, did not wait. Avoiding eye contact, he began speaking in his unemotional, disembodied voice.

"The account given by our returning member last week—"

"Name of Pam," interrupted Tony.

Philip nodded without looking up. "Pam's description of my list was incomplete. It was more than a simple list of the women with whom I had sex that month; it contained not only names but phone numbers—"

Pam interrupted, "Oh. Phone numbers! Oh, well then, excuse me—that makes it all okay!"

Undeterred, Philip continued, "The list also contained a brief description of the lovemaking preferences of each woman."

"Lovemaking preferences?" asked Tony.

"Yes, what each woman preferred in the sexual act. Such as, likes it from the rear . . . sixty-nine . . . long foreplay required . . . begin with lengthy back massage . . . massage oil . . . gets off on spanking . . . breast sucking . . . likes handcuffs . . . tied to bedposts a big turn-on."

Julius winced. Good God! Where was Philip going—was he heading in the direction of revealing Pam's preferences? Big trouble ahead.

Before he could head Philip off, Pam shot out, "You are truly disgusting. Repulsive." Pam leaned forward as if preparing to rise from her chair and leave.

Bonnie put her hand on Pam's arm to detain her and said to Philip, "I'm with Pam on this one. Philip, are you crazy? Why on earth would you brag about those things?"

"Yeah," said Gill, "I just don't get you. Look, here you are under blistering attack—I mean I'm wincing for you, man. I could not face what you're facing. But what do you do? You throw gasoline on the fire and you say, *'Burn me some more.'* No offense, Philip, but, shit, how can you do that?"

"Yeah, that's what I see too," said Stuart. "If I were in your situation, I'd want to put myself in the best possible light—not give the enemy more ammunition."

Julius tried to soothe the waters. "Philip, what have you been feeling the last few minutes?"

"Well, I had something important to say about that list and I said it—so naturally I feel entirely satisfied with the course of events."

Julius persevered. In his most gentle voice, he said, "Several people responded to you, Philip. What are you feeling about that?"

"That's where I don't go, Julius. That way lies despair. Better, far better, for me to keep my own counsel."

Julius pulled out another device from his grab bag—that venerable but reliable strategy of conditional voice. "Philip, try a thought experiment. Philosophers do that everyday. I understand your wish to retain your equanimity, but humor me for a moment and try to imagine that *you were going to have feelings* about others' responses today. *What might they be?"*

Philip considered Julius's question, smiled slightly, and nodded his head, perhaps as a token of admiration for the ingenuity of Julius's ploy.

"An experiment? Fair enough. If I *were* to have had feelings, I would have felt frightened by the ferocity of Pam's interruption. I am not unaware that she wishes to do me grievous harm."

Pam started to interject, but Julius immediately signaled her to be silent and allow Philip to continue.

"Then Bonnie inquired about the point of my bragging, and then Gill and Stuart asked about why I was attempting to immolate myself."

"Immo what?" asked Tony.

Pam opened her mouth to respond, but Philip instantaneously said, "*Immolate*—to sacrifice oneself by fire."

"Okay, you're partway there," Julius persisted. "You've accurately described what happened—what Bonnie, Gill, and Stuart said. Now try to continue with the experiment—*if you were going to have feelings about their comments.*"

"Right, I've gotten off track. No doubt you would conclude my unconscious is making an appearance."

Julius nodded. "Go on, Philip."

"I would feel entirely misunderstood. I would say to Pam, 'I wasn't trying to make it okay.' To Bonnie, I'd say, 'Bragging was the last thing in my mind.' To Gill and Stuart, I'd say, 'Thank you for the warning, but I was not attempting to injure myself.' "

"Okay, now we know what you *weren't* doing. So tell us what you *were* doing? I'm bewildered," said Bonnie.

"I was simply setting the record straight. Following the dictates of reason. Nothing less, nothing more."

The group lapsed into that state of mind that always ensued from an interaction with Philip. He was so rational, so imperially above the strife of everyday discourse. Everyone looked down, bewildered, disoriented. Tony shook his head.

"I comprehend every point you made," said Julius, "except the last one—that last phrase—'nothing less, nothing more.' That I cannot buy. Why volunteer that particular aspect of the truth *now,* today, at this juncture, in your relationship with us? You were eager to do it. You couldn't wait. I could feel your pressure to get it out. Despite the obvious negative consequences pointed out by the group, you were determined to jump in immediately today. Let's try to figure out why. What was the payoff for you?"

"That's not hard," responded Philip. "I know exactly why I said it."

Silence. Everyone waited.

"I'm getting pissed," said Tony. "Philip, you've got us hanging; you do this all the time. Do we have to beg you for the next sentence?"

"Sorry?" asked Philip, his face in a puzzled scrunch.

"You've got us all waiting to hear why you said it," said Bonnie. "Are you being deliberately inscrutable here?"

"Perhaps you think we don't want to know, that we have no curiosity about what you're going to say," suggested Rebecca.

"It's none of these," said Philip. "It's got nothing to do with you. It just happens that my focus fades and I turn inward."

"This sounds important," said Julius. "I think there's a reason for that—and it involves your interactions with the group. If you truly believe that your behavior is capricious, something like rain that just happens, then you're assuming a helpless stance. There is a reason you periodically avoid us and turn inward: I think it's because some anxiety has welled up in you. In this instance your loss of focus had to do with how you opened the meeting. Can you pursue that?"

Philip was silent, pondering Julius's words.

Julius had his ways of ratcheting up the pressure when treating other therapists: "Another thing, Philip, if you're going to be seeing clients or leading a group in the future, losing focus and turning inward is going to be a real liability in your work."

That did the trick. Philip immediately said, "I chose to reveal what I did for self-protection. Pam knew everything about the list, and I was uncomfortable about her being able to drop that bomb at any time. Revealing it myself was the lesser of two evils." Philip hesitated, inhaled, then continued: "There's more to say. I still haven't addressed Bonnie's accusation of bragging. I kept that list because I had been extremely sexually active that year. My three-week relationship with Pam's friend Molly was unusual; I preferred one-night stands, though I occasionally went back for seconds when I felt particularly sexually pressured and couldn't meet someone new. When I saw the same woman a second time, I needed the notes to refresh my memory and make the woman feel I remembered her. If she knew the truth—that she was just one of many—I might not succeed. No braggadocio whatsoever in these notes. They were meant for my private use only. Molly had the key to my apartment, invaded my privacy, forced open a locked desk drawer, and stole the list."

"You telling us," asked Tony, wide-eyed, "you had sex with so many women you had to keep notes so you wouldn't mix them up? I mean, what are we talking about here? How many? How'd you pull this off?"

Julius groaned to himself. Things were complicated enough already without Tony's envy-laced question. The tension between Pam and Philip was already unbearably high. It needed defusing, but Julius wasn't sure how to do it. Unexpected help arrived from Rebecca, who suddenly altered the entire course of the meeting.

"I'm sorry to interrupt, but I need some time in the group today," she said. "I've been thinking all week about revealing something I've never told anyone, not even you, Julius. This is, I think, my darkest secret." Rebecca paused, looked around the group. All eyes were on her. "This okay?"

Julius turned to Pam and Philip. "How about you two? Are we leaving you with too many strong feelings?"

"Okay with me," said Pam. "I need some time out."

"And you, Philip?"

Philip nodded.

"More than okay with me," said Julius, "unless you want to mention first about why you've decided to reveal this today."

"No, it's better for me to plunge in while I still have the courage. Here goes: About fifteen years ago, about two weeks before my wedding, my company sent me to the Las Vegas computer expo to do a presentation on their new product. I had already handed in my resignation, and this presentation was to be my last assignment—I was thinking then that perhaps it might be the last one in my life. I was already two months pregnant, and Jack and I had planned a month-long honeymoon and then I was to turn to house and baby. This was long before law school—I had no idea whether I'd ever work again.

"Well, I fell into in a strange mood in Vegas. One evening, to my surprise, I found myself in the bar of Caesar's Palace. I ordered a drink and soon fell into an intimate conversation with a well-dressed man. He asked if I was a working girl. I was unfamiliar with that phrase and nodded yes. Before I could say more about my job he asked me my fee. I gulped, looked him over—he was cute—and said, 'One hundred fifty dollars.' He nodded and up we went to his room. And then the next night I moved to the Tropicana and did it again. Same fee. And my last night there I did a freebie."

Rebecca took a deep breath, exhaled loudly. "And that's it. I've never told anyone about this. Sometimes I've considered telling Jack but never did. What would have been the point? Nothing but grief for him and precious little absolution for me. . . . And . . . Tony, you bastard . . . goddamnit, that's not funny!"

Tony, who had taken his wallet out and was counting his money, stopped in his tracks and, with a sheepish smile, said, "Just wanted to lighten things up."

"I don't want it to be made light of. This is heavy stuff for me." Rebecca flashed one of her remarkable smiles, which she could conjure up at will. "There it is—true confessions." She turned to Stuart, who on more than one occasion had referred to her as a porcelain doll. "So, what do *you* think? Maybe Rebecca's not the dainty doll she appears to be."

Stuart said, "I wasn't thinking that. You know where I went as you spoke? I flashed on a movie I rented a few nights ago—*The Green Mile.* There was an unforgettable scene of a condemned prisoner eating his last meal. Sounds to me that in Las Vegas you treated yourself to one last piece of freedom before marriage."

Julius nodded and said, "I agree. Sounds much like something you and I talked about a long time ago, Rebecca." To the group Julius explained, "Several years ago Rebecca and I worked together for about a year when she was wrestling with the decision of getting married." Turning back to Rebecca, he said, "I remember we spent weeks talking about your fears of giving up your freedom, your sense of your possibilities closing. Like Stuart, I think that those were the concerns that got played out in Las Vegas."

"One thing sticks out in my mind from those hours together, Julius. I remember your telling me about a novel where someone seeks a wise man who tells him that *alternatives exclude,* that for every *yes* there has to be a *no.*"

"Hey, I know that book—John Gardner's *Grendel,*" interrupted Pam. "It was Grendel, the demon, who sought out the wise man."

"Endless interconnections here," said Julius. "Pam first introduced me to that novel when I was seeing her for a few months about the same time. So, Rebecca, if that comment was helpful, you owe thanks to Pam."

Rebecca flashed Pam a big thank-you smile. "You were giving me indirect therapy. I pasted a note with that phrase on my mirror: *Alternatives exclude.* It explained my block in saying yes to Jack even though I believed he was the right man." Then, to Julius: "I remember your saying that to grow old gracefully I had to accept the limiting of possibilities."

"Long before Gardner," Philip interjected, "Heidegger," he turned to Tony, "an important German philosopher in the first half of last century . . ."

"An important Nazi, too," Pam interjected.

Philip ignored Pam's comment. "Heidegger spoke of confronting the limiting of possibility. In fact he linked it to the fear of death. Death, he suggested, was the *impossibility of further possibility.*"

"Death as the *impossibility of further possibility,*" Julius repeated, "a powerful thought. Maybe I'll paste *that* on *my* mirror. Thanks, Philip. There're so many things to look at here, including your feelings, Pam, but first, one more comment to you, Rebecca. This episode in Las Vegas must have happened while you and I were meeting, and you never mentioned it to me. That tells me how much shame you must have felt."

Rebecca nodded. "Yep, I decided to deep-six the whole episode." After pausing and considering whether to say anything else, she added, "There's more, Julius. I was ashamed, but even more . . . this feels risky . . . I felt even more shame when I fantasized about it afterward: it was a fantastic high—not a sexual high, no that's not right, not *just* a sexual high, but the excitement of being outside the law, of being primitive. And you know," Rebecca turned toward Tony, "that's always been part of my attraction to you, Tony—your jail time, your bar fights, your flaunting of the rules. But just now you went over the top; that stunt of pulling out your money was offensive."

Before Tony could reply, Stuart jumped in. "You've got a lot of guts, Rebecca. I admire you. And you've liberated me to reveal something I've never talked about—not with Julius or my previous shrink, not with anyone." He hesitated, looked in the eyes of each member. "Just checking out the safety factor here. This is high-risk stuff. I feel safe with everyone here with the exception of you, Philip, because I don't know you well yet. I'm sure Julius has talked to you about group confidentiality?"

Silence.

"Philip, your silence jams me up. I'm asking you something," said Stuart, who turned and faced Philip more directly. "What's going on? Why don't you answer?"

Philip looked up. "I didn't know an answer was required."

"I said I was sure that Julius told you about confidentiality, and then I raised my voice at the end of the sentence. That connotes a question—right? And also, didn't the context about trust signify that I needed an answer from you?"

"I understand," said Philip. "Yes, Julius told me about confidentiality, and, yes, I made a commitment to honor all the group basic ground rules, including confidentiality."

"Good," said Stuart. "You know, Philip, I'm beginning to change my mind—I used to think of you as arrogant, but now I'm beginning to think that you're just not housebroken or people-broken. And that does not require an answer—it's optional."

"Hey, Stuart—good!" said Tony, smirking. "You're showing up, man. I like it."

Stuart nodded. "I didn't mean that negatively, Philip, but I've got a story to tell and I need to make sure it's entirely safe here. So," he took a deep breath, "let's go. About thirteen or fourteen years ago—it was when I was just finishing my residency and was about to enter practice—I went to a pediatrics convention in Jamaica. The purpose of such conventions is to keep up with the latest in medical research, but you know many physicians go for other reasons: to look for a practice opportunity or an academic job . . . or just to have a good time and get laid. I struck out on all counts, and then, to make things worse, my plane back to Miami was late and I missed my connection to California. I had to spend the night in the airport hotel and was in a miserable mood."

There was rapt attention from the group members—this was a new side of Stuart.

"I checked into the hotel around eleven-thirty at night, took the elevator up to the seventh floor—funny how clear the details are—and was walking down a long silent corridor to my room when suddenly a door opened and a distraught, disheveled woman in a nightgown stepped out into the hallway—attractive, great body, about ten or fifteen years older than me. She grabbed my arm—her breath reeked of alcohol—and asked whether I had just seen anyone in the hall.

"'No one, why?' I answered. Then she told me a long, rambling story about a delivery man who had just swindled her out of six thousand dollars. I suggested she call the front desk or the police, but she seemed strangely uninterested in taking any action. Then she motioned me to come into her room. We talked, and I tried to calm her about her belief—obviously a delusion—that she had been robbed. One thing led to another, and we soon ended up in bed. I asked several times whether she wanted me there, whether she wanted me to make love to her. She did, and we did, and an hour or two later while she was sleeping I went to my room, got a few hours' sleep, and caught an early morning flight. Just before I got on the plane I made an anonymous phone call to the hotel telling them that they had a guest in room seven-twelve who might need medical attention."

After a few moments of silence, Stuart added, "That's it."

"That's *it?*" asked Tony. "A well-soused, good-looking broad invites you into her hotel room, and you give her what she's asking for? Man, no way I'd pass that up."

"No, that's not *it!*" said Stuart. "*It* is that I was a physician and someone sick, someone probably with incipient or full-blown alcoholic hallucinosis, crossed my path, and I end up screwing her. That's a violation of the Hippocratic oath, a grievous offense, and I've never forgiven myself for it. I can't let go of that evening—it's seared into my mind."

"You're too hard on yourself, Stuart," said Bonnie. "This woman's lonely, in her cups, steps out in the hallway, sees an attractive younger man, and invites him into her bed. She got just what she wanted, maybe what she needed. Probably you did her a world of good. She probably considers that a lucky night."

Others—Gill, Rebecca, Pam—were poised to speak, but Stuart preempted them: "I appreciate what you guys are saying—I can't tell you how many times I've said similar things to myself—but I'm really, truly, not asking for reassurance. What I wanted to do is just tell you about it, take this sordid act out of so many years of darkness and into the light—that's enough."

Bonnie responded, "That's good. It's good you told us, Stuart, but this ties in with something we've talked about before: your reluctance to accept help from us. You're terrific about giving help, not so good at letting us help you."

"Maybe just doctor reflexes," replied Stuart. "I had no med school courses on being a patient."

"Don't you ever get to go off duty?" asked Tony. "I think you were off duty that night in the Miami hotel. Midnight with a tipsy, horny broad—go for it, man, get laid, enjoy yourself."

Stuart shook his head. "A while ago I listened to a tape of the Dalai Lama speaking to Buddhist teachers. One of them asked him about burnout and whether they shouldn't have some regularly scheduled off-duty time. The Dalai Lama's reply was priceless: Off duty? The Buddha says, 'Sorry, I'm off duty!' Jesus is approached by a sufferer and replies, 'Sorry, I'm off duty today!' The Dalai Lama giggles all the time, but he found this particular idea absolutely hilarious and couldn't stop laughing."

"I'm not buying it," said Tony. "I think you're using your M.D. to avoid life."

"What I did in that hotel was wrong. No one will ever convince me otherwise."

Julius said, "Fourteen years ago and you can't let it go. What about the repercussions of this incident?"

"You mean besides self-excoriation and disgust?" said Stuart.

Julius nodded.

"I can tell you that I've been a damn good doctor, that I've never, not for an instant, ever again violated the ethics of my profession."

"Stuart, I decree that you've paid your debt," said Julius. "Case closed."

"Amen," echoed several others.

Stuart smiled and crossed himself. "This takes me back to Sunday Mass during my childhood. I feel like I've just come out of the confession booth absolved."

"Let me tell you a story," said Julius. "Years ago in Shanghai I visited a deserted cathedral. I'm an atheist, but I like visiting religious places—go figure. Well, I walked around and then sat down in the confession booth, on the priest's side, and found myself envying the father confessor. What power he had! I tried to mouth the words, 'You are forgiven, my son, my daughter.' I imagined the supreme confidence he enjoyed because he believed himself a vessel carrying the cargo of forgiveness straight from the man upstairs. And how puny my own techniques seemed in comparison. But later, after leaving the church, I came out of it by reassuring myself that at least I was living according to principles of reason and not infantilizing my patients by representing mythology as reality."

After a short silence, Pam said to Julius, "You know what, Julius? Something's changed. You're different from the way you were before I left. Telling stories about your life, stating opinions on religious belief, whereas you always avoided such things in the past. I gather it's the effect of your illness, but, nonetheless, I like it. I really like your being more personal."

Julius nodded. "Thanks. That silence gave me a sinking feeling that I had offended some religious sensibilities here."

"Not mine, Julius, if you're worried about me," said Stuart. "Those polls that say that ninety percent of Americans believe in God leave me bewildered. I left the Church in my teens, and if I hadn't then, I would leave now after what's come out about priests and pedophilia."

"Nor mine," said Philip. "You and Schopenhauer have something in common regarding religion. He believed the church leaders exploited man's ineradicable need for the metaphysical and that they infantilized the public and dwelled themselves in a state of perpetual deception by refusing to confess they had deliberately cloaked their truths in allegory."

Philip's comment interested Julius, but, noticing that only a few minutes remained, he steered the group back to process. "A lot happened today. A lot of risks were taken. Feelings? Some of you have been very quiet—Pam? Philip?"

"It hasn't escaped me," Philip said quickly, "that what has been revealed here today, what has caused so much needless torment, for me, for others, flows from the supreme and universal power of sex, which my other therapist, Schopenhauer, taught me is absolutely inbuilt, or, as we would say today, hardwired into us.

"I know many of Schopenhauer's words about this since I've often cited them in lectures. Let me quote a few: '[Sex is] the strongest and most active of all motives. . . . It is the ultimate goal of almost all human effort. It . . . interrupts every hour the most serious occupations, and sometimes perplexes . . . the greatest human minds.' 'Sex does not hesitate to intrude with its trash, and to interfere with . . . the investigations of the learned—' "

"Philip, this is important stuff, but, before we stop today, try to speak about *your* feelings rather than Schopenhauer's," interrupted Julius.

"I'll try, but let me continue—just one more last sentence: 'Every day it destroys the most valuable relationships. Indeed it robs of all conscience those who were previously honorable and upright.' " Philip stopped. "That's what I wanted to say; I'm finished."

"Haven't heard feelings, Philip," said Tony, grinning at the opportunity to confront Philip.

Philip nodded. "Just dismay about how we poor mortals, we fellow sufferers, are such victims of biology that we fill our lives with guilt about natural acts as Stuart and Rebecca have done. And that we all have the goal of extricating ourselves from the thralldom of sex."

After a few moments of the customary silence following one of Philip's pronouncements, Stuart turned to Pam: "I'd sure like to hear from you today. What do you feel about what I've laid on the group? You were on my mind when I thought about confessing here. I've been thinking that I've put you in a tough place because in a way you can't forgive me without also forgiving Philip."

"I feel as much respect for you as ever, Stuart. And don't forget that I'm sensitized to this issue. I was exploited by a doctor—Earl, my ex-husband, was my gynecologist."

"Exactly," said Stuart. "That compounds it. "How can you forgive me without also forgiving both Philip and Earl?"

"Not true, Stuart. You're a moral person—after listening to you today and hearing of your remorse, I feel that way even more. And that incident in the Miami hotel doesn't grab me—ever read *Fear of Flying*?"

Seeing Stuart shake his head, Pam went on, "Take a look at the book. Erica Jong would call what you had a simple 'zipless fuck'; it was mutual, spontaneous coupling, you were kind, no one got hurt, you took responsibility to make sure she was okay afterward. And you've used the incident as a moral compass since then. But Philip? What can one say about a man who models himself after Heidegger and Schopenhauer? Of all philosophers who ever lived, those were the two who were the most abject failures as human beings. What Philip did was unforgivable, predatory, without remorse—"

Bonnie interrupted, "Hold on, Pam, did you notice that when Julius tried to stop Philip, he absolutely insisted on one more sentence about sex robbing the person of conscience and destroying relationships. I wonder, wasn't that something about remorse? And wasn't that directed to you?"

"He has something to say? Let him say it to me. I don't want to hear it from Schopenhauer."

"Let me butt in here," said Rebecca. "I left the last meeting feeling bad for you and for all of us, including Philip, who, let's face it, has been pissed on here. At home I starting thinking of Jesus's remark about how he who is without sin should cast the first stone—that's got a lot to do with what I revealed today."

"We've got to stop," said Julius, "but, Philip, this is exactly what I was fishing for when I asked you about your feelings."

Philip shook his head in puzzlement.

"Have you understood that today you were given a gift by both Rebecca and Stuart?"

Philip continued to shake his head. "I don't understand."

"That's your homework assignment, Philip. I want you to meditate on the gifts you were given today."

If we do not want to be a plaything in the hands of every rogue and the object of every fool's ridicule, the first rule is to be reserved and inaccessible.

24

Philip walked for hours after the meeting, past the Palace of Fine Arts, that decaying colonnade built for the 1915 International Exposition, circled the adjoining lake twice while watching the swans patrolling their territory, and then strolled along the marina and Crissy Field path by San Francisco Bay until he reached the base of the Golden Gate Bridge. What was it Julius instructed him to think about? He recalled the instruction to think about Stuart's and Rebecca's gift, but before he could focus his mind he had already forgotten his assignment. Again and again he swept his mind clear of all thought and tried to focus on soothing and archetypal images—the wake of swans, the pirouetting of Pacific waves under the Golden Gate—but he continued to feel oddly distracted.

He walked through the Presidio, the former military base located on the overlook of the mouth of the bay, and down to Clement Street with its twenty blocks of wall-to-wall Asian restaurants. He chose a modest Vietnamese pho shop, and when his beef-and-tendon soup arrived, he sat quietly for a few minutes, inhaling the lemongrass vapor rising from the broth and staring at the glistening mountain of rice noodles. After only a few mouthfuls he requested the rest be packaged for his dog.

Generally inattentive to food, Philip had routinized his eating habits: breakfast of toast, marmalade, and coffee, a main meal at noon at the school student cafeteria, and a small inexpensive evening repast of soup or salad. All meals, by choice, were taken alone. He took solace, indeed sometimes broke into a full smile, when he thought of Schopenhauer's habit of paying for two at his eating club to ensure that no one sat next to him.

He turned homeward to his one-bedroom cottage, as sparsely furnished as his office, situated on the grounds of a grand house in Pacific Heights, not far from Julius's. The widow, who lived alone in the house, rented the cottage to him for a modest sum. She needed the additional income, valued her privacy but wanted an unobtrusive human presence nearby. Philip was the man for the job, and they had lived in isolated proximity for several years.

The enthusiastic greeting of yelps, barks, tail wagging, and acrobatic leaps into the air offered by Rugby, his dog, usually cheered Philip, but not on this evening. Nor did his evening dog walk nor any of his other routine leisure activities bring Philip tranquillity. He lit his pipe, listened to Beethoven's Fourth Symphony, read distractedly from Schopenhauer and Epictetus. His full attention was caught once, for only a few moments, by one particular Epictetus passage.

> If you have an earnest desire towards philosophy, prepare yourself from the very first to have the multitude laugh and sneer. Remember, if you are persistent, those very persons will afterwards admire you. . . . Remember if you ever happen to turn your attentions to externals, for the pleasure of anyone, be assured that you have ruined your scheme of life.

Yet his sense of uneasiness remained—an uneasiness that he had not experienced in some time, a state of mind that in years past had sent him out like a sexually crazed beast on the prowl. He strode into his tiny kitchen, cleaned his breakfast dishes from the table, turned on his computer, and submitted to his only addictive vice: he logged on to the Internet chess club and played five-minute blitz games silently and anonymously for the next three hours. Mostly, he won. When he lost it was usually through carelessness, but his irritation was short-lived: immediately he typed in "seeking a game," and his eyes lit up with childish delight as a brand-new game commenced.

By the time I was thirty I was heartily sick and tired of having to regard as my equals creatures who were not really so at all. As long as a cat is young it plays with paper pellets because it regards these as alive and as something similar to itself. It has been the same for me with human bipeds.

25

Porcupines, Genius, and the Misanthropist's Guide to Human Relationships

The porcupine fable, one of the best-known passages in all of Schopenhauer's work, conveys his frosty view of human relationships.

> One cold winter's day a number of porcupines huddled together quite closely in order, through their mutual warmth, to prevent themselves from being frozen. But they soon felt the effects of their quills on one another, which made them again move apart. Now, when the need for warmth once again brought them together, the drawback of the quills was repeated so they were tossed between two evils, until they discovered the proper distance from which they could best tolerate one another. Thus the needs for society, which

> springs from the emptiness and monotony of men's lives, drives them together but their many unpleasant and repulsive qualities once more drive them apart.

In other words, tolerate closeness only when necessary for survival and avoid it whenever possible. Most contemporary psychotherapists would unhesitatingly recommend therapy for such extreme socially avoidant stances. In fact the bulk of psychotherapy practice is addressed to such problematic interpersonal stances—not only social avoidance but maladaptive social behavior in all its many colors and hues: autism, social avoidance, social phobia, schizoid personality, antisocial personality, narcissistic personality, inability to love, self-aggrandizement, self-effacement.

Would Schopenhauer agree? Did he consider his feelings toward other people as maladaptive? Hardly. His attitudes were so close to his core, so deeply ingrained that he never viewed them as a liability. On the contrary, he considered his misanthropy and his isolation a virtue. Note, for example the coda of his porcupine parable: "Yet whoever has a great deal of internal warmth of his own will prefer to keep away from society in order to avoid giving or receiving trouble and annoyance."

Schopenhauer believed that a man of internal strength or virtue will not require supplies of any kind from others; such a man is sufficient unto himself. This thesis, interlocked with his unwavering faith in his own genius, served as a lifelong rationalization for the avoidance of closeness. Schopenhauer often stated that his position in the "highest class of mankind" imposed the imperative not to squander his gifts in idle social intercourse but instead to turn them to the service of humanity. "My intellect," he wrote, "belonged not to me but to the world."

Many of Arthur's writings about his supreme intelligence are so flamboyant that one might consider him grandiose were it not for the fact that his assessment of his intellectual prowess was accurate. Once Arthur applied himself to being a scholar, his prodigious intellectual gifts became evident to all about him. The tutors who prepared him for the university were astounded at his precocious progress.

Goethe, the one man of the nineteenth century whom Arthur

considered his intellectual equal, eventually came to respect Arthur's mind. Goethe had pointedly ignored the young Arthur at Johanna's salons when Arthur was preparing for the university. Later, when Johanna asked him for a letter of support for Arthur's application to the university, Goethe remained masterfully noncommittal in his note to an old friend, a professor of Greek: "Young Schopenhauer seems to have changed his studies and occupations a few times. How much he has achieved and in what discipline, you will readily judge for yourself if, out of friendship for me, you will give him a moment of your time."

Several years later, however, Goethe read Arthur's doctoral dissertation and was so impressed with the twenty-six-year-old, that during Arthur's next stay at Weimar, he regularly sent his servant to fetch him for long private discussions. Goethe wanted someone to critique his much-labored work on the theory of colors. Though Schopenhauer knew nothing of this particular subject, Goethe reasoned that his rare innate intelligence would make him a worthy discussant. He got rather more than he bargained for.

Schopenhauer, greatly honored at first, basked in Goethe's affirmation and wrote his Berlin professor: "Your friend, our great Goethe, is well, serene, friendly: praised be his name for ever and ever." After several weeks, however, discord arose between them. Arthur opined that Goethe had made some interesting observations on vision but had erred on several vital points and had failed to produce a comprehensive theory of color. Dropping his own professional writings, Arthur then applied himself to developing his own theory of colors, differing in several crucial ways from Goethe, which he published in 1816. Schopenhauer's arrogance eventually corroded their friendship. In his journal Goethe described the ending of his relationship with Arthur Schopenhauer: "We discussed a good many things in agreement; eventually, however, a certain separation proved unavoidable, as when two friends, having walked together so far, shake hands, one wanting to go north and the other south, and very soon losing sight of one another."

Arthur was hurt and angry at being dismissed, but internalized Goethe's respect for his intelligence and continued for the rest of his life to honor Goethe's name and to cite his works.

Arthur had much to say about the difference between men of genius and men of talent. In addition to his comment that men of talent could hit a target that others could not reach, whereas men of genius could hit a target that others could not see, Arthur pointed out that men of talent are called into being by the needs of the age and are capable of satisfying these needs, but their works soon fade away and disappear during the next generation. (Was he thinking of his mother's works?) "But the genius lights on his age like a comet into the paths of the planets. . . . he cannot go hand in hand with the regular course of the culture: on the contrary he casts his works far out onto the path in front."

Thus, one aspect of the porcupine parable is that men of true worth, particularly men of genius, do not require warmth from others. But there is another, darker aspect to the porcupine parable: that our fellow creatures are unpleasant and repulsive and, hence, to be avoided. This misanthropic stance is to be found everywhere in Schopenhauer's writings, which are studded with scorn and sarcasm. Consider the beginning of this passage from his insightful essay "On the Doctrine of the Indestructibility of Our True Nature by Death": "If in daily intercourse we are asked by one of the many who would like to know everything but who will learn nothing, about continued existence after death, the most suitable and above all the most correct answer would be: 'After your death you will be what you were before your birth.'"

The essay continues with a penetrating and fascinating analysis of the impossibility of two kinds of nothingness and in its entirety offers insights to every human who has ever contemplated the nature of death. But why begin with a gratuitous insult—"one of the many who would like to know everything but who will learn nothing"?—Why contaminate sublime thoughts with petty invective? Such dissonant juxtaposition is commonplace in Schopenhauer's writings. How disquieting to encounter a thinker so gifted yet so socially challenged, so prescient yet so blinded.

Throughout his writings Schopenhauer laments any time spent in socializing and conversation. "It is better," he says, "not to speak at all than to carry on a conversation as sterile and dull as is the ordinary conversation with bipeds."

He lamented that he had sought all his life for a "true human being" but found none but "miserable wretches, of limited intelligence, bad heart, and mean disposition." (Except Goethe, whom he always explicitly exempted from such diatribes.)

In an autobiographical note he states, "Almost every contact with men is a contamination, a defilement. We have descended into a world populated with pitiable creatures to whom we do not belong. We should esteem and honor the few who are better; we are born to instruct the rest, not to associate with them."

If we sift through his writings, it is possible to construct a misanthropist's manifesto: the rules of human conduct by which we should live. Imagine how Arthur, adhering to this manifesto, might have fared in a contemporary therapy group!

- "Do not tell a friend what your enemy ought not to know."
- "Regard all personal affairs as secrets and remain complete strangers, even to our close friends. . . . with changed circumstances their knowledge of the most harmless things about us may be to our disadvantage."
- "Giving way neither to love nor to hate is one half of world wisdom: to say nothing and believe nothing, the other half."
- "Distrust is the mother of safety" (a French proverb, cited approvingly).
- "To forget at any time the bad traits of a man's character is like throwing away hard-earned money. We must protect ourselves from foolish familiarity and foolish friendship."
- "The only way to attain superiority in dealing with men is to let it be seen you are independent of them."
- "To disregard is to win regard."
- "If we really think highly of a person we should conceal it from him like a crime."
- "Better to let men be what they are than to take them for what they are not."
- "We must never show anger and hatred except in our actions. . . . it is only the cold-blooded animals that are poisonous."
- "By being polite and friendly, you can make people pliable and obliging: hence politeness is to human nature what warmth is to wax."

There are few ways by which you can make more certain of putting people into a good humor than by telling them of some trouble that has recently befallen you, or by disclosing some personal weakness of yours.

26

At the next meeting Gill plunked himself down, his huge frame testing the limits of his chair, waited until everyone arrived, and started the meeting. "If no one else has something, I want to continue with the 'secrets' exercise."

"Let me insert a cautionary note here," said Julius. "I don't think it's a good idea to make this a prescribed exercise. I *do* believe that folks do better in the group when they reveal themselves fully, but it's important to move at our own pace and not feel pressured by any exercise to open up."

"I hear you," answered Gill, "but I don't feel pressured. I *want* to talk about this, and I also don't want to leave Rebecca and Stuart hanging out there alone. That okay?"

After noting the nods in the group, Gill continued: "My secret goes back to when I was thirteen. I was a virgin, barely into puberty, covered with acne, and Aunt Valerie, my father's youngest sister . . . she was late twenties or early thirties . . . used to stay with us from time to time—she was between jobs a lot. We got along great, played around a lot when my folks were out—wrestling, tickling, card games. Then one time, when I cheated at strip poker and got her naked, things got real sexual—no longer tickling but some serious feeling up. I was inexperienced and hormone-hot and didn't know exactly what was going on, but when she said to 'stick it in,' I said 'yes, ma'am' and followed instructions. After that we did it anytime we could until a couple of months later when my folks came home early and caught us red-handed, flat out in the act—what's that called . . . flagrant . . . flagrant something?"

Gill looked toward Philip, who opened his mouth to answer but was preempted by Pam, who said with lightning speed, "Flagrante delicto."

"Wow, fast . . . I forgot we have *two* professors here," murmured Gill, who continued his account: "Well, the whole thing kind of messed up the family. My dad didn't get too hot under the collar about it, but my mother was livid and Aunt Val didn't stay with us anymore, and my mother was furious with Dad for continuing to be friendly to her."

Gill stopped, looked around, and then added, "I can understand why my mother was upset, but, still, it was as much my fault as Aunt Val's."

"*Your* fault—at thirteen? Come on!" said Bonnie. Others—Stuart, Tony, Rebecca—nodded in agreement.

Before Gill could respond, Pam said, "I've got a response, Gill. Maybe not what you're expecting but something I've been holding back, something I wanted to say to you even before I left on my trip. I don't know how to put it tactfully, Gill, so I'm not going to try—just going to cut loose. Bottom line is that your story doesn't move me one bit, and, in most ways, *you just don't move me.* Even though you say you're revealing yourself like Rebecca and Stuart did, I don't experience you as being *personal.*

"I know that you're committed to the group," Pam continued. "You seem to work hard, you take a lot of responsibility for taking care of others, and, if someone runs out, it's usually you that runs to get them back. You seem to reveal yourself, but you don't—it's an illusion—you stay hidden. Yes, that's what you are—hidden, hidden, hidden. Your story about your aunt is so typical of what I mean. It *seems* personal, but it's not. It's a trick because it's not *your* story, it's your Aunt Val's story, and *of course* everyone is going to jump in and say, 'But you were just a child, you were thirteen, you were the victim.' What else could they say? And your stories about your marriage have *always* been about Rose, never about you. And they always get exactly the same response from us, '*Why* do you put up with that shit!'

"When I was meditating in India—bored out of my gourd—I thought a lot about this group. You can't believe how much. And I thought about each person here. Except for you, Gill. I hate to say this, but *I just didn't think about you*. When you talk, I never know who you're talking to—maybe the walls, or the floor, but I never experience you as speaking *personally* to me."

Silence. The members seemed bewildered about how to respond. Then Tony whistled and said, "Welcome back, Pam."

"No sense of being here if I'm not going to be honest," said Pam.

"What are you feeling, Gill?" asked Julius.

"Oh, just my typical feeling when I get a drop-kick to my belly—spitting out a few pieces of pancreas. Is *that* personal enough, Pam? Wait, wait, sorry, don't answer. I didn't mean that. I know you're giving me good straight stuff. And deep down, I know you're right."

"Say more about that Gill, about her being right," said Julius.

"She's right. I could reveal more. I know that. I have things I could say to people here."

"To who, for example?" asked Bonnie.

"Well, *you*. I really like you, Bonnie."

"Nice to hear, Gill, but it's still not too personal."

"Well, I got off on you calling me a hunk a couple of weeks ago. And I don't buy into your labeling yourself homely and so out of Rebecca's beauty league—I've always had a thing—maybe ever since Aunt Val—about older women. And I'll be honest, I had some juicy fantasies when you invited me to stay at your place when I didn't want to go home to Rose."

"That why you didn't take Bonnie up on her offer?" asked Tony.

"Other stuff came up."

When it became clear Gill was not going to elaborate, Tony asked, "You want to say more about the other stuff?"

Gill sat for a moment, his bald pate glistening with sweat, and then mustered resolve and said, "Tell you what, let me go around the rest of the group and talk about my feelings." He began with Stuart, who sat next to Bonnie. "For you, Stuart, I got nothing but admiration. If I had kids, I'd feel lucky to have you as their doctor. And what you described last week doesn't change any of my feelings.

"And you, Rebecca, tell you the truth, you intimidate me—you seem too perfect, too pretty, too clean. What you told us about the incident in Las Vegas doesn't change that—to me you're still pristine and spotless with tons of confidence. Maybe it's because I'm flustered now, but I can't even remember why you're in therapy. Stuart's image of you being a porcelain doll—that rings true—maybe you're a little too brittle, maybe you got some sharp edges—I don't know.

"And, Pam, you're a straight shooter, blunt, smartest person I'd ever met until Philip entered—he can give you a run for it. I know I don't want to get on the wrong side of either of you. But, Pam, you've got stuff to work on with men. They've given you hard times, but then, again, you hate us. All of us. Hard to know what's chicken, what's egg.

"Philip, you're way up there, like, in another whole layer or . . . or realm of *being*. But I wonder about you. I wonder if you've ever had a friend—I can't see you actually hanging out, having a beer, talking about the Giants. I can't see you having a good time or actually ever *liking* anyone. And I'll tell you the real question for me: *why aren't you lonely?*"

Gill continued on, "Tony, you're fascinating to me, you work with your hands, you really do things, not push numbers around like me. I wish you weren't so ashamed of your work."

"Well, that's everybody."

"No, it's not," said Rebecca, glancing toward Julius.

"Oh, Julius? He's of the group, not in the group."

"What's '*of* the group' mean?" asked Rebecca.

"Oh, I don't know, just a cute phrase I heard and been wanting to use. Julius—he's just there for me, for everyone, he's far above us. The way he . . ."

"He?" asked Julius, pantomiming searching about the group. "Where is this 'he' guy?"

"Okay, I mean *you*, Julius, the way you're handling your illness—I mean it's impressive—I'll never forget it."

Gill stopped. Everyone's attention remained riveted upon him, but he exhaled with a loud "whoosh." He looked as though he had had it and settled back in his chair, obviously fatigued, and took out a handkerchief and wiped his face and head.

Sentiments such as "good job, you took some risks" were voiced by Rebecca, Stuart, Tony, and Bonnie. Pam and Philip remained silent.

"How was that, Gill? You satisfied?" asked Julius.

Gill nodded. "I broke some new ground. Hope I didn't offend."

"How about you, Pam? You satisfied?"

"I've already put in my time today as the group bitch."

"Gill, let me ask you to do something," said Julius. "Imagine a continuum of self-revealing. At one pole, which we'll call 'one,' is the safest revealing, cocktail party stuff; and at the other pole, call it 'ten,' would be the deepest and riskiest revealing you can possibly imagine. Got that?"

Gill nodded.

"Now look back on your go-round just now. Tell me, Gill, what kind of score would you give yourself?"

Continuing to nod, Gill answered swiftly, "I'd give myself a 'four,' maybe a 'five'."

Julius, wanting to circumvent intellectualization or other defenses from Gill's arsenal of resistance, responded instantly, "And now tell me, Gill, what would happen if you were to ratchet it up a notch or two?"

"If I were to ratchet up a notch or two," Gill replied without hesitation, "I'd tell the group I was an alcoholic and that I drink myself to unconsciousness every night."

The group was stunned, Julius no less than the others. Before he had brought Gill into the group, he had seen him in individual therapy for two years and *never,* not once, had Gill mentioned an alcohol problem. How could this be? Julius was congenitally trusting of his patients. He was one of those optimistic souls who was greatly destabilized by duplicity; he felt wobbly and needed time to formulate a new vision of Gill. As he mused silently about his own naïveté and the tenuousness of reality, the mood of the group darkened and progressed from incredulousness to stridency.

"What, you're joking!"

"I can't believe it. How could you have come here week after week and withhold this?"

"You never took a drink with me, not even a beer. What was *that* all about?"

"Goddamn it! When I think of all the wild-goose chases you led us on, all the time we wasted."

"What kind of game were you playing?—everything a lie—I mean that stuff about Rose's problems—her bitchiness, her refusing sex, her refusal to have a child, and not a word about the real issue—your drinking."

Once Julius got his bearings, he understood what to do. A basic axiom that he taught to his group therapy students was: *Members should never be punished for self-disclosure. On the contrary, risk taking must always be supported and reinforced.*

With that in mind, he said to the group: "I understand your dismay that Gill never told us this before. But let's not forget one important thing: *today Gill did open up, he did trust us.*" As he spoke, he glanced, only for a moment, at Philip, hoping that Philip would learn something about therapy from this transaction. Then to Gill: "What I'm wondering about is *what made it possible for you to take this kind of chance today?*"

Gill, too ashamed to face the others, concentrated his attention on Julius and replied in a chastened tone. "I guess it was the risky revealing in the last couple of meetings—beginning with Pam and Philip and then Rebecca and Stuart—I'm pretty sure that was why I could say—"

"How long?" interrupted Rebecca. "How long have you been an alcoholic?"

"Creeps up on you, you know, so I'm not sure. I always liked the booze, but I guess I started meeting all the criteria about five years ago."

"You're what kind of an alcoholic?" asked Tony.

"My favorite poison is Scotch, cabernet, and black Russians. But I don't turn down anything—vodka, gin—totally ambidextrous."

"What I meant was 'when' and 'how much,'" said Tony.

Gill showed no defensiveness and seemed prepared to answer any question. "Mostly after hours. I start with Scotches as soon as I get home (or before I get home if Rose is giving me a hard time), and then I work my way through good wine the rest of the evening—at least a bottle, sometimes two, until I pass out in front of the TV."

"Where's Rose on this?" asked Pam.

"Well, we used to be big wine buffs together, built a two-thousand-bottle cellar, went to auctions. But she's not encouraging my drinking now—now she rarely has a glass at dinner and wants no part of any wine-related activities, except for some of her big social wine-tasting events."

Julius tried again to buck the current and bring the group back to the here-and-now. "I'm trying to imagine how you must have felt coming to meeting after meeting here and *not* talking about this."

"It wasn't easy," Gill admitted, shaking his head.

Julius always taught students the difference between *vertical* and *horizontal* self-disclosure. The group was pressing, as expected, for *vertical* disclosure—details about the past, including such queries as the scope and duration of his drinking—whereas *horizontal* disclosure, that is, *disclosure about the disclosure,* was always far more productive.

This meeting was vintage stuff for teaching, Julius mused, and he reminded himself to remember the sequence of events for future lectures and writing. And then, with a thud, he recalled that the future had no relevance for him. Though the poisonous black wart had been carved out of his shoulder, he knew that somewhere in his body lethal colonies of melanoma remained, voracious cells that craved life more than his own fatigued cells. They were there, pulsating, gulping oxygen and nutrients, growing and gathering strength. And his dark thoughts were always there also, percolating under the membrane of consciousness. Thank God for his one method of stilling his terror: entering into life as forcefully as possible. The extraordinarily intense life being lived in this group was very good medicine for him.

He pressed Gill, "Say more about what passed through your mind during all those months of group meetings."

"What do you mean?" said Gill.

"Well, you said, 'It wasn't easy.' Say more about that, about those meetings and why it wasn't easy."

"I'd come here all primed but never could unload; something always stopped me."

"Dig into that—the *something* that stopped you." Julius rarely was so directive in the group, but he was convinced that he knew how to move the discussion in a beneficial direction that the group might not take on its own.

"I like this group," Gill said. "These are the most important people in my life. I've never been a real member of anything before. I was afraid I'd lose my place, lose any credibility—exactly like what's happening now. Right now. People hate drunks . . . the group will want to boot me out . . . you'll tell me to go to AA. The group will judge me, not help me."

That was exactly the cue Julius had been waiting for. He moved quickly.

"Gill, look around the room—tell me, who are the judges here?"

"Everyone's a judge."

"All identically? I doubt it. Try to discriminate. Look around the group. Who are the main judges?"

Gill kept his gaze on Julius. "Well, Tony can come down on you pretty hard, but no, not on this—he likes his booze, too. That what you want?"

Julius nodded encouragement.

"Bonnie?" Gill continued to speak directly to Julius. "No, she's no judge—except of herself and, once in a while, of Rebecca—she's always gentle with me. Stuart, well, he's one of the judges; he definitely has a self-righteous streak. Pretty goody-goody sometimes. And Rebecca, for sure—I hear a lot of directives: be like me, be sure, be thorough, be dressed right, be washed, be neat. That's why I felt released when Rebecca and Stuart showed so much vulnerability: that made it possible for me to open up. And Pam—she's *the* judge. Chief justice. No doubt about it. I know she thinks I'm weak, unfair to Rose, you name it, everything about me is wrong. I don't have much hope of pleasing her—in fact, I don't have *any* hope." He halted. "Guess that's it," he said, scanning the group. "Oh yes, Philip." He spoke to Philip directly, unlike the other members. "Let's see . . . I don't think of you judging me, but I'm not sure if that's entirely a compliment. It's more that you wouldn't get close enough or involved enough with me even to bother judging me."

Julius was well pleased. He had defused the nonconstructive moan of betrayal and the punitive grilling of Gill. It was a matter of timing; sooner or later the details of his alcoholism would be aired, but not at this moment and in this manner.

What's more, Julius's focus on horizontal disclosure had yielded a bonus—Gill's ten-minute gutsy go-round was a bonanza of data—enough there to fuel a couple of good sessions.

Turning to the group, Julius said, "Reactions anyone?"

There was hesitation—not, he imagined, because there was so little to say but too much. The agenda groaned with its own weight: the members had to have reactions to Gill's confession, to his alcoholism, and his sudden toughness in the last few minutes. He waited expectantly. Good stuff was on its way.

He noted that Philip was looking at him, and, for a moment, their gazes met—that was unusual. Perhaps, Julius thought, Philip was signaling his appreciation of the finesse with which he had conducted this meeting. Or perhaps Philip was pondering Gill's feedback to him. Julius decided to inquire and nodded at Philip. No response. So he said, "Philip, your feelings so far about this meeting?"

"I've been wondering whether you were going to participate."

"Participate?" Julius was astounded. "I've been wondering if I were too active, too directive today."

"I meant *participate in the sharing of secrets,*" said Philip.

Will the time ever come, Julius thought, when Philip will say something even vaguely predictable? "Philip, I'm not evading your question, but there are some pressing loose ends here." He turned to Gill: "I'm concerned about where you are now."

"I'm on overload. My only issue is whether you'll allow me to stay in the group as an alcoholic," said Gill, whose forehead glistened with perspiration.

"Sounds like this is the time you need us most. I wonder, though, if your bringing it up today indicates that you're gathering resolve to do something about it. Perhaps entering a recovery program?"

"Yep. After this meeting, I can't keep doing what I'm doing. I may need to call you for an individual session. Okay?"

"Of course—as many as you'll need." Julius's policy was to honor requests for individual sessions with the proviso that members share the details of those sessions at the following group meeting.

Julius turned back to Philip. "Back to your question. There's an old therapist trick which provides a graceful evasion of embarrassing questions, and that is to reply, 'I wonder, why are you asking that question?' Well, I am going to ask you that, but I'm *not* going to evade you. Instead I'll offer you a proposition: I promise to answer your question fully if you agree first to explore your motivations for asking it. Do we have a deal?"

Philip hesitated, then responded. "Fair enough. My motivation for the question is not complicated. I want to understand your approach to counseling and, if possible, integrate any parts that might improve my own counseling practice. I work very differently from you: I don't offer an emotional relationship—I'm not there to love my client. Instead I am an intellectual guide. I offer my clients instruction in thinking more clearly and living in accord with reason. Now, perhaps belatedly, I'm beginning to understand what you're aiming for—a Buber-like I-thou encounter . . ."

"Buber? Who?" asked Tony. "Hate to keep sounding like a jerk, but I'm damned if I'm going to sit here and not know what's going on."

"Right on, Tony," said Rebecca. "Every time you ask a question, you're doing it for me too. I don't know who Buber is."

Others nodded agreement. Stuart said, "I've heard the name—something about 'I-thou'—but that's it."

Pam jumped in: "Buber's a German Jewish philosopher, died about fifty years ago, whose work explores the true encounter between two beings—the 'I-thou,' fully present, caring relationship—as opposed to the 'I-it' encounter that neglects the 'I-ness' of the other and uses rather than relates. The idea has come up a lot here—what Philip did to me years ago was to use me as an it."

"Thanks, Pam, I got it," said Tony, and then turned to Philip. "Are we all on the same page?"

Philip looked at Tony in a quizzical manner.

"You don't know what *that* means?" said Tony. "Gotta get you a dictionary of twentieth-century talk. Don't you ever turn on your TV?"

"I don't have a TV," said Philip in an even, nondefensive tone. "But if you are asking, Tony, whether I agree with Pam's response about Buber, the answer is yes—I could not have said it as well."

Julius was fascinated: *Philip uttering Tony's and Pam's name? Philip complimenting Pam?* Were these merely evanescent events, or might they be heralding a momentous change? How much he loved being alive, Julius thought—alive in this group.

"You still got the floor, Philip. I interrupted you," said Tony.

Philip continued, "So I was saying to Julius . . . I mean, I was saying to you"—he turned to Julius—"right?"

"Right, Philip," Julius replied. "I think you're going to be a fast learner."

"So," Philip went on, speaking in the measured tone of a mathematician, "First proposition: you wish to have an I-thou encounter with each client. Second proposition: an I-thou consists of a fully reciprocal relationship—by definition it cannot be a unilateral intimacy. Third: in the last couple of meetings people here have revealed a lot about themselves. Hence my entirely justifiable question to you: are you not required to reciprocate?"

After a moment of silence Philip added, "So that's the conundrum. I intended only to observe how a counselor of your persuasion handles a client's request for parity."

"So, your motivation is primarily a test of whether I'll be consistent in my approach?"

"Yes, not a test of *you,* personally, but of your *method."*

"Okay, I appreciate your position that the question is in the service of your intellectual understanding. Now just one further query and then I'll proceed to answer you. Why now? Why ask *this particular question at this particular time?"*

"First time it was possible. That was the first slight break in the pace."

"I'm not convinced. I think there's more. Again, *why now*?" Julius repeated.

Philip shook his head in confusion. "This may not be what you're asking, but I've been thinking of a point Schopenhauer made to the effect that there are few things that put people in a better humor than to hear of another's misfortune. Schopenhauer cites a poem of Lucretius"—"first century B.C. Roman poet," Philip said in an aside to Tony—"in which one takes pleasure from standing on the seashore and watching others at sea struggle with a terrible storm. 'It is a joy for us,' he says, 'to observe evils from which we are free.' Is this not one of the powerful forces taking place in a therapy group?"

"That's interesting, Philip," said Julius. "But entirely off the point. Let's stay focused now on the question of '*why now?*'"

Philip still appeared confused.

"Let me help, Philip," Julius prodded. "I'm belaboring this for a reason—one which will provide a particularly clear illustration of the differences between our two approaches. I'd suggest that the answer to *'why now?'* is intimately related to your interpersonal issues. Let me illustrate: can you summarize your experience in the last couple of meetings?"

Silence. Philip appeared perplexed.

Tony said, "Seems pretty obvious to me, Professor."

Philip looked at Tony with raised eyebrows. "Obvious?"

"Well, if you want it spelled it out, here it is: you enter this group and make a lot of deep-sounding pronouncements. You pull some things out of your philosophy bag that we all dig. Some people here think you're pretty wise—like Rebecca and Bonnie, for example. And me, too. You supply all the answers. You're a counselor yourself, and it looks like you're competing some with Julius. Same page?"

Tony looked questioningly at Philip, who nodded slightly, indicating that he should continue.

"So here comes good ole Pam back, and what does she do? Pulls your cover! Turns out you've got a messy past. Real messy. You're not Mister Clean after all. In fact you really fucked Pam over. You're knocked off your pedestal. Now you *got* to be upset about this. And so what do you do? You come in here today and say to Julius: what's *your* secret life? You want to knock *him* off his pedestal, level the playing ground. Same page?"

Philip nodded slightly.

"That's the way I see it. Hell, what else could it be?"

Philip fixed his eyes on Tony and responded, "Your observations are not without merit." He turned and addressed Julius: "Perhaps I owe you an apology—Schopenhauer always warned against allowing our subjective experience to contaminate objective observation."

"And an apology to Pam? How about Pam?" asked Bonnie.

"Yes, I suppose. That too." Philip glanced fleetingly in her direction. Pam looked away.

When it became apparent that Pam had no intention of responding, Julius said, "I'll let Pam speak for herself at her own pace, Philip, but as for me—no apology is necessary. The very reason you're here is to understand what you say and why you say it. And as for Tony's observations—I think they're right on target."

"Philip, I want to ask you something," said Bonnie. "It's a question that Julius has asked me many times. 'How'd you feel after you left the meeting the last couple of sessions?'"

"Not good. Distracted. Even agitated."

"That's what I imagined. I could see that," said Bonnie. "Any thoughts about Julius's final comment to you last week—about being given a gift by Stuart and Rebecca?"

"I didn't think about that. I tried but just felt tense. Sometimes I fear that all the strife and clamor here is a destructive distraction taking me away from the pursuits I really value. All this focus on the past and on our desires for change in the future only makes us forget the fundamental fact that life is nothing but a present moment, which is forever vanishing. What is the point of all this turmoil, given the ultimate destination of everything?"

"I see what Tony means about you never having any fun. It's so bleak," said Bonnie.

"I call it realism."

"Well, go back to that bit about life being only a present moment," Bonnie insisted. "I'm just asking about the present moment—your present response to being given a gift. Also, I've got a question about our postgroup coffee sessions. You charged out pretty quickly after the last two meetings. Did you think you weren't invited? No, let me put it this way: what is your present moment feeling about a coffee session after this meeting?"

"No, I am unaccustomed to so much talking—I need to recover. At the end of this meeting I will be very glad to be through for the day."

Julius looked at his watch. "We've got to stop—we're running over. Philip, I won't forget my contract with you. You fulfilled your part. I'll honor mine next meeting."

We should set a limit to our wishes, curb our desires, and subdue our anger, always mindful of the fact that the individual can attain only an infinitely small share of the things that are worth having . . .

27

After the session the group gathered for about forty-five minutes at their usual Union Street coffee shop. Because Philip was not present, the group did not talk about him. Nor did they continue to discuss the issues raised in the meeting. Instead they listened with interest to Pam's lively description of her trip to India. Both Bonnie and Rebecca were intrigued by Vijay, her gorgeous, mysterious, cinnamon-scented train companion, and encouraged her to respond to his frequent e-mails. Gill was upbeat, thanked everyone for their support, and said that he was going to meet with Julius, get serious about abstinence, and begin AA. He thanked Pam for her good work with him.

"Go Pam," said Tony. "The tough-love lady strikes again."

Pam returned to her condo in the Berkeley Hills just above the university. She often congratulated herself for having the good sense to hold on to this property when she married Earl. Perhaps, unconsciously, she knew she might need it again. She loved the blond wood in every room, her Tibetan scatter rugs, and the warm sunlight streaming into the living room in the late afternoon. Sipping a glass of Prosecco, she sat on her deck and watched the sun sink behind San Francisco.

Thoughts about the group swirled in her mind. She thought about Tony doffing the costume of the group jerk and, with surgical precision, showing Philip how clueless he was about his own behavior. That was priceless. She wished she had it on tape. Tony was an uncut gem—bit by bit, more of his real sparkle was becoming visible. And his comment about her dispensing "tough love"? Did he or anyone else sense how much the "tough" outweighed the "love" in her response to Gill? Unloading on Gill was a great pleasure, only slightly diminished by its having been helpful to him. "Chief justice," he had called her. Well, at least he had the guts to say that—but then he tried to undo it by unctuously complimenting her.

She recalled her first sight of Gill—how she was momentarily attracted to his physical presence, those muscles bulging out of his vest and jacket, and how quickly he had disappointed her by his pusillanimous contortions to please everyone and his whining, his endless whining, about Rose—his frigid, strong-willed, ninety-five-pound Rose—who had the good sense, it now turns out, not to be impregnated by a drunk.

After only a few meetings Gill had assumed his place in the long line of male losers in her life, beginning with her father, who wasted his law degree because he couldn't stand the competitive life of an attorney and settled for a safe civil service position of teaching secretaries how to write business letters and then lacked the fortitude to fight the pneumonia that killed him before he could start drawing his pension. Behind him in line there was Aaron, her acne-faced high school gutless boyfriend who passed up Swarthmore to live at home and commute to the University of Maryland, the school nearest home; and Vladimir, who wanted to marry her even though he had never gotten tenure and would be a journeyman English composition lecturer forever; and Earl, her soon-to-be ex, who was phony all the way from his Grecian Formula hair dye to his Cliff Note mastery of the classics and whose stable of women patients, including herself, offered easy pickings; and John, who was too much of a coward to leave a dead marriage and join her. And the latest addition, Vijay? Well, Bonnie and Rebecca could have him! She couldn't rouse much enthusiasm for a man who would need an all-day equanimity retreat to recover from the stress of ordering breakfast.

But these thoughts about all the others were incidental. The person who compelled her attention was Philip, that pompous Schopenhauer clone, that dolt sitting there, mouthing absurdities, pretending to be human.

After dinner Pam strolled to her bookshelves and examined her Schopenhauer section. For a time she had been a philosophy major and had planned a dissertation on Schopenhauer's influence on Becket and Gide. She had loved Schopenhauer's prose—the best stylist of any philosopher, save Nietzsche. And she had admired his intellect, his range, and his courage to challenge all supernatural beliefs, but the more she learned about Schopenhauer the person, the more revulsion she had felt. She opened an old volume of his complete essays from her bookshelf and began reading aloud some of her highlighted passages in his essay titled "Our Relation to Others."

- "The only way to attain superiority in dealing with men is to let it be seen you are independent of them."
- "To disregard is to win regard."
- "By being polite and friendly, you can make people pliable and obliging: hence politeness is to human nature what warmth is to wax."

Now she remembered why she had hated Schopenhauer. And Philip a counselor? And Schopenhauer his model? And Julius teaching him? It was all beyond belief.

She reread the last aphorism: *"Politeness is to human nature what warmth is to wax."* Hmm, so he thinks he can work me like wax, undo what he did to my life with a gratuitous compliment on my comments about Buber, or allowing me to pass through a door first. Well, fuck him!

Later she tried to find peace by soaking in her Jacuzzi and playing a tape of Goenka's chanting, which often soothed her with its hypnotic lilting melody, its sudden stops and starts and changes of tempo and timbre. She even tried Vipassana meditation for a few minutes, but she could not retrieve the equanimity it had once offered. Stepping out of the tub, she inspected herself in the mirror. She sucked in her abdomen, elevated her breasts, considered her profile, patted her pubic hair, crossed her legs in an alluring pose. Damn good for a woman of forty.

Images of her first view of Philip fifteen years ago swiveled into her mind. Sitting on his desk, casually handing out the class syllabus to students entering the room, flashing a big smile her way. He was a dashing man then, gorgeous, intelligent, otherworldly, impervious to distractions. What the fuck happened to *that* man? And that sex, that force, doing what he wanted, ripping off my underwear, smothering me with his body. Don't kid yourself, Pam—you loved it. A scholar with a fabulous grasp of Western intellectual history, and a great teacher, too, perhaps the best she ever had. That's why she first thought of a major in philosophy. But these were things he was never going to know.

After she was done with all these distracting and unsettling angry thoughts, her mind turned to a softer, sadder realm: Julius's dying. There was a man to be loved. Dying, but business as usual. How does he do it? How does he keep his focus? How does Julius keep caring? And Philip, that prick, challenging him to reveal himself. And Julius's patience with him, and his attempts to teach Philip. Doesn't Julius see he is an empty vessel?

She entertained a fantasy of nursing Julius as he grew weaker; she'd bring in his meals, wash him with a warm towel, powder him, change his sheets, and crawl into his bed and hold him through the night. There's something surreal about the group now—all these little dramas being played out against the darkening horizon of Julius's end. How unfair that he should be the one who is dying. A surge of anger rose within—but at whom could she direct it?

As Pam turned off her bedside reading light and waited for her sleeping pill to kick in, she took note of the one advantage to the new tumult in her life: the obsession with John, which had vanished during her Vipassana training and returned immediately after leaving India, was gone again—perhaps for good.

No rose without a thorn. But many a thorn without a rose.

28

Pessimism as a Way of Life

Schopenhauer's major work, *The World as Will and Representation,* written during his twenties, was published in 1818, and a second supplementary volume in 1844. It is a work of astonishing breadth and depth, offering penetrating observations about logic, ethics, epistemology, perception, science, mathematics, beauty, art, poetry, music, the need for metaphysics, and man's relationship to others and to himself. The human condition is presented in all its bleakest aspects: death, isolation, the meaninglessness of life, and the suffering inherent in existence. Many scholars believe that, with the single exception of Plato, there are more good ideas in Schopenhauer's work than in that of any other philosopher.

Schopenhauer frequently expressed the wish, and the expectation, that he would always be remembered for this grand opus. Late in life he published his other significant work, a two-volume set of philosophical essays and aphorisms, whose book title, *Parerga and Paralipomena,* means (in translation from the Greek) "leftover and complementary works."

Psychotherapy had not yet been born during Arthur's lifetime, yet there is much in his writing that is germane to therapy. His major work began with a critique and extension of Kant, who revolutionized philosophy through his insight that we constitute rather than perceive reality. Kant realized that all of our sense data are filtered through our neural apparatus and reassembled therein to provide us with a picture that we call reality but which in fact is only a chimera, a fiction that emerges from our conceptualizing and categorizing mind. Indeed, even cause and effect, sequence, quantity, space, and time are conceptualizations, constructs, not entities "out there" in nature.

Furthermore, we cannot "see" past our processed version of what's out there; we have no way of knowing what is "really" there—that is, the entity that exists prior to our perceptual and intellectual processing. That primary entity, which Kant called *Ding an sich* (the thing in itself), will and must remain forever unknowable to us.

Though Schopenhauer agreed that we can never know the "thing in itself," he believed we can get closer to it than Kant had thought. In his opinion, Kant had overlooked a major source of available information about the perceived (the phenomenal) world: *our own bodies*! Bodies are material objects. They exist in time and space. And each of us has an extraordinarily rich knowledge of our bodies—knowledge stemming *not* from our perceptual and conceptual apparatus but direct knowledge from inside, knowledge stemming from feelings.

From our bodies we gain knowledge that we cannot conceptualize and communicate because the greater part of our inner lives is unknown to us. It is repressed and not permitted to break into consciousness, because knowing our deeper natures (our cruelty, fear, envy, sexual lust, aggression, self-seeking) would cause us more disturbance than we could bear.

Sound familiar? Sound like that old Freudian stuff—the unconscious, primitive process, the id, repression, self-deception? Are these not the vital germs, the primordial origins, of the psychoanalytic endeavor? Keep in mind that Arthur's major work was published forty years before Freud's birth. When Freud (and Nietzsche as well) were schoolboys in the middle of the nineteenth century, Arthur Schopenhauer was Germany's most widely read philosopher.

How do we understand these unconscious forces? How do we

communicate them to others? Though they cannot be conceptualized, they can be experienced and, in Schopenhauer's opinion, conveyed directly, without words, through the arts. Hence he was to devote more attention to the arts, and particularly to music, than any other philosopher.

And sex? He left no doubt about his belief that sexual feelings played a crucial role in human behavior. Here, again, he was an intrepid pioneer: no prior philosopher had the insight (or the courage) to write about the seminal importance of sex to our internal life.

And religion? Schopenhauer was the first major philosopher to construct his thought upon an atheistic foundation. He explicitly and vehemently denied the supernatural, arguing instead that we live entirely in space and time and that all nonmaterial entities are false and unnecessary constructs. Though many others, Hobbes, Hume, even Kant, may have had agnostic leanings, none dared to be explicit about their nonbelief. For one thing, they were dependent for their livelihood upon the states and universities employing them and, hence, forbidden to express any antireligious sentiments. Arthur was never employed nor needed to be and was free to write as he wished. For precisely the same reason, Spinoza, a century and a half earlier, refused offers of exalted university positions, remaining instead a grinder of lenses.

And the conclusions that Schopenhauer reached from his inside knowledge of the body? That there is in us, and in all of nature, a relentless, insatiable, primal life force which he termed *will.* "Every place we look in life," he wrote, "we see striving that represents the kernel and 'in-itself' of everything." What is suffering? It is "hindrance to this striving by an obstacle placed in the path between the will and its goal." What is happiness, well-being? It is "attainment of the goal."

We want, we want, we want, we want. There are ten needs waiting in the wings of the unconscious for every one that reaches awareness. The will drives us relentlessly because, once a need is satisfied, it is soon replaced by another need and another and another throughout our life.

Schopenhauer sometimes invokes the myth of the wheel of Ixion or the myth of Tantalus to describe the dilemma of human existence. Ixion was a king who was disloyal to Zeus and punished by being bound to a fiery wheel which revolved in perpetuity. Tantalus, who dared to defy Zeus, was punished for his hubris by being eternally tempted but never satisfied. Human life, Schopenhauer thought, eternally revolves around an axle of need followed by satiation. Are we contented by the satiation? Alas, only briefly. Almost immediately boredom sets in, and once again we are propelled into motion, this time to escape from the terrors of boredom.

> Work, worry, toil and trouble are certainly the lot of almost all throughout their lives. But if all desires were fulfilled as soon as they arose, how then would people occupy their lives and spend their time? Suppose the human race were removed to Utopia where everything grew automatically and pigeons flew about ready-roasted; where everyone at once found his sweetheart and had no difficulty in keeping her; then people would die of boredom or hang themselves; or else they would fight, throttle, and murder one another and so cause themselves more suffering than is now laid upon them by nature.

And what is the most terrible thing about boredom? Why do we rush to dispel it? Because it is a distraction-free state which soon enough reveals underlying unpalatable truths about existence—our insignificance, our meaningless existence, our inexorable progression toward deterioration and death.

Hence, what is human life other than an endless cycle of wanting, satisfaction, boredom, and then wanting again? Is that true for all life-forms? Worse for humans, says Schopenhauer, because as intelligence increases, so does the intensity of suffering.

So is anyone ever happy? Can anyone ever be happy? Arthur does not think so.

> In the first place a man never is happy but spends his whole life in striving after something which he thinks will make him so; he seldom attains his goal and, when he does it is

> only to be disappointed: he is mostly shipwrecked in the end, and comes into harbor with masts and riggings gone. And then it is all one whether he has been happy or miserable; for his life was never anything more than a present moment, always vanishing; and now it is over.

Life, consisting of an inevitable tragic downward slope, is not only brutal but entirely capricious.

> We are like lambs playing in the field, while the butcher eyes them and selects first one then another; for in our good days we do not know what calamity fate at this very moment has in store for us, sickness, persecution, impoverishment, mutilation, loss of sight, madness, and death.

Are Arthur Schopenhauer's pessimistic conclusions about the human condition so unbearable that he was plunged into despair? Or was it the other way around? Was it his unhappiness that caused him to conclude that human life was a sorry affair best not to have arisen in the first place? Aware of this conundrum, Arthur often reminded us (and himself) that emotion has the power to obscure and falsify knowledge; the whole world assumes a smiling aspect when we have reason to rejoice, and a dark and gloomy one when sorrow weighs upon us.

I have not written for the crowd. . . . I hand down my work to the thinking individuals who in the course of time will appear as rare exceptions. They will feel as I felt, or as a shipwrecked sailor feels on a desert island for whom the trace of a former fellow sufferer affords more consolation than do all the cockatoos and apes in the trees.

29

"I'd like to continue where we left off," said Julius, opening the next meeting. Speaking stiffly, as though from a prepared text, he rushed on, "Like most therapists I know, I'm pretty open about myself to close friends. It's not easy for me to come up with a revelation as raw and pristine and right out there on the edge as those some of you have shared recently. But there is an incident I've revealed only once in my life—and that was years ago to a very close friend."

Pam, sitting next to Julius, interrupted. Putting her hand on his arm, she said, "Whoa, whoa, Julius. *You don't need to do this.* You've been bullied into this by Philip, and now, after Tony exposed his bullshit motives, even Philip has apologized for requesting it. I, for one, don't want you to put yourself through this."

Others agreed, pointing out that Julius shared his feelings all the time in the group and that Philip's I-thou contract was a setup.

Gill added, "Things are getting blurred here. All of us are here for help. My life's a mess—you saw that last week. But so far as I know, Julius, *you're* not having problems with intimacy. So what's the point?"

"The other week," Rebecca said, in her clipped precise speech, "you said I revealed myself in order to give Philip a gift. That was partially correct—but not the whole truth: now I realize I also wanted to shield him from Pam's rage. However, that said, my point is . . . what *is* my point? My point is that confessing what I did in Las Vegas was good therapy for me—I'm relieved to have gotten it out. But you're here to help me, and it's not going to help me one bit for you to reveal yourself."

Julius was taken aback—such strong consensus was an oddity in this group. But he thought he knew what was happening. "I sense a lot of concern about my illness—a lot of taking care of me, not wanting to stress me. Right?"

"Maybe," said Pam, "but for me there's more—there's something in me that doesn't *want* you to divulge something dark from your past."

Julius noted others signaling agreement and said, to no one in particular: "What a paradox. Ever since I've been in this field I've heard an ongoing chorus of complaints from patients that therapists were too distant and shared too little of their personal lives. So here I am, on the brink of doing just that, and I'm greeted by a united front saying, 'We don't want to hear. Don't do this.' So what's going on?"

Silence.

"You want to see me as untarnished?" asked Julius.

No one responded. "We seem stuck, so I'll be ornery today and just continue and we'll see what happens. My story goes back ten years ago to the time of my wife's death. I had married Miriam, my high school sweetheart, while I was in medical school, and ten years ago she was killed in a car crash in Mexico. I was devastated. To tell the truth, I'm not sure I've ever recovered from the horror of that event. But to my surprise, my grief took a bizarre turn: I experienced a tremendous surge in sexual energy. At that time I didn't know that heightened sexuality is a common response to confrontation with death. Since then I've seen many people in grief become suffused with sexual energy. I've spoken with men who've had catastrophic coronaries and tell me that they groped female attendants while careening to the ER in an ambulance. In my grief, I grew obsessed by sex, needed it—a lot of it—and when our friends, both married and unmarried women, sought to comfort me, I exploited the situation and took sexual advantage of some of them, including a relative of Miriam's."

The group was still. Everyone was uneasy, avoided locking gazes; some listened to the shrill chirping of a finch sitting in the scarlet Japanese maple outside the window. From time to time over many years of leading groups Julius had wished he had a cotherapist. This was one of those times.

Finally, Tony forced some words out: "So, what happened to those friendships?"

"They drifted away, gradually evaporated. I saw some of the women over the years by chance, but none of us ever spoke of it. There was a lot of awkwardness. And a lot of shame."

"I'm sorry, Julius," said Pam, "and sorry about your wife—I never knew that—and of course about . . . about those . . . relationships."

"I don't know what to say to you, Julius," said Bonnie. "This feels really awkward."

"Say more about the awkwardness, Bonnie," said Julius, feeling burdened by the chore of being his own therapist in the group.

"Well, this is brand new. This is the first time you've ever laid yourself out like this in the group."

"Go on. Feelings?"

"I feel very tense. I think it's because this is so ambiguous. If one of us," she waved her arm around, "brings something painful to the group, we know what we should do—I mean we get right to work even though we may not know exactly how to do it. But with you, I don't know . . ."

"Right, what's not clear is *why* you're telling us," said Tony, leaning forward, eyes squinting under his bushy eyebrows. "Let me ask something I learned from you. It came up last week in fact. *Why now?* Is it because you made a bargain with Philip? Most folks here say no about that—that the bargain makes no sense. Or do you want help with feelings remaining from that incident? I mean, your reasons for sharing aren't clear. If you want my personal reactions, I got no problem with what you did. I'll tell you straight out, I feel the same way I felt about Stuart and Gill and Rebecca—I personally don't see the big deal about what you did. I could see myself doing that. You're lonely, sexed up, some broads ask to comfort you, you let them, and everybody has a good time. They probably got off on it too. I mean, we're talking about ladies as though they only get used or exploited. I get riled, really riled, by this picture of men begging for some scrap of sex which women, sitting on their thrones, may or may not decide to toss out as a favor. As though they don't get off too."

Tony turned his head at the sound of Pam slapping her head as she covered her face with her hands and noted that Rebecca, too, had her hands to her head. "Okay, okay, maybe I'll toss those last cards and just stick with the cards saying, *Why now?*"

"Good question, Tony. I appreciate your getting me started. A few minutes ago I was wishing I had a cotherapist here to help me, and then you come along and do the job. You're good at this. Therapy could have been a good career for you. Let's see. *Why now?* I've asked that question so many times, and yet this may be the first time I've had it come my way. First, I think you're all right-on when you say it's not because of my bargain with Philip. Yet I can't dismiss that entirely because there is something to his point about the I-thou relationship. To quote Philip, the idea is 'not without merit.'" Julius smiled at Philip but received no smile in return.

Julius continued, "What I mean is, there *is* some problem with the lack of reciprocity in the authentic therapy relationship—it's a knotty question. So addressing that problem is part of my reason for accepting Philip's challenge."

Julius wanted a response. He felt he had been speaking too long. He turned to Philip. "How do *you* feel about what I've said so far?"

Philip jerked his head around, startled at Julius's question. After a moment's deliberation he said, "It seems generally agreed here that I'm one of those who have chosen to reveal a great deal. That's inaccurate. Someone in the group revealed something about her experience with me, and I revealed what I did only in the service of historical accuracy."

"Want to tell me what's that got to do with anything?" asked Tony.

"Exactly," said Stuart. "Talk about accuracy, Philip! First, for the record, I'm not one who's thought you've revealed yourself. But, mainly I want to say your answer is nowhere near the mark. It has zero to do with Julius's question about your feelings."

Philip seemed to take no offense. "Right. Okay, back to Julius's question—I think I was confounded by his question because I *had* no feelings. There was nothing in what he said to warrant an emotional response."

"*That* at least is relevant," said Stuart. "Your earlier response came out of left field."

"I am so tired of your pseudodementia game here!" Pam, slapping her thigh in exasperation, spit out her words to Philip. "And I'm pissed at your refusing to give me a name! This referring to me as 'someone in the group' is insulting and imbecilic."

"By *pseudodementia* you imply I feign ignorance?" said Philip, avoiding Pam's glare.

"Glory be," said Bonnie, raising her arms, "A first. The two of you are acknowledging one another, actually speaking."

Pam ignored Bonnie's remark and continued speaking to Philip. "Pseudodementia is a compliment compared to its alternative. You say you can find nothing in Julius's remark warranting a response. How *can anyone* have no responses to Julius?" Pam's eyes blazed.

"For example?" asked Philip. "You obviously have something in mind for me to feel."

"Let's try *gratitude* for taking you and your thoughtless and insensitive question seriously. Let's try *respect* for keeping his I-thou promise to you. Or how about *sorrow* for what he went through in the past. Or *fascination* or even *identification* with his unruly sexual feelings. Or *admiration* for his willingness to work with you, with all of us, despite his cancer. And that's just for starters." Pam raised her voice: "How could you *not* have feelings?" Pam looked away from Philip, breaking off their contact.

Philip didn't answer. He sat still as a Buddha, leaning forward in his chair, gazing at the floor.

In the deep silence following Pam's outburst Julius wondered how best to continue. Often it was better to wait—one of his favorite therapy axioms was *"strike when the iron is cold!"*

Viewing therapy, as he so often did, as a sequence of emotion activation followed by integration, Julius reflected upon the abundance of emotional expression today. Perhaps too much. Time to move on to understanding and integration. Choosing an oblique route, he turned to Bonnie, "So, what about the *'glory be!'*"

"Reading my thoughts again, Julius? How do you do it? I was just thinking about that crack and regretting it. I'm afraid it came out wrong and sounded mocking. Did it?" She looked at Pam and then Philip.

"I didn't think so at the time," said Pam, "but yeah, looking back, there's some mocking there."

"Sorry," said Bonnie. "But this boiling caldron here, you and Philip sniping, all those carom shots—I just felt relieved by the directness. And you?" she turned to Philip. "You resent my comment?"

"Sorry." Philip continued looking down. "It didn't register. I was only aware of the glare in her eyes."

"Her?" said Tony.

"In Pam's eyes." He turned to Pam, his voice quavered for an instant, "in your eyes, Pam,"

"Okay, man," said Tony, "*now* we're rolling."

"Were you scared, Philip?" asked Gill. "It's not easy to be on the receiving end of *that,* is it?"

"No, I was entirely preoccupied in my search for some way of not allowing her glare, her words, her opinion to matter to me. I mean, Pam, *your* words, *your* opinion."

"Sounds like you and I have something in common, Philip," said Gill. "You're like me—we both have our problems with Pam."

Philip looked at Gill and nodded, perhaps a nod of gratitude, Julius thought. When it seemed clear that Philip was not going to offer more, Julius looked around the group to bring in other members. He never passed up an opportunity to widen the interaction network: with the faith of an evangelist he believed that the more members involved in the interaction, the more effective the group. He wanted to engage Pam—her outburst toward Philip was still ringing in the air. To that end, he addressed Gill and said, "Gill, you say it's not easy to be on the receiving end of Pam's comments . . . and last week you referred to Pam as the chief justice—can you say more?"

"Oh, it's just my stuff, I know, I'm not sure and I'm not a good judge of this, but—"

Julius interrupted, "Stop! Let's freeze the action right here. At this instant." He turned to Pam: "Look at what Gill just said. Is that related to your saying you don't or can't listen to him?"

"Exactly," said Pam. "Quintessential Gill. Look, Gill, here's what you just announced: *'Don't pay any attention to what I'm about to say. It's not important—I'm not important—it's just my stuff. Don't want to offend. Don't listen to me.'* Not only do you disqualify yourself, but it is vapid. Downright tedious. Christ, Gill! You got something to say? Just stand up and say it!"

"So, Gill," Julius asked, "*if you were going* to say it straight out without preamble, what would it be?" That good old conditional voice ploy.

"I'd say to her—to you, Pam—*you* are the judge I fear here. You sit in judgment of me. I'm uneasy—no, I'm downright terrified, in your presence."

"That's straight, Gill. *Now* I'm listening," said Pam.

"So, Pam," said Julius, "that's two men here—Philip and Gill—who express fear of you. Do you have some reaction to that?"

"Yep—a big reaction. *'That's their problem.'* "

"Any possibility that it's also your problem?" said Rebecca. "Maybe other men in your life have felt this too."

"I'll think about it."

"Feedback, anyone, about this last interchange?" asked Julius.

"I think Pam's being a little dodgy," said Stuart.

"I agree. I get the feeling that you're not going to think too hard about it, Pam," said Bonnie.

"Yep, you're dead right. I think I'm still smarting from Rebecca saying she wanted to protect Philip from my rage."

"It's a dilemma, isn't it, Pam?" said Julius. "As you just said to Gill, you value no-bullshit feedback. Yet when you get it, ouch, how it smarts."

"That's true—so maybe I'm not as tough as I appear. And, Rebecca, that did hurt."

Rebecca said, "I'm sorry, Pam; that wasn't my intention. Supporting Philip is not identical to attacking you."

Julius waited and wondered in which direction to guide the group. There were many possibilities. Pam's rage and judgmentalism were on the table. And what about the other men, Tony and Stuart? Where were they? And the competitiveness between Pam and Rebecca was still on the table. Or should the group deal with the unfinished business with Bonnie and her mocking statement? Or perhaps focus more on the outburst from Pam to Philip? He knew it was best to be patient; it would be a mistake to push too fast. After only a handful of meetings there had been definite progress toward détente. Maybe they had done enough today. Hard to gauge, though; Philip gave little away. But then, to Julius's surprise, the group took an entirely unanticipated direction.

"Julius," said Tony, "I been wondering. You okay with the response to what you revealed?"

"Well, we didn't get very far. Let me think about what happened. You told me how you felt and so did Pam, and then she and Philip got into it about his not having feelings about my revelation. And, Tony, I never really answered your question about 'why now.' Let me go back to that." Julius took time to gather his thoughts, keenly aware that his self-revelation, or that of any therapist, always had double implications: first, whatever he got out of it for himself and, second, the modeling that it set for the group.

"I can tell you that I was not about to be deterred from revealing what I did. I mean, almost everyone here tried to stop me, but I felt bullheaded, absolutely determined to continue. This is very unusual for me and I'm not sure I understand it fully, but there's something important there. You inquired, Tony, whether I was asking for help with it—or maybe asking for forgiveness. No, that wasn't it; long ago I forgave myself after spending years working on it with my friends and with a therapist. One thing I can tell you for sure: in the past, I mean before my melanoma, I would never, not in a thousand years, have said what I said in the group today.

"Before my melanoma," Julius continued. "That's the key. We've all got a death sentence—I know you all pay me well for such cheery pronouncements—but the experience of having it certified, stamped, and even dated has sure caught my attention. My melanoma is giving me a strange sense of release that's got a lot to do with my revealing myself today. Maybe that's why I've been yearning for a co-therapist—someone objective who can make sure that I continue acting in your best interests."

Julius stopped. Then, he added, "I noted that none of you responded earlier when I commented on how you were taking care of me today."

After a few more moments of silence, Julius added, "And you're still not. You see, this is why I miss having a co-therapist here. I've always believed that if there's something big that's not being talked about, then nothing else that's important can be worked on either. My job is to remove obstacles; the last thing I want is to *be* an obstacle. Now, it's hard for me to get outside myself, but I feel you're avoiding me, or let me put it this way, avoiding *my mortal illness.*"

Bonnie said, "I *want* to discuss what's happening to you; but I don't want to cause you pain."

Others agreed.

"Yep, now you've put your finger right on it. Now listen hard to what I'm going to say: there's only one way you can hurt me—*and that is to cut yourself off from me.* It's hard to talk to someone with a life-threatening illness—I know that. People have a tendency to tread gently; they don't know the right thing to say."

"That's right-on for me," said Tony. "I don't know what to say. But I'm going to try to stay with you."

"I sense that, Tony."

"Isn't it so," said Philip, "that people fear contact with the afflicted because they wish not to be confronted with the death that awaits each of them?"

Julius nodded. "That sounds important, Philip. Let's examine it here." If anyone but Philip had said this, Julius would have been sure to ask whether they were expressing their own feelings. However, at this stage, he wanted only to support Philip's appropriateness. He scanned the group, awaiting a response.

"Maybe," said Bonnie, "there's something to what Philip said because I've had a couple of recent nightmares of something trying to kill me, and then there was that nightmare I described—trying to catch that train which was falling apart."

"I know that under the surface I'm more fearful than usual," said Stuart. "One of my tennis chums is a dermatologist, and twice now in the last month I've asked him to check out one of my skin lesions. Melanoma is on my mind."

"Julius," said Pam, "you've been on my mind ever since you told me about your melanoma. There is something to what I'm being told about my being tough on men, but you're the main exception—you are the dearest man I've ever known. And yes, I *do* feel protective of you. I felt it when Philip put you on the spot. I thought—and still think—it was callous and insensitive of him. And the question of whether I'm more conscious of my own death—well, that may be there, but I'm not aware of it. I *can* tell you that I'm on the lookout for consolatory things I might say to you. Last night I read something interesting, a passage in Nabokov's memoir, *Speak, Memory,* which described life as a spark between two identical pools of darkness, the darkness before we were born and the darkness after we die. And how odd it is that we have so much concern about the latter and so little about the former. I somehow found this enormously reassuring and immediately tagged it to give to you."

"That's a gift, Pam. Thank you. That's an extraordinary thought. And it *is* a reassuring thought, though I'm not quite sure why. I'm more comfortable with that first pool, before birth—it seems friendlier—perhaps I imbue it with promise, the potential of things to come."

"That thought," said Philip, "was also reassuring to Schopenhauer, from whom, incidentally, Nabokov undoubtedly lifted it. Schopenhauer said that after death we will be what we were before our birth and then proceeded to prove the impossibility of there being more than one kind of nothingness."

Julius never had a chance to reply. Pam glared at Philip and barked a response: "Right here we have a perfect illustration of why your desire to be a counselor is a monstrous joke. We're in the midst of tender feelings, and what matters most, what *only* matters to you, is accuracy of attribution. You think Schopenhauer once said something vaguely similar. Big fucking deal!"

Philip closed his eyes and began reciting: "'A man finds himself, to his great astonishment, suddenly existing after thousands and thousands of years of non-existence; he lives for a little while; and then, again, comes an equally long period when he must exist no more.' I've committed a great deal of Schopenhauer to memory: third paragraph of his essay 'Additional Remarks on the Doctrine of the Vanity of Existence.' Is that vague enough for you?"

"Children, children, you two quit that," said Bonnie, in a high-pitched voice.

"You're getting loose, Bonnie. I like it," said Tony.

"Other feelings, anybody?" asked Julius.

"I don't want to get caught in *this* crossfire. Some big cannons being wheeled out," said Gill.

"Yeah," said Stuart, "neither of them can resist the opportunity for a jab. Philip's got to comment on someone else using Schopenhauer's phrase, and Pam can't resist the opportunity to call Philip a monstrous joke."

"I didn't say *he* was a monstrous joke. I said . . ."

"Get off it, Pam, you're nitpicking. You know what I meant." Stuart held his ground. "And anyway that blowup about Nabokov—that was out of line, Pam. You bad-mouth his hero, and then you praise someone else who borrows Schopenhauer's words. What's so wrong with Philip setting you straight? What's the big crime with his pointing out Schopenhauer's priority?"

"I gotta say something," said Tony. "As usual I don't know who these dudes are—at least not Nabo . . . Nobo?"

"Nabokov," said Pam, in the soft voice she reserved for Tony. "He's a great Russian writer. You may have heard of his novel *Lolita.*"

"Yeah, I saw that. Well, in this kind of talk I get into a vicious circle—not knowing makes me feel stupid, then I clam up, and then I feel more stupid. I've got to keep trying to break that pattern by speaking out." He turned to Julius: "So to answer your question about feelings, *that's* one feeling—stupid. Another is that for one instant, when he said, 'is that vague enough for you?' I got a glimpse of Philip's teeth—and they're sharp teeth, real sharp. And some other feelings toward Pam," Tony turned to face her. "Pam, you're my girl—I really dig you, but I'll tell you something: *I sure don't want to get on your bad side.*"

"I hear you," said Pam.

"And, and . . ." said Tony, "I forgot the most important thing I was going to say—that this whole argument has gotten us off the track. We were talking about how we might be protecting or avoiding you, Julius. Then with Pam and Philip we got off the topic quick. So aren't we avoiding you again?"

"You know, I don't feel that now. When we work as intimately as we're doing now, we never stay on a single trail. The stream of thought keeps overflowing into new channels. And, incidentally,"

Julius turned to Philip, "I use that term—*intimately*—quite deliberately. I think your anger—which we see breaking through here for the first time—is truly a sign of intimacy. I think you care enough about Pam to be angry at her."

Julius knew Philip would not answer on his own and nudged him. "Philip?"

Shaking his head, Philip replied, "I don't know how to assess your hypothesis. But there is something else I want to say. I confess that, like Pam, I also have been looking for comforting or at least relevant things to say to you. I have followed Schopenhauer's practice of ending each day reading from the works of Epictetus or from the Upanishads." Philip glanced in Tony's direction. "Epictetus was a Roman philosopher of the second century, and the Upanishads are an ancient sacred Hindu text. The other night I read a passage from Epictetus that I thought would be of value, and I've made copies of it. I've translated it loosely from the Latin into current vernacular." Philip reached into his briefcase, handed out copies to each member, and then, eyes closed, recited the passage from memory.

> When, on a sea voyage, the ship is brought to anchor, you go out to fetch water and gather a few roots and shells by the way. But you always need to keep your mind fixed on the ship, and constantly to look around, lest at any time the master of the ship call, and you must heed that call and cast away all those things, lest you be treated like the sheep that are bound and thrown into the hold.
>
> So it is with human life also. And if there be available wife and children instead of shells and roots, nothing should hinder us from taking them. But if the master call, run to the ship, forsaking all those things, and without looking behind. And if thou be in old age, go not far from the ship at any time, lest the master should call, and thou be not ready.

Philip ended and held out his arms as though to say, "There it is."

The group studied the passage. They were bewildered. Stuart broke the silence, "I'm trying, but, Philip, I don't get it. What's the value of this for Julius? Or for us?"

Julius pointed to his watch. "Sorry to say we're out of time. But let me be teacherly and make one point. I often view a statement or act from two different points of view—from its *content* and from its *process*—and by *process* I mean *what it tells us about the nature of the relationship between the parties involved.* Like you, Stuart, I don't immediately understand the *content* of Philip's message: I've got to study it, and maybe the content can be a topic in another meeting. But I know something about the *process.* What I know, Philip, is that you, like Pam, were thinking about me, wanted to give me a gift, and you went to some lengths to do it: you memorized the passage and you made copies. And the meaning of that? It's got to reflect your caring about me. And what do I feel about it? I'm touched, I appreciate it, and I look forward to the time when you can express your caring in your own words."

Life can be compared to a piece of embroidered material of which, everyone in the first half of his time, comes to see the top side, but in the second half, the reverse side. The latter is not so beautiful, but is more instructive because it enables one to see how the threads are connected together.

30

When the group left, Julius watched them walk down his front stairs to the street. Rather than peel off singly to their parked cars, they continued in a clump, undoubtedly on their way to the coffee shop. Oh, how he would have liked to grab his windbreaker and go flying down the stairs to join them. But that was another day, another life, another pair of legs, he thought, as he crept down the hall heading toward his office computer to enter his notes on the meeting. Suddenly, he changed his mind, walked back into the group room, took out his pipe, and enjoyed the aroma of rich Turkish tobacco. He had no particular purpose other than simply to bask for a few minutes more in the embers of the group session.

This meeting, like the last three or four, had been riveting. His thoughts drifted back to the groups of breast cancer patients he had led so long ago. How often had those members described a golden period once they overcame the panic of realizing that they were truly going to die. Some said living with cancer had made them wiser, more self-realized, while others had reordered their priorities in life, grown stronger, learned to say no to activities they no longer valued and yes to things that really mattered—such as loving their family and friends, observing the beauty about them, savoring the changing seasons. But what a pity, so many had lamented, that it was only after their bodies were riddled with cancer that they had learned how to live.

These changes were so dramatic—indeed one patient had proclaimed, "Cancer cures psychoneurosis"—that on a couple of occasions Julius impishly described only the psychological changes to a class of students and then asked them to guess what kind of therapy was involved. How shocked students were to learn it was not therapy or medication but a confrontation with death that had made the difference. He owed a lot to those patients. What a model they were for him in his time of need. What a pity he couldn't tell them. Live right, he reminded himself, and have faith that good things will flow from you even if you never learn of them.

And how are you doing with your cancer? he asked himself. I know a lot about the panic phase which, thank God, I'm now coming out of even though there are still those 3 A.M. times when panic grips with a nameless terror that yields to no reasoning or rhetoric—it yields to nothing except Valium, the light of breaking dawn, or a soothing hot-tub soak.

But have I changed or grown wiser? he wondered. Had my golden period? Maybe I'm closer to my feelings—maybe that's growth. I think, no, *I know* I've become a better therapist—grown more sensitive ears. Yes, definitely I'm a different therapist. Before my melanoma I would never have said that I was in love with the group. I would never have dreamed of revealing such intimate details of my life—Miriam's death, my sexual opportunism. And my irresistible compulsion to confess to the group today—Julius shook his head in amazement—*that's* something to wonder about, he thought. I feel a push to go against the grain, against my training, my own teaching.

One thing for sure, they did *not* want to hear me. Talk about resistance! They wanted no part of my blemishes or my darkness. But, once I put it out, some interesting stuff emerged. Tony was something else! Acted like a skilled therapist—inquiring whether I was satisfied with the group's response, trying to normalize my behavior, pressing about "why now." Terrific stuff. I could almost imagine him leading the group after I'm gone—that would be something—a college drop-out therapist with jail time in his past. And others—Gill, Stuart, Pam—stepped up, took care of me, and kept the group focused. Jung had other things in mind when he said that only the wounded healer can truly heal, but maybe honing the patients' therapeutic skills is a good enough justification for therapists to reveal their wounds.

Julius moseyed down the hall to his office and continued thinking about the meeting. And Gill—did he show up today! Calling Pam "the chief justice" was terrific—and accurate. I have to help Pam integrate that feedback. Here's a case when Gill's vision is sharper than mine. For a long time I've liked Pam so much that I overlooked her pathology—maybe that's why I couldn't help her with her obsession about John.

Julius turned on his computer and opened a file titled, "Short Story Plots"—a file which contained the great unfulfilled project in his life: to be a real writer. He was a good, contributing professional writer (he had published two books and a hundred articles in the psychiatric literature), but Julius yearned to write literature and for decades had collected plots for short stories from his imagination and his practice. Though he had started several, he never found the time, nor the courage, to finish and submit a story for publication.

Scrolling down the lists of plots he clicked on "Victims confront their enemies" and read two of his ideas. The first confrontation took place on a posh ship cruising off the Turkish coast. A psychiatrist enters the ship's casino and there across the smoke-filled room sees an ex-patient, a con man who had once swindled him out of seventy-five thousand dollars. The second confrontation plot involved a female attorney who was assigned a pro bono case to defend an accused rapist. On her first jail interview with him she suspects he is the man who raped her ten years before.

He made a new entry: "In a therapy group a woman encounters a man who, many years before, had been her teacher and sexually exploited her." Not bad. Great potential for literature, Julius thought, though he knew it would never be written. There were ethical issues: he'd need permission from Pam and Philip. And he'd need, also, the passage of ten years, which he didn't have. But potential, too, for good therapy, thought Julius. He was certain that something positive could come of this—if only he could keep them both in the group and could bear the pain of opening up old wounds.

Julius picked up Philip's translation of the tale of the ship's passengers. He reread it several times, trying to understand its meaning or relevance. But still he ended up shaking his head. Philip offered it as comfort. But where was the comfort?

Even when there is no particular provocation, I always have an anxious concern that causes me to see and look for dangers when none exist; for me it magnifies to infinity the tiniest vexation and makes association with people most difficult.

31

How Arthur Lived

After obtaining his doctorate, Arthur lived in Berlin, briefly in Dresden, Munich, and Mannheim, and then, fleeing a cholera epidemic, settled, for the last thirty years of his life, in Frankfurt, which he never left aside from one-day excursions. He had no paid employment, lived in rented rooms, never had a home, hearth, wife, family, intimate friendships. He had no social circle, no close acquaintances, and no sense of community—in fact he was often the subject of local ridicule. Until the very last few years of his life he had no audience, readership, or income from his writings. Since he had so few relationships, his meager correspondence consisted primarily of business matters.

Despite his lack of friends, we nonetheless know more about his personal life than that of most philosophers because he was astonishingly personal in his philosophical writings. For example, in the opening paragraphs of the introduction to his major work, *The World as Will and Representation,* he strikes an unusually personal note for a philosophic treatise. His pure and clear prose makes it immediately evident that he desires to communicate personally with the reader. First he instructs the reader how to read his book, starting with a plea to read the book twice—and to do so with much patience. Next he urges the reader to first read his previous book, *On the Fourfold Root of Sufficient Reason,* which serves as an introduction to this book and assures the reader that he will feel much gratitude toward him for his advice. He then states that the reader will profit even more if he is familiar with the magnificent work of Kant and the divine Plato. He notes that he has, however, discovered grave errors in Kant, which he discusses in an appendix (which should also be read first), and lastly notes that those readers familiar with the Upanishads will be prepared best of all to comprehend his book. And, finally, he remarks (quite correctly) that the reader must be growing angry and impatient with his presumptuous, immodest, and time-consuming requests. How odd that this most personal of philosophic writers should have lived so impersonally.

In addition to personal references inserted into his work, Schopenhauer reveals much about himself in an autobiographical document with a title written in Greek, "Ειζεαυτον" (About Myself), a manuscript shrouded in mystery and controversy whose strange story goes like this:

Late in his life there gathered around Arthur a very small circle of enthusiasts, or "evangelists," whom he tolerated but neither respected nor liked. These acquaintances often heard him speak of "About Myself," an autobiographical journal in which he had been jotting observations about himself for the previous thirty years. Yet after his death something strange happened: "About Myself" was nowhere to be found. After searching in vain, Schopenhauer's followers confronted Wilhelm Gwinner, the executor of Schopenhauer's will, about the missing document. Gwinner informed them that "About Myself" no longer existed; as Schopenhauer had instructed him he had burned it immediately after his death.

Yet a short time later the same Wilhelm Gwinner wrote the first biography of Arthur Schopenhauer, and in it Schopenhauer's evangelists insisted they recognized sections of the "About Myself" document either in direct quotes or in paraphrase. Had Gwinner copied the manuscript before burning it? Or not burned it all and instead plundered it for use in his biography? Controversy swirled for decades, and ultimately another Schopenhauer scholar reconstituted the document from Gwinner's book and from other of Schopenhauer's writings and published the forty-seven-page "Ειζεαυτον" at the end of the four-volume *Nachlass* (Manuscript Remains). "About Myself" is an odd reading experience because each paragraph is followed by a description of its Byzantine provenance, often longer than the text itself.

Why was it that Arthur Schopenhauer never had a job? The story of Arthur's kamikaze strategy for obtaining a position at the university is another one of those quirky anecdotes included in every biographical account of Schopenhauer's life. In 1820, at the age of thirty-two, he was offered his first teaching job, a temporary, very low-salaried position (*Privatdozent*) to teach philosophy at the University of Berlin. What did he do but immediately and deliberately schedule his lecture course (titled "The Essence of the World") at the exact same hour as the course offered by Georg Wilhelm Hegel, the departmental chairman and the most renowned philosopher of the day?

Two hundred eager students crammed into Hegel's course, whereas only five came to hear Schopenhauer describe himself as an avenger who had come to liberate post-Kantian philosophy from the empty paradoxes and the corrupting and obscure language of contemporary philosophy. It was no secret that Schopenhauer's targets were Hegel and Hegel's predecessor, Fichte (remember, the philosopher who had begun life as a gooseherd and walked across all of Europe in order to meet Kant). Obviously, none of this endeared the young Schopenhauer to Hegel or to the other faculty members, and when no students at all materialized for Schopenhauer's course the following semester, his brief and reckless academic career was over: he never again gave a public lecture.

In his thirty years at Frankfurt until his death in 1860, Schopenhauer adhered to a regular daily schedule, almost as precise as Kant's daily routine. His day began with three hours of writing followed by an hour, sometimes two, of playing the flute. He swam daily in the cold Main River, rarely missing a day even in the midst of winter. He always lunched at the same club, the Englischer Hof, dressed in tails and white tie, a costume that was high fashion in his youth but conspicuously out of style in mid-nineteenth century Frankfurt. It was to his luncheon club that any curious person wanting to meet the odd and querulous philosopher would go.

Anecdotes about Schopenhauer at the Englischer Hof abound: his enormous appetite, often consuming food for two (when someone remarked upon this, he replied that he also thought for two), his paying for two lunches to ensure no one sat next to him, his gruff but penetrating conversation, his frequent outbursts of temper, his blacklist of individuals to whom he refused to speak, his tendency to discuss inappropriate shocking topics—for example, praising the new scientific discovery that allowed him to avoid venereal infection by dipping his penis after intercourse into a dilute solution of bleaching powder.

Though he enjoyed serious conversation, he rarely found dining companions he deemed worthy of his time. For some time, he regularly placed a gold piece on the table when he sat down and removed it when he left. One of the military officers that usually lunched at the same table once asked him about the purpose of this exercise. Schopenhauer replied that he would donate the gold piece for the poor the day that he heard officers have a serious conversation that did not entirely revolve around their horses, dogs, or women. During his meal he would address his poodle, Atman, as "You, Sir," and if Atman misbehaved he redressed him by calling him "You Human!"

Many anecdotes of his sharp wit are told. Once a diner asked him a question to which he simply responded, "I don't know." The young man commented, "Well, well, I thought you, a great sage, knew everything!" Schopenhauer replied, "No, knowledge is limited, only stupidity is unlimited!" A query to Schopenhauer from or about women or marriage elicited without fail an acerbic response. He was once forced to endure the company of a very talkative woman, who described in detail the misery of her marriage. He listened patiently, but when she asked if he understood her, he replied, "No, but I do understand your husband."

In another reported exchange he was asked if he would marry.

> "I have no intention to get married because it would only cause me worries."
>
> "And why would that would be the case?"
>
> "I would be jealous, because my wife would cheat on me."
>
> "Why are you so sure of that?"

"Because I would deserve it."
"Why is that?"
"Because I would have married."

He also had sharp words to say about physicians, once remarking that doctors have two different handwritings: a barely legible one for prescriptions and a clear and proper one for their bills.

A writer who visited the fifty-eight-year-old Schopenhauer at lunch in 1846 described him thus:

> Well built . . . invariably well dressed but an outmoded cut . . . medium height with short silvery hair . . . amused and exceedingly intelligent blue-flecked eyes . . . displayed an introverted and, when he spoke, almost baroque nature, whereby he daily supplied considerable material to the cheap satire of . . . the table company. Thus, this often comically disgruntled, but in fact harmless and good-naturedly gruff, table companion became the butt of the jokes of insignificant men who would regularly—though admittedly not ill-meaningly—make fun of him.

After lunch Schopenhauer habitually took a long walk, often carrying on an audible monologue or a conversation with his dog which elicited jeers from children. He spent evenings reading alone in his rooms, never receiving visitors. There is no evidence of romantic relationships during his years in Frankfurt, and in 1831, at the age of forty-three, he wrote in "About Myself," "The risk of living without work on a small income can be undertaken only in celibacy."

He never saw his mother after their break when he was thirty-one, but twelve years later, in 1831, they began to exchange a few business-related letters until her death in 1835. Once when he was ill, his mother wrote a rare personal comment: "Two months in your room without seeing a single person, that is not good, my son, and saddens me. A man cannot and should not isolate himself in that manner."

Occasional letters passed back and forth between Arthur and his sister, Adele, in which she again and again tried to move closer to her brother, all the while offering reassurances that she would never make demands on him. But he repeatedly backed away. Adele, who never married, lived in great despair. When he told her of moving from Berlin to escape cholera, she wrote back that she would have welcomed getting the cholera which would have put an end to her misery. But Arthur pulled away even further, absolutely refusing to be drawn into her life and her depression. After Arthur left home, they saw each other only once, in 1840, in a brief and unsatisfactory meeting, and Adele died nine years later.

Money was a continual source of concern throughout Schopenhauer's life. His mother left her small estate to Adele, and Adele died with virtually no remaining estate. He tried, in vain, to get a job as a translator, and until the very last years of his life his books neither sold nor were reviewed by the press.

In short, Arthur lived without any of the comforts or rewards that his culture held so necessary to equilibrium, even to survival. How did he do it? What price did he pay? These, as we shall see, were the secrets he confided to "About Myself."

The monuments, the ideas left behind by beings like me are my greatest pleasure in life. Without books I would long ago have been in despair.

32

Julius entered the group room the following week to an odd scene. The members, sprawled in their seats, were intently studying Philip's parable. Stuart had placed his copy on a clipboard and underlined as he read. Having forgotten his copy, Tony was reading over Pam's shoulder.

Rebecca, with a hint of exasperation in her voice, began the meeting: "I've read this with due diligence." She held up Philip's handout, then folded it and put it in her purse. "I've given it enough time, Philip, in fact, too much time, and now I'd like you to disclose the relevance of this text to me or the group or Julius."

"I think it would be a richer exercise if the class discussed it first," responded Philip.

"Class? That's what this feels like—a class assignment. Is this the way you do counseling, Philip?" she asked, snapping her purse shut. "Like a teacher in a classroom? This is not why I'm here; I came for treatment, not for adult education."

Philip took no note of Rebecca's huffiness. "At best there exists only a vague boundary between education and therapy. The Greeks—Socrates, Plato, Aristotle, the Stoics and Epicureans—all believed that education and reason were the tools needed to combat human suffering. Most philosophical counselors consider education to be the foundation of therapy. Almost all ascribe to Leibniz's motto, *Caritas sapientis* meaning 'wisdom and care.'" Philip turned toward Tony. "Leibniz was a German philosopher of the seventeenth century."

"I'm finding this tedious and presumptuous," said Pam. "Under the guise of helping Julius, you"— she raised her voice an octave— "Philip, I'm talking to you . . ." Philip, who had been tranquilly staring upward, jerked upright and turned toward Pam. "First, you pass out this sophomoric assignment and now try to control the group by coyly withholding your interpretation of the passage."

"Here you go once again trying to de-ball Philip," said Gill. "For God's sake, Pam, he's a philosopher and counselor. You don't need to be a rocket scientist to figure out that he'll try to contribute to the group by drawing from his own expertise. Why begrudge him everything?"

Pam opened her mouth to speak but closed it, seemingly at a loss for words. She stared at Gill, who added: "You asked for straight feedback, Pam. You got it. And no, I've not been drinking, if that's what you're thinking. I'm in my fourteenth day of sobriety—I've been meeting with Julius twice a week—he's turned on the heat, tightened the screws, and got me going to an AA meeting every day, seven days a week, fourteen meetings in fourteen days. I didn't mention it last week because I wasn't sure I could stick it out."

All the members, save Philip, reacted strongly with nods and congratulations. Bonnie told him she was proud of him. Even Pam managed a "good for you." Tony said, "Maybe I should join you." He pointed to his bruised cheek. "My boozing leads to bruising."

"Philip, how about you? You got a response to Gill?" asked Julius.

Philip shook his head. "He's already had a good bit of support from others. He's sober, speaking out, gaining strength. Sometimes more support is less."

"I like that motto of Leibniz you cited, *Caritas sapientis*—wisdom and care," said Julius. "But I urge you not to forget the *'caritas'* part. If Gill deserves support, *why should you always be last in line?* And, what's more, you've got unique information: who else but you can express *your* feelings about his coming to your defense and confronting Pam on your behalf?"

"Well said," responded Philip. "I have mixed feelings. I liked Gill's support, and at the same time I'm wary of liking it. Rely on others to do battle for you, and your own musculature will atrophy."

"Well, I'm going to reveal more of my ignorance," said Tony, pointing to the handout. "This boat story, Philip—I really don't understand it. You told us last week you were going to give Julius something comforting, and yet this story about a boat and passengers—I mean, to put it bluntly, I don't know what the fuck gives here."

"Don't apologize," said Bonnie. "I told you, Tony, that you almost always speak for me—I'm as confused as you are about this ship and gathering shells."

"Me too," said Stuart. "I don't get it."

"Let me help," said Pam. "After all, interpreting literature is how I earn a living. First step is to go from the concrete—that is, the ship, the shells, the sheep, and so on—to the abstract. In other words, ask yourself: what does this ship or voyage or harbor represent?"

"I think the ship stands for death—or the journey toward death," said Stuart, glancing at his clipboard.

"Okay," said Pam. "So, where do you go from there?"

"Seems to me," Stuart replied, "the main point is *don't pay so much attention to details on shore that you'll miss the boat's sailing.*"

"So," said Tony, "if you get too caught up in shore stuff—even having a wife and kids—then the boat might sail without you—in other words, you might miss your death. Big deal—is that such a catastrophe?"

"Yeah, yeah, you're right, Tony," said Rebecca, "I also understood the boat to be death, but when you put it that way I see it doesn't make sense."

"I don't get it either," said Gill, "but it doesn't say you'll miss death; it says you'll go to it trussed up like the sheep."

"Whatever," said Rebecca, "but this still doesn't feel like therapy." She turned to Julius, "This is supposed to be for you. Do you find any comfort in this?"

"I'll repeat what I said to you last week, Philip. What I get is the knowledge that you want to give me something to ease my ordeal. And also that you shy away from doing that directly. Instead, you choose a less personal approach. Sets a future agenda, I think, for you to work on expressing your caring in a more personal way.

"As for the content," Julius continued, "I'm confused also, but this is how I understand it: since the boat might sail at any time—that is, since death could call us at any point—we should avoid getting too attached to the things of the world. Perhaps it warns us that deep attachments would make dying more painful. Is this the message of consolation you're trying to give me, Philip?"

"I think," Pam interjected before Philip could answer, "that it falls into place better if you think of the ship and the journey not as representing death but what we might call the authentic life. In other words, we live more authentically if we keep focused on the fundamental fact of sheer being, the miracle of existence itself. If we focus on "being," then we won't get so caught up in the diversions of life, that is, the material objects on the island, that we lose sight of existence itself."

A brief silence. Heads turned toward Philip.

"Exactly," responded Philip with a hint of enthusiasm in his tone. "My view exactly. The idea is that one has to beware of losing oneself in life's distractions. Heidegger called it falling or being absorbed in the *everydayness* of life. Now, I know you can't abide Heidegger, Pam, but I don't believe his misguided politics should be permitted to deprive us of the gift of his philosophical insights. So, to paraphrase Heidegger, falling into *everydayness* results in one's becoming unfree—like the sheep.

"Like Pam," Philip continued, "I believe the parable warns us against attachment and urges us to stay attuned to the miracle of being—not to worry about *how* things are but to be in a state of wonderment *that things are*—that things exist at all."

"Now I think I'm getting your meaning," said Bonnie, "but it's cold, abstract. What comfort is there in that? For Julius, for anyone?"

"For me, there is comfort in the idea that my death informs my life." Philip spoke with uncharacteristic fervor as he continued, "There is comfort in the idea of not allowing my core being to be devoured by trivialities, by insignificant successes or failures, by what I possess, by concerns about popularity—who likes me, who doesn't. For me, there is comfort in the state of remaining free to appreciate the miracle of being."

"Your voice sounds energized," said Stuart, "but I also think this seems steely and bloodless. It's cold consolation. Makes me shiver."

The members were puzzled. They sensed that Philip had something of value to offer but, as usual, were confused by his bizarre manner.

After a brief silence Tony asked Julius, "Does this work for you? I mean in terms of offering you something. Does it help you in some way?"

"It doesn't work for me, Tony. Yet, as I've said," he turned toward Philip, "you're reaching out to give me something that works for you. I'm aware, too, this is the second time you've offered me something I've not been able to make use of, and that must be frustrating for you."

Philip nodded but remained silent.

"A second time! I don't recall another time," said Pam. "Did it happen when I was away?"

Several heads shook no. No one else remembered a first time, and Pam asked Julius, "Are there blanks that need to filled in here?"

"There's old history between Philip and me," said Julius. "A lot of the puzzlement today could be removed by relating this history. But I feel it's up to you, Philip. When you're ready."

"I'm willing for all to be discussed," said Philip. "You have carte blanche."

"No, what I mean is, it's not for me to do that. To paraphrase your words, *it would be a richer exercise if you would discuss it yourself.* I think it's your call and your responsibility."

Philip tilted his head upward, closed his eyes, and, using the same tone and manner as when reciting a memorized passage, began: "Twenty-five years ago I consulted Julius for what is now termed *sexual addiction*. I was predatory, I was driven, I was insatiable, I thought of little else. My whole being was caught up in the pursuit of women—new women, always new women, because once I bedded a woman I rapidly lost interest in her. It was as though the epicenter of my existence was that moment of ejaculating inside the woman. And once that happened I had a brief respite from my compulsion, but soon—sometimes only hours later—I felt the call to prowl again. Sometimes I had two or three women in a day. I was desperate. I wanted to get my mind out of the trough, to think about other things, to touch some of the great minds of the past. I was educated in chemistry then, but I yearned for real wisdom. I sought help, the best and most expensive available, and met with Julius weekly, sometimes twice weekly, for three years, without benefit."

Philip paused. The group stirred. Julius asked, "How is this going for you, Philip? Can you go farther, or is it enough for one day?"

"I'm fine," replied Philip.

"With your closed eyes it's hard to read you," said Bonnie. "I'm wondering if you keep them closed because you fear disapproval."

"No, I close my eyes to look within and collect my thoughts. And surely I've made it clear that only my own approval matters to me."

Again there settled onto the group that strange otherworldly sense of Philip's untouchability. Tony tried to dispel it by whispering loudly, "Nice try, Bonnie."

Without opening his eyes, Philip continued. "Not too long after I gave up therapy with Julius, I inherited a fair sum of money from the maturation of a trust account my father had set up for me. The money enabled me to leave my profession as a chemist and devote myself to reading all of Western philosophy—in part because of my enduring interest in that field, but primarily because I believed that somewhere in the collective wisdom of the world's great thinkers I would find a cure for my condition. I felt at home in philosophy and soon realized that I had found my true calling. I applied and was accepted in the philosophy doctoral program at Columbia. It was at that time that Pam had the misfortune of crossing my path."

Philip, eyes still closed, paused and inhaled deeply. All eyes were on him except for furtive glances toward Pam, who stared at the floor.

"As time went by I chose to concentrate my attention on the trinity of truly great philosophers: Plato, Kant, and Schopenhauer. But, in the final analysis, it was only Schopenhauer who offered me help. Not only were his words pure gold for me, but I sensed a strong affinity with his person. As a rational being I cannot accept the idea of reincarnation in its vulgar sense, but if I *had* lived before it would have been as Arthur Schopenhauer. Simply knowing of his existence has tempered the ache of my isolation.

"After reading and rereading his work for several years, I found that I had overcome my sexual problems. By the time I received my doctorate, my father's bequest was exhausted and I needed to earn a living. I taught at a few places around the country and a few years ago moved back to San Francisco to accept a position at Coastal University. Eventually I lost interest in teaching because I never found students worthy of me or my subject, and then, about three years ago, it occurred to me that, since philosophy had healed me, I might be able to use philosophy to heal others. I enrolled in and completed a counseling curriculum and then began a small clinical practice. And that brings me to the present."

"Julius was useless to you," said Pam, "yet you contacted him again. Why?"

"I didn't. He contacted me."

Pam muttered, "Oh, yeah, right out of the blue Julius contacted *you?*"

"No, no, Pam," said Bonnie, "that part is true; Julius confirmed it when you were away. I can't fill you in on it because I've never really understood it myself."

"Right, let me come in here," said Julius. "I'll reconstruct it as best I can. The first few days after receiving the bad news from my doctor I was staggered and tried to find a way to come to terms with having a lethal cancer. One evening I got into a very morose mood as I thought about the meaning of my life. I got to thinking about being destined to slip into nothingness and remaining there forever. And that being so, then what difference did anyone or any activity make?

"I can't remember the whole chain of my morbid thinking, but I knew I had to clutch some kind of meaning or I would drown on dry land, then and there. As I surveyed my life, I realized that I *had* experienced meaning—and that it always involved stepping outside of myself, helping others to live and to fulfill themselves. More clearly than ever before I realized the centrality of my work as a therapist and then I thought for hours about those I had helped; all my patients, old and new, paraded through my imagination.

"Many I *knew* I had helped but had I had an *enduring* impact on their lives? That was the question that plagued me. I think I told the rest of group before Pam returned that I had to know the answer to this question so badly I decided to contact some of my old patients to find out whether I had truly made a difference. Seems crazy, I know.

"Then, while browsing through the charts of my long-ago patients,

I also began thinking of those I had failed to help. What had happened to *them*? I wondered. Could I have done more? And then the thought, the wishful thought, arose that maybe some of my failures were late bloomers, maybe they had gotten some delayed benefit from our work together. Then my eye fell upon Philip's chart, and I remember saying to myself, 'If you want failure, *there* is failure—there is someone you *really* didn't help—you couldn't make even a dent in his problems.' From that moment on, I had an irresistible impulse to contact Philip and find out what happened to him, to see if, in some way, I had been useful to him after all."

"So that's how it came about that you called him," said Pam. "But how did it come about that he entered the group?"

"You want to pick it up from here, Philip?" said Julius.

"I believe it would be a richer exercise if you continued," said Philip with the slightest trace of a smile on his lips.

Julius quickly filled the group in on the subsequent events: Philip's appraisal that his therapy had been without value and that Schopenhauer had been his real therapist, the e-mail invitation to the lecture, Philip's request for supervision . . .

"I don't get it, Philip," interrupted Tony. "If you didn't get anything from Julius in therapy, then why in hell would you want his supervision?"

"Julius posed that exact question, several times," said Philip. "My answer is that even though he didn't help me, I could still appreciate his superior skills. Perhaps I was a recalcitrant, resistive patient, or perhaps my particular type of problem would not yield to his particular approach."

"Okay, got it," said Tony. "I interrupted you, Julius."

"I'm about finished. I agreed to become his supervisor with one condition: that he first spend six months in my therapy group."

"I don't think you've ever explained why you made that condition," said Rebecca.

"I observed the way he related to me and to his students and told him that his impersonal and uncaring manner would interfere with his becoming a good therapist. Is that your view of it, Philip?"

"Your precise words to me were: 'How can you be a therapist

when you don't know what the fuck is going on between you and other people?'"

"Bingo," said Pam.

"Sounds like Julius, all right," said Bonnie.

"Sounds like Julius when his buttons are being pushed," said Stuart. "Were you pushing his buttons?"

"Not intentionally," replied Philip.

"I'm still not clear, Julius," said Rebecca. "I understand why you called Philip, and why you advised him to get group therapy. But why did you put him in your group or agree to supervise him? You have plenty on your plate now. Why take on this additional task?"

"You guys are tough today. That's the big question and I'm not sure I can answer it, but it's got something to do with redemption and setting things right."

"I know a lot of this discussion was to fill me in and I appreciate that," said Pam. "I have just one more query. You said Philip twice offered you comfort—or tried to. I still haven't heard about the first time."

"Right, we started toward there but never got to it," Julius responded. "I attended one of Philip's lectures and gradually understood that he had constructed it specifically to offer me some help. He discussed at length a passage from a novel in which a dying man obtained much consolation from reading a passage by Schopenhauer."

"Which novel?" asked Pam.

"*Buddenbrooks,*" replied Julius.

"And it wasn't helpful? Why not?" asked Bonnie.

"For several reasons. First, Philip's mode of giving me comfort was very indirect—much like the way he just presented the passage by Epictetus . . ."

"Julius," said Tony, "I'm not being a smart-ass, but wouldn't it be better to speak directly to Philip—and guess who I learned this from?"

"Thanks, Tony—you are one hundred percent right." Julius turned to face Philip. "Your mode of offering me counsel in the course of a lecture was off-putting—so indirect and so public. And so unexpected because we had just spent an hour in private face-to-face talk in which you seemed utterly indifferent to my condition. That was one thing. And the other was the actual content. I can't repeat the passage here—I don't have your photographic memory—but essentially it described a dying patriarch having an epiphany in which the boundaries dissolved between himself and others. As a result he was comforted by the unity of all life and the idea that after death he would return to the life force whence he came and hence retain his connectedness with all living things. That about right?" Julius looked at Philip, who nodded.

"Well, as I tried to tell you before, Philip, that idea offers me no comfort—zero. If my own consciousness is extinguished, then it matters little to me that my life energy or my bodily molecules or my DNA persists in deep space. And if connectivity is the quest, then I'd rather do it in person, in the flesh. So"—he turned and scanned the group and then faced Pam—"that was the first consolation Philip offered, and the parable in your hands is the second."

After a brief silence Julius added, "I'm feeling I've been doing too much talking today. How are you all responding to what's been happening so far?"

"I'm interested," said Rebecca.

"Yeah," said Bonnie.

"This is some pretty high-level stuff going on," said Tony, "but I'm staying with it."

"I'm aware," noted Stuart, "of ongoing tension here."

"Tension between . . . ?" asked Tony.

"Between Pam and Philip, of course."

"And lots between Julius and Philip," added Gill, again taking up Philip's cause. "I'm wondering, Philip, do you feel listened to? Do you feel your contributions get the consideration they merit?"

"It seems to me, that . . . that . . . well . . ." Philip was unusually tentative but soon regained his characteristic fluency. "Isn't it precipitous to dismiss so quickly—"

"Who are you talking to?" asked Tony.

"Right," answered Philip. "Julius, isn't it precipitous to dismiss so quickly a concept that has offered consolation to much of humanity for millennia? It is Epictetus's idea, and Schopenhauer's as well, that excessive attachment either to material goods, to other individuals, or even attachment to the concept of 'I' is the major source of human suffering. And doesn't it follow that such suffering can be ameliorated by avoiding the attachment? Indeed, these ideas are at the very heart of the Buddha's teaching as well."

"That's a good point, Philip, and I will take it to heart. What I hear you saying is that you're giving me good stuff which I dismiss out of hand—and that leaves you feeling unvalued. Right?"

"I said nothing about feeling unvalued."

"Not out loud. I'm intuiting that—it would be such a human response. I've a hunch if you will look inside you'll find it there."

"Pam, you're rolling your eyes," said Rebecca. "Is this talk about attachment reminding you of your meditation retreat in India? Julius, Philip—both of you missed the postgroup coffee when Pam described her time at the ashram."

"Yep, exactly," said Pam. "I had a bellyful of talk about the relinquishment of all attachments including the inane idea that we can sever our attachment to our personal ego. I ended up with strong feelings that it was all so life-negating. And that parable Philip handed out—what's the message? I mean, what kind of voyage, what kind of life, is it if you are so focused on the departure that you can't enjoy your surroundings and can't enjoy other people? And that's what I see in you, Philip." Pam turned to address him directly. "Your solution to your problems is a pseudosolution; it's no solution at all—it's something else—it's a relinquishment of life. You're not in life; you don't really listen to others, and when I hear you speak I don't feel I'm listening to a living, breathing person."

"Pam," Gill sprang to Philip's defense, "talk about listening—I'm not sure *you* do much listening. Did you hear that he was miserable years ago? That he had overwhelming problems and impulses? That he did not respond to *three full years* of therapy with Julius? That he did what you just did last month—what any of us would do—seek another method? That he finally got help from a different approach—one which is no freakish New Age pseudosolution? And that now he's trying to offer something to Julius by using the approach that helped him?"

The group was silenced by Gill's outburst. After a few moments Tony said, "Gill, you are something else today! Sticking it to my girl

Pam—I don't like that, but, man, I sure do like the way you're talking here—hope it rubs off on your home life with Rose."

"Philip," said Rebecca, "I want to apologize for being so dismissive earlier today. I want to say that I'm changing my mind about this . . . story by . . . by . . . Epihetus . . ."

"Epictetus," said Philip in a softer tone.

"Epictetus, thanks." Rebecca continued, "The more I think about it, this whole thing about attachment throws a light on some of my stuff. I think I *am* suffering from excessive attachment—not to things or possessions but to my looks. All my life I've had a free pass because of a pretty face—got lots of affirmation—prom queen, homecoming queen, beauty contests—and now that it's fading . . ."

"Fading?" said Bonnie. "Just pass the faded remnants on to me."

"Me, too, I'll trade you anytime and throw in all my jewelry . . . and kids, if I had any," said Pam.

"I appreciate that. I really do. But it's all relative." Rebecca went on, "I *am* too attached. I *am* my face, and now that it's become less, I feel *I* am less. I'm having a lot of trouble giving up my free pass."

"One of Schopenhauer's formulations that helped me," said Philip, "was the idea that relative happiness stems from three sources: what one is, what one has, and what one represents in the eyes of others. He urges that we focus only on the first and do not bank on the second and third—on *having* and *our reputation*—because we have no control over those two; they can, and will, be taken away from us—just as your inevitable aging is taking away your beauty. In fact, 'having' has a reverse factor, he said—*what we have often starts to have us.*"

"Interesting, Philip. All three parts of that—what you are, have, and stand for in the eyes of others—hits home for me. I've lived too much of my life for that last part—what others will think of me. Let me confess another secret: my magic perfume. I've never talked to anyone about this, but ever since I can remember I've daydreamed about manufacturing a perfume called Rebecca made up of my essence which lingers indefinitely and causes anyone who inhales it to think of my beauty."

"Rebecca, you're taking so many more risks now. I love it," said Pam.

"Me too," said Stuart. "But let me tell you something that's never registered before. I like to look at you, but I'm realizing now that your good looks are a barrier to seeing or knowing *you,* maybe even as much of a barrier as when a woman is ugly or misshapen."

"Wow, that's a shocker. Thanks, Stuart."

"Rebecca, I want you to know," said Julius, "that I too am touched by your trusting us with your daydream about the perfume. It points out what a vicious circle you've set up. You confuse your beauty with your essence. And then what happens, as Stuart points out, is that others do not relate to your essence but to your beauty."

"A vicious circle which leaves me doubting whether there's anything there. I'm still struck by your phrase the other week, Julius, 'the beautiful empty woman'—that's me in spades."

"Except the vicious circle may be breaking down," said Gill. "I know I've seen more of you—that is, something deeper, in the last few weeks than in the whole previous year."

"Yeah, me too," agreed Tony, "and, I'm being serious now, I want to say I'm really sorry about counting out money when you told us about that time in Las Vegas—I acted like a real jerk."

"Apology noted and accepted," said Rebecca.

"You've gotten a lot of feedback today, Rebecca," said Julius. "How're you feeling about it?"

"I feel great—it's good. I feel people are treating me differently."

"It's not us," said Tony, "it's you. Put real stuff in—get real stuff out!"

"*Put real stuff in—get real stuff out.* I like that, Tony," said Rebecca. "Hey, you're getting good at this therapy business; maybe *I* should start counting out money. What are your fees?"

Tony smiled broadly. "Since I'm on a roll, let me give you my guess, Julius, about why you went out of your way to work with Philip again. Maybe when you first saw Philip years ago you were closer to that state of mind you told us about last week—you know, having strong sex desires for other women."

Julius nodded. "Go on."

"Well, here's what I'm wondering: if you had issues similar to Philip's—not the same but something in that ballpark—could that have gotten in the way of your therapy with him?"

Julius sat up straight in his chair. Philip, too, straightened up. "You are sure catching my attention, Tony. Now I'm beginning to remember why therapists are hesitant to reveal themselves—I mean it doesn't go away—what you reveal comes back to haunt you again and again."

"Sorry, Julius, I definitely didn't mean to put you on the spot."

"No, no, it's okay. I really mean that. I'm not complaining; maybe I'm just stalling. Your observation is good—maybe it's *too* good, too close, and I'm resisting a bit." Julius paused and thought a moment. "Okay, here's what comes up for me: I remember that I was surprised and dismayed that I hadn't helped Philip. I *should* have helped him. When we began, I would have taken a big bet that I would have helped him a lot. I thought I had an inside track on helping him. I was sure that my own personal experience would grease the rails of therapy."

"Maybe," said Tony. "Maybe that's why you invited Philip into this group—give it another try, getting another chance. Right?"

"You took the words out of my mouth," said Julius. "I was just going to say that. This may be the reason why a few months ago when I was wondering about who I helped and who I didn't, I got so fixated on Philip. In fact, when Philip came to mind I began to lose interest in contacting other patients.

"Hey, look at the time. I hate to bring this meeting to an end, but we've got to stop. Good meeting—I know I've got a lot to think about—Tony, you opened up some things for me. Thanks."

"So," said Tony with a grin, "am I excused from paying today?"

"Blessed is he who gives," said Julius. "But who knows?—keep on like this and that day may come."

After leaving the group room the members chattered on the outside steps of Julius's home before dispersing. Only Tony and Pam headed toward the coffee shop.

Pam was fixated on Philip. She was not mollified by Philip's statement that she had been unlucky to have met him. Moreover, she hated his compliment on her interpretation of the parable and hated even more that she had enjoyed getting it. She worried that the group was swinging over to Philip—away from her, away from Julius.

Tony felt elated—he voted himself the MVP—the meeting's most valuable player; maybe he'd skip the bar scene tonight—try to read one of the books Pam had given him.

Gill watched Pam and Tony walk down the street together. He (and Philip of course) were the only ones Pam had not hugged at the end of the meeting. Had he crossed her too much? Gill turned his attention to tomorrow's wine-tasting event—one of Rose's big nights. A group of Rose's friends always got together at this time of the year for a sampling of the year's best wines. How to negotiate that? Just swish the wine and spit it out? Pretty tough to pull that off. Or come right out with the truth? He thought of his AA sponsor: he knew how the conversation between them would go:

Sponsor: Where're your priorities? Skip the event, go to a meeting.
Gill: But wine tasting is the reason these friends get together.
Sponsor: Is it? Suggest another activity.
Gill: Won't work. They won't do it.
Sponsor: Then get new friends.
Gill: Rose won't like it.
Sponsor: So?

Rebecca said to herself: *Real stuff in, real stuff out. Real stuff in, real stuff out.* Must remember that. She smiled when she thought about Tony counting his money when she had talked about her flirtation with whoredom. Secretly she had gotten a kick out of that. Was it bad faith to accept an apology from him?

Bonnie, as always, hated to see the meeting come to an end. She was alive those ninety minutes. The rest of her life seemed so tepid. Why was that? Why *must* librarians lead dull lives? Then she thought about Philip's statement about what you are, what you have, and what you represent to others. Intriguing!

Stuart relished the meeting. He was entering full-bodied into the group. He repeated to himself the words he had said to Rebecca about how her looks served as a barrier to knowing her and that he had recently seen something deeper than her skin. That was good. That was good. And telling Philip that his cold kind of consolation had made him shiver. *That* was being more than a camera. And then there was the way he had pointed out the tension between Pam and Philip. No, no, that was camera stuff.

On his walk home Philip struggled to avoid thinking of the meeting, but the events were too heady to screen out. In a few minutes he caved in and permitted his thoughts free rein. Old Epictetus had caught their attention. He always does. Then he imagined hands reaching out and faces turned toward him. Gill had become his champion—but not to be taken seriously. Gill wasn't *for* him but instead was *against* Pam, trying to learn how to defend himself against her, and Rose, and all other women. Rebecca had liked what he had said. Her handsome face lingered briefly in his mind. And then he thought of Tony—the tattoos, the bruised cheek. He had never met anyone like him—a real primitive, but a primitive who is beginning to comprehend a world beyond everydayness. And Julius—was he losing his sharpness? How could he defend attachment while acknowledging his problems of overinvestment in Philip as a patient?

Philip felt jittery, uncomfortable in his skin. He sensed that he was in danger of unraveling. Why had he told Pam that she was unlucky to have met him? Is that why she had spoken his name so often in the meeting—and demanded that he face her? His former debased self was hovering like a ghost. He sensed its presence, thirsting for life. Philip quieted his mind and slipped into a walking meditation.

To the learned men and philosophers of Europe: for you, a windbag like Fichte is the equal of Kant, the greatest thinker of all time, and a worthless barefaced charlatan like Hegel is considered to be a profound thinker. I have therefore not written for you.

33

Suffering, Rage, Perseverance

If Arthur Schopenhauer were alive today, would he be a candidate for psychotherapy? Absolutely! He was highly symptomatic. In "About Myself" he laments that nature endowed him with an anxious disposition and a "suspiciousness, sensitiveness, vehemence, and pride in a measure that is hardly compatible with the equanimity of a philosopher."

In graphic language he describes his symptoms:

> Inherited from my father is the anxiety which I myself curse and combat with all the force of my will. . . . As a young man I was tormented by imaginary illnesses. . . . When I was studying in Berlin I thought I was a consumptive. . . . I was haunted by the fear of being pressed into military service. . . . From Naples I was driven by the fear of smallpox and from Berlin by the fear of cholera. . . . In Verona I was seized by the idea I had taken poisoned snuff . . . in Manheim I was overcome by an indescribable feeling of fear without any external cause. . . . For years I

> was haunted by the fear of criminal proceedings. . . . If there was a noise at night I jumped out of bed and seized sword and pistols that I always had ready loaded. . . . I always have an anxious concern that causes me to look for dangers where none exist: it magnifies the tiniest vexation and makes association with people most difficult for me.

Hoping to quell his suspiciousness and chronic fear, he employed a host of precautions and rituals: he hid gold coins and valuable interest-bearing coupons in old letters and other secret places for emergency use, he filed personal notes under false headings to confuse snoopers, he was fastidiously tidy, he requested that he always be served by the same bank clerk, he allowed no one to touch his statue of the Buddha.

His sexual drive was too strong for comfort, and, even as a young man, he deplored being controlled by his animal passions. At the age of thirty-six a mysterious course of illness confined him to his room for an entire year. A physician and medical historian suggested in 1906 that his illness had been syphilis, basing the diagnosis only upon the nature of the medication prescribed, coupled with Schopenhauer's history of unusually great sexual activity.

Arthur longed to be released from the grip of sexuality. He savored his moments of serenity when he was able to observe the world with calm in spite of the lust tormenting his corporeal self. He compared sexual passion to the daylight which obscures the stars. As he aged he welcomed the decline of sexual passion and the accompanying tranquillity.

Since his deepest passion was his work, his strongest and most persistent fear was that he should lose the financial means enabling him to live the life of the intellect. Even into old age he blessed the memory of his father, who had made such a life possible, and he spent much time and energy guarding his money and pondering his investments. Accordingly, he was alarmed by any unrest threatening his investments and became ultraconservative in his politics. The 1848 rebellion, which swept over Germany as well as the rest of Europe, terrified him. When soldiers entered his building to gain a vantage point from which to fire on the rebellious populace in the street, he offered them his opera glasses to increase the accuracy of their rifle fire. In his will, twelve years later, he left almost his entire estate to a fund established for the welfare of Prussian soldiers disabled fighting that rebellion.

His anxiety-driven letters about business matters were often laced with anger and threats. When the banker who handled the Schopenhauer family money suffered a disastrous financial setback and, to escape bankruptcy, offered all his investors only a small fraction of their investment, Schopenhauer threatened him with such draconian legal consequences that the banker returned to him 70 percent of his money while paying other investors (including Schopenhauer's mother and sister) an even smaller portion than originally proposed. His abusive letters to his publisher eventually resulted in a permanent rupture of their relationship. The publisher wrote: "I shall not accept any letters from you which in their divine rudeness and rusticity suggest a coachman rather than a philosopher. . . . I only hope that my fears that by printing your work I am printing only waste paper will not come true."

Schopenhauer's rage was legendary: rage at financiers who handled his investments, at publishers who could not sell his books, at the dolts who attempted to engage him in conversations, at the bipeds who regarded themselves his equal, at those who coughed at concerts, and at the press for ignoring him. But the real rage, the white-hot rage whose vehemence still astounds us and made Schopenhauer a pariah in his intellectual community, was his rage toward contemporary thinkers, particularly the two leading lights of nineteenth-century philosophy: Fichte and Hegel.

In a book published twenty years after Hegel succumbed to cholera during the Berlin epidemic, he referred to Hegel as "a commonplace, inane, loathsome, repulsive, and ignorant charlatan, who with unparalleled effrontery, compiled a system of crazy nonsense that was trumpeted abroad as immortal wisdom by his mercenary followers."

Such intemperate outbursts about other philosophers cost him heavily. In 1837 he was awarded first prize for an essay on the freedom of the will in a competition sponsored by the Royal Norwegian Society for Learning. Schopenhauer showed a childlike delight in the prize (it was his very first honor) and greatly vexed the Norwegian consul in Frankfurt by impatiently clamoring for his medal. However, the very next year, his essay on the basis of morality submitted to a competition sponsored by the Royal Danish Society for Learning met a different fate. Though the argument of his essay was excellent and though it was the only essay submitted, the judges refused to award him the prize because of his intemperate remarks about Hegel. The judges commented, "We cannot pass over in silence the fact that several outstanding philosophers of the modern age are referred to in so improper a manner as to cause serious and just offense."

Over the years many have agreed entirely with Schopenhauer's opinion that Hegel's prose is unnecessarily obfuscating. In fact, he is so difficult to read that an old joke circulating around philosophy departments is that the most vexing and awesome philosophical question is not "does life have meaning?" or "what is consciousness?" but "who will teach Hegel this year?" Still, the level, the vehemence of Schopenhauer's rage set him apart from all other critics.

The more his work was neglected, the shriller he became, which, in turn, caused further neglect and, for many, made him an object of mockery. Yet, despite his anxiety and loneliness, Schopenhauer survived and continued to exhibit all the outward signs of personal self-sufficiency. And he persevered in his work, remaining a productive scholar until the end of his life. He never lost faith in himself. He compared himself to a young oak tree who looked as ordinary and unimportant as other plants. "But let him alone: he will not die. Time will come and bring those who know how to value him." He predicted his genius would ultimately have a great influence upon future generations of thinkers. And he was right; all that he predicted has come to pass.

Seen from the standpoint of youth, life is an endlessly long future; from that of old age it resembles a very brief past. When we sail away, objects on the shore become ever smaller and more difficult to recognize and distinguish; so, too, is it with our past years with all their events and activities.

34

As time raced by, Julius looked forward with increasing anticipation to the weekly group meeting. Perhaps his experiences in the group were more poignant because the weeks of his "one good year" were running out. But it was not just the events of the group; everything in his life, large and small, appeared more tender and vivid. Of course, his weeks had *always* been numbered, but the numbers had seemed so large, so stretched into a forever future, that he had never confronted the end of weeks.

Visible endings always cause us to brake. Readers zip through the thousand pages of *The Brothers Karamazov* until there are only a dozen remaining pages, and then they suddenly decelerate, savoring each paragraph slowly, sucking the nectar from each phrase, each word. Scarcity of days caused Julius to treasure time; more and more he fell into astonished contemplation of the miraculous flow of everyday events.

Recently, he had read a piece by an entomologist who explored the cosmos existing in a roped-off, two-by-two piece of turf. Digging deeply, he described his sense of awe at the dynamic, teeming world of predators and prey, nematodes, millipedes, springtails, armor-plated beetles, and spiderlings. If perspective is attuned, attention rapt, and knowledge vast, then one enters everydayness in a perpetual state of wonderment.

So it was for Julius in the group. His fears about the recurrence of his melanoma had receded, and his panics grew less frequent. Perhaps his greater comfort stemmed from taking his doctor's estimate of "one good year" too literally, almost as a guarantee. More likely, though, his mode of life was the active emollient. Following Zarathustra's path, he had shared his ripeness, transcended himself by reaching out to others, and lived in a manner that he would be willing to repeat perpetually throughout eternity.

He had always remained curious about the direction the therapy groups would take the following week. Now, with his last good year visibly shrinking, all feelings were intensified: his curiosity had evolved into an eager childlike anticipation of the next meeting. He remembered how, years ago, when he taught group therapy the beginning students complained of boredom as they observed ninety minutes of talking heads. Later, when they learned how to listen to the drama of each patient's life and to appreciate the exquisitely complex interaction between members, boredom dissolved and every student was in place early awaiting the next installment.

The looming end of the group propelled members to address their core issues with increased ardor. A visible end to therapy always has that result; for that reason pioneer practitioners like Otto Rank and Carl Rogers often set a termination date at the very onset of therapy.

Stuart did more work in those months than in three previous years of therapy. Perhaps Philip had jump-started Stuart by serving as a mirror. He saw parts of himself in Philip's misanthropy and realized that every member of the group, except the two of them, took pleasure in the meetings and considered the group a refuge, a place of support and caring. Only he and Philip attended under duress—Philip in order to obtain supervision from Julius, and he because of his wife's ultimatum.

At one meeting Pam commented that the group never formed a true circle because Stuart's chair was invariably set back a bit, sometimes only a couple of inches, but big inches. Others agreed; they had all felt the seating asymmetry but never connected it to Stuart's avoidance of closeness.

In another meeting Stuart launched into a familiar grievance as he described his wife's attachment to her father, a physician who rose from chairman of a surgery department, to medical school dean, to president of a university. When Stuart continued, as he had in previous meetings, to discuss the impossibility of ever winning his wife's regard because she continually compared him to her father, Julius interrupted to inquire whether he was aware that he had often told this story before.

After Stuart responded, "But surely we should be bringing up issues that continue to be bothersome. Shouldn't we?" Julius then asked a powerful question: "How did you think we would feel about your repetition?"

"I imagine you'd find it tedious or boring."

"Think about that, Stuart. What's the payoff for you in being tedious or boring? And then think about why you've never developed empathy for your listeners."

Stuart did think about that a great deal during the following week and reported feeling astonished to realize how little he ever considered that question. "I know my wife often finds me tedious; her favorite term for me is *absent,* and I guess the group is telling me the same thing. You know, I think I've put my empathy into deep storage."

A short time later Stuart opened up a central problem: his ongoing inexplicable anger toward his twelve-year-old son. Tony opened a Pandora's box by asking, "What were you like when you were your son's age?"

Stuart described growing up in poverty; his father had died when he was eight, and his mother, who worked two jobs, was never home when he returned from school. Hence, he had been a latch-key child, preparing his own dinner, wearing the same soiled clothes to school day after day. For the most part, he had succeeded in suppressing the memory of his childhood, but his son's presence propelled him back to horrors long forgotten.

"Blaming my son is crazy," he said, "but I just keep feeling envy and resentment when I see his privileged life." It was Tony who helped crack Stuart's anger with an effective reframing intervention: "What about spending some time feeling proud at providing that better life for your son?"

Almost everyone made progress. Julius had seen this before; when groups reach a state of ripeness, all the members seem to get better at once. Bonnie struggled to come to terms with a central paradox: her rage toward her ex-husband for having left her and her relief that she was out of a relationship with a man she so thoroughly disliked.

Gill attended daily AA meetings—seventy meetings in seventy days—but his marital difficulties increased, rather than decreased, with his sobriety. That, of course, was no mystery to Julius: whenever one spouse improves in therapy, the homeostasis of the marital relationship is upset and, if the marriage is to stay solvent, the other spouse must change as well. Gill and Rose had begun couples' therapy, but Gill wasn't convinced that Rose could change. However, he was no longer terrified at the thought of ending the marriage; for the first time he truly understood one of Julius's favorite *bon mots: "The only way you can save your marriage is to be willing (and able) to leave it."*

Tony worked at an astonishing pace—as though Julius's depleting strength were seeping directly into him. With Pam's encouragement, strongly reinforced by everyone else in the group, he decided to stop complaining of being ignorant and, instead, do something about it—get an education—and enrolled in three night courses at the local community college.

However thrilling and gratifying these widespread changes, Julius's central attention remained riveted on Philip and Pam. Why their relationship had taken on such importance for him was unclear, though Julius was convinced the reasons transcended the particular. Sometimes when thinking about Pam and Philip, he was visited by the Talmudic phrase "to redeem one person is to save the whole world." The importance of redeeming their relationship soon loomed large. Indeed it became his raison d'être: it was as though he could save his own life by salvaging something human from the wreckage of that horrific encounter years before. As he mused about the meaning of the Talmudic phrase, Carlos entered his mind. He had worked with Carlos, a young man, a few years ago. No, it must have been longer, at least ten years, since he remembered talking to Miriam about Carlos. Carlos was a particularly unlikable man, crass, self-centered, shallow, sexually driven, who sought his help when he was diagnosed with a fatal lymphoma. Julius helped Carlos make some remarkable changes, especially in the realm of connectivity, and those changes allowed him to flood his entire life retrospectively with meaning. Hours before he died he told Julius, "Thank you for saving my life." Julius had thought about Carlos many times, but now at this moment his story assumed a new and momentous meaning—not only for Philip and Pam, but for saving his own life, as well.

In most ways Philip appeared less pompous and more approachable in the group, even making occasional eye contact with most members, save Pam. The six-month mark came and went without Philip raising the subject of dropping because he had fulfilled his six-month contract. When Julius raised the issue, Philip responded, "To my surprise group therapy is a far more complex phenomenon than I had originally thought. I'd prefer you supervise my work with clients while I was also attending the group, but you've rejected that idea because of the problems of 'dual relationships.' My choice is to remain in the group for the entire year and to request supervision after that."

"I'm fine with that plan," Julius agreed, "but it depends, of course, on the state of my health. The group has four more months before we end, and after that we'll have to see. My health guarantee was only for one year."

Philip's change of mind about group participation was not uncommon. Members often enter a group with one circumscribed goal in mind, for example, to sleep better, to stop having nightmares, to overcome a phobia. Then, in a few months, they often formulate different, more far-reaching goals, for example, to learn how to love, to recapture zest for life, to overcome loneliness, to develop self-worth.

From time to time the group pressed Philip to describe more precisely how Schopenhauer had helped so much when Julius's psychotherapy had so utterly failed. Because he had difficulty answering questions about Schopenhauer without providing the necessary philosophical background, he requested the group's permission to give a thirty-minute lecture on the topic. The group groaned, and Julius urged him to present the relevant material more succinctly and conversationally.

The following session Philip embarked upon a brief lecturette which, he promised, would succinctly answer the question of how Schopenhauer had helped him.

Though he had notes in his hand, he spoke without referring to them. Staring at the ceiling, he began, "It's not possible to discuss

Schopenhauer without starting with Kant, the philosopher whom, along with Plato, he respected above all others. Kant, who died in 1804 when Schopenhauer was sixteen, revolutionized philosophy with his insight that it is impossible for us to experience reality in any veritable sense because all of our perceptions, our sense data, are filtered and processed through our inbuilt neuroanatomical apparatus. All data are conceptualized through such arbitrary constructs as space and time and—"

"Come on, Philip, get to the point," interrupted Tony. "How did this dude help you?"

"Wait, I'm getting there. I've spoken for all of three minutes. This is not the TV news; I can't explain the conclusions of one of the world's greatest thinkers in a sound bite."

"Hey, hey, right on, Philip. I like that answer," said Rebecca.

Tony smiled and backed off.

"So Kant's discovery was that, rather than experience the world as it's really out there, we experience our own personalized processed version of what's out there. Such properties as space, time, quantity, causality are *in us,* not out there—we impose them on reality. But, then, what *is* pure, unprocessed reality? What's really out there, that raw entity before we process it? *That* will always remain unknowable to us, said Kant."

"Schopenhauer—how he helped you! Remember? Are we getting warm?" asked Tony.

"Coming up in ninety seconds. In his future work Kant and others turned their entire attention to the ways in which we process primal reality.

"But Schopenhauer—and see, here we are already!—took a different route. He reasoned that Kant had overlooked a fundamental and immediate type of data about ourselves: our own bodies and our own feelings. We can know ourselves from the *inside,* he insisted. We have direct, immediate knowledge, not dependent on our perceptions. Hence, he was the first philosopher to look at impulses and feelings from the *inside,* and for the rest of his career he wrote extensively about interior human concerns: sex, love, death, dreams, suffering, religion, suicide, relations with others, vanity, self-esteem. More than any other philosopher, he addressed those dark impulses deep within that we cannot bear to know and, hence, must repress."

"Sounds a little Freudian," said Bonnie.

"The other way around. Better to say that Freud is Schopenhauerian. So much of Freudian psychology is to be found in Schopenhauer. Though Freud rarely acknowledged this influence, there is no doubt he was quite familiar with Schopenhauer's writings: in Vienna during the time Freud was in school, the 1860s and '70s, Schopenhauer's name was on everyone's lips. I believe that without Schopenhauer there could have been no Freud—and, for that matter, no Nietzsche as we know him. In fact, Schopenhauer's influence on Freud—particularly dream theory, the unconscious, and the mechanism of repression—was the topic of my doctoral dissertation.

"Schopenhauer," Philip continued, glancing at Tony and hurrying to avoid being interrupted, "normalized my sexuality. He made me see how ubiquitous sex was, how, at the deepest levels, it was the central point of all action, seeping into all human transactions, influencing even all matters of state. I believe I recited some of his words about this some months ago."

"Just to support your point," Tony said, "I read in the newspaper the other day that pornography takes in more money than the music and the film industry combined. That's huge."

"Philip," said Rebecca, "I can guess at it, but I still haven't heard you say exactly how Schopenhauer helped you recover from your sexual compulsion or . . . uh . . . *addiction.* Okay if I use that term?"

"I need to think about that. I'm not persuaded it's entirely accurate," said Philip.

"Why?" asked Rebecca. "What you described sounds like an addiction to me."

"Well, to follow up on what Tony said, have you seen the figures for males watching pornography on the Internet?"

"Are you into Internet porno?" asked Rebecca.

"I'm not, but I could have taken that route in the past—along with the majority of men."

"Right about that," said Tony. "I admit it, I watch it two or three times a week. Tell you the truth, I don't know anyone who doesn't."

"Me, too," said Gill. "Another of Rose's pet peeves."

Heads turned toward Stuart. "Yes, yes, mea culpa—I've been known to indulge a bit."

"This is what I mean," said Philip. "So is everyone an addict?"

"Well," said Rebecca, "I can see your point. There's not just the porn, but there's also the epidemic of harassment suits. I've defended quite a few in my practice. I saw an article the other day about a dean of a major law school resigning because of a sex harassment charge. And, of course, the Clinton case and the way his potentially great voice has been stilled. And then look at how many of Clinton's prosecutors were behaving similarly."

"Everybody's got a dark sex life," said Tony. "Some of it's like—who's unlucky? Maybe males are just being males. Look at me, look at my jail time in being too pushy in my demands for a blow job from Lizzie. I know a hundred guys who did worse—and no consequences—look at Schwarzenegger."

"Tony, you're not endearing yourself to the females here. Or at least to this female," said Rebecca. "But I don't want to lose focus. Philip, go on, you're still not making your point."

"First of all," Philip continued without a hitch, "rather than tsk-tsking about all this awful depraved male behavior, Schopenhauer two centuries ago understood the underlying reality: the sheer awesome power of the sex drive. It's the most fundamental force within us—the will to live, to reproduce—and it can't be stilled. It can't be reasoned away. I've already spoken of how he describes sex seeping into everything. Look at the Catholic priest scandal, look at every station of human endeavor, every profession, every culture, every age bracket. This point of view was exquisitely important to me when I first encountered Schopenhauer's work: here was one of the greatest minds of history, and, for the first time in my life, I felt completely understood."

"And?" asked Pam, who had been silent throughout this discussion.

"And what?" said Philip, visibly nervous as always when addressed by Pam.

"And what else? That was it? That did it? You got better because Schopenhauer made you feel understood?"

Philip seemed to take no note of Pam's irony and responded in an even tone with a sincere manner. "There was a great deal more. Schopenhauer made me aware that we are doomed to turn endlessly on the wheel of will: we desire something, we acquire it, we enjoy a brief moment of satiation, which rapidly fades into boredom, which then, without fail, is followed by the next 'I want.' There is no exit by way of appeasing desire—one has to leap off the wheel completely. That's what Schopenhauer did, and that's what I've done."

"Leaping off the wheel? And what does that mean?" Pam asked.

"It means to escape from willing entirely. It means to fully accept that our innermost nature is an unappeasable striving, that this suffering is programmed into us from the beginning, and that we are doomed by our very nature. It means that we must first comprehend the essential nothingness of this world of illusion and then set about finding a way to deny the will. We have to aim, as all the great artists have, at dwelling in the pure world of platonic ideas. Some do this through art, some through religious asceticism. Schopenhauer did it by avoiding the world of desire, by communion with the great minds of history, and by aesthetic contemplation—he played the flute an hour or two every day. It means that one must become observer as well as actor. One must recognize the life force that exists in all of nature, that manifests itself through each person's individual existence, and that will ultimately reclaim that force when the individual no longer exists as a physical entity.

"I've followed his model closely—my primary relationships are with great thinkers whom I read daily. I avoid cluttering my mind with everydayness, and I have a daily contemplative practice through chess or listening to music—unlike Schopenhauer, I have no ability to play an instrument."

Julius was fascinated by this dialogue. Was Philip unaware of Pam's rancor? Or frightened of her wrath? And what of Philip's solution to his addiction? At times Julius silently marveled at it; more often he scoffed. And Philip's comment that when he read Schopenhauer he felt entirely understood *for the first time* felt like a slap in the face. *What am I,* thought Julius, *chopped liver? For three years I worked my ass off trying to understand and empathize with him.* But Julius kept silent; Philip was gradually changing. Sometimes it is best to store things and return to them at some propitious time in the future.

A couple of weeks later the group raised these issues for him during a meeting which began with Rebecca and Bonnie both telling Pam that she had changed—for the worse—since Philip had entered the group. All the sweet, loving, generous parts of her had disappeared from sight, and, though her anger was not as vicious as in her first confrontation with him, still, Bonnie said, it was always present and had frozen into something hard and relentless.

"I've seen Philip change a great deal in the past few months," said Rebecca, "but you're so stuck—just like you were with John and Earl. Do you want to hold on to your rage forever?"

Others pointed out that Philip had been polite, that he had responded fully to every one of Pam's inquiries, even to those laced with sarcasm.

"Be polite," said Pam, "then you will be able to manipulate others. Just like you can work wax only after you have warmed it."

"What?" asked Stuart. Other members looked quizzical.

"I'm just quoting Philip's mentor. That's one of Schopenhauer's choice tidbits of advice—and that's what I think of Philip's politeness. I never mentioned it here, but when I first considered grad school I considered working on Schopenhauer. But after several weeks of studying his work and his life, I grew to despise the man so much I dropped the idea."

"So, you identify Philip with Schopenhauer?" said Bonnie.

"*Identify*? Philip *is* Schopenhauer—twin-brained, the living embodiment of that wretched man. I could tell you things about his philosophy and life that would curdle your blood. And, yes, I do believe Philip manipulates instead of relating—and I'll tell you this: it gives me the shivers to think of him indoctrinating others with Schopenhauer's life-hating doctrine."

"Will you ever see Philip as he is now?" said Stuart. "He's not the same person you knew fifteen years ago. That incident between you distorts everything; you can't get past it, and you can't forgive him."

"That 'incident'? You make it sound like a hangnail. It's more than an incident. As for forgiving, don't you think some things exist that are not forgivable?"

"Because you are unforgiving does not mean that things are unforgivable," said Philip in a voice uncharacteristically charged with emotion. "Many years ago you and I made a short-term social contract. We offered each other sexual excitement and release. I fulfilled my part of it. I made sure you were sexually gratified, and I did not feel I had further obligation. The truth is that I got something and you got something. I had sexual pleasure and release, and so did you. I owe you nothing. I explicitly stated in our conversation following that event that I had a pleasurable evening but did not wish to continue our relationship. How could I have been clearer?"

"I'm not talking about clarity," Pam shot back, "I'm talking about charity—love, *caritas,* concern for others."

"You insist that I share your worldview, that I experience life the same way as you."

"I only wish you had shared the pain, suffered as I did."

"In that case I have good news for you. You will be pleased to know that after that incident your friend Molly wrote a letter condemning me to every member of my department as well as to the university president, provost, and the faculty senate. Despite my receiving a doctorate with distinction and despite my excellent student evaluations, which incidentally included one from you, not one member of the faculty was willing to write me a letter of support or assist me in any way to find a position. Hence I was never able to get a decent teaching position and for the past years have struggled as a vagabond lecturer at a series of unworthy third-rate schools."

Stuart, working hard on developing his empathic sense, responded, "So you must feel you've served your time and that society exacted a heavy price."

Philip, surprised, raised his eyes to look at Stuart. He nodded. "Not as heavy as the one I exacted from myself."

Philip, exhausted, slumped back in his chair. After a few moments, eyes turned to Pam, who, unappeased, addressed the whole group: "Don't you get that I'm not talking about a single past criminal act. I'm talking about an ongoing way of being in the world. Weren't you all chilled just now when Philip described his behavior in our act of love as his 'obligations to our social contract'? And what about his comments that, despite three years with Julius, he felt understood for the 'first time' only when he read Schopenhauer. You all know Julius. Can you believe that after three years Julius did not understand him?"

The group remained silent. After several moments Pam turned to Philip. "You want to know the reason you felt understood by

Schopenhauer and not Julius? I'll tell you why: because Schopenhauer is dead, dead over one hundred and forty years, and Julius is alive. And you don't know how to relate to the living."

Philip did not look as though he would respond, and Rebecca rushed in, "Pam, you're being vicious. What will it take to appease you?"

"Philip's not evil, Pam," said Bonnie, "he's broken. Can't you see that? Don't you know the difference?"

Pam shook her head and said, "I can't go any further today."

After a palpably uncomfortable silence Tony, who had been uncharacteristically quiet, intervened. "Philip, I'm not pulling a rescue here, but I've been wondering something. Have you had any follow-up feelings to Julius's telling us a few months ago about his sexual stuff after his wife died?"

Philip seemed grateful for the diversion. "What feelings *should* I have?"

"I don't know about the '*should*.' I'm just asking what you *did* feel. Here's what I'm wondering: when you were first seeing him in therapy, would you have felt Julius understood you more if he had revealed that he too had personal experience with sexual pressure?"

Philip nodded. "That's an interesting question. The answer is, maybe, yes. It might have helped. I have no proof, but Schopenhauer's writings suggest that he had sexual feelings similar to mine in intensity and relentlessness. I believe that's why I felt so understood by him.

"But there's something I've omitted in talking about my work with Julius, and I want to set the record straight. When I told him that his therapy had failed to be of value to me in any way, he confronted me with the same question raised in the group a little while ago: why would I want such an unhelpful therapist for a supervisor? His question helped me recall a couple of things from our therapy that stuck with me and had, in fact, proved useful."

"Like what?" asked Tony.

"When I described my typical routinized evening of sexual seduction—flirtation, pickup, dinner, sexual consummation—and asked him whether he was shocked or disgusted, he responded only that it seemed like an exceptionally boring evening. That response shocked me. It got me realizing how much I had arbitrarily infused my repetitive patterns with excitement."

"And the other thing that stuck with you?" asked Tony.

"Julius once asked what epitaph I might request for my tombstone. When I didn't come up with anything, he offered a suggestion: 'He fucked a lot.' And then he added that the same epitaph could serve for my dog as well."

Some members whistled or smiled. Bonnie said, "That's mean, Julius."

"No," Philip said, "it wasn't said in a mean way—he meant to shock me, to wake me up. And it *did* stick with me, and I think it played a role in my decision to change my life. But I guess I wanted to forget these incidents. Obviously, I don't like acknowledging that he's been helpful."

"Do you know why?" asked Tony.

"I've been thinking about it. Perhaps I feel competitive. If he wins, I lose. Perhaps I don't want to acknowledge that his approach to counseling, so different from mine, works. Perhaps I don't want to get too close to him. Perhaps she," Philip nodded toward Pam, "is right: I can't relate to a living person."

"At least not easily," said Julius. "But you're getting closer."

And so the group continued over the next several weeks: perfect attendance, hard productive work, and, aside from repeated anxious inquiries into Julius's health and the ongoing tension between Pam and Philip, the group felt trusting, intimate, optimistic, even serene. No one was prepared for the bombshell about to hit the group.

When a man like me is born there remains only one thing to be desired from without—that throughout the whole of his life he can as much as possible be himself and live for his intellectual powers.

35

Self-Therapy

More than anything else, the autobiographical "About Myself" is a dazzling compendium of self-therapy strategies that helped Schopenhauer stay afloat psychologically. Though some strategies, devised in anxiety storms at 3 A.M. and rapidly discarded at dawn, were fleeting and ineffective, others proved to be enduring bulwarks of support. Of these, the most potent was his unswerving lifelong belief in his genius:

> Even in my youth I noticed in myself that, whereas others strived for external possessions, I did not have to turn to such things because I carried within me a treasure infinitely more valuable than all external possessions; and the main thing was to enhance the treasure for which mental development and complete independence are the primary conditions. . . . Contrary to nature and the rights of man, I had to withdraw my powers from the advancement of my own well-being, in order to devote them to the service of mankind. My intellect belonged not to me but to the world.

The burden of his genius, he said, made him more anxious and uneasy than he already was by virtue of his genetic makeup. For one thing, the sensibility of geniuses causes them to suffer more pain and anxiety. In fact, Schopenhauer persuades himself, there is a direct relationship between anxiety and intelligence. Hence, not only do geniuses have an obligation to use their gift for mankind, but, because they are meant to devote themselves entirely to the fulfilling of their mission, they are compelled to forego the many satisfactions (family, friends, home, accumulation of wealth) available to other humans.

Again and again he calmed himself by reciting mantras based on the fact of his genius: "My life is heroic and not to be measured by the standards of Philistines, shopkeepers or ordinary men. . . . I must therefore not be depressed when I consider how I lack those things that are part of an individual's regular course of life. . . . therefore it cannot surprise me if my personal life seems incoherent and without any plan." Schopenhauer's belief in his genius served also to provide him with a perduring sense of life meaning: throughout his life he regarded himself as a missionary of truth to the human race.

Loneliness was the demon that most plagued Schopenhauer, and he grew adept at constructing defenses against it. Of these, the most valuable was the conviction that he was master of his destiny—that he chose loneliness; loneliness did not choose him. When he was younger, he stated, he was inclined to be sociable, but thereafter: "I gradually acquired an eye for loneliness, became systematically unsociable and made up my mind to devote entirely to myself the rest of this fleeting life." "I am not," he reminded himself repeatedly, "in my native place and not among beings who are my equal."

So the defenses against isolation were powerful and deep: he voluntarily chose isolation, other beings were unworthy of his company, his genius-based mission in life mandated isolation, the life of geniuses must be a "monodrama," and the personal life of a genius must serve one purpose: facilitating the intellectual life (hence, "the smaller the personal life, the safer, and thus the better").

At times Schopenhauer groaned under the burden of his isolation. "Throughout my life I have felt terribly lonely and have always sighed from the depths of my heart, 'now give me a human being' but, alas in vain. I have remained in solitude but I can honestly and sincerely say it has not been my fault, for I have not shunned or turned away anyone who was a human being."

Besides, he said, he was not really alone because—and here is another potent self-therapy strategy—he had his own circle of close friends: the great thinkers of the world.

Only one such being was a contemporary, Goethe; most of the others were from antiquity, especially the Stoics, whom he quoted frequently. Almost every page of "About Myself" contains some aphorism spawned by a great mind supporting his own convictions. Typical examples:

> The best aid for the mind is that which once for all breaks the tormenting bonds that ensnare the heart. —Ovid

> Whoever seeks peace and quiet should avoid women, the permanent source of trouble and dispute. —Petrarch

> It is impossible for anyone not to be perfectly happy who depends entirely upon himself and who possesses in himself all that he calls his. —Cicero

A technique used by some leaders of therapy or personal growth groups is the "who am I?" exercise; members write seven answers to the question "who am I?" each on a different card, and then arrange the cards in order of importance. Next they are asked to turn over one card at a time, beginning with the most peripheral answer and to meditate upon what it would be like to let go of (that is, disidentify with) each answer, until they get to the attributes of their core self.

In an analogous manner, Schopenhauer tried on and discarded various self-attributes until he arrived at what he considered his core self:

> When, at times, I felt unhappy it was because I took myself to be other than I was and then deplored that other person's misery and distress. For example, I took myself to be a lecturer who does not become a professor and has no one to hear his lectures; or to be one about whom this Philistine

> speaks ill or that scandalmonger gossips; or to be the lover who is not listened to by the girl with whom he is infatuated; or to be the patient who is kept home by illness; or to be other persons afflicted with similar miseries. I have not been any of these; all this is the stuff from which the coat has been made which I wore for a short time and which I then discarded in exchange for another.
>
> But, then, *who am I?* I am the man who has written *The World as Will and Representation* which has given a solution to the great problem of existence which perhaps will render obsolete all previous solutions. . . . I am that man, and what could disturb him in the few years in which he has still to draw breath.

A related soothing strategy was his conviction that sooner or later, probably after his death, his work would become known and would drastically alter the course of philosophic inquiry. He first began expressing this opinion early in life, and his belief in ultimate success never wavered. In this he was similar to both Nietzsche and Kierkegaard, two other independent and unappreciated thinkers who were entirely (and correctly) convinced that they would have posthumous fame.

He eschewed any supernatural consolations, embracing only those based on a naturalistic worldview. For example, he believed that pain ensues from the error of assuming that many of life's exigencies are accidental and, hence, avoidable. Far better to realize the truth: that pain and suffering are inevitable, inescapable, and essential to life—"that nothing but the mere form in which it manifests itself depends on chance, and that our present suffering fills a place . . . which, without it, would be occupied by some other suffering. If such a reflection were to become a living conviction, it might produce a considerable degree of stoical equanimity."

He urged us to live and experience life *now* rather than live for the "hope" of some future good. Two generations later Nietzsche would take up this call. He considered hope our greatest scourge and pilloried Plato, Socrates, and Christianity for focusing our attention away from the only life that we have and toward some future illusory world.

Where are there any real monogamists? We all live for a time and, most of us, always, in polygamy. And since every man needs many women, there is nothing fairer than to make it incumbent upon him to provide for many women. This will reduce woman to her true and natural position as a subordinate being.

36

Pam opened the next meeting. "I've got something to announce today."

All heads turned toward her.

"Today is confession time. Go ahead, Tony."

Tony bolted upright, stared at Pam for a long moment, then leaned back in his chair, crossed his arms, and closed his eyes. If he had been wearing a fedora, he would have pushed it down over his face.

Pam, surmising that Tony had no intention of commenting, continued in her clear bold voice, "Tony and I have been sexually involved for a while, and it's hard for me to keep coming here and be silent about it."

After a short charged silence came stuttered questions: "Why?" "What started this?" "How long?" "How could you?" "Where is it going?"

Quickly, coolly, Pam responded, "It's been going on for several weeks. I don't know about the future, don't know what started it; it wasn't premeditated but just happened one evening after a meeting."

"You going to join us today, Tony?" Rebecca asked gently.

Tony slowly opened his eyes. "It's all news to me."

"News? You saying that this is not true?"

"No. I mean confession day. This 'go ahead, Tony'—*that* was news to me."

"You don't look happy about it," said Stuart.

Tony turned to address Pam: "I mean, I was over at your place last night. Being intimate, you know. Intimacy—how many times have I heard here that broads are more sensitive and want more intimacy than plain old sexual intimacy? So why not be intimate enough to talk to me, to run this 'confession day' by me first?"

"Sorry," Pam said, without sounding sorry, "things weren't sitting right with me. After you left I was up much of the night brooding and thinking about the group, and I realized time was too short—we've got only six more meetings left. Am I counting right, Julius?"

"Right. Six more meetings."

"Well, it just hit me how much I was betraying you, Julius. And my contract here with everyone else. And betraying myself, too."

"I never put it all together," said Bonnie, "but I've had a feeling that something wasn't right the last several meetings. You've been different, Pam. I remember Rebecca sensing that more than once. You rarely talk about your own issues—I have no idea what's going on between you and John or whether your ex-husband's in the picture or not. Mostly what you've been doing is attacking Philip."

"And Tony, you too," added Gill. "Now that I think about it, you've been real different. You've been hiding out. I've missed the old free-swinging Tony."

"I've got some thoughts here," said Julius. "First, something Pam touched off with her use of the word *contract.* I know this is repetitious, but it bears repeating for any of you who may be in a group in the future"—Julius glanced at Philip—"or even lead a group. The *only* contract any of us have is to do our best to explore our relationship with everyone in the group. The danger of an out-of-group relationship is that *it jeopardizes the therapy work.* How does it do that? *Because people in a tight relationship will often value that relationship more than the therapy work.* Look, it's precisely what's happened here: not only have Pam and Tony hidden their own relationship—that's understandable—but as a result of their personal involvement they've backed off from their therapy work here."

"Until today," said Pam.

"Absolutely, until today—and I applaud what you've done, and applaud your decision to bring it to the group. You know what my question's going to be for both you and Tony: *why now*? You've known each other in the group about two and a half years. Yet *now* things change. Why? What happened a few weeks ago that prompted the decision to get together sexually?"

Pam turned to Tony, raising her eyebrows, cueing him to answer. He complied. "Gentlemen first? My turn again? No problem; I know exactly what changed: Pam crooked her finger and signaled 'okay.' I've had a perpetual hard-on for her since we started, and if she'd crooked her finger six months ago or two years ago I would've come then too. Call me 'Mister Available.' "

"Hey, that's the Tony I know and love," said Gill. "Welcome back."

"It's not hard to figure out why you've been different, Tony," said Rebecca. "You're getting it on with Pam, and you didn't want to do anything to screw it up. It's reasonable. So you hide out, cautious about showing any of your not-so-nice parts."

"The jungle part, you mean?" said Tony. "Maybe, maybe not—it's not all that simple."

"Meaning?" asked Rebecca.

"Meaning the 'not-so-nice part' is a turn-on for Pam. But I don't want to get into that."

"Why not?"

"Come on, Rebecca, it's obvious. Why are you putting me on the spot? If I keep talking like this, I can kiss my relationship with Pam good-bye."

"You sure?" persisted Rebecca.

"What do you think? I figure her bringing it up at all in the group says it's a done deal, that she's made up her mind. It's getting warm here—hot seat's getting hot."

Julius repeated his question to Pam about the timing of her affair with Tony, to which Pam was uncharacteristically tentative. "I can't get perspective on it. I'm too close. I do know that there wasn't any forethought, no planning—it was an impulsive act. We were having coffee after a meeting, just the two of us, because all you guys went off in your own directions. He invited me to get some dinner—he's done that often, but this time I suggested he come to my place and have some homemade soup. He did, and things got out of hand. Why that day and not earlier? I can't say. We've hung out together in the past: I've talked to Tony about literature, given him books to read, encouraged him to go back to school, and he's taught me about woodwork and helped me build a TV stand, a small table. You've all known that. Why it got sexual now? I don't know."

"Are you okay about trying to find out? I know it's not easy to talk about something so intimate in the presence of a lover," said Julius.

"I've come here resolved to work today."

"Good, here's the question: think back to the group—what were the important things going on when this began?"

"Since I returned from India, two things have loomed large. Your health is number one. I once read a crackpot article stating that people pair in groups in the unconscious hope their offspring will provide a new leader, but that's far out. Julius, I don't know about how your illness might have prompted me to get more involved with Tony. Maybe the fear of the group ending caused me to seek a more personal permanent bond; maybe I irrationally thought this might keep the group continuing after the year. I'm guessing."

"Groups," said Julius, "are like people: they don't want to die. Perhaps your relationship with Tony *was* a convoluted way to keep it alive. All therapy groups try to continue, to have regular reunions—but they rarely do so. Like I've said many times here, the group is not life; *it's a dress rehearsal for life.* We've all got to find a way to transfer what we learn here to our life in the real world. End of lecture.

"But, Pam," Julius continued, "you mentioned *two* things loom large: one was my health and the other was . . ."

"It's Philip. I've been preoccupied with him. I hate that he's here. You've said that his presence may ultimately be a boon to me, and I trust you, but so far he's been nothing but a blight, with maybe one exception; I'm so caught up in my hatred for him that my preoccupation with Earl and John has vanished. And I don't think it's coming back."

"So," Julius persisted, "so Philip looms large. Is it possible that Philip's presence plays some role in the timing of your affair with Tony?"

"Anything's possible."

"Any hunches?"

Pam shook her head. "I don't see it. I'd vote for sheer horniness. I haven't been with a man for months. That's rare for me. I think it's no more complicated than that."

"Reactions?" Julius scanned the room.

Stuart jumped in, his keen, orderly mind clicking. "There's more than conflict between Pam and Philip—there's a lot of competition. Maybe I'm stretching it, but here's my theory: Pam always had a key place, a central position, in the group—the professor, the erudite one, the one who took Tony in hand to educate him. So, what happens? She goes away for a few weeks and returns to find Philip squatting in her place. I think this was disorienting." Stuart turned to Pam. "Whatever other grievances you had about him from fifteen years ago got compounded."

"And the connection to Tony?" asked Julius.

"Well, that might have been one way of competing. If my recollections are right, it was around then that Pam and Philip both tried to give you comforting gifts. Philip passed out that story about the ship stopping at an island, and I remember Tony got really caught up in the discussion." He turned to Pam. "Maybe that was threatening to you; maybe you didn't want to lose your influence over Tony."

"Thanks, Stuart, mighty enlightening," shot back Pam. "Your point is that to compete with this zombie I have to fuck all the guys in the group! That's your view of women's abilities?"

"*That's* going to encourage feedback," said Gill, "and that zombie crack is out of line. I prefer Philip's even-mindedness over hysterical name-calling any day! Pam, you are one angry lady. Can you be anything else but mad?"

"Those are strong feelings, Gill. What's happening?" asked Julius.

"I think I see a lot of my wife in this new angry Pam, and I'm determined not to let any vicious stuff pass—from either of them."

Then Gill added, "And there's something else. I think I'm miffed at continuing to be so invisible to Pam." He turned to her. "I'm being personal and upfront with you; I've let you know what I'm feeling about you, I tell you how I see you as the chief justice, but nothing registers—I still don't matter. You've only got eyes for Philip . . . and

Tony. And I think I'm giving you important stuff—and here's another piece: I think I know why your John bailed out: *it wasn't because he was a coward; it was because of your rage."*

Pam, lost in thought, remained silent.

"There are lots of powerful feelings coming out. Let's keep looking at them and try to understand them. Ideas?" asked Julius.

"I admire Pam's honesty today," said Bonnie, "and I can understand how raw she feels. I also appreciate Gill taking her on. That's an amazing change for you, Gill, and I applaud it, but sometimes I wish you'd let Philip defend himself. I don't understand why he doesn't." She turned to Philip. "Why don't you?"

Philip shook his head and remained silent.

"If he won't speak, I'll answer for him," said Pam. "He's following instructions from Arthur Schopenhauer." She took a note from her purse, scanned it, and read:

- *Speak without emotion.*
- *Don't be spontaneous.*
- *Remain independent of others.*
- *Think of yourself as living in a town in which you have the only watch that keeps time—it will serve you well.*
- *To disregard is to win regard.*

Philip nodded appreciatively and replied, "I approve of your reading material. Sounds like pretty good advice to me."

"What's going on?" asked Stuart.

"Doing a little browsing in Schopenhauer," said Pam, holding up her notes.

After a silence, Rebecca broke the impasse. "Tony, where are you? What's going on with you?"

"Hard for me to talk today," said Tony, shaking his head. "I feel tied up, like I'm frozen solid."

To everyone's surprise, Philip responded, "I think I understand your bind, Tony. It's like Julius said, you're caught between two conflicting requirements: you're expected to work in the group by freely expressing yourself, and at the same time you're trying to honor your allegiance to Pam."

"Yep, I see that," Tony replied, "but seeing is not enough, doesn't free me up. But still, thanks. And here's one back to you. What you just said a minute ago—you know, supporting Julius's point—well, that's a first for you—I mean not challenging him—a big change, man."

"Understanding, you say, is not enough. What else is needed?" Philip asked.

Tony shook his head. "This ain't easy today."

"I think I know what would help," said Julius, turning toward Tony. "You and Pam are avoiding one another, not expressing your feelings. Maybe you're saving it to talk about later. I know it's awkward, but can you make a start on doing it here? Perhaps try talking to each other, not to us."

Tony took a deep breath and turned to Pam. "I don't feel good about this, feel off balance. I'm pissed at the way all this played out. I can't get my mind around why not a phone call to me first, to talk it over, get me on board for today?"

"Sorry. But we both knew this had to come out sometime. We talked about that."

"That's it? That's all you got to say? And what about tonight? Are we still on?"

"It would be too awkward to see you. The rules here are to talk about all relationships, and I want to honor my contract with the group. I can't go on with this; maybe after the group ends—"

"You have a most convenient and flexible relationship to contracts," interrupted Philip, showing uncharacteristic signs of agitation. "You honor them when it suits you. When I discuss honoring my past social contract with you, you revile me. Yet you break the rules of the group, you play secret games, you use Tony capriciously."

"Who are you to speak of contracts?" Pam shot back loudly. "What about the contract between teacher and student?"

Philip looked at his watch, stood up, and announced, "Six o'clock. I have fulfilled my time obligations." He left the room muttering, "Enough wallowing in muck today."

It was the first time anyone other than Julius had ever ended a meeting.

Everyone who is in love will experience an extraordinary disillusionment after the pleasure is finally attained; and he will be astonished that what was desired with such longing achieves nothing more than what every other sexual satisfaction achieves, so that he does not see himself very much benefited by it.

37

Leaving the group room did not clear the muck from Philip's mind. He walked down Fillmore Street assailed by anxiety. What had happened to his arsenal of self-soothing techniques? Everything that had for so long provided him structure and serenity was unraveling—his mental discipline, his cosmic perspective. Struggling for equanimity, he instructed himself: Don't struggle, don't resist, clear your mind; do nothing but watch the passing show of your thoughts. Just let thoughts drift into consciousness and then drift away.

Things drifted in all right, but there was no drifting out. Instead, images unpacked their bags, hung up their clothes, and set up housekeeping in his mind. Pam's face drifted into view. He focused on her image, which, to his astonishment, transformed itself by shedding years: her features grew younger, and soon the Pam he had known so many years ago stood before him. How strange it was to descry the young in the old. He usually imagined the opposite trajectory—seeing the future in the present, the skull underlying the unblemished skin of youth.

How radiant her face! And such astonishing clarity! Of all the hordes, the hundreds, of women whose bodies he had entered and whose faces had long faded, melding into one archetypal visage, how was it possible that Pam's face persisted in such remarkable detail?

Then, to his amazement, sharper memory snippets of the young Pam slipped into view: her beauty, her giddy excitement as he tied her wrists with his belt, her cascade of orgasms. His own sexual excitement remained as a vague body memory—a wordless, heaving sensation of pelvic thrusting and exultation. He remembered, too, lingering in her arms for much too long. It was for that precise reason he had regarded her as dangerous and had resolved on the spot not to see her again. She represented a threat to his freedom. The quarry he sought was quick sexual release—that was his license to blessed peace and solitude. He never wanted carnality. He wanted freedom; he wanted to escape from the bondage of desire in order to enter, however briefly, the true philosophers' will-free clearing. Only after sexual release could he think elevated thoughts and join his friends—the great thinkers whose books were personal letters to him.

More fantasies came; his passion enveloped him and, with a great whoosh, sucked him from the philosophers' distant observing grandstand. He craved; he desired; he wanted. And more than anything, he wanted to hold Pam's face in his hands. Tight orderly connections between thoughts loosened. He imagined a sea lion surrounded by a harem of cows, then a yelping mongrel flinging himself again and again against a steel link fence separating him from a bitch in heat. He felt himself a brutish, club-wielding caveman, grunting, warning off competitors. He wanted to possess her, lick her, smell her. He thought of Tony's muscular forearms, of Popeye gulping his spinach and chucking the empty can behind him. He saw Tony mounting her—her legs splayed, her arms encircling him. That pussy should be his, his alone. She had no right to defile it by offering it to Tony. Everything she did with Tony sullied his memory of her, impoverished his experience. He felt sick to his stomach. He was a biped.

Philip turned and walked along the marina, then through Crissy Field to the bay and along the edge of the Pacific, where the calm surf and the timeless aroma of ocean salt soothed him. He shivered and buttoned his jacket. In the fading light of day, the cold Pacific wind streamed through the Golden Gate and rushed by him, just as the hours of his life would forever rush past without warmth or pleasure. The wind presaged the frost of endless days to come, arctic days of rising in the morning with no hope of home, love, touch, joy. His mansion of pure thought was unheated. How strange that he had never before noticed. He continued walking but with the glimmering knowledge that his house, his whole life, had been built on foundations flimsy and false.

We should treat with indulgence every human folly, failing, and vice, bearing in mind that what we have before us are simply our own failings, follies, and vices.

38

In the following meeting Philip shared neither his frightening experiences nor his reasons for abruptly leaving the previous meeting. Though he now participated more actively in the group discussions, he always did so at his own choosing and the members had learned that energy invested in prying Philip open was energy wasted. Hence they shifted their attention to Julius and inquired whether he felt usurped by Philip's ending the meeting last week.

"Bittersweet," he replied. "The bitter part is being replaced. Losing my influence and my role is symbolic of all impending endings and renunciations. I had a bad night after the last meeting. Everything feels bad at 3 A.M. I had a rush of sorrow at all the endings ahead of me: the ending of the group, of my therapy with all my other patients, the ending of my last good year. So, that's the bitter. The sweet is my pride in you guys. And that includes you, Philip. Pride in your growing independence. Therapists are like parents. A good parent enables a child to gain enough autonomy to leave home and function as an adult; in the same way a good therapist's aim is to enable patients to leave therapy."

"Lest there be a misunderstanding, I want to clarify the record," Philip proclaimed. "It was not my intention to usurp you last week. My actions were entirely self-protective: I felt inexpressibly agitated by the discussion. I forced myself to remain till the end of the meeting, and then I had to leave."

"I understand that, Philip, but my preoccupation with endings is so strong now that I may see portents of endings and replacement in benign situations. I'm also aware that, tucked into your disclaimer, is some caring for me. For that I thank you."

Philip bowed his head slightly.

Julius continued, "This agitation you describe sounds important. Should we explore it? There are only five meetings left; I urge you to take advantage of this group while there's still time."

Though Philip silently shook his head as if to indicate that exploration was not yet possible for him, he was not destined to stay silent permanently. In the following meetings Philip was inexorably drawn in.

Pam opened the next meeting by pertly addressing Gill: "Apology time! I've been thinking about you and think I owe you one . . . no, I *know* I owe you one."

"Say more." Gill was alert and curious.

"A few months ago I blasted you for never being present, for being so absent and impersonal that I could not bear to listen to you. Remember? That was pretty harsh stuff—"

"Harsh, yes," interrupted Gill, "but necessary. It was good medicine. It got me started on my path—do you realize I haven't had a drink since that day?"

"Thanks, but *that's* not what I'm apologizing for—it's what's happened since. You *have* changed: you've been *present;* you've been more upfront and more straight with me than anyone else here, and yet I've just been too self-absorbed to acknowledge you. For that I'm sorry."

Gill accepted the apology. "And what about the feedback I've given you? Was any of it helpful?"

"Well, your term *chief justice* shook me up for days. It hit home; it made me think. But the thing that sticks most in my mind was when you said John refused to leave his wife not because of cowardice but because he didn't want to deal with my rage. *That* got to me, *really* got me thinking. I couldn't get your words out of my mind. And you know what? I decided you were dead right and John was right to turn away from me. I lost him not because of *his* deficits but because of mine—he had had enough of me. A few days ago I picked up the phone, called him, and said these things to him."

"How'd he take it?"

"Very well—after he picked himself off the floor. We ended up having a nice amiable talk: catching up, discussing our courses, mutual students, talking about doing some joint teaching. It was good. He told me I sounded different."

"That's great news, Pam," said Julius. "Letting go of anger is major progress. I agree you've too much attachment to your hates. I wish we could take an internal snapshot of this letting-go process for future reference—to see exactly how you did it."

"It was all nonvolitional. I think your maxim—*strike when the iron is cold!*—had something to do with it. My feelings about John have cooled enough to step back and permit rational thought."

"And what about" asked Rebecca, "your attachment to your Philip-hatred?"

"I think you've never appreciated the monstrous nature of his actions to me."

"Not true. I felt for you . . . I *ached* for you when you first described it—an awful, awful experience. But fifteen years? Usually things cool in fifteen years. What keeps *this* iron red-hot?"

"Last night—during a very light sleep—I was thinking about my history with Philip and had this image of reaching into my head and grabbing the entire awful cluster of thoughts about him and smashing it on the floor. Then I saw myself bending over, examining the fragments. I could see his face, his seedy apartment, my soiled youth, my disillusionment with academic life, I saw my lost friend Molly—and as I looked at this heap of wreckage I knew what had happened to me was just . . . just . . . unforgivable."

"I remember Philip saying that unforgiving and unforgivable were two different things," said Stuart. "Right, Philip?"

Philip nodded.

"Not sure I get that," said Tony.

"Unforgivable," said Philip, "keeps the responsibility outside of oneself, whereas unforgiving places the responsibility on one's own refusal to forgive."

Tony nodded. "The difference between taking the responsibility for what you do or blaming it on someone else?"

"Precisely," said Philip, "and, as I've heard Julius say, therapy begins when blame ends and responsibility emerges."

"Quoting Julius again, Philip, I like it," said Tony.

"You make my words sound better than I do," said Julius. "And again I experience you drawing closer. I like that."

Philip smiled almost imperceptibly. When it was clear he was not planning to respond further, Julius addressed Pam: "Pam, what are you feeling?"

"To be honest, I'm floored by how hard everyone struggles to see change in Philip. He picks his nose, and everyone oohs and aahs. It's a joke how his pompous and trite remarks arouse such reverence." Mimicking Philip, she said in a singsong cadence, *"Therapy begins when blame ends and responsibility emerges."* Then, in a raised voice: "And what about *your* responsibility, Philip? Not a goddamn word about it except some bullshit about all your brain cells changing and therefore it wasn't you who did anything. No, *you* weren't there."

After an awkward silence, Rebecca said softly, "Pam, I want to point out that you *are* able to forgive. You've forgiven a lot of things. You said you forgave me for my excursion into prostitution."

"No victim there—except you," responded Pam quickly.

"And," continued Rebecca, "we've all taken note of how you forgave Julius, instantly, for his indiscretions. You forgave him without knowing or inquiring whether some of his friends were injured by his actions."

Pam softened her voice. "His wife had just died. He was in shock. Imagine losing someone you had loved since high school. Give him a break."

Bonnie pitched in, "You forgave Stuart for his sexual adventure with a troubled lady and even forgave Gill for withholding his alcoholism from us for so long. You've done a lot of forgiving. Why not Philip?"

Pam shook her head. "It's one thing to forgive someone for an offense to someone else—quite another thing when you're the victim."

The group listened sympathetically but nonetheless continued. "And, Pam," said Rebecca, "I forgive you for trying to make John leave his two young children."

"Me, too," said Gill. "And I'll eventually forgive you for what you did with Tony here. How about you? Do you forgive yourself for springing that 'confession day' and dumping him in public? That was humiliating."

"I've apologized publicly for not consulting with him about the confession. I was guilty there of extreme thoughtlessness."

Gill persisted, "There's something else, though: do you forgive yourself for using Tony?"

"Using Tony?" said Pam." *I* used *Tony*? What are you talking about?"

"Seems like your whole relationship was one thing—and a far more important thing—to him than to you. Seems like you weren't relating so much to Tony but to others, perhaps even to Philip, *through* Tony."

"Oh, Stuart's cockamamie idea—I've never bought into that," said Pam.

"Used?" interjected Tony. "You think I was used? No complaints here about that—I'm up for being used like that any time."

"Come on, Tony," said Rebecca, "stop playing games. Stop thinking with your little head."

"Little head?"

"Your cock!"

When Tony broke into a big lascivious smile, Rebecca barked, "You bastard, you knew what I meant! You just wanted to hear me talk dirty. Get serious, Tony, we don't have much time left here. You can't really be saying you weren't affected by what happened with Pam."

Tony stopped smiling, "Well, being suddenly dumped felt . . . you know, thrown away. But I'm still hoping."

"Tony," said Rebecca, "you've still got a lot of work to do on relating to a woman. Quit begging—it's demeaning. I hear you saying they can use you in any goddamned way they want because there's only one thing you want from them: to get laid. That's belittling yourself—and them too."

"I didn't think I was using Tony," said Pam. "Everything felt mutual to me. But, to be honest, at the time I didn't reflect much. I just acted on automatic pilot."

"As did I, long ago. Automatic pilot," Philip said softly.

Pam was startled. She looked at Philip for a few seconds and then gazed downward.

"I have a query for you," said Philip.

When Pam did not look up, he added, "A query for *you*, Pam."

Pam raised her head and faced him. Other members exchanged glances.

"Twenty minutes ago you said '*disillusionment* with academic life.' And yet a few weeks ago you said that when you applied to grad school, you seriously considered philosophy, even working on Schopenhauer. If that is so, then I put this question to you: *could I have been that disastrous a teacher?*"

"I *never* said you were a bad teacher," replied Pam. "You were one of the best teachers I've ever had."

Astonished, Philip stared hard at her.

"Talk about what you're feeling, Philip," urged Julius.

When Philip refused to answer, Julius said, "You remember everything, every word, Pam says. I think she matters a great deal to you."

Philip remained silent.

Julius turned toward Pam. "I'm thinking about your words—that Philip was one of the best teachers you ever had. That must have compounded your sense of disappointment and betrayal."

"Amen. Thanks, Julius, you're always there."

Stuart repeated her words, "*One of the best teachers you ever had!* I'm absolutely floored by that. I'm floored by your saying something so . . . so generous, to Philip. That's a huge step."

"Don't make too much of it," said Pam. "Julius hit the nail on the head: if anything, his being a good teacher made what he did even more egregious."

Tony, taking to heart Gill's comments about his relationship with Pam, opened the next meeting by addressing Pam directly. "This is . . . like awkward, but I been holding something back. I want to say that I'm feeling more bummed out about us than I've admitted. I haven't done anything wrong to you—you and I were . . . uh, together . . . mutual about the sex, and yet now I'm the person non grata—"

"Per*sona* non grata," whispered Philip gently.

"Persona non grata." Tony continued, "And I feel I'm being punished. We're not close anymore, and I guess I miss that. It seems like we were once friends, then lovers, and now . . . it's like . . . in limbo . . . nothing . . . you avoid me. And Gill's right: getting dumped in public was humiliating as hell. Right now I get nothing from you—not getting laid, not being friends."

"Oh Tony, I am so so sorry. I know. I made a mistake—I—we—should never have done this. It's awkward for me, too."

"So how about our going back to where we were before?"

"Back to?"

"Just friends, that's all. Just hanging out after the group, like all the others do here, except for my buddy, Philip, who's coming around." Tony reached over and gave Philip's shoulder an affectionate squeeze. "You know, talking about the group, your telling me about books, all that stuff."

"That sounds adult," answered Pam. "And . . . it would be a first for me—usually after an affair I make a clean tumultuous break."

Bonnie volunteered, "I wonder, Pam, if you keep your distance from Tony because you fear he will interpret a friendly overture as a sexual invitation."

"Yeah, exactly—there is that—that's an important part of it. Tony does get a bit single-minded."

"Well," said Gill, "there's an obvious remedy: just clear the air. Be straight with him. Ambiguity makes things worse. Couple of weeks ago I heard you raise the possibility that maybe the two of you can get together later after the group ends—is that real or just a phony way of softening the let-down? It just muddies the waters. Keeps Tony hanging."

"Yep, right on!" said Tony. "That statement a couple weeks ago about our possibly continuing sometime in the future was big for me. I'm trying to keep everything on an even keel so I can keep that possibility open."

"And," said Julius, "in so doing, you forfeit the opportunity of doing some work on yourself while this group and I are still available to you."

"You know, Tony," said Rebecca, "getting laid is not the most important thing, not the *only* thing, in the world."

"I know, I know, that's why I'm bringing this up today. Give me a break."

After a short silence Julius said, "So, Tony, keep working on this."

Tony faced Pam. "Let's do what Gill said—clear the air—as adults. What do you want?"

"What I want is to go back to where we were before. I want you to forgive me for embarrassing you by springing the confession. You're a dear man, Tony, and I care for you. The other day I overheard my undergraduate students using this new term, *fuck-buddies*—perhaps that's what we were and it was fun then but it's a bad idea now or in the future—the group takes precedence. Let's concentrate on working on our stuff."

"Okay by me. I'm up for it."

"So, Tony," said Julius, "you're liberated—you're now free to talk about all the thoughts you've been holding back lately—about yourself, Pam, or the group."

In the remaining meetings the liberated Tony returned to his instrumental role in the group. He urged Pam to deal with her feelings about Philip. When the potential breakthrough following her praise of Philip as a teacher never materialized, he pressed her to work harder on why she kept her resentment of Philip red-hot yet could find forgiveness for others in the group.

"I've already said," Pam answered, "that obviously it's much easier to forgive others, like Rebecca, or Stuart, or Gill, because I was not a personal victim of their offenses. My life wasn't altered by what they did. But there's more. I can forgive others here because they've shown remorse and, above all, because they've changed.

"I've changed. I do believe, now, it's possible to forgive the person but not the act. I think I might be capable of forgiving a changed Philip. *But he hasn't changed.* You ask why I can forgive Julius—well, look at him: he never stops giving. And, as I'm sure you've all figured out, he's been giving us a final gift of love: he's teaching us how to die. I knew the old Philip, and I can attest he's the same man you see sitting here. If anything, he's colder and more arrogant."

After a short pause she added, "And an apology from him wouldn't hurt."

"Philip, not changed?" said Tony. "I think you're seeing what you want to see. All those women he used to chase—*that's* changed." Tony turned to Philip. "You haven't really spelled it out, but it's different. Right?"

Philip nodded. "My life has been very different—I have been with no woman in twelve years."

"You don't call *that* change?" Tony asked Pam.

"Or reform?" said Gill.

Before Pam could respond, Philip interjected, "Reform? No, that's inaccurate. The idea of *reformation* played no role. Let me clarify: I have not changed my life, or, as it's been put here, my sex addiction, by virtue of some moral resolution. I changed because my life was agony—no longer bearable."

"How did you take that final step? Was there a last-straw event?" asked Julius.

Philip hesitated as he considered whether to answer Julius. Then he inhaled deeply and began, speaking mechanically as though wound up with a key: "One night I was driving home after a long orgy with an exceptionally beautiful woman and thought that now, if ever in my life, I had gotten all I wanted. I had had my surfeit. The aroma of sexual juices in the car was overpowering. Everything reeked of fetid flesh: the air, my hands, my hair, my clothes, my breath. It was as though I had just bathed in a tub of female musk. And then, on the horizon of my mind I could spot it—desire was gathering strength, readying to rear its head again. *That* was the moment. Suddenly my life made me sick, and I began to vomit. And it was then," Philip turned to Julius, "when your comment about my epitaph came to mind. And *that* was when I realized that Schopenhauer was right: life is forever a torment, and desire is unquenchable. The wheel of torment would spin forever; I had to find a way to get off the wheel, and it was then I deliberately set about patterning my life after his."

"And it's worked for you all these years?" said Julius.

"Until now, until this group."

"But you're so much better now, Philip," said Bonnie. "You're so much more in touch, so much more approachable. I'll tell you the truth—the way you were when you first started here . . . I mean I could never have imagined me or anyone else consulting you as a counselor."

"Unfortunately," Philip responded, "being 'in touch' here means that I must share everyone's unhappiness. That simply compounds my misery. Tell me, how can this 'being in touch' possibly be useful? When I was 'in life' I was miserable. For the past twelve years I have been a visitor to life, an observer of the passing show, and"—Philip spread his fingers and raised and lowered his hands for emphasis—"I have lived in tranquillity. And now that this group has compelled me to once again be 'in life,' I am once again in anguish. I mentioned to you my agitation after that group meeting a few weeks ago. I have not regained my former equanimity."

"I think there's a flaw in your reasoning, Philip," said Stuart, "and that has to do with your statement that you were 'in life.'"

Bonnie leaped in, "I was going to say the same thing. I don't believe you were ever in life, not *really* in life. You've never talked about having a real loving relationship. I've heard nothing about male friends, and, as for women, you say yourself that you were a predator."

"That true, Philip?" asked Gill. "Have there never been any real relationships?"

Philip shook his head. "Everyone with whom I've interacted has caused me pain."

"Your parents?" asked Stuart.

"My father was distant and, I think, chronically depressed. He took his own life when I was thirteen. My mother died a few years ago, but I had been estranged from her for twenty years. I did not attend her funeral."

"Brothers? Sisters?" asked Tony.

Philip shook his head. "An only child."

"You know what comes to my mind?" Tony interjected. "When I was a kid, I wouldn't eat most things my mother cooked. I'd always say 'I don't like it,' and she'd always come back with 'How do you know you don't like it if you've never tasted it?' Your take on life reminds me of that."

"Many things," Philip replied, "can be known by virtue of pure reason. All of geometry, for example. Or one may have some partial exposure to a painful experience and extrapolate the whole from that. And one may look about, read, observe others."

"But your main dude, Schopenhauer," said Tony, "didn't you say he made a big deal about listening to your own body, of relying on—what did you say?—your instant experience?"

"Immediate experience."

"Right, *immediate experience.* So wouldn't you say you're making a major decision on second-rate, secondhand info—I mean info that's not your own immediate experience?"

"Your point is well taken, Tony, but I had my fill of direct experience after that 'confession day' session."

"Again you go back to that session, Philip. It seems to have been a turning point," said Julius. "Maybe it's time to describe what happened to you that day."

As before, Philip paused, inhaled deeply, and then proceeded to relate, in a methodical manner, his experience after the end of that meeting. As he spoke of his agitation and his inability to marshal his mind-quieting techniques, he grew visibly agitated. Then, as he described how his mental flotsam did not drift away but lodged in his mind, drops of perspiration glistened on his forehead. And then, as Philip spoke of the reemergence of his brutish, rapacious self, a pool of wetness appeared in the armpits of his pale red shirt and rivulets of sweat dripped from his chin and nose and down his neck. The room was very still; everyone was transfixed by Philip's leakage of words and of water.

He paused, took another deep breath, and continued: "My thoughts lost their coherence; images flooded pell-mell into my mind: memories I had long forgotten. I remembered some things about my two sexual encounters with Pam. And I saw her face, not her face now but her face of fifteen years ago, with a preternatural vividness. It was radiant; I wanted to hold it and . . ." Philip was prepared to hold nothing back, not his raw jealousy, not the caveman mentality of possessing Pam, not even the image of Tony with the Popeye forearms, but he was now overcome by a massive diaphoresis, which soaked him to the skin. He stood and strode out of the room saying, "I'm drenched; I have to leave."

Tony bolted out after him. Three or four minutes later the two of them reentered the room, Philip now wearing Tony's San Francisco Giants sweater, and Tony stripped to his tight black T-shirt.

Philip looked at no one but simply collapsed into his seat, obviously exhausted.

"Bring 'em back alive," said Tony.

"If I weren't married," said Rebecca, "I could fall in love with both you guys for what you just did."

"I'm available," said Tony.

"No comment," said Philip. "That's it for me today—I'm drained."

"Drained? Your first joke here, Philip. I love it," said Rebecca.

Some cannot loosen their own chains yet can nonetheless liberate their friends.

—*Nietzsche*

39

Fame, at Last

There are few things that Schopenhauer vilified more than the craving for fame. And, yet, oh how he craved it!

Fame plays an important role in his last book, *Parerga and Paralipomena,* a two-volume compilation of incidental observations, essays, and aphorisms, completed in 1851, nine years before his death. With a profound sense of accomplishment and relief, he finished the book and said; "I will wipe my pen and say, 'the rest is silence.'"

But finding a publisher was a challenge: none of his previous publishers would touch it, having lost too much money on his other unread works. Even his magnum opus, *The World as Will and Representation,* had sold only a few copies and received only a single, lackluster review. Finally, one of his loyal "evangelists" persuaded a Berlin bookseller to publish a printing of 750 copies in 1853. Schopenhauer was to receive ten free copies but no royalties.

The first volume of *Parerga and Paralipomena* contains a striking triplet of essays on how to gain and maintain a sense of self-worth. The first essay, "What a Man Is," describes how creative thinking results in a sense of inner wealth. Such a path provides self-esteem and enables one to overcome the basic vacuity and boredom of life, which results in a ceaseless pursuit of sexual conquests, travel, and games of chance.

The second essay, "What a Man Has," dissects one of the major techniques used to compensate for inner poverty: the endless accumulation of possessions, which ultimately results in one becoming possessed by one's possessions.

It is the third essay, "What a Man Represents," that most clearly expresses his views on fame. A person's self-worth or inner merit is the essential commodity, whereas fame is something secondary, the mere shadow of merit. "It is not fame but that whereby we merit it that is of true value. . . . a man's greatest happiness is not that posterity will know something about him but he himself will develop thoughts that deserve consideration and preservation for centuries." Self-esteem that is based on inner merit results in personal autonomy which cannot be wrested from us—it is in our power—whereas fame is never in our power.

He knew that ablating the desire for fame was not easy; he likened it to "extracting an obstinate painful thorn from our flesh" and agreed with Tacitus, who wrote, "The thirst for fame is the last thing of all to be laid aside by wise men." And he, himself, was never able to lay aside the thirst for fame. His writings are permeated with bitterness about his lack of success. He regularly searched newspapers and journals for some mention, any mention, of himself or his work. Whenever he was away on a trip, he assigned this scanning task to Julius Frauenstädt, his most loyal evangelist. Though he could not stop chafing at being ignored, he ultimately resigned himself to never knowing fame in his lifetime. In later introductions to his books he explicitly addressed the future generations who would discover him.

And then the unthinkable came. *Parerga and Paralipomena,* the very book in which he described the folly of pursuing fame, made him famous. In this final work he softened his pessimism, staunched his flow of jeremiads, and offered wise instruction on how to live. Though he never renounced his belief that life is but a "mouldy film on the surface of the earth," and "a useless disturbing episode in the blissful repose of nothingness," he took a more pragmatic path in the *Parerga and Paralipomena.* We have no choice, he said, but to be condemned to life and must therefore attempt to live with as little pain as possible. (Schopenhauer always viewed happiness as a negative state—an absence of suffering—and treasured Aristotle's maxim "Not to pleasure but to painlessness do the prudent aspire.")

Accordingly, *Parerga and Paralipomena* offers lessons on how to think independently, how to retain skepticism and rationality, how to avoid soothing supernatural emollients, how to think well of ourselves, keep our stakes low, and avoid attaching ourselves to what can be lost. Even though "everyone must act in life's great puppet play and feel the wire which sets us into motion," there is, nonetheless, comfort in maintaining the philosopher's lofty perspective that, from the aspect of eternity, nothing really matters—everything passes.

Parerga and Paralipomena introduces a new tone. While it continues to emphasize the tragic and lamentable suffering of existence, it adds the dimension of connectivity—that is, through the commonality of our suffering, we are inexorably connected to one another. In one remarkable passage the great misanthrope displays a softer, more indulgent, view of his fellow bipeds:

> The really proper address between one man and another should be, instead of Sir, Monsieur, . . . *my fellow sufferer.* However strange this may sound, it accords with the facts, puts the other man in the most correct light, and reminds us of that most necessary thing, tolerance, patience, forbearance, and love of one's neighbor, which everyone needs and each of us therefore owes to another.

A few sentences later he adds a thought that could serve well as an opening paragraph in a contemporary textbook of psychotherapy:

> We should treat with indulgence every human folly, failing, and vice, bearing in mind that what we have before us are simply our own failings, follies, and vices. For they are just the failings of mankind to which we also belong and accordingly we have all the same failings buried within ourselves. We should not be indignant with others for these vices simply because they do not appear in us at the moment.

Parerga and Paralipomena was a great success, generating several compilations of selections published separately under more popular titles *(Aphorisms on Practical Wisdom, Counsels and Maxims, The Wisdom of Life, Living Thoughts of Schopenhauer, The Art of Literature, Religion: A Dialogue)*. Soon Schopenhauer's words were on the tongue of the entire educated German public. Even in neighboring Denmark, Kierkegaard wrote in his 1854 journal that "all the literary gossips, journalists, and authorlings have begun to busy themselves with S."

Praise ultimately appeared in the press. Great Britain, Arthur's almost-birthplace, was the first to honor him with a stunning review of all of his work (titled "Iconoclasm in German Philosophy") in the prestigious *Westminister Review.* Shortly afterward this review was translated and widely read in Germany. Similar articles quickly appeared in France and Italy, and Schopenhauer's life changed dramatically.

Curious visitors flocked to the Englischer Hof to eye the philosopher at lunch. Richard Wagner sent him the original libretto of the *Ring of the Nibelungs* with a dedication. Universities began to teach his work, learned societies issued invitations for membership, eulogistic letters arrived in the post, his previous books reappeared in bookstores, townspeople greeted him on his walks, and pet stores had a run on poodles similar to Schopenhauer's.

Schopenhauer's rapture and delight were very evident. He wrote, "If a cat is stroked it purrs; and just as inevitably if a man is praised, sweet rapture and delight are reflected in his face," and expressed the hope that "the morning sun of my fame will gild with its first rays the evening of my life and dispel its gloom." When the eminent sculptress Elisabeth Ney visited Frankfurt for four weeks to do a bust of him, Arthur purred, "She works all day at my place. When I get home we have coffee together, we sit together on the sofa, and I feel as if I were married."

Not since the best years of his life—the two years spent as a child in Le Havre with the de Blesimaire family—had Arthur spoken so tenderly and contentedly of domestic life.

> **At** the end of his life, no man, if he be sincere and in possession of his faculties, would ever wish to go through it again. Rather than this, he will much prefer to choose complete nonexistence.

40

Members filed in for the penultimate meeting with contrasting feelings: some felt sorrow about the looming end of the group, some thought about personal work they had left undone, some scanned Julius's face as though to imprint it in their minds, and all were enormously curious about Pam's response to Philip's revelations of the previous meeting.

But Pam did not offer satisfaction; instead she extracted a sheet of paper from her purse, slowly unfolded it, and read aloud:

> A carpenter does not come up to me and say, "listen to me discourse about the art of carpentry." Instead he makes a contract for a house and builds it. . . . Do the same thing yourself: eat like a man; drink like a man. . . . get married, have children, take part in civic life, learn how to put up with insults, and tolerate other people.

Then, turning to Philip, she said, "Written by . . . guess who?"

Philip shrugged.

"Your man, Epictetus. That's why I bring it here. I know you revere him—you brought Julius one of his fables. Why am I quoting him? I'm merely speaking to the point raised by Tony and Stuart and others last week that you've never been 'in life.' I believe that you selectively pick and choose various passages from philosophers to support your position and—"

Gill interrupted, "Pam, this is our next-to-last meeting. If this is another one of your get-Philip tirades, I don't personally feel I've got time for it. Do what you tell me to do. Get real and talk about your feelings. You must have had strong reactions to what Philip said about you last meeting."

"No, no, hear me out," Pam said quickly. "This is not 'get-Philip' stuff. My motivations are different. The iron is cooling. I'm trying to say something helpful to Philip. I think he's compounded his life avoidance by selectively gathering support from philosophy. He draws from Epictetus when he needs him and overlooks the same Epictetus when he doesn't."

"That's a great point, Pam," said Rebecca. "You're putting your finger on something important. You know, I bought a copy of a little paperback called the *Wisdom of Schopenhauer* at a used-book store and have been skimming it the last couple of nights. It's all over the place: some of it's fabulous and some outrageous. There's a passage I read yesterday that floored me. He says that if we go into any cemetery, knock on the tombstones, and ask the spirits dwelling there if they'd like to live again, every one of them would emphatically refuse." She turned to Philip. "You believe this?" Without waiting for him to respond, Rebecca continued, "Well, I don't. He's not speaking for me. I'd like to check it out. Could we get a vote here?"

"I'd choose to live again. Life's a bitch, but it's a kick too," said Tony. A chorus of "me too" spread around the group. "I hesitate for one reason," explained Julius. "The idea of once again bearing the pain of my wife's death; but, even so, I'd say yes. I love being alive." Only Philip held silent.

"Sorry," he said, "but I agree with Schopenhauer. Life is suffering from start to finish. It would have been better if life, all life, had never been."

"Better not have been *for whom*?" asked Pam. "For Schopenhauer, you mean? Apparently not for the folks in this room."

"Schopenhauer is hardly alone in his position. Consider the millions of Buddhists. Remember that the first of the Buddha's four noble truths is that life is suffering."

"Is that a serious answer, Philip? What's happened to you? When

I was a student you lectured brilliantly on modes of philosophical argument. What kind of argument is this? Truth by proclamation? Truth by appeal to authority? That's the way of religion, and yet surely you follow Schopenhauer in his atheism. And has it occurred to you that Schopenhauer was chronically depressed and that the Buddha lived in a place and at a time when human suffering—pestilence, starvation—was rampant and that, indeed, life then was unmitigated suffering for most? Has it occurred—"

"What kind of philosophic argument is *that*?" retorted Philip. "Every halfway literate sophomore student knows the difference between genesis and validity."

"Wait, wait," interjected Julius. "Let's pause for a minute and check in." He scanned the group. "How are the rest of you guys feeling about the last few minutes?"

"Good stuff," said Tony. "They were really duking it out. But with padded gloves."

"Right, better than silent glares and hidden daggers," said Gill.

"Yeah, I liked it a lot better," agreed Bonnie. "Sparks were flying between Pam and Philip but cooler sparks."

"Me, too," said Stuart, "until the last couple of minutes."

"Stuart," said Julius, "in your first meeting here you said your wife accused you of talking in telegrams."

"Yep, you're stingy today. A few more words won't cost you any more," said Bonnie.

"Right. Maybe I'm regressing because . . . you know, this being the next-to-last meeting. Can't be sure—I don't feel sad; as usual I have to infer my feelings. Here's something I do know, Julius. I love your taking care of me, calling on me, staying on my case. How's that?"

"That's great, and I'll keep doing it. You said you liked Pam and Philip talking 'until the last couple of minutes.' So, what about those last minutes?"

"At first it felt good-natured—more like a family squabble. But that last comment by Philip—that had a nasty edge to it. I mean the comment starting with "Every halfway literate sophomore student." I didn't like that, Philip. It was a put-down. If you said that to me, I'd have felt insulted. And threatened—I'm not even sure what philosophical argument means."

"I agree with Stuart," said Rebecca. "Tell me, Philip, what *were* you feeling? Did you want to insult Pam?"

"Insult her? No, not at all. That was the last thing I wanted to do," responded Philip. "I felt . . . uh . . . *uplifted* or *released*—not sure of the right word—by her saying the iron was no longer red-hot. Let's see, what else? I knew that one of her motives in bringing in the quote by Epictetus was to trap and confound me. That was obvious. But I kept in mind what Julius said to me when I brought in that fable for him—that he was pleased by the effort and the caring behind the act."

"So," said Tony, "let me pull a Julius. Here's what I hear: you intended one thing but your words resulted in another thing entirely."

Philip looked quizzical.

"I mean," said Tony, "you said that insulting Pam was the last thing in the world you wanted to do. Yet that was exactly what you did, wasn't it?"

Philip, reluctantly, nodded agreement.

"So," Tony continued, sounding like a triumphant attorney in cross-examination, "you need to get your intentions and your behavior on the same page. You need to get them *congruent*—do I have the word right?" Tony looked at Julius who nodded his head. "And *that's* why you should be in therapy. Congruence is what therapy is all about."

"Well argued," said Philip. "I have no counterargument. You're right. That is why I need therapy."

"What?" Tony could not believe his ears. He glanced at Julius, who gave him an "attaboy" nod.

"Catch me, I'm going to faint," said Rebecca who slumped back in her chair.

"Me, too," echoed Bonnie and Gill, slumping back as well.

Philip looked around at the sight of half the group in mock unconsciousness and, for the first time since entering the group, grinned.

Philip ended the group's levity by returning to the issue of his personal approach to counseling. "Rebecca's discussion of Schopenhauer's tombstone comment implies that my approach or any approach based on his point of view is invalid. Lest you forget, I struggled for years with a serious affliction which Julius failed to cure, and I was only healed by patterning my path upon Schopenhauer's."

Julius instantly supported Philip. "I don't deny you've done good work. Most therapists today would say it's not possible to overcome a severe sex addiction on your own. Contemporary treatment involves long-term work—I mean many years—in a structured recovery program consisting of individual therapy and groups meeting multiple times a week, often along twelve-step principles. But no such recovery program existed back then, and, frankly, I doubt whether you would have found it compatible.

"So," Julius continued, "I want to go on record as saying that your feat is remarkable: the techniques by which you controlled your runaway drives worked—better than anything I offered, even though I gave it my best shot."

"I've never thought otherwise," said Philip.

"But, here's a question, Philip: Is there a possibility your methods are now superannuated?"

"Super . . . what?" asked Tony.

"Superannuated," whispered Philip, who was sitting next to Tony—super (Latin for *beyond*) plus annus (*years*)—in other words, *outmoded, obsolete.*"

Tony nodded his thanks.

"The other day," Julius continued, "when I was wondering how to bring this home to you, an image came to mind. Imagine an ancient city that built a high wall to protect it from the wild torrents of an adjacent river. Centuries later, though the river had long dried up, the city still invested considerable resources in maintaining that wall."

"You mean," said Tony, "continuing to use some solution even when the problem had gone away—like wearing a bandage long after the cut had healed."

"Precisely," said Julius. "Maybe the bandage is a better metaphor—right to the point."

"I don't agree," Philip addressed both Julius and Tony, "that my wound is healed or that containment is no longer necessary. For proof one need only look at my extreme discomfort levels in this group."

"That's not a good measure," said Julius. "You've had little experience with intimacy, with expressing feelings directly, with getting feedback and disclosing yourself. This is new for you; you've been in seclusion for years, and I toss you into this high-powered group. *Of course* that's going to feel uncomfortable. But what I'm really referring to is the overt problem, the sexual compulsion—and perhaps that's gone. You're older, been through a lot, maybe you've entered the land of gonadal tranquillity. Nice place, good sunny climate. I've dwelled there comfortably for many years."

"I would say," Tony added, "that Schopenhauer has cured you, but now you need to be saved from the Schopenhauer cure."

Philip opened his mouth to respond but then closed it and pondered Tony's statement.

"Another thing," Julius added, "when you think about your stress in the group, don't forget the heavy-duty pain and guilt you've faced here as a result of a chance encounter with a person from your past."

"I've heard nothing about guilt from Philip," said Pam.

Philip responded instantly, facing Pam. "If I had known *then* what I know *now* about the years of pain you've suffered, *I would never have done what I did.* As I said before, you were unlucky to have crossed my path. The person I was then did not think of consequences. Automatic pilot—that person was on automatic pilot."

Pam nodded and caught his glance. Philip held it for a moment and then turned his attention back to Julius. "I grasp your point about the magnitude of the interpersonal stress in this group, but I insist that is only part of the picture. And it is here that our basic orientations are at odds. I agree there is stress in relationships with other beings. And possibly reward as well—I'll grant you that last point though I myself have never known it. Nonetheless, I'm convinced that in the very state of existing there is tragedy and suffering. Permit me to cite Schopenhauer for only two minutes."

Without waiting for a response, Philip, staring upward, began reciting:

> In the first place a man never is happy but spends his whole life in striving after something which he thinks will make him so; he seldom attains his goal and, when he does it is

> only to be disappointed: he is mostly shipwrecked in the end, and comes into harbor with masts and riggings gone. And then it is all one whether he has been happy or miserable; for his life was never anything more than a present moment, always vanishing; and now it is over.

After a long silence Rebecca said, "That sends shivers up my back."

"I know what you mean," said Bonnie.

"I know I'm sounding like an uptight English professor," said Pam, addressing the entire group, "but I urge you, don't be misled by rhetoric. That quote adds nothing of substance to what Philip has been saying all along; it only says it more persuasively. Schopenhauer was a brilliant stylist and wrote the best prose of any philosopher. Except for Nietzsche, of course—no one wrote better than Nietzsche."

"Philip, I want to respond to your comment about our basic orientations," said Julius. "I don't believe we're as far apart as you think. I don't disagree with much that you and Schopenhauer have said about the tragedy of the human condition. Where you go east and I go west is when we turn to the question of *what to do about it.* How shall we live? How to face our mortality? How to live with the knowledge that we are simply life-forms, thrown into an indifferent universe, with no preordained purpose?

"As you know," Julius continued, "though I'm more interested in philosophy than most therapists, I'm no expert. Yet, I'm aware of other bold thinkers who have not flinched from these raw facts of life and who have arrived at entirely different solutions than Schopenhauer. I'm thinking particularly of Camus, Sartre, and Nietzsche, who all advocate life engagement rather than Schopenhauer's pessimistic resignation. The one I know best is Nietzsche. You know, when I first received my diagnosis and was in a state of panic, I opened *Thus Spoke Zarathustra* and was both calmed and inspired—especially by his life-celebratory comment that we should live life in such a manner that we'd say yes if we were offered the opportunity to live our life again and again in precisely the same manner."

"How did that relieve you?" asked Philip.

"I looked at my life and felt that I had lived it right—no regrets from *inside,* though, of course, I hated the *outside* events that took my wife from me. It helped me decide how I should live my remaining days: I should continue doing exactly what had always offered me satisfaction and meaning."

"I didn't know that about you and Nietzsche, Julius," said Pam. "It makes me feel even closer to you because *Zarathustra,* melodramatic as it is, remains one of my absolutely favorite books. And I'll tell you my favorite quote from it. It's when Zarathustra says, '*Was that life? Well, then, once again!*' I love people who embrace life and get turned off by those who shrink away from it—I'm thinking of Vijay in India. Next ad I run in a personal column maybe I'll post that Nietzsche quote and the Schopenhauer tombstone quote side-by-side and ask respondents to choose between them. That would winnow out the nay-sayers.

"I have another thought I want to share." Pam turned to face Philip. "I guess it's obvious that after the last meeting I thought about you a lot. I'm teaching a course on biography, and in my reading last week I ran across an amazing passage in Erik Erikson's biography of Martin Luther. It goes something like this: '*Luther elevated his own neurosis to that of a universal patient-hood and then tried to solve for the world what he could not solve for himself.*' I believe that Schopenhauer, like Luther, seriously fell into this error and that you've followed his lead."

"Perhaps," responded Philip in a conciliatory fashion, "neurosis is a social construct, and we may need a different kind of therapy and a different kind of philosophy for different temperaments—one approach for those who are replenished by closeness to others and another approach for those who choose the life of the mind. Consider, for example, the large numbers who are drawn to Buddhist meditation retreats."

"That reminds me of something I've been meaning to say to you, Philip," said Bonnie. "I think your view of Buddhism misses something. I've attended Buddhist retreats where the focus has been directed outwards—on loving kindness and connectivity—not on solitude. A good Buddhist can be active, in the world, even politically active—all in the service of loving others."

"So it's becoming clearer," said Julius, "that your selectivity error involves human relationships. To give another example: you've cited the views about death or solitude of several philosophers but never speak of what these same philosophers—and I'm thinking of the Greek philosophers—have said about the joys of *philia,* of friendship. I remember one of my own supervisors quoting me a passage from Epicurus saying that friendship was the most important ingredient for a happy life and that eating without a close friend was living the life of a lion or a wolf. And Aristotle's definition of a friend—one who promotes the better and the sounder in the other—comes close to my idea of the ideal therapist."

"Philip," Julius asked, "how is this all feeling today? Are we laying too much on you at once?"

"I'm tempted to defend myself by pointing out that not one of the great philosophers ever married, except Montaigne, who remained so disinterested in his family that he was unsure how many children he had. But, with only one remaining meeting, what's the point? It's hard to listen constructively when my entire course, everything I plan to do as a counselor, is under attack."

"Speaking for myself, that's not true. There's a great deal you can contribute, much that you *have* contributed to the members here. Right?" Julius scanned the group.

After lots of strenuous head-nodding affirmation for Philip, Julius continued: "But, if you're to be a counselor, you *must* enter the social world. I want to remind you that many, I would bet *most,* of those who will consult you in your practice will need help in their interpersonal relationships, and if you want to support yourself as a therapist, you *must* become an expert in these matters—there's no other way. Just take a look around the group: everyone here entered because of conflicted relationships. Pam came in because of problems with the men in her life, Rebecca because of the way her looks influenced her relations with others, Tony because of a mutually destructive relationship with Lizzy and his frequent fights with other men, and so on for everyone."

Julius hesitated, then decided to include all the members. "Gill entered because of marital conflict. Stuart because his wife was threatening to leave him, Bonnie because of loneliness and problems with her daughter and ex-husband. You see what I mean, relationships cannot be ignored. And, don't forget, that's the very reason I insisted you enter the group before offering you supervision."

"Perhaps there's no hope for me. My slate of relationships, past and present, is blank. Not with family, not with friends, not with lovers. I treasure my solitude, but the extent of it would, I think, be shocking to you."

"A couple times after group," said Tony, "I've asked if you wanted to have a bite together. You always refused, and I figured it was because you had other plans."

"I haven't had a meal with anyone for twelve years. Maybe an occasional rushed sandwich lunch, but not a real meal. You're right, Julius, I guess Epicurus would say I live the life of a wolf. A few weeks ago after that meeting when I got so upset, one of the thoughts that circled in my mind was that the mansion of thought I had built for my life was unheated. The group is warm. This room is warm but my living places are arctic cold. And as for love, it's absolutely alien to me."

"All those women, hundreds of them, you told us," said Tony, "there must have been some love going around. You must have felt it. Some of them must have loved you."

"That was long ago. If any had love for me, I made sure to avoid them. And even if they felt love, it was not love, for me, the real me—it was love for my act, my technique."

"What's the real you?" asked Julius.

Philip's voice grew deadly serious. "Remember what I did for a job when we first met? I was an exterminator—a clever chemist who invented ways to kill insects, or to render them infertile, by using their own hormones. How's that for irony? The killer with the hormone gun."

"So the real you is?" Julius persisted.

Philip looked directly into Julius's eyes: "A monster. A predator. Alone. An insect killer." His eyes filled with tears. "Full of blind rage. An untouchable. No one who has known me has loved me. Ever. No one *could* love me."

Suddenly, Pam rose and walked toward Philip. She signaled Tony to change seats with her and, sitting down next to Philip, took his hand in hers, and said in a soft voice, "*I* could have loved you, Philip.

You were the most beautiful, the most magnificent man I had ever seen. I called and wrote you for weeks after you refused to see me again. I could have loved you, but you polluted—"

"Shhh." Julius reached over and touched Pam on the shoulder to silence her. "No, Pam, don't go there. Stay with the first part, say it again."

"I could have loved you."

"And you were the . . ." prompted Julius.

"And you were the most beautiful man I had ever seen."

"Again," whispered Julius.

Still holding Philip's hand and seeing his tears flow freely, Pam repeated, "I could have loved you, Philip. You were the most beautiful man . . ."

At this Philip, with his hands to his face, rose and bolted from the room.

Tony immediately headed to the door. "That's my cue."

Julius, grunting as he too rose, stopped Tony. "No, Tony, this one's on me." He strode out and saw Philip at the end of the hall facing the wall, head resting on his forearm, sobbing. He put his arm around Philip's shoulder and said, "It's good to let it all out, but we must go back."

Philip, sobbing more loudly and heaving as he tried to catch his breath, shook his head vigorously.

"You must go back, my boy. This is what you came for, this very moment, and you mustn't squander it. You've worked well today—exactly the way you have to work to become a therapist. Only a couple of minutes left in the meeting. Just come back with me and sit in the room with the others. I'll watch out for you."

Philip reached around and briefly, just for a moment, put his hand atop Julius's hand, then raised himself erect and walked alongside Julius back to the group. As Philip sat down, Pam touched his arm to comfort him, and Gill, sitting on the other side, clasped his shoulder.

"How are *you* doing, Julius?" asked Bonnie. "You look tired."

"I'm feeling wonderful in my head, I'm so swept away, so admiring of the work this group has done—I'm so glad to have been a part of this. Physically, yes, I have to admit I am ailing, and weary. But I have more than enough juice left for our last meeting next week."

"Julius," said Bonnie, "okay to bring a ceremonial cake for our last meeting?"

"Absolutely, bring any kind of carrot cake you wish."

But there was to be no formal farewell meeting. The following day Julius was stricken by searing headaches. Within a few hours he passed into a coma and died three days later. At their usual Monday-afternoon time the group gathered at the coffee shop and shared the ceremonial carrot cake in silent grief.

I can bear the thought that in a short time worms will eat away my body but the idea of philosophy professors nibbling at my philosophy makes me shudder.

41

Death Comes to Arthur Schopenhauer

Schopenhauer faced death as he faced everything throughout his life—with extreme lucidity. Never flinching when staring directly at death, never succumbing to the emollient of supernatural belief, he remained committed to reason to the very end of his life. It is through reason, he said, that we first discover our death: we observe the death of others and, by analogy, realize that death must come to us. And it is through reason that we reach the self-evident conclusion that death is the cessation of consciousness and the irreversible annihilation of the self.

There are two ways to confront death, he said: the way of reason or the way of illusion and religion with its hope of persistence of consciousness and cozy afterlife. Hence, the fact and the fear of death is the progenitor of deep thought and the mother of both philosophy and religion.

Throughout his life Schopenhauer struggled with the omnipresence of death. In his first book, written in his twenties, he says: "The life of our bodies is only a constantly prevented dying, an ever deferred death. . . . Every breath we draw wards off the death that constantly impinges on us, in this way we struggle with it every second."

How did he depict death? Metaphors of death-confrontation abound in his work; we are sheep cavorting in the pasture, and death is a butcher who capriciously selects one of us and then another for slaughter. Or we are like young children in a theater eager for the show to begin and, fortunately, do not know what is going to happen to us. Or we are sailors, energetically navigating our ships to avoid rocks and whirlpools, all the while heading unerringly to the great final catastrophic shipwreck.

His descriptions of the life cycle always portray an inexorably despairing voyage:

> What a difference there is between our beginning and our end! The former in the frenzy of desire and the ecstasy of sensual pleasure; the latter in the destruction of all the organs and the musty odor of corpses. The path from birth to death is always downhill as regards well-being and the enjoyment of life; blissfully dreaming childhood, lighthearted youth, toilsome manhood, frail and often pitiable old age, the torture of the last illness, and finally the agony of death. Does it not look exactly like existence were a false step whose consequences gradually become more and more obvious?

Did he fear his own death? In his later years he expressed a great calmness about dying. Whence his tranquillity? If the fear of death is ubiquitous, if it haunts us all our life, if death is so fearsome that vast numbers of religions have emerged to contain it, how did the isolated and secular Schopenhauer quell its terror for himself?

His methods were based on intellectual analysis of the sources of death-anxiety. Do we dread death because it is alien and unfamiliar? If so, he insists we are mistaken because death is far more familiar than we generally think. Not only have we a taste of death daily in our sleep or in states of unconsciousness, but we have all passed through an eternity of nonbeing before we existed.

Do we dread death because it is evil? (Consider the gruesome iconography commonly depicting death.) Here, too, he insists we are mistaken: "It is absurd to consider nonexistence as an evil: for every evil, like every good, presupposes existence and consciousness. . . . to have lost what cannot be missed is obviously no evil." And he asks us to keep in mind that life is suffering, that it is an evil in itself. That being so, how can losing an evil be an evil? Death, he says, should be considered a blessing, a release from the inexorable anguish of biped existence: "We should welcome it as a desirable and happy event instead of, as is usually the case, with fear and trembling." Life should be reviled for interrupting our blissful nonexistence, and, in this context, he makes his controversial claim: "If we knocked on the graves and asked the dead if they would like to rise again, they would shake their heads." He cites similar utterances by Plato, Socrates, and Voltaire.

In addition to his rational arguments, Schopenhauer proffers one that borders on mysticism. He flirts with (but does not marry) a form of immortality. In his view, our inner nature is indestructible because we are but a manifestation of the life force, the will, the thing-in-itself which persists eternally. Hence, death is not true annihilation; when our insignificant life is over, we shall rejoin the primal life force that lies outside of time.

The idea of rejoining the life force after death apparently offered relief to Schopenhauer and to many of his readers (for example, Thomas Mann and his fictional protagonist Thomas Buddenbrooks), but because it does not include a continued personal self, strikes many as offering only chilly comfort. (Even the comfort experienced by Thomas Buddenbrooks is short-lived and evaporates a few pages later.) A dialogue that Schopenhauer composed between two Hellenic philosophers raises the question of just how much comfort Schopenhauer drew from these beliefs. In this conversation, Philalethes attempts to persuade Thrasymachos (a thoroughgoing skeptic) that death holds no terror because of the individual's indestructible essence. Each philosopher argues so lucidly and so powerfully that the reader cannot be sure where the author's sentiments lay. At the end the skeptic, Thrasymachos, is unconvinced and is given the final words:

> Philalethes: "When you say I, I, I want to exist, it is not you alone that says this. Everything says it, absolutely everything that has the faintest trace of consciousness. It is the cry not of the individual but of existence itself. . . . only thoroughly recognize what you are and what your existence really is, namely, the universal will to live, and the whole question will seem to you childish and most ridiculous."
>
> Thrasymachos: You're childish yourself and most ridiculous, like all philosophers, and if a man of my age lets himself in for a quarter hour's talk with such fools it is only because it amuses me and passes the time. I've more important business to attend to, so goodbye.

Schopenhauer had one further method of keeping death-anxiety at bay: death-anxiety is least where self-realization is most. If his position based on universal oneness appears anemic to some, there is little doubt about the robustness of this last defense. Clinicians who work with dying patients have made the observation that death-anxiety is greater in those who feel they have lived an unfulfilled life. A sense of fulfillment, at "consummating one's life," as Nietzsche put it, diminishes death-anxiety.

And Schopenhauer? Did he live rightly and meaningfully? Fulfill his mission? He had absolutely no doubt about that. Consider his final entry in his autobiographical notes:

> I have always hoped to die easily, for whoever has been lonely all his life will be a better judge than others of this solitary business. Instead of going out amid the tomfooleries and buffooneries that are calculated for the pitiable capacities of human bipeds, I shall end happily conscious of returning to the place whence I started . . . and of having fulfilled my mission.

And the same sentiment—the pride of having pursued his own creative path—appears in a short verse, his authorial finale, the very last lines of his final book:

I now stand weary at the end of the road
The jaded brow can hardly bear the laurel
And yet I gladly see what I have done
Ever undaunted by what others say.

When his last book, *Parerga and Paralipomena,* was published, he said, "I am deeply glad to see the birth of my last child. I feel as if a load that I have borne since my twenty-fourth year has been lifted from my shoulders. No one can imagine what that means."

On the morning of the twenty-first of September 1860 Schopenhauer's housekeeper prepared his breakfast, tidied up the kitchen, opened the windows, and left to run errands, leaving Schopenhauer, who had already had his cold wash, sitting and reading on the sofa in his living room, a large, airy, simply furnished room. On the floor by the sofa lay a black bearskin rug upon which sat Atman, his beloved poodle. A large oil painting of Goethe hung directly over the sofa, and several portraits of dogs, Shakespeare, Claudius, and daguerreotypes of himself hung elsewhere in the room. On the writing desk stood a bust of Kant. In one corner a table held a bust of Christoph Wieland, the philosopher who had encouraged the young Schopenhauer to study philosophy, and in another corner stood his revered gold-plated statue of the Buddha.

A short time later his physician, making regular rounds, entered the room and found him leaning on his back in the corner of the sofa. A "lung stroke" (pulmonary embolus) had taken him painlessly out of this world. His face was not disfigured and showed no evidence of the throes of death.

His funeral on a rainy day was more disagreeable than most due to the odor of rotting flesh in the small closed mortuary. Ten years earlier Schopenhauer had left explicit instructions that his body not be buried directly but left in the mortuary for at least five days until decay began—perhaps a final gesture of misanthropy or because of a fear of suspended animation. Soon the mortuary was so close and the air so foul that several of the assembled people had to leave the room during a long pompous eulogy by his executor, Wilhelm Gwinner, who began with the words:

> This man who lived among us a lifetime, and who nevertheless stayed a stranger amongst us, commands rare feelings. Nobody is standing here who belongs to him through the bond of blood; isolated as he lived, he died.

Schopenhauer's tomb was covered with a heavy plate of Belgian granite. His will had requested that only his name, Arthur Schopenhauer, appear on his tombstone—"nothing more, no date, no year, no syllable."

The man lying under this modest tombstone wanted his work to speak for him.

Mankind has learned a few things from me which it will never forget.

42

Three Years Later

The late-afternoon sun streamed through the large open sliding windows of the Café Florio. Arias from *The Barber of Seville* flowed from the antique jukebox, accompanied by the hissing of an expresso machine steaming milk for cappuccinos.

Pam, Philip, and Tony sat at the same window table they had been using for their weekly coffee meeting since Julius's death. Others in the group had joined them for the first year, but for the past two years only the three of them had met. Philip halted their conversation to listen to an aria and hum along with it. "'*Una voce poco fa,*' one of my favorites," he said, when they resumed their conversation. Tony showed them his diploma from his community college program. Philip announced he was now playing chess two evenings a week at the San Francisco Chess Club—the first time he had played opponents face-to-face since his father's death. Pam spoke of her mellow relationship with her new man, a Milton scholar, and also of her Sunday attendances at the Buddhist services at Green Gulch in Marin.

She glanced at her watch. "And now, it's showtime for you guys." She looked them over. "Handsome dudes, you two. You both look great, but, Philip, that jacket," she shook her head, "it has got to go—

uncool—corduroy is dead, twenty years passé, those elbow patches too. Next week we go shopping." She looked at their faces. "You're going to do great. If you get nervous, Philip, remember the chairs. Remember Julius loved you both. And I do, too." She planted a kiss on each of their foreheads, left a twenty-dollar bill on the table, saying, "Special day, my treat," and walked out.

An hour later seven members filed into Philip's office for their first group meeting and warily sat down in Julius's chairs. Philip had wept twice as an adult: once during that last meeting of Julius's therapy group and again upon learning that Julius had bequeathed him these nine chairs.

"So," Philip began, "welcome to our group. We've tried to orient you to the group procedures during our screening session with each of you. Now it's time to begin."

"That's it. Just like that? No further instructions?" said Jason, a short, wiry middle-aged man wearing a tight black Nike T-shirt.

"I remember how scared I was in my first group therapy session," said Tony, who leaned forward in his seat. He was neatly dressed in a white short-sleeved shirt, khaki trousers, and brown loafers.

"I didn't say anything about being scared," replied Jason. "I'm referring to the lack of guidance."

"Well, what would help get you started?" asked Tony.

"Info. That's what makes the world go round now. This is supposed to be a philosophical consultation group—are both of you philosophers?"

"I'm a philosopher," said Philip, "with a doctorate from Columbia, and Tony, my co-leader, is a counseling student."

"A student? I don't get it. How will you two operate here?" shot back Jason.

"Well," answered Tony, "Philip will bring in helpful ideas from his knowledge of philosophy, and me, well, I'm here to learn and to pitch in any way I can—I'm more of an expert in emotional accessibility. Right, partner?"

Philip nodded.

"Emotional accessibility? Am I supposed to know what that means?" asked Jason.

"Jason," interrupted another member, "my name is Marsha, and I want to point out that this is about the fifth challenging thing you've said in the first five minutes of our group."

"And?"

"And you're the kind of macho-exhibitionistic guy I have a lot of trouble with."

"And you're the kind of Miss Prissy who gives me a major pain in the ass."

"Wait, wait, let's freeze the action for a moment," said Tony, "and get some feedback on our first five minutes from the other members here. First, I want to say something to you, Jason, and to you, Marsha—something that Philip and I learned from Julius, our teacher. Now, I'm sure you two feel like this is a stormy beginning but I've got a hunch, a very strong hunch, that by the end of this group, each of you are going to prove very valuable to the other. Right, Philip?"

"Right you are, partner."

Notes

Page 1. "Every breath we draw wards . . .": Arthur Schopenhauer, *The World as Will and Representation,* trans. E. F. J. Payne, 2 vols. (New York: Dover Publications, 1969), vol. 1., p. 311 / § 57.

Page 17. "Ecstasy in the act of copulation . . .": Arthur Schopenhauer, *Manuscript Remains in Four Volumes,* ed. Arthur Hübscher, trans. E. F. J. Payne (Oxford: Berg Publishers, 1988–90), vol. 3. p. 262 / § 111.

Page 23. "Life is a miserable thing . . .": Eduard Grisebach, ed., *Schopenhauer's Gespräche und Selbstgespräche* (Berlin: E. Hofmann,1898), p. 3.

Page 31. "Talent is like a marksman . . .": Schopenhauer, *World as Will,* vol. 2, p. 391 / chap. 31, "On Genius."

Page 33. "No one helped me, . . .": Rüdiger Safranski, *Schopenhauer and the Wild Years of Philosophy,* trans. Ewald Osers (Cambridge: Harvard University Press, 1991), p. 11.

Page 35. "A happy life is impossible . . .": Arthur Schopenhauer, *Parerga and Paralipomena,* trans. E. F. J. Payne, 2 vols. (Oxford: Clarendon Press, 2000), vol. 2, p. 322 / § 172a.

Page 41. "The solid foundations of our view . . .": Ibid., vol. 1, p. 478 / chap. 6, "On the Different Periods of Life."

Page 42. "Splendor, rank, and title exercise . . .": Safranski, *Schopenhauer,* p. 14.

Page 42. "I no more pretended ardent love . . .": Ibid., p. 13.

Page 43. "If we look at life in its small details . . .": T. Bailey Saunders, trans., *Complete Essays of Schopenhauer: Seven Books in One Volume* (New York: Wiley, 1942), book 5, p. 24. See also Schopenhauer, *Parerga and Paralipomena*, vol. 2, p. 290 / § 147a.

Page 48. "in the near and penetrating eye of death . . .": Thomas Mann, *Buddenbrooks*, trans. H. T. Lowe-Porter (New York: Vintage Books, 1952), p. 509.

Page 49. "A master-mind could lay hold . . .": Ibid., p. 510.

Page 49. "Have I hoped to live on . . .": Ibid., p. 513.

Page 50. "so perfectly consistently clear . . .": Thomas Mann, *Essays of Three Decades*, trans. H. T. Lowe-Porter (New York: Alfred A. Knopf, 1947), p. 373.

Page 50. "emotional, breath-taking, playing between violent contrasts . . .": Ibid., p. 373.

Page 50. "letting that dynamic, dismal genius work . . .": Ronald Hayman, *Nietzsche: A Critical Life* (New York: Penguin, 1982), p. 72.

Page 55. "Religion has everything on its side . . .": Schopenhauer, *World as Will*, vol. 2, p. 166 / chap. 17, "On Man's Need for Metaphysics."

Page 57. "Could we foresee it . . .": Saunders, *Complete Essays*, book 5, p. 3. See also Schopenhauer, *Parerga and Paralipomena*, vol. 2, p. 298 / § 155a.

Page 59. "In endless space countless luminous spheres . . .": Schopenhauer, *World as Will*, vol. 2, p. 3 / chap. 1, "On the Fundamental View of Idealism."

Page 71. "Just because the terrible activity . . .": Ibid., vol. 2, p. 394 / chap. 31, "On Genius."

Page 71. "by far the happiest part . . .": Safranski, *Schopenhauer*, p. 26.

Page 71. "Remember how your father permits . . .": Ibid., p. 29.

Page 72. "feeling of two friends meeting . . .": Schopenhauer, *Parerga and Paralipomena*, vol. 2, p. 299 / § 156.

Page 72. "I found myself in a country unknown to me . . .": Safranski, *Schopenhauer*, p. 280.

Page 73. "The greatest wisdom is to make . . .": Schopenhauer, *Parerga and Paralipomena*, vol. 2, p. 284 / § 143.

Page 87. "The kings left their crowns and scepters behind . . .": Safranski, *Shopenhauer,* p. 44.

Page 88. "put aside all these authors for a while . . .": Ibid., p. 37.

Page 90. "In my seventeenth year . . .": Ibid., p. 41.

Page 90 "This world is supposed to have been made . . .": Ibid., 58.

Page 91. "When, at the end of their lives . . .": Schopenhauer, *Parerga and Paralipomena,* vol. 2, p. 285 / § 145.

Page 107. "A person of high, rare mental gifts . . .": Schopenhauer, *World as Will,* vol. 2, p. 388 / chap. 31, "On Genius."

Page 108. "Noble, excellent spirit to whom I owe everything . . .": Safranski, *Shopenhauer,* p. 278.

Page 109. "Dancing and riding do not make . . ." and other quotations from Heinrich's letters: Ibid., pp. 52–53.

Page 109. "I know too well how little you had . . .": Ibid., p. 81.

Page 109. "I continued to hold my position . . .": Ibid., p. 55.

Page 109. "Your character. . .": Arthur Schopenhauer. Johanna Schopenhauer to Arthur Schopenhauer (April 28, 1807). In *Der Briefwechsel Arthur Schopenhauer Hrsg. v. Carl Gebbart Drei Bände. Erste Band* (1799) München: R. Piper & Co. p.129ff. Trans. by Felix Reuter and Irvin Yalom.

Page 109. "I will always choose the most exciting option . . .": Der Briefwechsel Arthur Schopenhauers. Herausgegeben von Carl Gebhardt. Erster Band (1799–1849). Munich: R. Piper, 1929. Aus: Arthur Schopenhauer: Sämtliche Werke. Herausgegeben von Dr. Paul Deussen. Vierzehnter Band. Erstes und zweites Tausend. Munich: R. Piper, 1929. pp. 129ff. Nr.71. Correspondence, Gebhardt and Hübscher, eds. Letter from Johanna Schopenhauer, April 28, 1807, trans. by Felix Reuter and Irvin Yalom.

Page 110. "The serious and calm tone . . .": Ibid.

Pages 111–12. "That you have so quickly come to a decision . . .": Safranski, *Schopenhauer,* p. 84.

Page 113. "It is noteworthy and remarkable to see . . .": Schopenhauer, *World as Will,* vol. 1, p. 85 / § 16.

Page 121. "Only the male intellect . . .": Schopenhauer, *Parerga and Paralipomena,* vol. 2, p. 619 / § 369.

Page 121. "Your eternal quibbles, your laments . . .": Safranski, *Schopenhauer,* pp. 92, 94.

Page 125. "I know women. They regard marriage only . . .": Arthur Schopenhauer: Gespräche. Hrsg. v. Arthur Hübscher, Stuttgart-Bad Cannstatt 1971, p.152. Trans. by Felix Reuter and Irvin Yalom.

Page 125. "Mark now on what footing . . .": Safranski, p. 94.

Page 126. "Fourfold root? No doubt this . . .": Ibid., p. 169.

Page 127. "The door which you slammed so noisily . . .": Paul Deusen, ed., *Journal of the Schopenhauer Society, 1912–1944,* trans. Felix Reuter, Frankfurt: n.p. 1973, p. 128.

Page 127. "Most men allow themselves to be seduced . . .": Schopenhauer, *Manuscript Remains,* vol. 4, p. 504 / "Ειζεαυτον," § 25. Trans. modified by Felix Reuter and Irvin Yalom.

Page 129. "Great sufferings render lesser ones . . .": Schopenhauer, *World as Will,* vol. 1, p. 316 / § 57. Trans. modified by Walter Sokel and Irvin Yalom.

Page 141. "Nothing can alarm or move him any more . . . ": Ibid., vol. 1, p. 390/ § 68.

Page 152. "One must have chaos . . .": Friedrich Nietzsche, *Thus Spoke Zarathustra,* trans. R. J. Hollingdale (New York: Penguin, 1961), p. 46.

Page 155. "The flower replied: . . .": Schopenhauer, *Parerga and Paralipomena,* vol. 2, p. 649 / chap. 314 § 388."

Page 171. "The cheerfulness and buoyancy of our youth . . .": Ibid., vol. 1, p. 483 / chap. 6, "On the Different Periods of Life."

Page 172. "half mad through excesses . . .": Arthur Hübscher, *Arthur Schopenhauer: Ein Lebensbild. Dritte Auflage, durchgesehen von Angelika Hübscher, mit einer Abbildung und zwei Handschriftproben.* (Mannheim: F. A. Brockhaus, 1988), S. 12.

Page 172. "little though I care for stiff etiquette . . .": Safranski, *Schopenhauer,* p. 40.

Page 172. "I only wish you had learned . . .": Ibid., p. 40.

Page 172. "Next to the picture were . . .": Ibid., p. 42.

Page 172. "I find that a panorama from a high mountain . . .": Ibid., p. 51.

Page 173. "Philosophy is a high mountain road . . .": Schopenhauer, *Manuscript Remains,* vol. 1, p. 14 / § 20.

Page 173. "We entered a room of carousing servants . . .": Safranski, *Schopenhauer,* p. 51.

Page 173. "The strident singing of the multitude . . ." and subsequent quotations in this paragraph: Ibid., p. 43.

Page 174. "I am sorry that your stay . . .": Ibid., p. 45.

Page 174. "Every time I went out among men . . .": Schopenhauer, *Manuscript Remains,* vol. 4, p. 512 / "Ειζεαυτον," § 32.

Page 174. "Be sure your objective judgments . . .": Safranski, *Schopenhauer,* p. 167.

Page 175. "He is a happy man . . .": Saunders, *Complete Essays,* book 2, p. 63. See also Schopenhauer, *Parerga and Paralipomena,* vol. 1, p. 445 / chap. 5, "Counsels and Maxims."

Page 185. "Sex does not hesitate to intrude . . .": Schopenhauer, *World as Will,* vol. 2, p. 533 / chap. 44, "The Metaphysics of Sexual Love."

Page 186. "Obit anus, abit onus . . .": Bryan Magee, *The Philosophy of Schopenhauer* (Oxford: Clarendon Press, 1983; revised 1997), p. 13, footnote.

Page 186. "Industrious whore": Safranski, *Schopenhauer,* p. 66.

Page 186. "I was very fond of them . . .": Ibid., p. 67.

Page 187. "But I didn't want them, you see . . .": Arthur Schopenhauer: Gespräche. Herausgegeben von Arthur Hübscher. Neue, stark erweiterte Ausg. Stuttgart-Bad Cannstatt, 1971, p. 58. Trans. by Felix Reuter.

Page 187. "May you not totally lose the ability . . .": Safranski, *Schopenhauer,* p. 245.

Page 187. "For a woman, limitation to one man . . .": Ibid., p. 271.

Page 187. "Man at one time has too much . . .": Ibid., p. 271.

Page 187. "All great poets were unhappily married . . .": Schopenhauer, *Manuscript Remains,* vol. 4, p. 505 / "Ειζεαυτον," § 25.

Page 188. To marry at a late age . . . : Schopenhauer, *Manuscript Remains,* vol. 4, p. 504 / "Ειζεαυτον," § 24.

Page 188. "Next to the love of life . . .": Schopenhauer, *World as Will,* vol. 2, p. 513 / chap. 42, "Life of the Species."

Page 189. "If we consider all this . . .": Ibid., vol. 2, p. 534 / chap. 44, "The Metaphysics of Sexual Love."

Page 189. "The true end of the whole love story . . .": Ibid., vol. 2, p. 535 / chap. 44, "The Metaphysics of Sexual Love."

Page 189. "Therefore what here guides man . . .": Ibid., vol. 2, p. 539 / chap. 44, "The Metaphysics of Sexual Love."

Page 189. "The man is taken possession of by the spirit . . .": Ibid., vol. 2, pp. 554, 555 / chap. 44, "The Metaphysics of Sexual Love."

Page 189. "For he is under the influence . . .": Ibid., vol. 2, p. 556 / chap. 44, "The Metaphysics of Sexual Love."

Page 189. "What is not endowed with reason . . .": Ibid., vol. 2, p. 557 / chap. 44, "The Metaphysics of Sexual Love."

Page 191. "If I maintain silence about my secret . . .": Schopenhauer, *Parerga and Paralipomena,* vol. 1, p. 466 / chap. 5, "Counsels and Maxims."

Page 205. "If we do not want to be a plaything . . .": Schopenhauer, *Manuscript Remains,* vol. 4, p. 499 / "Ειζεαυτον," § 20.

Page 206. "If you have an earnest desire . . .": Epictetus: *Discourses and Enchiridion,* trans. Thomas Wentworth Higginson (New York: Walter J. Black, 1944), p. 338.

Page 207. "By the time I was thirty . . .": Schopenhauer, *Manuscript Remains,* vol. 4, p. 513 / "Ειζεαυτον," § 33.

Page 207. "One cold winter's day . . .": Schopenhauer, *Parerga and Paralipomena,* vol. 2, p. 651 / § 396.

Page 208. "Yet whoever has a great deal of internal warmth . . .": Ibid., vol. 2, p. 652 / § 396.

Page 208. "highest class of mankind": Schopenhauer, *Manuscript Remains,* vol. 4, p. 498 / "Ειζεαυτον," § 20.

Page 208. "My intellect belonged not to me . . .": Ibid., vol. 4, p. 484 / "Ειζεαυτον," § 3.

Page 209. "Young Schopenhauer seems to have changed . . .": Safranski, *Schopenhauer,* p. 120.

Page 209. "Your friend, our great Goethe . . .": Ibid., p. 177.

Page 209. "We discussed a good many things . . .": Ibid., p. 190.

Page 210. "But the genius lights on his age . . .": Schopenhauer, *World as Will,* vol. 2, p. 390 / chap. 31, "On Genius."

Page 210. "If in daily intercourse we are asked . . .": Schopenhauer, *Parerga and Paralipomena,* vol. 2, p. 268 / § 135.

Page 210. "It is better not to speak . . .": Schopenhauer, *Manuscript Remains,* vol. 4, p. 512 / "Ειζεαυτον," § 32.

Page 211 "miserable wretches, of limited intelligence . . .": Ibid., vol. 4, p. 501 / "Ειζεαυτον," § 22.

Page 211. "Almost every contact with men . . .": Ibid., vol. 4, p. 508 / "Ειζεαυτον," § 29.

Page 211. "Do not tell a friend what your enemy . . .": Schopenhauer, *Parerga and Paralipomena,* vol. 1, p. 466 / chap. 5, "Counsels and Maxims."

Page 211. "Regard all personal affairs as secrets . . .": Ibid., vol. 1, p. 465 / chap. 5 "Counsels and Maxims."

Page 211. "Giving way neither to love nor to hate . . .": Ibid., vol. 1, p. 466/ chap. 5, "Counsels and Maxims."

Page 211. "Distrust is the mother of safety . . ." Schopenhauer, *Manuscript Remains,* vol. 4, p. 495 / "Ειζεαυτον," § 17.

Page 211. "To forget at any time the bad traits . . .": Schopenhauer, *Parerga and Paralipomena,* vol. 1, p. 466/ chap. 5, "Counsels and Maxims."

Page 211. "The only way to attain superiority . . .": Saunders, *Complete Essays,* book 2, p. 72. See also Schopenhauer, *Parerga and Paralipomena,* vol. 1, p. 451 / § 28.

Page 211. "To disregard is to win regard": Ibid., p. 72. See also Schopenhauer, *Parerga and Paralipomena,* vol.1, p. 451 / § 28.

Page 211. "If we really think highly . . .": Ibid., p. 72. See also Schopenhauer, *Parerga and Paralipomena,* vol.1, p. 451 / § 28.

Page 211. "Better to let men be what they are . . .": Schopenhauer, *Manuscript Remains,* vol. 4, p. 508 / "Ειζεαυτον," § 29, footnote.

Page 211. "We must never show anger and hatred . . .": Schopenhauer, *Parerga and Paralipomena,* vol. 1, p. 466 / chap. 5, "Counsels and Maxims."

Page 211. "By being polite and friendly . . .": Ibid., p. 463.

Page 213. "There are few ways by which . . .": Schopenhauer, *Parerga and Paralipomena,* vol. 1, p. 459 / chap. 5, "Counsels and Maxims."

Page 227. "We should set a limit to our wishes . . .": Ibid., vol. 1, p. 438 / chap. 5, "Counsels and Maxims."

Page 231. "No rose without a thorn . . .": Saunders, *Complete Essays,* book 5, p. 97. See also Schopenhauer, *Parerga and Paralipomena,* vol. 2, p. 648 / § 385.

Page 232. Bodies are material objects . . . : See discussion in Magee, *Philosophy of Schopenhauer,* pp. 440–53.

Page 233. "Every place we look in life . . .": Schopenhauer, *World as Will,* vol. 1, p. 309 / § 56.

Page 234. "Work, worry, toil and trouble . . .": Schopenhauer, *Parerga and Paralipomena,* vol. 2, p. 293 / § 152.

Page 234. "In the first place a man never is happy . . .": Saunders, *Complete Essays,* book 5, p. 21. See also Schopenhauer, *Parerga and Paralipomena,* vol. 2, p. 284 / § 144.

Page 235. "We are like lambs playing in the field . . .": Schopenhauer, *Parerga and Paralipomena,* vol. 2, p. 292 / § 150.

Page 237. "I have not written for the crowd . . .": Schopenhauer, *Manuscript Remains,* vol. 4, p. 207 / "Pandectae II," § 84.

Page 246. "A man finds himself . . .": Saunders, *Complete Essays,* book 5, p. 19. See also Schopenhauer, *Parerga and Paralipomena,* vol. 2, p. 283 / § 143.

Page 248. "When, on a sea voyage . . .": Epictetus, *Discourses and Enchiridion,* p. 334.

Page 251. "Life can be compared to a piece of embroidered material . . .": Schopenhauer, *Parerga and Paralipomena,* vol. 1, p. 482 / chap. 6, "On the Different Periods of Life."

Page 255. "Even when there is no particular provocation . . .": Schopenhauer, *Manuscript Remains,* vol. 4, p. 507 / "Ειζεαυτον," § 28.

Page 257. Schopenhauer's daily schedule: Magee, *Philosophy of Schopenhauer,* p. 24.

Page 258. Schopenhauer's table talk: Safranski, *Schopenhauer,* p. 284.

Page 258. The gold piece for the poor: Arthur Hübscher, ed., *Schopenhauer's Anekdotenbuchlein* (Frankfurt, 1981), p. 58. Trans. Felix Reuter and Irvin Yalom.

Page 258. Many anecdotes of his sharp wit . . . : Ibid.

Page 259. "Well built . . . invariably well dressed . . .": Safranski, *Schopenhauer,* p. 284.

Page 259. "The risk of living without work . . .": Schopenhauer, *Manuscript Remains,* vol. 4, p. 503 / "Ειζεαυτον," § 24.

Page 259. "Two months in your room . . .": Safranski, *Schopenhauer,* p. 288.

Page 261. "The monuments, the ideas left behind . . .": Schopenhauer, *Manuscript Remains,* vol. 4, p. 487 / "Ειζεαυτον," § 7.

Page 277. "To the learned men and philosophers of Europe . . .": Ibid., vol. 4, p. 121 / "Cholera-Buch," § 40.

Page 277. "suspiciousness, sensitiveness, vehemence, and pride . . .": Ibid., vol. 4, p. 506 / "Ειζεαυτον," § 28.

Page 277. "Inherited from my father . . .": Ibid., vol. 4, p. 506 / "Ειζεαυτον," § 28.

Page 278. Schopenhauer's precautions and rituals: Safranski, *Schopenhauer,* p. 287.

Page 278. A physician and medical historian suggested . . . : Iwan Bloch, "Schopenhauers Krankheit im Jahre 1823" in *Medizinische Klinik,* nos. 25–26 (1906).

Page 279. "I shall not accept any letters . . .": Safranski, *Schopenhauer,* p. 240.

Page 279. "commonplace, inane, loathsome, repulsive . . .": Schopenhauer, *Parerga and Paralipomena,* vol. 1, p. 96 / § 12.

Page 280. "We cannot pass over in silence . . .": Safranski, *Schopenhauer,* p. 315.

Page 280. "But let him alone . . .": Saunders, *Complete Essays,* book 5, p. 97. See also Schopenhauer, *Parerga and Paralipomena,* vol. 2, p. 647, para. 387.

Page 281. "Seen from the standpoint of youth . . .": Ibid., vol. 1, pp. 483–84 / chap. 6, "On the Different Periods of Life."

Page 289. "It means to escape from willing entirely": See discussion in Magee, *Philosophy of Schopenhauer,* pp. 220–25.

Page 295. "When a man like me is born . . .": Schopenhauer, *Manuscript Remains,* vol. 4, p. 510 / "Ειζεαυτον," § 30.

Page 295. "Even in my youth I noticed . . .": Ibid., vol. 4, p. 484 / "Ειζεαυτον," § 3.

Page 296. "My life is heroic . . .": Ibid., vol. 4, pp. 485–86 / "Ειζεαυτον," § 4.

Page 296. "I gradually acquired an eye . . .": Ibid., vol. 4, p. 492 / "Ειζεαυτον," § 12.

Page 296. "I am not in my native place . . .": Ibid., vol. 4, p. 495 / "Ειζεαυτον," § 17.

Page 296. "the smaller the personal life . . .": Grisenbach, *Schopenhauer's Gespräche,* p. 103.

Page 296. "Throughout my life I have felt terribly lonely . . .": Schopenhauer, *Manuscript Remains,* vol. 4, p. 501 / "Ειζεαυτον," § 22.

Page 297. "The best aid for the mind . . .": Ibid., vol. 4, p. 499 / "Ειζεαυτον" § 20.

Page 297. "Whoever seeks peace and quiet . . .": Ibid., vol. 4, p. 505 / "Ειζεαυτον" § 26.

Page 297. "It is impossible for anyone . . .": Ibid., vol. 4, p. 517 / "Ειζεαυτον—Maxims and Favourite Passages."

Page 297. "When, at times, I felt unhappy . . .": Ibid., vol. 4, p. 488 / "Ειζεαυτον," § 8.

Page 298. "that nothing but the mere form . . .": Schopenhauer, *World as Will,* vol. 1, p. 315 / § 57.

Page 299. "Where are there any real monogamists? . . .": Saunders, *Complete Essays,* book 5, p. 86. See also Schopenhauer, *Parerga and Paralipomena,* vol. 2, p. 624 / § 370.

Page 307. "Everyone who is in love . . .": Schopenhauer, *World as Will,* vol. 2, p. 540 / chap. 44, "The Metaphysics of Sexual Love."

Page 309. "We should treat with indulgence . . .": Schopenhauer, *Parerga and Paralipomena,* vol. 2, p. 305 / chap. 11, § 156a.

Page 321. "Some cannot loosen their own chains . . .": Nietzsche, *Thus Spake Zarathustra,* p. 83. F. Nietzche, *Thus Spake Zarathustra* (New York: Penguin Books, 1961), p.83. Translation modified by Walter Sokel and Irvin Yalom.

Page 321. "I will wipe my pen and say . . .": Magee, *Philosophy of Schopenhauer,* p. 25.

Page 322. "It is not fame . . .": Schopenhauer, *Parerga and Paralipomena,* vol. 1, pp. 397, 399 / chap. 4, "What a Man Represents."

Page 322. "extracting an obstinate painful thorn . . .": Ibid., vol. 1, p. 358 / chap. 4, "What a Man Represents."

Page 322. "mouldy film on the surface of the earth . . .": Schopenhauer, *World as Will,* vol. 2, p. 3 / chap. 1, "On the Fundamental View of Idealism."

Page 322. "A useless disturbing episode . . .": Schopenhauer, *Parerga and Paralipomena,* vol. 2, p. 299 / § 156

Page 322. "Not to pleasure but to painlessness . . .": Schopenhauer, *Manuscript Remains,* vol. 4, p. 517 / "Ειζεαυτον—Maxims and Favourite Passages."

Page 323. "everyone must act in life's great puppet play . . .": Schopenhauer, *Parerga and Paralipomena,* vol. 2, p. 420 / § 206.

Page 323. "The really proper address . . .": Ibid., vol. 2, pp. 304, 305 / § 156, 156a.

Page 323, "We should treat with indulgence . . . Schopenhauer, *Parerga and Paralipomena,* vol.2, p. 305 / chap. 11, § 156a.

Page 324. "all the literary gossips . . .": Magee, *Philosophy of Schopenhauer,* p. 26.

Page 324. "If a cat is stroked it purrs . . .": Schopenhauer, *Parerga and Paralipomena,* vol. 1, p. 353 / chap. 4, "What a Man Represents."

Page 324. "the morning sun of my fame . . .": Schopenhauer, *Manuscript Remains,* vol. 4, p. 516 / "Ειζεαυτον," § 36.

Page 324. "She works all day at my place . . .": Safranski, *Schopenhauer,* p. 348.

Page 325. "At the end of his life, no man . . .": Schopenhauer, *World as Will,* vol. 1, p. 324 / § 59.

Page 325. "A carpenter does not come up to me . . .": Pierre Hadot, *Philosophy as a Way of Life: Spiritual Exercises from Socrates to Foucault,* ed. Arnold Davidson, trans. Michael Chase (Oxford: Blackwell, 1995).

Page 330. "In the first place a man . . .": Schopenhauer, *Parerga and Paralipomena,* vol. 2, p. 284 / § 144.

Page 337. "I can bear the thought . . .": Schopenhauer, *Manuscript Remains,* vol. 4, p. 393, "Senilia," § 102.

Page 338. "The life of our bodies . . .": Schopenhauer, *World as Will,* vol. 1, p. 311 / § 57.

Page 338. "What a difference there is . . .": Schopenhauer, *Parerga and Paralipomena,* vol. 2, p. 288 / § 147.

Page 338. Schopenhauer's final thoughts on death . . . : Safranski, *Schopenhauer,* p. 348.

Page 339. "It is absurd to consider nonexistence . . .": Schopenhauer, *World as Will,* vol. 2, p. 467 / chap. 41, "On Death and Its Relation to the Indestructibility of Our Inner Nature."

Page 339. "We should welcome it . . .": Schopenhauer, *Parerga and Paralipomena,* vol. 2, p. 322 / § 172a.

Page 339. "If we knocked on the graves . . .": Schopenhauer, *World as Will,* vol. 2, p. 465 / chap. 41, "On Death and Its Relation to the Indestructibility of Our Inner Nature."

Page 339. The dialogue between two Hellenic philosophers: Schopenhauer, *Parerga and Paralipomena,* vol. 2, p. 279 / § 141.

Page 340. "When you say I, I, I . . .": Ibid., vol. 2, p. 281 / § 141.

Page 340. "I have always hoped to die easily . . .": Schopenhauer, *Manuscript Remains,* vol. 4, p. 517 / "Ειζεαυτον," § 38.

Page 341. "I now stand weary at the end of the road . . .": Schopenhauer, *Parerga and Paralipomena,* vol. 2, p. 658 / "Finale."

Page 341. "I am deeply glad to see . . .": Magee, *Philosophy of Schopenhauer,* p. 25.

Page 342. "This man who lived among us a lifetime . . .": Karl Pisa, *Schopenhauer* (Berlin: Paul Neff Verlag, 1977), p. 386.

Page 343. "Mankind has learned . . .": Schopenhauer, *Manuscript Remains,* vol. 4, p.328, "Spicegia," § 122.

About the author

2 A Conversation with Irvin D. Yalom

3 Meet Irvin D. Yalom

About the book

8 Writing *The Schopenhauer Cure*

Read on

14 Have You Read?
More by Irvin D. Yalom

Insights,
Interviews
& More . . .

About the author

A Conversation with Irvin D. Yalom

Where did you grow up?

In Washington, DC. My parents owned a small liquor and grocery store there.

What is your earliest memory?

The summer heat rising from the torrid pavement; the heat slamming you in the face as you left the home even early in the morning; the heat, which often drove my parents—and hordes of other inner-city families—to spend the night on the "speedway," a park on the banks of the Potomac. I remember my father taking me with him to the sprawling outdoor market in southeast DC at 5:00 A.M. to buy produce for the store. And I remember the Sylvan, a tiny cinema around the corner, where my parents deposited me three or four times a week to keep me off the unsafe streets. For the same reason, each summer they sent me to camp for eight weeks, which generated by far the most delicious memories of my childhood.

I remember Sundays, always a time of family gatherings. A group of my parents' relatives and friends from the old country stayed connected and met every Sunday for picnics and dinners, which were always followed by card playing—the women, canasta or poker; the men, pinochle. And Sunday mornings were mellow times, etched clearly in my mind. Usually I played chess with my father—often with him singing in

"'I remember the Sylvan, a tiny cinema around the corner, where my parents deposited me three or four times a week to keep me off the unsafe streets.'"

accompaniment to Yiddish songs played on the phonograph—or Victrola, as we called it then.

Where are your ancestors and parents from? Did they leave behind any interesting stories

My father came from a small shtetl near the Russian-Polish border. Sometimes they said they were from Russia, sometimes, from Poland. My father joked that they'd change the country to Poland when they decided they couldn't bear another long severe Russian winter. My father came from Selz and my mother from Prussina, about fifteen kilometers away. All the shtetls in the area were destroyed by the Nazis and several of my relatives, including my father's sister and his brother's wife and children, were all murdered in concentration camps. My father's father was a bootmaker who often shopped at my maternal grandfather's feed and grain story. My parents met as teenagers and married after immigrating to the United States in 1921. They arrived penniless in New York and for most of their lives struggled for economic survival. My father's brother had opened a small postage-stamp-sized store in Washington, DC, and encouraged my parents to move there. They owned a series of grocery and then liquor stores, each one slightly larger and more successful.

Did both of your parents work in the liquor and grocery store? What memories of the store do you have?

Both parents worked impossibly hard in the store six days a week from 8:00 A.M. to 10:00 P.M.—Fridays and Saturdays until ▶

Meet Irvin D. Yalom

Reid Yalom

IRVIN D. YALOM is the bestselling author of *Love's Executioner*, *Momma and the Meaning of Life*, and *The Gift of Therapy*, as well as several classic textbooks on psychotherapy, including the monumental work that has long been the standard text in the field, *The Theory and Practice of Group Psychotherapy*.

“'My parents met as teenagers and married after immigrating to the United States in 1921.'”

A Conversation with Irvin D. Yalom
(continued)

midnight. An incident of which I used in *Lying on the Couch* is a true story about my father:

> *He had a tiny, six-by-six, grocery store on Fifth and R streets in Washington, DC. We lived upstairs over the store. One day a customer came in and asked for a pair of working gloves. My father pointed to the back door saying he had to get them out of the back room and that it would take him a couple of minutes. Well, there was no back room—the back door opened onto the alley—and my father slipped out and galloped to the open market two blocks down, bought a pair of gloves for twelve cents, rushed back, and sold them to the customer for fifteen cents.*

Where were you educated? Have you any good collegiate anecdotes?

At George Washington University, which offered me a full-tuition scholarship—three hundred dollars. I lived at home and drove or bussed to school each day. College years were lost years with few good memories. I was a major grind, taking only pre-med courses and completing my studies in three years. One of my great regrets in life is having missed out on those glorious college days so often portrayed in films and literature. Why the rush and the grind? In those years medical school admission was extremely difficult for Jews: all medical schools had a fixed five-percent class quota. I and four of my close friends were admitted to George Washington School of Medicine and three of us have

“‘One of my great regrets in life is having missed out on those glorious college days so often portrayed in films and literature.’”

remained close to this day—all of us, incidentally, in our original and stable marriages. Much of the sense of urgency stemmed from my relationship with Marilyn, whom I met when fifteen; I wanted to nail down our relationship in marriage as quickly as possible—before she changed her mind.

> "'I owned a fireworks stand for many Fourth of July seasons.'"

What does your wife do?

Marilyn was a professor of French, then director of the Stanford Women's Research Center. She is also a writer of cultural history. Her works include *A History of the Wife, A History of the Breast,* and *Birth of the Chess Queen.*

What are some of the jobs you had before settling into your medical profession?

I worked extensively in my parents' store throughout childhood as well as delivering *Liberty* magazines and—at a nearby Safeway—helping to carry shoppers' bags to cars. I passed a summer as a soda jerk for Peoples Drug Store—for money to buy a microscope—and passed another summer on a dairy farm—the classified ad had a typo, "fine" work instead of "farm" work, but I took the job anyway. I worked Saturdays for three years as a clothing and shoe salesman at Bonds Clothing store. I owned a fireworks stand for many Fourth of July seasons. Several summers were spent as a camp counselor and tennis instructor. I tutored organic chemistry in college. Once I began medical school, extra income was available only from laboratory ▶

jobs, selling blood and sperm, and assisting professors with library research. I held a myriad of post-MD consultation jobs at prisons and psychiatric hospitals.

What recent work of fiction would you recommend?

The best new fiction I've read in several years is the novel *Cloud Atlas,* by David Mitchell—a work of genius. I've been reading and loving several books by Murakami and Paul Auster. And I've just reread *Our Mutual Friend,* by Charles Dickens, and *The German Lesson,* by Siegried Lenz—what masterpieces!

Have you any writerly quirks?

I write every morning starting early—7:00 A.M.—till early afternoon, when I begin seeing patients. I get lots of material from my dreams. I'm very single-minded when writing and always put the writing first. I do a lot of active planning for my next day's work on a bicycle and while soaking in a hot tub.

What do you rely upon for stimulation—do you observe any beverage rituals?

My stimulation as a writer is mental, from reading philosophy and fiction, and from my clinical work—hardly an hour of therapy with a patient goes by without some ideas being generated that will find their way into my writing. I don't mean that there is content from the patient that I use, but that the issues discussed raised jog some thoughts about the way our mind works.

“‘My stimulation as a writer is mental, from reading philosophy and fiction, and from my clinical work.’”

What are your hobbies or outdoor pursuits?

Biking, chess, walks in San Francisco, and reading, always reading. My wife and I enjoy walks in Palo Alto and San Francisco; we go to the theater, meet with friends, and stay close to our four children. We are often engrossed in their careers: Eve is a gynecologist; Reid, a talented art photographer; Victor, a psychologist and entrepreneur; and Ben, a theatre director. And we have an annual vacation with all the children and grandchildren, often in Hawaii.

What are you working on now?

I just finished a revision—fifth edition—of my textbook, *The Theory and Practice of Group Psychotherapy,* and am recovering from word-weariness. For the last few months I've been plunging into the study of Hellenistic Philosophy, especially Epicurus. I've been preparing and fertilizing the soil and hoping that sooner or later, some green shoots of a new writing project will burst forth. I'm waiting. . . .

Writing *The Schopenhauer Cure*

BEFORE DISCUSSING WHY I chose to write this particular novel, I shall address a more fundamental question: why am I writing a novel at all? For my entire career I've been a teacher and practitioner of psychotherapy: how does writing fiction articulate with that identity?

My first fifteen years of life were spent in a menacing neighborhood in Washington, DC, where the safest place was the public library at Seventh and K streets; it was there that I routinely spent my Saturdays and first experienced the enchantment of spending time in an alternative imaginative world. Ever since, I have always been in the midst of some work of fiction. By adolescence I had developed the notion—which I hold to this day—that writing a good novel was one of the very best things a person can do in life.

Now let me explain why I write a particular type of novel. In my career as a psychiatrist I have had two major separate but parallel interests: group therapy and existential therapy. Each of these two approaches has a different frame of reference.

Group therapy, based on interpersonal theory, makes the assumption that individuals fall into despair because they are unable to establish enduring, meaningful, sustaining relationships with others. Hence the therapy is directed toward exploring what goes awry in the patient's attempt to make contact with others. The group is the ideal arena for such explorations since it can focus powerfully on the way that members relate to one another.

The point is *not* that members will continue to know and to befriend one another after the group. That rarely happens. The point is that the group is a *social microcosm*—that is, the problems that individuals have in relationships are, over time, invariably replicated in the here-and-now of the group. So when leaders focus on the relationship between members, they are addressing the major relationship problems of the members (assuming, and leaders try to make this happen, that members will transfer what they have learned in the group to their situations "back home"). What's more, a focus on the here-and-now, on the real-time developments in the group, provides richer, more powerful, and far more accurate data: therapists no longer have to rely on the members' (often inaccurate) descriptions of past and present interpersonal problems; instead, therapists are presented with a vibrant tapestry as all the interpersonal problems are played out in living color before their eyes in the group meetings.

Existential therapy makes a different assumption: that individuals fall into despair because of their confrontation with the pain inherent in the human condition. Individuals have pain *not only* because of inbuilt unbridled destructive drives, *not only* because of parents who were too caught up in their own pain and neurotic struggles to provide the child the necessary support and cherishment, *not only* because of half-forgotten shards of traumatic experience, *not only* because of current interpersonal, economic, occupational stress *but also* because of the anxiety inherent in the raw facts of existence. What are these raw facts? That we are mortal, that we face inevitable death, that we enter and leave existence alone, that we are, to a greater extent than we realize, the authors of our life design and of the shape of reality itself, and that we are, by nature, meaning-seeking creatures, who have the misfortune to be thrown into a universe without any intrinsic meaning and hence must set about constructing our own meaning—one strong enough to support a life.

In the first part of my career I did what university professors are expected to do. I conducted research in my areas of interest and published ephemeral articles in professional journals. I wrote two heavy textbooks: one on group therapy *(The Theory and Practice of Group Psychotherapy)* and one an existential approach to psychotherapy *(Existential Psychotherapy)*.

Though both of these books were successful texts and became widely used in training institutes, I felt they left something undone: they failed to present the human side of what *really* happened in therapy. Professional ▸

Writing *The Schopenhauer Cure* *(continued)*

prose did not permit me to convey what was truly the critical part of the therapy experience—the deep, intimate, human, risky, caring (even loving) texture of the therapist-client relationship. I searched for another way to write and ultimately settled upon a literary conveyance: I would entirely jettison professional prose and jargon and teach through literature using the techniques of fiction to illuminate the inner world of both the client and the therapist. I had good models: other existential thinkers have taken the same path. Consider Sartre and Camus. Few today read or remember their formal philosophical works: it is their fiction and drama that brings brought their thoughts to life, and it is in this medium that they are remembered.

And so, in 1990, I began to write differently. Two volumes of teaching stories *(Love's Executioner* and *Momma and the Meaning of Life)* and three teaching novels *(When Nietzsche Wept, Lying on the Couch,* and *The Schopenhauer Cure)* were intended to explicate various aspects of an existential approach to psychotherapy. For example, *When Nietzsche Wept* examined what therapy might look like if it had been invented by Nietzsche, the philosopher-poet, rather than Freud, the physician-scientist. *Lying on the Couch* explored the nature of the therapist-patient relationship and, particularly, whether (and to what extent) the therapist should be self-disclosing.

I wrote each of these books with a particular audience in mind: young psychotherapists. But since psychotherapy is such a human process and so many individuals have the desire for self-exploration and personal growth, there has been a large crossover readership consisting of both therapists and the general public.

Unlike writers who begin a project with a certain plot in mind (or the development of a certain character, or a particular place), my starting place has always been a cluster of ideas. I hoped in *The Schopenhauer Cure* to explore four topics:

1) How group therapy works
2) How philosophy in general, and the philosophy of Arthur Schopenhauer in particular, might influence the practice of psychotherapy
3) How Schopenhauer's strange life history and his significant personal pathology influenced his philosophical conclusions
4) How the awareness of death influences one's life conduct

For forty years I've led and written about therapy groups and have great respect for the power and efficacy of this therapy format. In recent years, however, I have grown increasingly concerned about the state of the group therapy field. Two developments particularly disturb me: first, the gross misrepresentation of group therapy in the media; second, the pernicious influence of medical economics upon the practice of group therapy.

The mass media occasionally portray individual therapy in an accurate and sympathetic manner (who wouldn't want to be in individual treatment with the therapist portrayed by Robin Williams in *Good Will Hunting*?), but group therapy is invariably portrayed in a ridiculing and, more to the point, highly inaccurate fashion. (Consider, for example, the therapy group in *The Bob Newhart Show*).

Moreover, there has been considerable regression in the professional field. The HMOs have chosen, for economic reasons, to use therapy groups in a limited fashion. The great majority of groups now offered by large health care organizations are "psycho-information"—devoted mostly to conveying information about psychological disorders to group members. Although this has some limited value in treatment, therapy groups have far more powerful mechanisms of rendering help. Every skilled group therapist knows about the healing experience of groups in which members dedicate themselves to exploring all facets of their relationships with one another. One may compare the group therapy experience to a mercy ship conveying many individuals to a better and safer place. In *The Schopenhauer Cure,* I've taken great pains to portray group therapy in an accurate and realistic fashion. In my new edition of my group therapy textbook I have often referred student therapists to certain pages of *The Schopenhauer Cure* for graphic illustrations of many aspects relating to clinical theory and practice.

Why Arthur Schopenhauer? And what is his connection to therapy? (He died in 1860, decades before the emergence of contemporary psychotherapy.) I first grew interested in his work while researching Nietzsche for my novel *When Nietzsche Wept.* Although they never met—Nietzche was sixteen when Schopenhauer died— Nietzsche learned much from Schopenhauer and at first wrote admiringly about him. Later, however, he turned vehemently against him. I became fascinated by that schism. Nietzsche and Schopenhauer had many similarities: they were fearless and unrelenting in their investigations of the human condition, ▸

Writing *The Schopenhauer Cure* *(continued)*

eschewed all authority, and abandoned all illusions about existence. Yet they arrived at diametrically different attitudes toward life: Nietzsche embraced and celebrated it; Schopenhauer was grim, pessimistic, life-negating.

What accounted for this? To what extent did their life circumstances and personality structure determine philosophic conclusions? The more I studied Schopenhauer's life and work, the more impressed I was by the extraordinary range and depth of his vision. It was not difficult to understand why some philosophers posit that Schopenhauer's work contains more interesting ideas than the work of any other philosopher, save Plato. And yet there is no doubt that he was a deeply troubled and most peculiar man.

I first intended to write a historical novel about Schopenhauer and the implications of his work for the field of psychotherapy. This idea, however, was later abandoned. For one thing, I was never able to overcome the obstacle of Schopenhauer's dying in 1860, some thirty years before psychotherapy appeared upon the historical scene. (I consider 1895, the publication date of Freud and Breuer's *Studies in Hysteria,* to be the birth-year of modern psychotherapy. The final chapter of that book is an astoundingly prescient meditation in which Freud anticipates many of the developments in therapy that were to unfold over the next century.) Yet Schopenhauer's influence on psychotherapy is considerable: he was *the* German philosopher during Freud's education and many of his insights were to inform such later concepts as the unconscious, the id, repression, the role of sexuality, and the necessity of self-exploration sans supernatural illusions.

Schopenhauer's life itself proved another obstacle. His life, as he put it, was a monodrama, and monodramas do not make good fiction. He was one of the most embittered and isolated individuals in history, without friends, wife, family, or colleagues. I needed some other figure, a fictional foil, and for several weeks I experimented with the creation of a philosophically erudite Jesuit. However, I never could find the plot I wanted and eventually abandoned the project and turned to another book: *The Gift of Therapy.*

When I returned, two years later, to the embryo of my Schopenhauer novel I was pleased to find it still alive, and soon arrived at another idea entirely: I would write a contemporary novel set in a therapy group in which one of the members, Philip, would be both a living incarnation of

Arthur Schopenhauer and a repository of his ideas, many of which he would introduce into the therapy group discussion. I would also maintain my ties with the historical Schopenhauer by presenting, in alternate chapters, a psychobiography of Schopenhauer.

Make no mistake Schopenhauer was seriously misanthropic. Pessimistic, arrogant, secretive, manipulative and disdainful of others ("bipeds" was his term for humans), he might be one of the most unlikely characters in history to enter a therapy group. But suppose he did! What a challenge he would present be for a group therapist! And what a kick it might be to have him in a group! And just think—if a group could help Arthur Schopenhauer, it could help anyone!

Lastly, a few words about this novel's dark horizon—Julius's fatal illness. I wanted my protagonist not only to cope with his personal death but to help his clients confront their own. The reasons for choosing to introduce death into the therapeutic process stretch back to my years of working with patients who had untreatable cancer. I encountered many patients who did not shrivel in the face of death but, on the contrary, underwent changes that can only be called personal growth, maturation, or the development of wisdom. They rearranged their priorities, trivialized the trivia, and developed a greater appreciation of the things that mattered—the people they loved, the changing seasons, the music and poetry they had so long ignored. As one patient put it, "Cancer cures psychoneurosis." But what a pity it was they had to wait until the end, when their body was riddled with cancer, to learn how to live.

What would happen, I wondered, if one starkly introduced death into the therapy process? Might the members be driven away? Might they decide it was best not to scratch where it didn't itch? Might death loom too large for them to work on their personal quotidian problems? Or might the opposite occur? Might the awareness of inevitable death lend a vital perspective, seriousness, and power to the process of change?
I wasn't sure how the plot would develop. I constructed the stage, set the characters in motion, and had the delicious pleasure of recording what happened.

Read on

Have You Read?
More by Irvin D. Yalom

WHEN NIETZSCHE WEPT

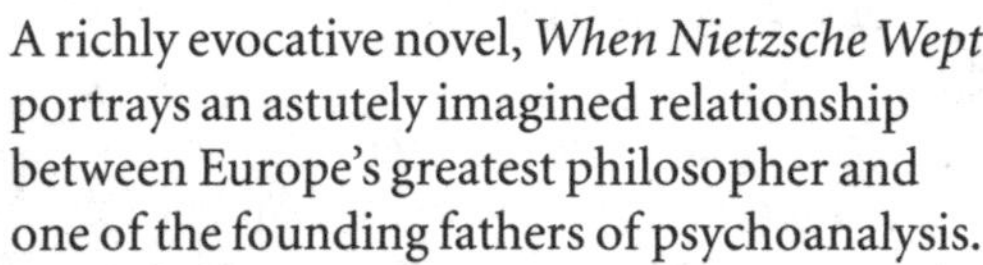

A richly evocative novel, *When Nietzsche Wept* portrays an astutely imagined relationship between Europe's greatest philosopher and one of the founding fathers of psychoanalysis.

"The best dramatization of a thinker's thought since Sartre." —*Chicago Tribune*

LYING ON THE COUCH

A provocative exploration of the unusual doctor-patient relationships formed by three therapists: Seymour, who blurs the boundary of sexual propriety with one of his clients; Marshal, who worries about the role money plays in his dealings with his patients; and Ernest, who, driven by his sincere faith in psychoanalysis, invents a radical, and potentially devastating, approach to therapy.

"If Freud or Jung had set out to write a psychological thriller, I doubt that either one could have come up with a yarn as taut and telling." —*Los Angeles Times*

LOVE'S EXECUTIONER

In this bestselling collection of absorbing tales, Irvin D. Yalom uncovers the mysteries, frustrations, pathos, and humor at the heart of the therapeutic encounter.

"Dr. Yalom demonstrates once again that in the right hands, the stuff of therapy has the interest of the richest and most inventive fiction."

—*New York Times*

MOMMA AND THE MEANING OF LIFE

The long-awaited follow-up to *Love's Executioner* probes the marvels at the heart of the therapeutic encounter, revealing the confrontations of both the author and his patients with life's most profound challenges.

"These six engrossing narratives are very valuable gleanings from a master therapist's professional and personal experience."

—*Kirkus Reviews*

Have You Read? *(continued)*

THE GIFT OF THERAPY

Distilling thirty-five years of clinical practice, Irvin D. Yalom proposes eighty-five often idiosyncratic "tips" for beginning therapists.

"An absorbing guide." —*Boston Globe*

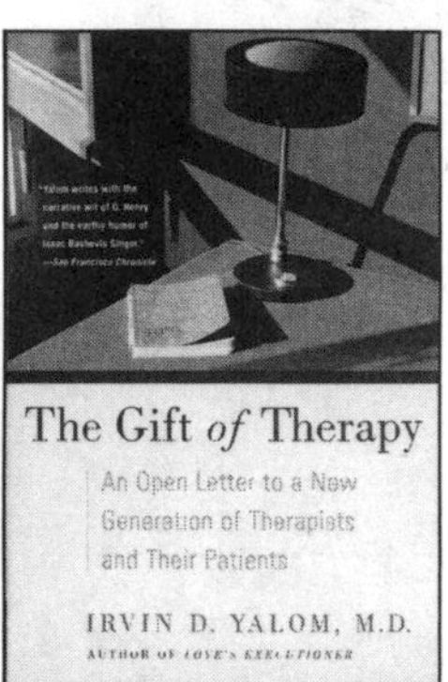